STATION

THE STATION TRILOGY: BOOK ONE

JARRETT BRANDON EARLY

Dedicated to:

*My father, Timothy Jon Early, who taught me that the dreamer doesn't
have to wake, but he has to get his shit done.*

*My mother, Maureen Brearton Early, who keeps the dreamer from flying
off into space.*

TO THE READER

Because music played a significant role in the creation of Station, I have carefully put together a novel "soundtrack" to accompany the text. This soundtrack not only represents the music I was listening to when I wrote Station, but also creates an atmospheric backdrop to accentuate certain sections and chapters.

On my website, you will find the Station soundtrack and those of other books in the series. There is both a Spotify playlist and YouTube links to each song, organized by chapter and chapter section. I hope you enjoy listening and reading. Thanks again!

www.JarrettBrandonEarly.com

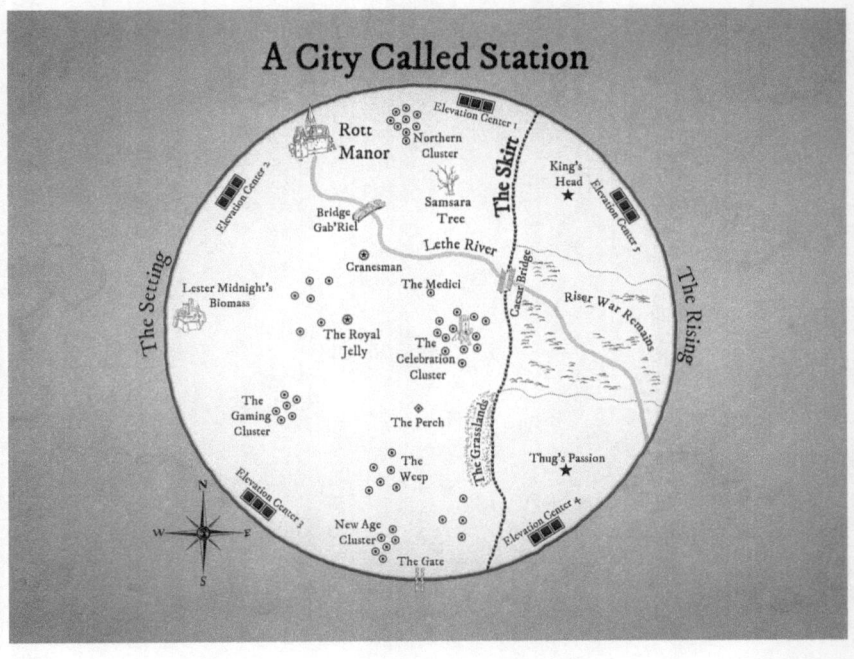

A City Called Station

PROLOGUE

The melancholy sounds of Peter Gabriel's "I Grieve" began to fade into the background as alcohol and pills, finishing their seductive dance, took giant steps forward. Consciousness gave ground as both breathing and heart rate commenced with inevitable declines. Fear receded as a calm acceptance took hold.

Minutes later, he felt as if he could fit a symphony between heartbeats. Each slow breath contained a complete requiem. The music was beautiful and intoxicating. And then both pieces fell silent.

And Marlin Hadder died.

Upon his death, Hadder felt a light fall over him, lifting him through and above the encroaching darkness. Up he went, surrounded by the warmth of a thousand familiar hugs, coming to rest on a soft canvas that caressed his feet like a lover's touch.

An iridescent figure approached, tall and powerful, and painfully beautiful. It looked down at Hadder and presented an honest smile before offering its hand. Hadder looked down at the perfect hand and wanted nothing more than to take it, to kiss it and hold it tightly, begging it to lead him on and promising to follow. These are the things that Hadder wanted to do.

But he found that he could not, not with the Rage that remained, buried deep within him, bubbling to the surface at this most inopportune time. Instead, inexplicably and reflexively, Hadder punched out at the entity, catching it in the neck. Its hand fell slowly as smile faded into frown, confusion and sadness falling over it like a shroud. The two stood motionless and stared at each other, the guilt of one reflecting the sorrow of the other. They may have remained like that for eternity.

A cackling laughter cut into the moment, however, emanating from all around, echoing in Hadder's soul. All went red. And Hadder fell back to earth, a silent scream marking his descent, ending in heartbeats and deep inhalations.

PART I

A CITY CALLED STATION

1

The bar called Station was a shit hole. To call it unremarkable would be a misuse of the word, as one would certainly offer remarks upon visiting the place. Dirt and grime caked the few windows of the small building, forcing one to view the establishment through the filter of a brown lens. Wooden tables and chairs littered the room in varying degrees of disrepair, many serving no use other than as an instrument to bludgeon your fellow man.

The neighborhood bar and grill it was not. Instead of kitsch posters and antiques, torn pages of Barely Legal littered the walls, girls' eyes poked out alongside hand-drawn dialogue bubbles that presented the reader with a myriad of sinister requests.

The actual bar at which Hadder sat was an island of angrily carved words and phrases, a sanctuary for splinters lying in wait for an unwary hand. Every move elicited a wooden moan accompanied by the odor of rot. The beer that had been given to Hadder was warm and lonely, with no condensation to keep it company and no mouth in a rush to welcome it.

In short, there was plenty to remark about in the bar called Station. Marlin Hadder, however, paid attention to none of these details, any one of which would have been rich fodder for later conversations.

Instead, Hadder was entirely focused on the knifepoint dancing danger-ously close to his left eye. The blade was being brandished by the white-bearded barkeep whose gas station shirt identified his name as Shirley and whose trucker hat identified him as a fan of Dr. Hook.

Uncomfortable seconds passed as the two held eyes across the desecrated wooden divider. Finally, silence hanging heavy and taut, threatening to suffocate, Hadder decided that he must give voice to his concern.

"What are you about?" Hadder managed through gritted teeth, afraid that even the slightest jaw movement could spring whatever dark trap into which he had wandered. His full effort was put forth in refusing his body the shaking that it so wanted to perform.

"How did you find your way here, you little shit?" Shirley asked, his tone a strange mix of anger and fear tickled with notes of bewildered curiosity. "And don't you dare fucking lie to me. Lies begat eyes here. You give me one, I take the other."

Hadder's mind began to spin. How could he explain to this hillbilly inter-rogator the bizarre series of events, both imagined and bafflingly real, that brought him to this place? A place that seemed suitable only for horror movie villains and failed backyard wrestlers. How many sentences would he get in before that shaky blade pierced his eye and plunged deep into his brain? What did Shirley want or need to hear?

Pieces of responses, starts and stops, tore through Hadder's head like tornadoes of razor wire, faster and faster, turning his thoughts to mush until there was nothing, just an empty whiteness that blanketed the world. It was then that Hadder spoke without thinking, words that were not his own.

"I had a dream where I met God. He reached in to shake my hand, and I punched him in the throat. For this betrayal, he showed me a door. That door led here."

When the white blanket tore free, revealing reality once more, there was no longer a knife swaying dangerously before Hadder's face. Instead, it was buried deep into the damaged bar, just a few precious inches from Hadder's suddenly delicate left hand.

Shirley had pulled back a bit but was still wearing his scowl like a boa.

Slowly, he let it slide off his shoulders, turned his head, and sent a foul-looking brown substance spinning towards the dirty floor. Wiping his mouth with the back of one hairy arm, the smirk of a hunter who had just bagged his quarry lit up Shirley's weathered countenance. It was enough to make Hadder lean back slightly; he hoped imperceptibly.

"Well, shit, that wasn't quite a dream now, was it, boy? Decisions were made, and now consequences need to be dealt with."

"I don't understand," Hadder said truthfully.

"Yes, you do. You just don't know that you do." Shirley began to limp back towards Hadder, his face brandishing a smile that was surprisingly more imposing than the knife he held moments before. "You were given a path, and you rejected it." Shirley's dirty finger was now acting as the blade's proxy, so close that Hadder could smell that morning's Marlboros radiating from it. "You were then presented with another path, and you rejected that, as well." Shirley's pointing finger transformed into an upheld palm that flashed more than a few pale scars. "Now you've been gifted one more. A last one. Show it to me." Desperation curled up at the corners of his words.

Hadder almost asked. Almost played dumb. Almost invoked the wrath of this relic of Americana. But they both knew what Shirley wanted to see. And they both knew that it laid at the center of this burgeoning relationship. So Hadder did the only thing he could; he reached into his pants pocket and retrieved it.

Hadder's right fist came up to hover over Shirley's palm. He hesitated for just a moment before painfully opening his hand, letting the object drop into Shirley's possession, away from him for the first time since it came into his being. Shirley looked down but was unfazed by what he saw there, expecting it to appear no less than he would expect another cigarette to grace his lips in the coming minutes.

Shirley limped over and held his hand under one of the few working lights, studying that which he now held - a small key. He ran his fingers over the dark, pitted metal. Brought it to his nose for a deep inhale. Traced the crude etchings that adorned one side. Tongued the key's rudimentary teeth.

Slowly, Shirley turned back towards Hadder, the light causing deep shadows to dance across his ragged face, falling into the ravine of a wide smile. "This is the real thing, son." His voice had softened noticeably. "Please, tell me how it came to you."

Disturbing memories rose to the surface. An ache in Hadder's stomach like he subsisted on a diet of glass. A fountain of bile pours from his mouth, the toilet only partially catching the spray. A lump carried on the foul river lodges itself in his throat, cutting off his access to sweet oxygen. A panic. A desperate act. He slams his sternum into the corner of the sink repeatedly, bruising some ribs and cracking others. A release. A grotesque ball of blackish, brownish, yellowish biomaterial swan dives into the empty sink, rolls around like a salted slug before coming to rest. Hadder leans in, horrorstricken, to get a closer look. He pokes at the ball with a trembling finger. It surrenders a sickening sound, like a bullet being torn from meaty flesh, as a rapid meltdown commences. An acrid smell of sulfurous vomit crashes into Hadder, sending him back on his heels. He raises his hand to defend himself against the specter, foreign gases bending the light in front of him. It dissipates quickly. Hadder inches forward again, hesitantly peers into the sink, where he sees it for the first time.

There is nothing special about the key, except for its biological origins. It's small and aged like it endured a thousand thunderstorms. It's not fanciful, could very well come from a 1982 Civic or someone's backyard shed lock. Hadder picks it up for further inspection, emotions flashing too quickly to register, from revulsion to curiosity to disappointment. He raises the key closer to the lone bathroom light, turning it slowly in an attempt to unveil all possible mysteries. None appear, save six crudely hewn numerals, one set of three atop the other.

Shock wearing off, Hadder begins to shiver, dropping the key to the tiled floor. He turns on the sink's hot water, and steam quickly fills the bathroom. Hadder forces his hands under the scalding water, cupping hands to splash his head, face, and neck in an attempt to cleanse himself of recent events. He rinses out his mouth and takes giant gulps, convinced that the liquid fire will consume any alien residuals.

Several minutes pass, and Hadder is spent. Head still buried in the sink, he turns off the water, collects himself. Hands holding onto opposite edges of the sink, Hadder ventures to look up for the first time, fearful that the mirror will reveal further, perhaps more visible, changes. He looks up, but a curtain of steam prevents him from observing his reflection. Hadder hits the fan switch, and steam rushes towards the ceiling like a choreographed flock moving south, giving Hadder an unencumbered view ahead. Completely fogged over, a single word has been clearly drawn on the bathroom mirror with an oily finger, waiting for the heat to reveal its secret. Hadder stares blankly at the reflective canvas, at a loss once again, a recurring theme. He traces each letter over and over in his mind, feels the word burrowing into his soul. What did it mean? Who had written it? Why him? What was it? *Station.*

"Son, you in there?" Shirley's words were like ice water thrown over the hot embers of memory. Hadder sat upright in a jolt. Maybe the simplest form of narrative would do best.

"I puked it up. That's how the key came to me." It rang ridiculously in his ears. Another knife was sure to make an appearance.

But a second blade did not appear. A shadow of empathy touched Shirley's words. "That must have really sucked."

"It did."

Shirley chuckled. "Still, you should count your blessings. It could've been much worse. The last person who came in with one of these, a pretty girl, had to carve it from her forehead. Poor girl had a goddam key-shaped lump sitting atop her eyes for days before she worked up the nerve. Cut was still fresh when I seen her. Still lovely, though. Lady before that, well, let's just say Brad fucking Pitt himself couldn't have gotten her pants off anytime soon after that ordeal."

Hadder's stool became unstable as he fought to process this new information. "You mean, there are others? Others with keys like this? That came here?"

Shirley placed the key on the bar between himself and Hadder. Hadder felt strangely relieved that it was out of another's possession. Shirley reached for the pack of cigarettes in his shirt pocket, took out a Marlboro Red, and lit it. "Well, of course, there are others." A judgmental eye was sent Hadder's way. "Did you think you were special? Did I hurt your feelings?"

"I didn't know what to think. I don't even know what's real anymore."

Another laugh escaped Shirley, this one lasting longer, uncomfortably so. "You might want to get used to that feeling. And don't worry, you are special. Just not that special. There are others, to be sure, but not that many. And none have entered this hallowed ground in quite some time. To be honest, I believed no more would. But here you are, as sad and confused and resigned as all that came before you. Unsure if this is an end or a beginning."

"And which is it?

"That's entirely up to you, son."

"So, what now?"

Shirley bent down and began to rummage behind the bar. Hadder heard clinking as he shuffled through bottles of booze. Rising back up, Shirley held an indeterminate bottle of caramel liquid. He placed two relatively clean glasses between Hadder and himself and filled them both with two fingers of the swirling fluid. "Now, we drink."

"I still have my beer."

"That ain't drinking. I make this myself. Cheers. To close calls." Each took long sips. Although it was remarkably smooth, Hadder felt its effects almost immediately, tickling the inside of this skull. Shirley let out a long breath, took one last moment to admire his creation, and set down his glass. "Now I have to render a decision. Your key checks out. Your hangdog expression and overall shit stain demeanor check out. And your responses, even though you don't even know what the fuck you're saying, check out. That means that YOU check out. And since YOU check out, it's time for you to discover why you're here."

"I'm here because I Google Mapped the coordinates on that vile key. This is the only building in the vicinity."

"That's HOW you got here. It ain't WHY you're here."

"Mister, I haven't understood shit in my life for the past few years." A flash of a woman's bloodied face and a child's unmoving hand amidst twisted steel and gore-covered concrete assaulted Hadder. His hands went reflexively to his face, rubbing hard as if he could physically remove the painful image, the annihilation of a once-beautiful life. "Please help me. Either with explanations or with that knife of yours. I didn't come all this way for homemade whiskey and secondhand smoke."

"Very well, son." A sense of seriousness draped itself over Shirley. He straightened, ran his hands down his shirt in an attempt to look more presentable, and breathed in deeply. "Stay calm, son. It gets a little strange from here on out."

And strange it got.

Clouds of white assailed Shirley's eyes, transforming them into milky marbles staring into the distance. Shirley's mouth slowly opened and continued to open well past the intentions of human biology. Hadder, wide-eyed and tense, winced at the sounds of muscles tearing and ligaments snapping filling the empty room, echoing off bare walls to bombard him from multiple angles. The lower jaw continued to drop as Shirley's head tilted back, creating a cavernous maw that looked as if it could swallow the world.

Just as Hadder thought he could take no more, that he would run from the building screaming, searching for a stone with which he could bash out his ruined brains, the terrifying transfiguration ceased. Both men stood unmoving, one set of eyes glued to one giant mouth.

"Shirley?"

As if in response, noise began to emanate from deep within Shirley, a needle being dropped on the human phonograph. A voice boomed from the living speaker, containing none of Shirley's country twang or cigarette roughness. Instead, it was distinguished and ancient, with a cadence that lulled Hadder like a cobra in the face of a seasoned charmer. The words filled all - room, ears, and mind, alike.

Greetings and salutations, my invited guest. You have been chosen amongst millions to receive the greatest gift that can be bestowed upon an individual of your ilk – a second chance, a new life. I know it has been hard for you, struggling with issues both unique to yourself and common to all. For whatever reasons, real or imagined, significant or trivial, you have proven unable to cope with that which has been presented to you by this current world. Your recent actions have demonstrated your contempt, or at least apathy, towards this existing life of yours. I do not judge you for this. On the contrary, I empathize with you and, in some of your cases, even admire you for it. I want to help you. In your possession is a key, granting you access to a better place where you can remake yourself into the person you always wanted to be. Accept my gracious offer and the bar representative before you will reveal the path to a fresh beginning. This world is not for you, and you are not for it. Join us in utopia, where dreams blossom rather than withering on the vine. Join me and help me remake you into the person you should have always been. I hope to see you soon. Godspeed.

The needle rose, and the record stopped. The chasm of Shirley's face began to shrink back to its original state, the impossibly stretched muscles and ligaments falling back into place until it finally started to resemble the mask of a man once more. The twin snowstorms that had encased Shirley's eyes began to clear, the bright blues of his retinas appearing like the morning sun. Seconds that felt like hours passed and Hadder feared that he had just born witness to the death of a man. Finally, however, Shirley took a massive breath before succumbing to a fit of coughing, desperately holding the bar to remain upright. It took several moments for the older man to compose himself enough to speak.

Hadder had let entire ordeal pass without saying a word. What does one say to incredible absurdity?

Shirley, seeming thankful for the silence, refilled both their glasses with a quaking hand. "Fuck, that never gets any easier. Apologies for the graphic show; there's no way around it. Kudos, though, you handled it quite well. Some have run for the hills."

"I might have, but I still can't feel my fucking legs. And I may have pissed myself a little."

"An honest man. Probably hasn't served you well in life, but I appreciate it nonetheless."

"This doesn't seem like the sort of place that rewards or even suffers fake bravado."

Another Shirley chuckle followed. Another cigarette was lit. "Quite right, you are, son! Now let me respond to your honesty with some of my own in kind. I'll try to cut through the mysticism and smoke and mirrors that my boss, this fine establishment's glorious benefactor, favors and shoot you straight. You have a choice to make, one that will fundamentally alter your existence."

"For the good or bad."

"That's not for me to know. I can only offer options. Tell me you wanna move forward, and I take you on. Tell me you want no part of this madness, and you relinquish that key, and I tell you to get fucking lost. But given the circumstances that must have driven you and your fellow key holders here, could any reformation be anything but positive or at least par for the course?"

Hadder's recurring nightmare of taking an unforeseen exam for a class he had skipped all semester came to life in real-time. "Any details to assist me with this decision, Shirley? Anything at all you can tell me?"

Shirley rubbed his beard uncomfortably. "I'm just a tool, son. A pawn in some cosmic game that's too big for an old country boy to comprehend. I play my role and keep my head down. I sold my soul a long time ago, and this is my purgatory. Yours is elsewhere, far above my pay grade."

"Is that what I'm doing, selling my soul?"

The deep, sad sigh that fell from Shirley almost brought tears to Hadder's eyes. "No, that's what I did. You're being offered something else entirely. A new path. A different life. An escape from all this."

"Anything else, Shirley?" Hadder felt sickened by the desperate plea he could hear in his own question.

"Yeah, just one thing. It's like a river, son. Moves only in one direction, if you catch my drift."

"I don't."

"If you go forward, there ain't no going back. There ain't no peeking in and seeing if you like it or not. This ain't no holiday, it's a permanent vacation."

Hadder had not been good at making big decisions in recent years. He either overthought, procrastinating until choices were made for him or all options ceased being possible. Or he made choices in the span of a breath, weighing no alternatives and giving no fucks.

"I think I'm in, Shirley."

Shirley delivered his patented, serious look. "You think? Why don't you take a minute and think this over, kid? I ain't trying to rush you."

"I don't think. I know. There's nothing for me here, hasn't been in some time. I'm already on that river, and it's only flowing in one direction. I need to see where these waters are leading. Let's go. Now, please, before I lose my nerve or shit my pants."

Shirley slammed both fists onto the bar, which threatened to become sawdust beneath them. "Fucking right! Follow me, you cavalier bastard."

Shirley marched towards the back of the tavern, slipping out from behind the bar and past a small bathroom hidden from view. Hadder scooped up his terrible key and trailed, giving the toilets a wide berth and offering a silent thanks that he didn't have to use the facilities. Shirley pushed open the rear door and held it open. "Dead men first," he teased, motioning Hadder through the exit. As he walked out, Hadder was immediately blinded by the wash of sunlight that engulfed him and cursed its severity.

Had he known that it would be last sunlight he would see, he might have treated its warm rays a bit more gently.

But Hadder did not treat them as such, throwing his arms in front of his eyes and cursing the sun and its damnable insistence on showing things as they really are, warts and all. His pupils shrank before its enormity, and he slowly lowered his shields, blinking a few times in surrender.

Hoping to discover some secret garden or mystical pool hiding behind the bar called Station, Hadder couldn't help but frown when faced with a wasteland of discarded engines, cinderblock-supported frames, and rusty remnants of once-great voices of American ingenuity. There was only an automobile junkyard, just as one would expect to find in this armpit of the country.

Shirley limped ahead. The wind began to kick up, lifting dust to sting the side of Hadder's face as he followed. He turned to block the onslaught, and when it ceased, he looked ahead to see that Shirley had stopped at an old

Lincoln Town Car. It appeared to be an early 90's model, similar to his grandfather's, except instead of being a brilliant midnight blue, it was blood brown and covered with rust holes. The Lincoln was buried in the ground, showing only the top two-thirds of the car. The bottom of the trunk appeared to be level with the sun-battered ground.

Shirley must have noticed the "are you serious" look that had crawled up to sit on Hadder's face.

"It's not much to look at, I'll grant you that. But here we are, nonetheless."

"I don't get it."

"Pretty simple, really. Just take your key and open the trunk. Climb in, and that's it."

"What's in there?"

"Hell if I know, son; I just work here. You're the twenty-seventh person I ever let in, although you're the first in a long while. But I tell you this, I've yet to open this here trunk to find any skulls, bones, or dried blood. It must go somewhere."

"Anyone ever come back out."

"I told you, it's a one-way trip, son." The wind increased. Whether it was trying to push Hadder towards or away from the trunk portal, he had no idea. Shirley protected his eyes from the cutting sand.

"Let's hurry it up if you don't mind. Shit or get off the pot, as my daddy used to say. What'll it be?"

Hadder briefly thought of his old life, how meaningless it had become. How no light had appeared in the proverbial tunnel to show him the way. Perhaps this was the light he was so desperately waiting on. Despite the crew of butterflies that had found their way into his stomach, he saw no other alternative. "Guess I'm shitting."

Hadder removed the key from his pocket, knelt down, and inserted it into the trunk's keyhole. His breath caught as he slowly turned the key.

Momentary doubt fell away as the trunk popped open. It was wholly unremarkable, just a filthy Lincoln trunk, graciously void of any decomposing predecessors. As a child, Hadder remembered thinking how easy it would be to fit three bodies in the trunk of his grandfather's Lincoln. This trunk only had to accommodate one.

"In you go," Shirley yelled, the wind now having risen to point where the conversation was becoming difficult. Demonstrating a determination that belied his recent character, Hadder dropped to all fours and crawled into the trunk.

Or was it a tomb? It certainly was the end of one life, but would there be another on its heels? Or would he find only darkness and a dearth of oxygen?

Hadder looked up at Shirley, his hands resting on the top of the trunk. "Well, son, end of the line!" The wind was a storm now, sending garbage wrappers and old newspapers alongside the dust and dirt to pepper Shirley and the other forgotten residents of the impromptu junkyard. "Tell that fucking devil Albany, 'hello and go fuck yourself,' for me!" he called through rumbles of laughter.

"Wait!" Hadder screamed. "What was that about a devil?! Shirley!"

The top slammed shut, immediately cutting off the sounds of gusting winds and maniacal laughter, ushering in the kind of silence that one encounters in deep caves or space. And then the darkness that Hadder feared fell. Like the bottom of an ocean trench, it pressed and suffocated. Like the hateful words from a loved one, it was tangible. Like lights out at the end of the first day of a prison sentence, it was the realization that things would never be the same.

2

I t took Hadder several moments to move. Left alone in the absolute dark and silence, he felt mildly relaxed considering the circumstances, as if back in the womb. And maybe that was the point, a rebirth of sorts. Poking around the trunk in the darkness, his hands felt only the cold hard metal of the Lincoln's exoskeleton to the sides and near the trunk entrance. It seemed his only option was to push on, backward, delving deeper into the belly of the rustic incubator.

Hadder slithered towards the back of the trunk, feeling his way in the blackness, hoping to avoid the sharp bite of a rabies-infected rat. At worst, he would encounter nothing more than a solid barrier typically found between trunk and carriage, truly rendering this a tomb and finishing the job that he started but failed to complete.

Hadder reached hesitantly, unsure what he truly cared about more, finding a door to a new life or an end to this one.

After what seemed like endless advancement, his fingers finally encountered resistance. But it wasn't the firmness of felt upon steel that his fingers touched, but rather the silkiness that one would imagine surrounds white sand resorts that interrupt unhappy but otherwise tolerable lives. It kissed Hadder's fingertips but let him through. First, his fingers were allowed entrance, followed by his wrist, arm, and shoulder. Despite not feeling any open area beyond and knowing that any end might be preferable to a stifling death in the back of a junked Lincoln, Hadder pushed ahead, rolling his whole body through the sand curtain. At least, he hoped it was a curtain and not a pure block of suffocating matter.

Two rolls in and Hadder was still surrounded by the soft substance. Daring not to open his eyes or breathe in, the idea formed that he would die in limbo, no physical body or family to ever recount his existence. Just as well, he mused. Hadder wanted to be forgotten.

And with that thought painfully dry humping his mind, Hadder rolled again, this time feeling dead air rather than more velveteen silt. In the nanosecond it took for gravity to wrest control of the situation, Hadder found time to consider which was worse, suffocation or the splatter from a long fall. And again, he wondered, why God didn't those pills work?

Hadder fell heavily, but not damagingly so, onto the cool, sandy floor of what he assumed to be a cave. Having gone spelunking in his younger days, Hadder recognized the deep level of absolute blackness that surrounded him. He rose unsteadily to his feet and felt around blindly. Behind, there was no hint of the ledge from where he fell, only the rough, impenetrable surface of a rock wall. He hand-walked along the wall, searching for anything that may offer a way back or out. Finding none, Hadder took a calming breath, already sensing the weight of darkness beginning to breed claustrophobia.

It seemed Hadder was at the tail end of a tunnel, with only one real direction to travel, which was comforting. He moved slowly, now and then tripping over a rock formation or small pothole in the floor surface, everything threatening to snap ankles and create a permanent mummified addition to the dry cave. Hadder walked, scooted, crawled, and crept forward, unable to decipher seconds from minutes or feet from yards. But like Columbus's crew, on the cusp of permanent hopelessness and mania, he forced himself to believe that there was an end to the vast nothingness.

Mid-step Hadder froze, then sat down, unsure that what he had just felt was real or only a malicious phantom of his own conjuring. He held perfectly still.

There! This time he was sure of it. A gentle breeze caressed Hadder's cheek like a Thai kiss. On he went, emboldened and stooped in a half-walk, half-crawl like some crazed calisthenics exercise. Excited by the promise of the same light he had cursed earlier, Hadder almost ran headfirst into the cave wall, putting out his left hand just in time to save himself the indignity of leaving a bloody faceprint on the rock.

The cave doglegged hard to the right, so Hadder kept his hand attached to the wall, sliding it along as he was herded into an almost 90-degree curve.

Coming out of the turn, Hadder was immediately flooded with relief that only accompanies a life that narrowly dodged a turn for the absolute worse. There, maybe one hundred yards away, was the faint opening of the cave. It must have been night out, with minimal light filtering in, but Hadder's pinhole pupils picked it up immediately, giving him renewed purpose and speeding his crawl-walk into a crawl-run.

Hadder slowed as he approached the cave mouth. Dry vegetation cascaded down from above the cavern, obstructing the view of the outside.

Some thoughts bubbled up before Hadder snaked his way through the dry creepers. It was midday when he submitted his fate to the long-dead Lincoln. How long had he been stumbling along in that cave? Did he pass out at some point, unable to determine unconsciousness in the lightless tunnel? And most troublesome – although he was by no means an expert in the topography of the region, Hadder didn't recall it being a hotbed of dry cave systems. In which case, where the hell was he?

While these questions were both perplexing and worrisome, next to the fears of suffocation, falling from an unseen height, and becoming permanently lost in the perpetual darkness of an unknown cave, he shook these concerns off reasonably quickly.

Mustering his courage, Hadder clapped his hands together and plowed forward through the parched plants. A stiff breeze, barely perceptible inside the cavern, blew back his hair as he stepped out from the protection of the earth, his feet slipping from the hard rock onto soft sand.

Hadder looked out at the landscape and had to remind himself to breathe as he stared into the barren face of an uninviting desert that spread out in all directions, disappearing into the horizon.

Dumbfounded, Hadder shuffled ahead and slid down a small hillock that rose up to greet the cave opening. Reaching the bottom, he noted that the ground was not soft and giving, but rather hard-baked dirt, void of foliage, with a thin layer of sand atop it, like the boardwalk leading down to a busy beach. The wind whipped around him, creating small sand devils that swept up dead weeds and sent them on cyclone carnival rides, depositing them dozens of feet away. The twisters seemed appropriate sentinels, warning Hadder not to continue on this path, but unaware that this was the only option available to him.

Hadder's eyes rose, and he was awestruck by the clarity and size of the moon in this wasteland. Never before had he seen it play such a role in the night sky, as if he were viewing it from another, much closer world. He felt unsubstantial standing under its gaze, fighting the urge to prostrate himself before the great satellite.

Dark, wispy clouds cruised across the sky, late for a meeting with a beautiful woman. Occasionally, lightning streaked between clouds, connecting them momentarily by a leash of electricity, brightening the desolate world in a flash before fading away in surrender to the night.

The air was crisp and dry, with a clean, pleasant smell indicative of areas not yet tarred by man. With open sand all around, Hadder had no idea which way to travel. Only dark shadow could be perceived in three directions, with the hill-cave dominating the fourth view. Lighting continued to shriek across the sky, shining a spotlight on various areas at a time. One bolt illuminated the skeletal remains of a dead tree far ahead. A second raged behind the hillock, and Hadder looked back to discover that the hill continued to rise far above the cave entrance. A third struck in the distance to Hadder's left, lifting the veil along the horizon.

And it was there that Hadder found it, backlit by startling light and submerged in shadow. But he saw it clearly, like catching eyes with a good friend in a crowded room. It looked back with the beckoning call of an old habit that promised one more good time while bringing nothing but pain.

But Hadder had nowhere else to go. And was fucking curious. And needed answers.

He marched towards the city in the distance, hopeful that it was more dream than nightmare, more heaven than hell.

————

WHEN JUDGING DISTANCES, most people quickly learn that they don't know shit about it. Hadder was no different. He walked and walked; footprints instantly erased by the secretive winds. His form created an array of shadows, long and short in every direction, the show above painting the canvas below with dark and light.

As he walked, Hadder's mind was blank, stripped clean of both thought and emotion from the trials of the past years. Electronic soundtracks echoed in his head, playing off wind-sound and emptiness. He strode with purpose, eyes focused solely on the city before him, getting slightly more substantial by the step, slightly less invisible, slightly more real.

After what could have been an hour, the details of Hadder's destination began to fall into focus. At least, one significant feature became clear – the wall.

The place was fucking walled in.

Still too removed to approximate the actual height of the enclosure, Hadder was close enough to decide that two words could be used to adequately describe it - vast and imposing. But was it to keep the desert out, or something else in?

As he continued, Hadder noticed a significant brightening of his desert surroundings. He looked up, expecting to see the moon receding in fear of the incoming sun. But there the moon still sat, arrogant in its rule of the night sky. It remained in the exact location as before, a Japanese flag draped over the heavens. It appeared larger, however, and was now radiating significantly more light than when he first set out onto the desert plateau, like a sun with the volume turned down. Hadder kept walking, willing to accept that an oversized moon that alternates size and brightness was par for the course here.

Finally, under the serene face of the eccentric moon, Hadder arrived at what he prayed was a city. He stood in awe of the high wall before him, reminded of those that surrounded great cities of antiquity. Its earthen quality matched that of the desert floor, blending in with the barren land-scape. It appeared to be more than two hundred feet in height, with a surface that would give no purchase for foot or hand.

Hadder placed his left hand on the wall, leaving it there as he walked its length, much as he did back at the cave portal. It gently turned in a massive circle large enough to encompass several of America's great amusement parks, and Hadder wondered about the rides awaiting him.

Thousands of steps later, Hadder's hand, still held fast to the wall face, ran over an almost unnoticeable seam in the earthen material. Like finding the end of a roll of tape, it was easier to feel the seam than see it. A slight difference in rock color was all that distinguished one slab from the other. Something else, however, clearly marked this area as something special, something necessary.

Two feet above Hadder's head, painted in a red scrawl, rested the words for which he had risked what was left of his diminished life, seemingly traversing worlds and wandering aimlessly. In a slight double arch, much like a grandmother's wooden welcome sign over the front door, laid what he needed to read to believe.

Welcome to Station.

3

M arlin Hadder's eyes followed the faint outline of the door but were unable to locate keyhole, handle, or knocker. Seeing no alternative, he simply pressed both palms against the slab's cold surface. Almost immediately, Hadder felt a strange vibration flow through his arms as the barrier warmed to an uncomfortable level. Just before having to remove his hands from the now blistering wall, something invisible clicked, and the door swung in silently. If there were hinges present, they were entirely hidden and immaculately greased, leaving Hadder to believe that something more than sophisticated engineering was at play here.

Slowly adjusting to the new shadow created by the open doorway, Hadder stood for a moment, still unable to wrap his head around where he was and how he had gotten here. A common mantra - *this is fucking crazy* – played incessantly in his head. As his pupils dilated once more, he began to make out another, deeper shadow in the darkness. Two golden eyes appeared as the shadow grew, moving closer at a measured pace. One hand was held up in an affectation of peace.

"Greetings, greetings," came a calming voice like the bubbling creek behind Hadder's childhood home. The sound, still emanating from a golden-eyed shadow, continued. "Welcome to your new home. I know you've been through some real trials to find us. We all share in your suffering."

Words stuck in Hadder's throat like a key as the man stepped out into the strange moonlight. He was a slight black man just shy of middle age, wearing trendy, well-fitting casual clothing that made him immediately appear engaging and credible. Smallish in stature, he barely reached Hadder's chin. What really stood out, however, were those golden eyes of his, two beacons that seemed to penetrate meat and bone to peer into one's soul. Hadder had yet to speak a word by the time the man was upon him. He held out his hand. And this time, Hadder took it.

"Welcome to Station, my new friend. I'm sure you're feeling a mix of confusion and fear and curiosity and a million other emotions. I wish I could assuage all your concerns at once, here and now, but things don't get any more normal from this point on."

Hadder heard the man's words but found himself failing to comprehend them all, so transfixed he was by the golden orbs that swam in the night air.

The man noticed and cleared his throat. "I apologize for how my eyes must appear to you. One of the little perks of our fair community. Trust me, these will be the least of things to catch your eye by this time tomorrow."

Hadder shook off the stupid look he was sure to be wearing. "Sorry for staring. My name's Marlin. Marlin Hadder."

"No need for sorries. I'm sure you're quite flummoxed right now. Who wouldn't be, with that nastiness with the key and that musty cave and that trackless desert and this King Kong wall? It's almost enough to make a black man white and a white man honest." He smiled. "That was what we call a joke around here. Don't worry, you'll loosen up soon enough. My name's Miles, and I've been granted the pleasure of showing you around. We're all so very intrigued. You're the first new resident in quite a long time, and there will be real chatter about what that means. So please come in, there's a world for you to explore. Make sure to keep an open mind, lest you lose yours."

With that, Miles turned and walked back into shadow. After a brief moment to collect his thoughts before realizing he had none, Hadder followed, completing the journey from one world into another.

––––––––

THERE REALLY WAS a city behind that wall of earth. If one found the term city to be a bit strong, none could argue that it was, at the very least, a large town. Squat buildings, no more than three or four stories, sprouted up to Hadder's left and right. He turned around to glimpse one final view of the outside desert, only to find that the door had moved ninja-quiet back in place, leaving only the barest impression that it even existed.

A monster moved to stand before the sealed entrance, and Hadder quickly came to understand Miles's veiled words.

"Jesus Christ," he shouted, shuffling backward so fast that he tripped over his own feet to land hard on his ass. The man or thing that stood over Hadder was around eight feet tall and swathed in a thick layer of muscle not seen outside of film special effects.

The monstrosity's skin was the color of a drowning victim, a pale blue with white scars crisscrossing his bare chest and face. He wore sturdy, calf-high boots into which were tucked pants that seemed to sparkle with starlight. He wore a jacket of the same material that was accented with a fur collar. No undershirt, of course, that would detract from the effect. To complete the look, his long hair was held tight atop his head in an odd pony-tail, which fell to the side to tickle his cheek.

If Hadder weren't about to shit himself, he would have had to admit that he sat before a striking specimen of the highest order.

Miles began to giggle from above and behind, an annoying high pitch laugh that sounded more witch than man, a break from his projected poise. "I'm so sorry. I should have told you about the guardians of Station. Most are gentle giants, really, as long as you do as they say. And they rarely say anything at all. They don't bite unless you're truly unruly. Then they leave permanent marks." Miles lent Hadder a hand and helped him up. "This one's

Galba. He's an alright fellow. Some of them can be real thugs at times, but Galba's courteous enough." Galba stared down at Hadder.

"You mean there's more than one of him?"

"There used to be twelve of them. Now there's eleven."

"What are they?"

"They guard the Skirt and maintain a general peace here in Station."

Hadder caught the use of "general peace," but thought better of asking about it. "What's the Skirt?"

"We're getting a little ahead of ourselves. Let's get moving, and I'll try to explain along the way. We haven't had a new resident in a long, long time. Many are going to want to meet you. Many are going to have questions. Best that you're somewhat informed about your surroundings before the bombardment commences. This way...Marlin? Or do you prefer Hadder?"

"Either is fine."

"Well, just so you know, you can call yourself anything you want here. This place is a hard reset, in more ways than one. We were all obviously unhappy out there, so we've been given the gift to rebuild ourselves in Station. Here, you can become the person you always wanted to be but were unable to become. But make sure you select a name quickly, or some humorist in the group will christen you with a name you may find unbecoming. He or she will place it around your neck like a garrote, and there it will sit uncomfortably for the entirety of your time here. Pick one before it gets picked for you."

"Is that how you became Miles? Or is that your real name?"

Miles hesitated a moment, his face betraying something deep beneath those calm waters. "You have to understand something before we continue. Out there is no more "real" than in here. The Before - time prior to arriving at Station - is now the dream, was the nightmare. Station is real. Station is the now. Station is the reality."

Hadder involuntarily flinched at the small rant, the speeding up towards a mania buried deep within the otherwise composed man who called himself Miles.

Miles took a deep breath in and straightened his already immaculate clothing. "But to answer your question, I gave myself the name Miles. It is mine now, and it is who I am. Who are you? Who do you want to be?"

Hadder needed no pause. "You can call me Hadder. I never hated who I was, just what I was."

Miles delivered a smile that was not quite easy nor forced. "Up to you, my caucasian friend. And we continue." Miles motioned around as he walked. "So, this is Station, Hadder. Do you know what that is?"

Hadder shook his head in the negative. "Still trying to process."

"It's the end of the line. Well, it's the end, or it could be the beginning depending on your perspective. Some look at it as an opportunity, others as a curse. Which of those it will be for you will be of your own making."

As they walked, the two began passing short buildings on the left, the size of small restaurants. The names of the buildings had similar themes, ranging from *Live Again* and *Energizer* to *Good Vibes*. Outside of several, people in loose white garb performed a kind of bastardized Tai Chi, chanting as they went through ridiculous motions.

Miles shook his head. "I see you've spotted the Haight-Ashbury section of Station. These gentle souls are still searching as if Station isn't already the end of their quest. Crystals and energy and wavelengths and whatever other flavors of the month. Happy as heck to be here. Tiresome, but they can be a good time if you're in the right mindset."

One of the white-dressed figures, a middle-aged woman with wild gray hair, ran up to Hadder excitedly. "Your aura! It's all fire. Wait, no! It's blood on fire! Who are you? I think Station has big plans for you. Or maybe you for it! Here, take this crystal; it will help focus your chakra."

Miles intercepted her. "Please, Miss Star, let the man settle in before you hit him with your mumbo jumbo. Come on, Hadder."

They walked on. Star continued to stare; Hadder could feel her eyes burrowing into his back. She shouted after them, "I see you, young man! And Father sees you, too!"

Hadder shouted behind him. "I'm not that young, but thanks!" He turned back to Miles, "Father? Some Station deity, I presume?"

Miles continued walking, staring straight ahead. He seemed to get a bit more rigid, but it was hard to tell. "In some ways. But don't get me wrong, Father is quite real, in the physical sense. That's what some call Mister Rott, creator of Station. Others consider him a god or a devil depending on your take on the city."

Hadder almost tripped on a loose cobblestone in the walkway. "So, some don't like it here, I gather. Seems pleasant enough." And it really did. The footpaths were clean, the buildings in good repair. The air was crisp and clear. Looking around, Harder could see workers dressed in tight black skin suits tending gardens, fixing structures, and carrying loads. All in all, it seemed the sort of charming town that one might find in Canada, that wondrous land to the North, brimming with beauty and healthcare.

Miles thought for a long moment. "Station's like a partially filled glass. Some say its half-empty, others half-full. Up to your outlook, I guess."

"Looks like summer camp to me."

"Only if summer never ended. And there were no parents to call to come pick you up."

They kept walking along the cobbled footpath. Plentiful bushes and flowers bordered the path, all well-manicured and kept. "Looks like the grounds crew does a nice job," Hadder remarked.

Miles laughed politely again. "They aren't complaining."

While the landscape remained the image of tranquility, the characters that dotted the stage changed almost immediately. Where there were overly polite Tai Chi practitioners frolicking, there were now people in various forms of disarray, passed out on lawns in an impossible medley of positions. In other areas, drunken men and women hunched over crying, catching their tears in dirty hands. Far to the left, a man screamed at the large moon, accusing it of stealing his child.

"Miles, what the hell?"

"Oh sorry, Hadder, I've been here so long I forget how strange it can appear at first glance. Station tends to organize itself according to the disposition of its residents. Back there are the new age energy riders. This here is what we lovingly refer to as the Weep. You know the weepy fools that frequent daytime bars across America?"

"The ones that never let me drink in peace."

"Yeah, well, this is an entire area of them. Most got kicked out of the other areas. So here they are, feeding off each other's misery. Really should have done themselves in when they had the chance. The free booze, drugs, and time aren't good for their distinct dispositions. And the rest of us have our own problems; we don't need to listen to theirs."

"Seems like a terrible place."

"Looks like small-town America to me." Hadder couldn't disagree with Miles's take.

Miles continued walking, his pace unrelenting. "Where are we going, Miles?"

"My job right now, Hadder, is to orientate you to this bizarre new world. I'm taking you to the best place to do that, so bear with me. But if our destination has you worried, that's where we're going." Hadder followed Miles's pointing finger, past numerous other squat buildings. In the near distance stood a cylinder-like structure with a flat observation area at the top, a middle finger pointing to the heavens. "Please hold all questions until we get there. Better to see it for yourself. Otherwise, I'm tinkling into the wind here. For every drop that goes forward, another flies back to sprinkle my face, and I'm not into that. But if that's your bag, some Bars will accommodate you."

"Bars?"

"We're almost there." He took off faster without answering Hadder's question.

ON THEY WALKED through the Weep, passing men and women alike, but predominantly older males, a depressing slice of ennui in an otherwise lovely environment. Even amidst this melancholy, however, everything was maintained but the people. More squat buildings faded in and out of view. *Broken Dreams* on Hadder's left, *The Regret* to his right.

Hadder squinted to read other names. "Miles, what are these buildings?"

"Bars. You can call them whatever you want to call them, but most of us refer to them as Bars. Places to relax, sleep, and party. For some, places to get completely messed up in. For others, carnal pleasures dominate their time in a Bar."

Hadder couldn't keep the wonder from his voice. "These are all bars? I haven't seen so many in one place since Thailand. Is there anything else here?"

"Yeah." Hadder could tell that Miles wanted to get to the Perch fast, hoping to deliver a speech that would answer all questions in one fell swoop instead of providing the information piecemeal.

The Perch was reached several minutes after an inebriated man screamed, "Why did she do it?" over and over again as he sat Indian style in front of a bar called *Better Times*. Miles had no reaction to the outburst.

Like a simplified, miniature version of Seattle's Space Needle, what the Perch had in height, it made up for with a lack in charm. It was a simple metal cylinder with a spiral staircase entwining it, speeding its way to the top. At its pinnacle, there was a simple circular platform with a polished guardrail protecting its edges.

Up they went, more than 75 feet above the ground. Miles had scampered up ahead and was leaning dramatically against the rail when Hadder broached the platform. "Glad you could make it." Miles threw his arm out and turned in a circle, ending with a theatrical flourish that would have made any two-bit magician proud. "Welcome to Station. This is your city. This is your life. There is nothing else."

4

Hadder took a slow, methodical turn atop the Perch, attempting to digest everything in a single, sweeping gaze. From his vantage point, Hadder could clearly see Station's walls in two of the four primary directions - from where he came and to his left. Directly ahead, and more so to his right, the wall could barely be made out in the distance.

The great moon still hung huge and bright above, seemingly unmoved since his arrival. It cast moonbeam shadows across Station's relatively flat terrain, giving the city a ghostlike quality that was apropos given the citizenry. Squat buildings continued to litter the ground in most directions, with the occasional taller, more impressive construct piercing the night in a few select locations.

Miles waited patiently as Hadder looked upon his new city, breathing in the fresh air and accepting the small moonlit breeze, imagining that they contained hidden energy that would once again bring vitality to his current husk of a body. Forms moved below him in all directions, none in a seeming hurry. From his admittedly uneducated perspective, it seemed that Station was full, but not packed with people. Enough to avoid feeling lonely, but not so many that the weight of strangers would press heavy on one's chest.

Miles finally cleared his throat, evidently ready to give his prepared spiel. "Listen, Hadder, it would be impossible for me to tell you everything about this city of secrets here and now. Understanding Station is like becoming a surgeon. You can listen to all the lectures, read all the journals, and watch all the videos you want, but until you've held a man's organs and life in your hands, you don't know what is going on."

"Driving may have been a less intense metaphor for a new city."

Miles smirked. "And therefore, less appropriate. Station is a complex creature with moving parts and shifting dynamics. Those, unfortunately, you'll have to figure out for yourself alongside where you belong and how you want to spend your time here."

"Time here? Is there an end to this place? How long are we expected to stay here?"

Miles's face shifted uncomfortably. Whether it was sadness, frustration, or anger, Hadder was unable to decipher. "I don't know, Hadder. And that is perhaps Station's greatest mystery. But let's not dwell on the potentially morose. As I said before, Station is what you make of it. I, myself, have had some of the best times of my life here. You'll want for nothing; everything is provided for you, from clothes to food to entertainment."

"What kind of entertainment?"

A genuine smile this time. "Anything from your wildest dreams, my friend. Sex? Yes. Drugs? Sure. Music? Absolutely. But here you can go much deeper, to satiate those desires that you were scared to indulge in during the Before. All you have to do is ask here, and things will be put in motion."

Miles could see the confusion in Hadder's eyes. "These are things you will find out on your own, of course. Let me tell you what you need to know to get started. A tutorial of sorts, the basic buttons of the place. How does that sound?"

"Please."

Miles pointed up. "As you've no doubt noticed, sunlight never falls on Station."

"Why is that?"

"There have been many theories. My own? I think Mister Rott, when creating this place and envisioning who would live here, felt that sunlight showed too many scars, highlighted too many difficult truths. So, he found a workaround. The great moon, which we call the Idol Moon, is our sun as well as our moon. It changes size and brightness to mark days and nights, but never shifts location in the sky. Right now, it is our day, referred to as the Solay. In a bit, the moon will fold in on itself and usher in our night, the Haela."

Hadder looked up at the mysterious body that dominated the heavens. "Where are we, Miles?"

"Wrong question. First, because I don't know and, second, because it doesn't matter. Now, as the Idol Moon doesn't move, there are no classic directions in Station. Therefore, we use the Gate, the entrance you recently passed through, as our southernmost point. Please remember this as I continue."

Hadder turned back towards where they had walked from, hoping to get his bearings before Miles moved on. "See the small buildings that make up the majority of Station's construction, Hadder? As I mentioned before, these are Bars. One or more of them is where you will spend the vast majority of your time. Each one is unique and caters to varying tastes, personalities, and desires. While they are all different, however, many share qualities and attract similar patrons. In this way, Station organically organizes itself through the Bar system. While there are no rigid lines or defined borders, Bars of a feather naturally flock together. Think back to the two areas we passed. The new-age groups tend to stay in one Cluster while Station's sadder individuals have congregated to the Cluster others call the Weep."

"How many of these Clusters are there?"

Miles had to think for a moment. "Maybe a dozen or so, but most are undefined, and there is a lot of crossover. Additionally, just like neighborhoods in the Before, demographics and trends adjust over time. And people change. Just because you're here doesn't mean you stop growing and learning and changing. You may spend significant time in one Bar or Cluster to wake up one day and discover that it's not for you anymore." Something lit a fire behind Miles's golden eyes. "But that's the beauty of Station!

There're no families to consider. There's no property to worry about. There's no paperwork to fill out. Tired of where you are? Pick up and move on, no questions asked. Station is a playground with all the toys you could ever want."

"But where do I go, Miles?"

"You'll have to experiment, try to get in where you fit in. That's the scariest but also the most exciting part of coming to Station. You mentioned Thailand earlier. I assume you've been?"

"Yes, right after..." Hadder hesitated, rewound. "I mean, I've been."

"And when you arrived, did you know exactly where to go and what to do? Who to ask and what to avoid?"

"No, I just figured it out as I went."

"Exactly, you'll have to do the same here. But unlike in the Before, Station is quite tolerant of bad behavior and mistakes. Now, the majority of the city is called the Setting, which is everything west of the Skirt. That's all you need to acquaint yourself with right now."

"What is the Skirt?"

Miles turned to the "east," and Hadder trailed his gaze. In the distance, Hadder could make out a wide swath of land scraped clean of any Bars or other buildings. "The Skirt is the border between the Setting and the Rising. You just stay on this side, and you'll have no worries."

"But why are the two sides separated?"

Miles quickly turned back to face Hadder. "Sorry, not part of the tutorial. To the north, you'll find Mister Rott's manor and the Elevation Centers are at the city's edges. Before you ask, others should explain, or better yet show, what Elevations are. Too much information too quickly, and your brain can fry like an earthworm on hot cement."

Hadder couldn't hold back any longer. "How long have you been here, Miles? How long has everyone been here?"

A frown was followed by a non-committal shrug. "Time works differently here, Hadder. We don't have names for things like weeks, months, or years. Time is measured in short bursts of Solays and Haelas. I don't know how long I've been here, whether months or years or decades, in terms of

Before time. Here, we just live for the present. In the Before, many of us couldn't escape the past. Others were too fearful of the future. Station tries to change that for all its residents, it really does."

"But you said I was the first newcomer in a long time."

"That's right. Everyone had come to think that the doors were closed forever, that we were the chosen ones, for good or bad. You may find mixed reactions to your arrival."

"How did you know I was coming?"

"Well, Mister Rott told me, of course."

"And how did he know?"

Miles's golden eyes flashed again. "He knows everything, Hadder." A deep sigh. "And with that, my friend, I will leave you to your thoughts. You have much to consider and a new life to prepare for."

Panic struck Hadder like cold water. "Wait, Miles, I have so many more questions. Where do I sleep? What is expected of me?"

Miles had already started moving towards the steps of the Perch. "Any-where and nothing, my friend. Each Bar is larger than it looks. Living quar-ters and other necessities can be found under each; just look for a space that's uninhabited at the moment." Hadder began to ask another question, but Miles held up his hand. "I really must be going, Hadder. I was supposed to play at *The Royal Jelly* this Solay, and this unplanned tutorial has already made me late. Not that I'm upset, mind you. Anything for Mister Rott."

"What's *The Royal Jelly*?"

"A Bar to the northwest. Nice place. But if I may suggest, jumpstart your new life by visiting the Celebration Cluster just east of here. They'll give you a proper welcome." Miles began to descend the stairs but stopped suddenly. "Oh, I almost forgot. Don't worry about your health here. There're no diseases, no one gets sick, no STDs or genital warts to keep you from a good time. Heck, no one even ages as far as I can tell. So, go out and lose yourself. You'll always find yourself again." Miles continued down.

"Wait! No one ages or gets sick? So, no one dies here in Station?" Hadder called out.

"I didn't say that," came the reply from beneath, Miles's voice fading away, replaced by another chill breeze that cut through Hadder's worn t-shirt and jeans.

Hadder went to the railing and faced west, looking down at the various Bars and wondering which would be his, watching Station's residents as they crossed between buildings, hollering greetings to each other and exchanging laughter.

Hadder's mind wandered. Could this strange city really prove a new beginning? Could it make him finally forget his old life that was lost in the wreckage? Is that what he needed? Is that what he really wanted?

As Hadder stood pondering these questions, time passed. He didn't know how long he remained there, but a shifting of moon shadows told him that Solay was slowly transitioning into Haela. It was time to go down, to face this new reality. Looking out at his new city, one full of limitless possibility and with a cast of unique characters to meet, Hadder felt as alone as he did on that couch, counting heartbeats and begging them to stop.

Hadder breathed in deeply, holding in the air until his lungs burned, before exhaling loudly, as if to remind himself that he still lived. Slapping the cold handrail, he set off down the Perch's stairs, spiraling into a dark new world.

———

HADDER REACHED the bottom of the Perch and looked around. Given the twisting nature of the staircase, he had to reacquaint himself with his surroundings to identify south. He agreed with Miles's inference that he needed a jolt to his central nervous system, a hard reboot. The Celebration Cluster sounded like the ideal place to accomplish this. With only a basic understanding of where he was going, Hadder began walking an approximation of east, hoping that answers would come as more of the city was revealed. Keeping the Perch at his back, Hadder marched in a steady but unhurried pace, trying not to stick out as the new kid in school. Because while some enjoyed meeting the new boy, there were always others waiting to pounce.

5

H adder marveled at the nocturnal beauty of the city. Cobblestone paths lined with blueish lichen wove through manicured lawns and gardens. Small, handcrafted signs, carved with care and detailed with a steady hand, helped guide one along the many paths. This way to the Perch. That way to the Lethe River. Straight ahead, and you would find yourself at something called *The Soiree Noire*.

Unsure of where he was going, Hadder simply plunged forward, stopping to take in Station's bizarre but enchanting horticulture. A grouping of brightly iridescent white blossoms took turns shooting brilliant, multicolored spores into the air, making the area around them light up like the Fourth of July. Tall yellow flowers shaped like phonograph horns belted out air that made dulcet sounds and released sweet fragrances as Hadder passed.

Hadder had to pause for a moment as two distinct flowers, one a striking red and the other midnight blue, leaned into each other from opposite ends of the pathway, locked in a passionate kiss. Sitting just below Hadder's eye line, they created an arch that he could have quickly passed under, but he decided against this, choosing instead to remain still for the bawdy blossom show. After several minutes, the flowers separated, returning to their respective sides of the pathway. Once there, each flower, in tandem, launched purple seeds into the night sky that came down gently on glowing green propellers. A light evening breeze caught the lot and sent them in various directions to start new lives in other parts of the city.

Station's mysteries didn't end with its plant life. The air was filled with translucent butterflies that graced various flowers with their beauty. The size of a human hand, Hadder thought he could make out small, human-like faces at the tops of the insect bodies, smiling at him as they passed teasingly close to his face.

For a short while, a box turtle with flashlight eyes walked along the path with a slow-moving Hadder. On the turtle's rather large shell sat an ecosystem of its own, complete with a black soil foundation, peat moss topping, and an assortment of shrubbery comprised of unique shapes and colors. Circling the vegetation was a potpourri of chromatic insects that would take turns landing on and taking off from the variegated leaves. One insect, a large yellow bee that left pink trails in its wake, swooped down and plucked a crimson berry from a particular plant. Struggling a bit with the weight, the bee hefted the seed into the air and flew towards the box turtle's head. When in range, it dropped the berry, which was quickly picked out of the air by a snapping maw. A small tip, Hadder thought, for the reptilian conveyance.

Leaving the turtle and its self-contained world behind, Hadder went right at the next fork in the path, too entranced by the scenes around him to pay attention to the small signs. Long glow-worms could be seen on several of the larger leaves, hungrily having their fill. As they ate, a neon gas escaped their worm asses and hung for a second before coalescing into distinct shapes and images. One worm created a small ballerina pirouetting in the air while another formed a fist with only its middle finger up. Hadder flicked that one deep into the adjacent bush and continued to move forward, wowed by everything he was experiencing.

After gaping at Station's natural curiosities for what felt like hours, Hadder got the definite feeling that he was moving in circles and decided that he needed to take a more active approach in finding his way. While the signs should be helpful, Hadder had no idea about the landmarks or Bars to which they referred. None referenced actual Clusters, probably in line with Miles's assertion that Clusters could change and blend into each other over time.

Coming around a corner in an unusually steep garden section, Hadder spotted the first person he had seen on his unplanned nature hike. It was one of the black-garbed workers he had spied earlier, bending low to tend to some plants that sat on the edge of a small pond. Back towards the cobble-stones, Hadder could see the man's impossibly pale hands working at a furious speed to dig holes and deposit saplings. If the man heard Hadder's approach, he gave no sign.

Hadder, growing tired of sightseeing, decided it was best to ask for direc-tions before his thirst grew any stronger. He moved to stand close behind the black-on-white figure. "Excuse me, I seem to be a bit lost. Can you point me towards the Celebration Cluster?"

No reaction came as the speed planting continued. Hadder moved around to the other side of the man, hoping to catch his eye and attention. Head down towards his work, Hadder was unable to make out the face, but took note of the man's snowy white hair that loudly reflected the Solay's intense moon rays. Hadder knelt down beside the man and, seeing no other way to distract him from his duties, placed his hand carefully on the other's working arm. His progress now halted; the man looked up to stare at Hadder.

Half a second of shock was followed by an instinctive revulsion that, instead of being vocalized, manifested itself as Hadder falling backward on his ass before hurriedly crab-walking until he was a safe distance away. There he remained on his back, determined to ensure that what he saw was indeed real and not the hallucination of some alien pollen in his lungs.

The man's face was the same as his hands - porcelain white. But this inhuman color was not limited to the man's visage. His eyes were two color-less marbles, making him appear as an animated Roman bust. Tearing away from those empty eyes, Hadder was equally appalled by what he found inches below, where instead of a mouth, there was only perfectly smooth skin.

With no scar or stitching or divot, one could only assume that no mouth had ever graced that blank face.

"I'm so sorry to bother you," Hadder stammered from his backside, unable to know if the creature understood him, viewed him as friend or foe.

And he didn't wait to find out as the white creature stood up, revealing sinewy muscle under the black skinsuit. Flipping onto his stomach, Hadder rose quickly and began to run blindly around the next corner. He didn't make it far before tripping over a raised cobblestone to fall headfirst into a broad thoroughfare that had been concealed by a curtain of ivy falling from branches that hung over the path.

Hadder hit the ground hard, driving wind from his lungs and scraping his palms. Raising his eyes slowly, Hadder noticed two things. First, the larger, more polished stones that made up this new path. Second, the two pairs of shoes that stood uncomfortably close to his head. One was shiny black Beatle boots while the other was a tiny duo of intricate high-tops that changed colors like a lava lamp as the wearer shifted from one foot to the other.

The owner of the boots spoke first. "Easy there, old chap. My goodness, but what's the hurry?" Hadder detected a posh British accent.

Hands wrapped around Hadder's arms and helped him to his feet. The man, whose outfit continued the Beatles theme with a smart-looking black suit with pants that just touched the ankles, continued as he brushed the dirt off of Hadder's stained t-shirt. "There, there, nothing broken, I presume. Oh, but look at that face, Reena! My good sir, you look like you've seen a ghost. Were you running from someone?"

Reena chimed in. "Or something?" Hadder looked over and had to do a double-take of the alluring girl who donned the artistic high-tops. She was a tiny dark-skinned Asian with fuchsia hair styled in a cute bob. Her makeup accented the look, with glowing rose-colored lines that outlined silver eyes that gleamed similarly to Miles's golden optics. She wore a youthful jumper of white on which messages changed continuously, from *YOLT* to *Station Brat* to *The Before = Dream*.

"I asked what you were running from." The man's musical voice ripped

Hadder's attention from the lovely girl. Hadder, unable to put what he saw into words, simply pointed down the side-path with a shaky hand. "I'll check it out," the man said to Reena before sprinting away.

"See something you like," Reena giggled.

Hadder realized that he was gawking at the girl again. This time, he had noticed a quarter-sized comet revolving above Reena's head. It tore through the air at a steady pace, leaving in its wake a pink tail that created a perfect circle above Reena. Ideal headwear for an angel.

"I was just admiring your..." Again, a loss of words. Hadder pointed.

"Oh, my Light Crown? Thanks so much, I just had it made. It's gonna be all the rage at *The Soiree* tonight. Remember that you saw it on me first, alright?"

The man returned, looking perplexed. Reena spoke first. "You see anything, Jonny?"

"Nothing. Sorry old chap, all I found was a manikin working on the gardens. Just some generic glume, Reena, not even a strange model. Cat release your tongue, yet? Can you tell me what you saw?"

Hadder tried to explain. "There was a man back there. A pale one. With white eyes and, and, and, no mouth. He..."

Jonny interrupted. "Yes, the manikin, I saw him. I'm asking, what has you so absolutely frazzled?"

Hadder stood open-mouthed. Recognition struck Reena.

"Wait a minute, Jonny." To Hadder, "Who are you? I don't think I've seen you around before. Jonny, have you ever seen this man?"

"Can't say that I have, love. I would have remembered that handsome jawline and wild-eyed bewilderment."

Reena took Hadder's hand. Her hands were soft like two doves. "You've never seen a manikin before, have you?" A broad smile revealed pink braces. "Because you just got here. Because you're a..."

"My god!" Jonny cut in excitedly. "You're a new resident! Oh, how truly delightful. Oh, poor thing, no wonder you look so Edvard Munch. Did no one explain manikins to you? Who's running this travesty of an operation?"

"I bet it was that Miles. He can't concentrate on anything besides his music for any length of time. We should've been asked to do it."

"You know Mister Rott loves his original Keys, my dear. From which we are far removed. But enough of the past, where are our manners? My good sir, I am Jonston Van Vleet, also known as Jonny VV, and this is my dearest friend and esteemed equal Reena Song. What might your name be?"

Hadder forced himself to speak, working hard to remove his eyes from Jonny's suit, which he noticed subtly danced with green embers as if logs had just been thrown on a Christmas fire. "I'm Hadder. Marlin Hadder. And yes, I just arrived, although I'm not too sure how long ago. And yes, Miles took me to the Perch, but he left me with more questions than answers. And finally, yes, that thing back there, that manikin, scared the shit out of me."

Jonny VV slapped his hand together loudly. "Oh, how marvelous, Reena! How absolutely wonderful! We have a project on our hands. It's so great to meet you, Hadder. It's been too long since someone new showed up. Honestly, most of us thought the books were closed, but how happy I am to know that we were wrong. Where were you trying to go, Hadder, if you don't mind me asking."

"Miles thought the Celebration Cluster might be a good place to start."

Reena hooked her left arm around Hadder's right. "Well, at least boring Miles got that part right."

Jonny took Hadder's left arm. "Indeed, he did, my Asian blossom. Hadder, the Celebration Cluster happens to be where the striking Miss Reena and I were heading, as we do on the eve of every Haela. We would be honored if you would walk with us. Perhaps we can shed a bit more light on this dark place."

"I would like that."

"Then we're off," said Reena, pulling Hadder and Jonny with her.

Hadder's feet moved, but his mind remained frozen, unable to comprehend the things he had witnessed in the past few hours. Too many questions and still too few answers. Still clinging to a world now closed to him. But at least he was no longer alone, as he distinctively felt two arms helping him along this new, evidently more traveled road.

———

THEY WALKED in silence briefly before Jonny, already showing himself to be the verbose gentleman that he was, began the lesson.

"So, tell me, Hadder, did that scoundrel Miles tell you anything of value?"

"He told me about the Bar system. Said I had to get in where I fit in."

Jonny laughed. "Well, at least he shed some light on that. Life in Station is similar to the Before."

"Miles mentioned the Before."

"Yes, our lives before Station. Anyway, think of Bars as groups of friends. Sometimes you would like to hang out with this group, other times you prefer that group. This group you can live with, another you can party with. There's no laws or contracts here, so it's all a bit of a loosey-goosey arrangement, but we like it like that, don't we Reena."

"Of course. Who needs restrictions?"

"Well, some do, don't they, love?" Both laughed at a joke Hadder didn't catch. Jonny continued. "Some Bars are just places to meet up and have a good time, while others are for nesting, with living quarters beneath them. Rooms are first-come, first-serve, but most people respect if an individual has remained in the same room for a while, meaning it becomes theirs permanently, or as long as he or she wishes. Some like to create new homes here, not like Reena and I. True rolling stones, isn't that right, darling?"

"No moss here, Jonny."

Hadder's curiosity could be kept silent no longer. "And that thing back there, the manikin?"

Jonny stopped walking. "Well now, look around, new friend Hadder." He waited for Hadder to take in his surroundings before pressing on. "How would you describe Station so far?"

Hadder thought for a moment. "Clean. Manicured. Beautiful. Dim. Alien."

"Well said. The last two are products of the place itself, but the first three we owe to the hundreds of manikins that service Station."

"But what are they? Slaves?" Hadder involuntarily shuddered at the idea.

"Oh no, dear man, you have to have a soul to be a slave. Manikins are just human-shaped husks preprogrammed with instructions. Wind-up men and women. They tend the gardens, prepare our food, pour our drinks, and clean up our filth."

"They do more than that, Jonny."

"Quite right you are, my exotic berry. The more advanced ones can do wondrous things, like creating breathtaking ensembles such as those being worn by your two guides."

"Who do you think made me this Light Crown?"

"Some can play moving music that will make you sob like an infant. Others can paint haunting portraits of loved ones from the Before." Jonny leaned in close to Hadder's ear. "And others can bring you to the mountain-tops of sexual ecstasy."

"Jonny! Oh my god, gross!"

"Sorry, love, just an observation," stated Jonny, throwing a wink towards Hadder for good measure.

"So, manikins do all the work in Station?" asked Hadder, still trying to come to grips with these creatures.

Reena responded, "Well, Station wouldn't be much of a Xanadu if we all had jobs to do, now would it?"

Hadder halted the walk. "Is that what this is supposed to be? Some kind of Utopia?"

Jonny and Reena exchanged wary glances, the first crack in their other-wise optimistic projections. Reena answered with a question. "What is a Utopia, Marlin? Is it a place that is perfect for everyone all the time? This seems impossible. Or is it a place that merely offers the complete freedom of life and expression, the elements necessary so that one may craft the perfect life for herself? I think you'll find like so many of us have that Station is not the former. But it can be the latter."

Hadder still looked confused.

Jonny took his hand. "Come, maybe it's best you see for yourself. We're almost there."

———

As the trio walked, their shadows were becoming simultaneously deeper and yet less defined. Hadder looked up to find that the Idol Moon was marginally smaller and giving off noticeably less light than when he first entered the city, clearly transitioning from Solay to Haela.

The broader path they were now on - Hadder thought it resembled more of a road than the small paths through the gardens - was lined with large trees whose many branches went up, out, and down in gentled arcs. At the end of each branch were baseball-sized fruits that emanated soft, purplish light, lighting the way for Station's transient populace.

Jonny, following Hadder's eyes, commented. "These are Monarch Trees. They can be found straddling most of Station's larger walkways. If you observe them carefully, you can see how their fruits grow brighter as Haela falls and dim during Solay. Just another of Mister Rott's wonderful creations."

"Who is this Mister Rott? Miles mentioned him as well, but I didn't get anything concrete out of him."

Another nervous exchange between Jonny and Reena. "That's a difficult one, Hadder, old boy. Like describing *Starry Night* to a blind person or trying to hold back a river with your hands."

Reena snickered. "Those are terrible explanations, Jonny. Someone explained it to me at a party many Haelas ago. Mister Rott is like dark matter. We rarely see him, his true impact is nearly impossible to measure, and yet he pulls all the strings on this contained universe of ours. Therefore, we know he exists. We know he crafted all of this. We know he handpicked each of us. But the why of it all?" Reena shrugged helplessly. "Many theories are floating around, some plausible and most others preposterous. But these are *big* questions, sweet, handsome Marlin, better left for later times, to be digested piece by piece lest you choke on too much awareness."

"Well said and quite right," said Jonny. "You have eternity for these philosophical queries, old chap. This upcoming Haela? This is a time for jubilation! For meeting new friends and grabbing up new lovers!" Jonny jogged ahead to stand under a large, darkened archway that marked the end of the current thoroughfare, which was opening into a vast courtyard beyond. "This!" He threw his arms up dramatically. "This is the Celebration Cluster!"

On cue, the archway lit up like a Roman candle, forcing Hadder to shield his eyes in the growing dimness. Upon adjustment, Hadder found that weaved throughout the arch was a medley of glowing flowers that released all the colors of the spectrum while systematically discharging fiery seeds that disappeared skyward before exploding into blasts of light, creating the perfect backdrop for Jonny VV's immaculate pose.

Reena stood on her toes to kiss Hadder's cheek. She smelled like vanilla cookies fresh out of the oven. "In case you couldn't tell, we're here." And with that, she screamed into the air, ran, and jumped into Jonny's waiting arms. Together, they beckoned Hadder forward, dragging him deep into a Haela he would never forget.

6

H adder passed under the blinding archway and into a paved central clearing that was vaguely circular, and onto which were situated nearly a dozen Bars of differing sizes and shapes. In the center of the clearing was the largest of the buildings, a nine-story monstrosity covered in vines and red roses whose glow made the entire structure look as if it were made of pure fire. The sign over the entrance, although unlit, read *Inferno*.

"Is that where we're going?" Hadder asked, pointing towards the conspicuous Bar. Jonny and Reena shared a nervous laugh.

"Not there, my virgin friend. *Inferno* is the craziest, most grotesque Bar in the Celebration Cluster. Best to stay away from there, or you'll end up catatonic on one of your first Haelas. In fact, just stay away from it forever. That's the best policy. But not to worry, we'll have a grand time elsewhere."

The trio walked to the left of the clearing, keeping *Inferno* on their right. Two Bars passed by on the western edge of the Cluster, one smaller establishment called *The 1999* and the other a majestic building whose sign read *The Soiree Noire*. In direct contrast to *Inferno*, *The Soiree Noire* was a classically built marble building bathed in beautiful white light by barrel-shaped bushes with shining megaphone blossoms that surrounded the Bar, spotlighting it. Hadder recalled Reena mentioning a Bar with a similar name.

They came upon the ivory Bar but, to Hadder's surprise, continued past. "Aren't we going in? To *The Soiree Noire*, I mean."

Reena answered this time. "We will, for sure, but not yet. *The Soiree* doesn't open until full Haela, so we have some time to kill."

"And a better place to ease ourselves into the true night," piggybacked Jonny.

They kept walking, continuing past several more Bars; *Inferno* was now at their backs. During the stroll, Hadder could see the plaza begin to fill as residents started to pour in from other thoroughfares that fed into the Cluster. Each resident, from what Hadder could tell, was as smartly dressed as his two companions, with colorful designs, illuminated fabrics, and exotic materials. Most yelled out in greeting to Jonny and Reena, who were obviously well-liked. Hadder sighed deeply, feeling for the first time since the accident that he was in good hands, being taken care of.

The Celebration Cluster woke up as they walked, reacting no doubt to the Idol Moon's reduction. The world grew darker and brighter in succession as radiant moonbeams were traded for opening petals that released a Solay's worth of pent-up spectral energy that painted the Cluster. Looking around, Hadder held back tears, imagining that such a canvas would be more at home in the Louvre, for these places didn't really exist, especially for wretches like himself. Hadder heard his name from far away but growing closer.

"Hadder. Hadder." It was Jonny. Hadder didn't know how many times he had called him. He realized that he had stopped walking, was now merely standing and staring wide-eyed at the wonderment of his surroundings.

"Sorry, Jonny, I was..." Another loss for words, a growing habit.

Jonny smiled sweetly. "No, I'm sorry. We've been here so long we all forget how truly remarkable it all is." Jonny and Reena joined Hadder, and together the three stood in silence, staring at an alien realm as it transitioned from bizarrely beautiful to beautifully bizarre. Finally, Hadder turned to his new friends. "I'm ready."

Together, they swept Hadder away towards a simple two-story Bar that looked as if it didn't exist. No flower lights were highlighting the building, for none were needed. The entire exterior looked to be made of mirrored glass, which powerfully reflected the breathtaking portrait of the Celebration Cluster and created a startling effect on the observer.

"Here we are, Hadder, my boy. This is *Morning's Echo*, the perfect place to start another memorable Haela."

Hadder looked at the building, and in it, he saw himself, Jonny VV, and Reena Song as they approached. He smiled at the image, three friends backlit by a psychedelic, fantastical Vegas, ready to take on the night. "I'm ready," repeated Hadder. They were the first confident words he had spoken in years.

ALTHOUGH ENTIRELY DISSIMILAR, the inside of *Morning's Echo* matched its exterior in terms of attractiveness and warmness. A large central, ovular bar dominated the main room, behind which were three manikins who took turns either frantically pouring beverages, cleaning, or staring blankly into space. Everything was made from a light-colored wood that gave the area a relaxed, calming appeal. Looking up, Hadder noticed that he could see clear to the beamed ceiling, for the second floor was nothing more than a 360-degree mezzanine that allowed those above an unencumbered view of the first floor.

Several groups sitting at various tables, sipping colorful drinks from geometric glasses, greeted the trio as they entered. One woman stood up. With dark caramel skin and an afro that was blown back into a tear shape, she looked like she had stepped out from the pages of a leading fashion magazine. Her tailored white apron dress contrasted perfectly with her dark skin and showed off her athletic, impossibly long legs. "Reena! Who is that dingy, Reality Bites, tasty morsel you got with you? Hey boo! Long-time, never see!"

Hadder could feel the blood rushing to his face in a blush. Jonny swiftly

came to his defense. "Not yet, Sonja," he called out. "We'll do a proper introduction in a bit." Jonny now appeared to be talking to everyone in the Bar.
"When *Echo* fills up, I'll introduce our new man here to everyone."

Sonja looked confused. "New man? What's that supposed..." the words
faded out as realization settled in. "Oh, child," were the last words Hadder
could hear as Sonja covered her mouth and dramatically collapsed back into
her chair, falling into hushed conversation with her tablemates. Hadder
couldn't help but see all the other occupied tables falling into similar quiet
talks that were followed by furtive glances in his direction.

Jonny walked him to the circular bar, helping him into a tall stool that
was topped and backed with cushioned white leather. Hadder settled in as
Jonny and Reena took seats beside him.

"That was necessary, old chap, or you'll be facing the firing squad all
night. Honestly, you still will, but after I announce you to an audience, I'm
hoping you'll later be staring down one barrel at a time rather than an arsenal. Glume!"

Hadder was forced back into his chair as one of the three manikins
approached from the other side of the bar and waited. It was nearly identical
to the one he had stumbled upon in the garden, only this one had spiked
white hair atop its head. A head that held a face that contained no mouth.

"What will it be, Hadder?"

"Just beer is fine."

Another chuckle from Reena. Jonny worked to address Hadder's
confused look. "This is Station, Hadder. The miracles don't stop with our
surroundings. The drinks provided have all sorts of properties, can make
you feel any number of ways. Uppers, downers? Want to think more or less?
Need to calm down? Need to cheer up? Want to sleep? Want to wake up?
Need to remember? Have to forget? Behind this bar are potions carefully
crafted to match whatever mood you're in - or want to be in."

"How do I know which to take?"

"I think there's a list behind the bar somewhere," answered Reena. "But
no one ever uses it. Not sure it's even accurate. The best way is to ask someone, especially someone who's been around."

"Which is literally everyone except you at this point," added Jonny. "Which is why maybe it's best if I order for you, if you don't mind."

Hadder motioned in the affirmative, and Jonny looked to begin going through concoctions in his mind. "What do you think, Reena? The old Number 7?"

Reena smiled and rubbed Hadder's shoulder. "I think that one would be perfect, Jonny."

"And how about you, my love."

"Let me get a Number 9."

Jonny seemed surprised. "Number 9? This early in the Haela?"

Reena's Light Crown began to rotate faster. "Marlin has inspired me. It's gonna be a special night."

"By God, you're right! It will be a special night. Glume! Two 9's and a 7 for my new friend!"

The manikin quickly dipped behind the bar, coming up with three glasses, two cylindrical and one round. It turned quickly and walked to a long rectangular table that was centered inside the ovular bar. From the table rose various taps, each with a distinct number. With practiced hands and efficient movement, the manikin filled all three glasses in short order and returned them to the patrons. Jonny and Reena had before them thin-looking orange elixirs while Hadder stared at a thick golden substance that sloshed slowly in his round crystalline glass.

Jonny lifted his glass, and Reena did the same. "Hadder, my friend. This is how we toast here in Station. *The Before is no more, we've all closed that door. To Station, our home, where new dreams are born.* Cheers!"

Hadder put the Number 7 to his lips and drank deeply. He was happy to discover that the beverage was mildly sweet and much lighter than it appeared. It went down quick and smooth, and Hadder felt it warm his belly and massage his brain almost instantly. A relaxing chemical drifted through his bloodstream, loosening muscles and lessening inhibitions. For the first time in memory, a small smile crept onto Hadder's face.

Reena noticed it almost immediately. "Ahh, there it is, Jonny. That's what we've been looking for."

"Yes, love, the Number 7 always does the trick. Orientation periods always require potent relaxants."

As they made small talk, people continued to enter *Morning's Echo*, joining others at the round side tables and filling chairs around the large bar. Jonny seemed to be taking a lay of the land when he spoke. "When do you think I should make the introduction, Miss Song?"

Reena looked Hadder up and down, failing to hide her rating of his current attire. "Jonny, you absolutely have to let me clean him up before you do. And get some proper Celebration Cluster garments on him. We don't want everyone judging the poor thing before they've even met him."

"Right you are, yet again, love. I'll meet you both upstairs in what feels like an hour."

Reena pulled Hadder from his stool. "Come with me, Marlin. Please."

Reena led Hadder down and past the central bar towards the back of the *Echo*, where he noticed two large double doors. They gave way quickly under Reena's soft push. To the left, stairs rose to the upper mezzanine, while the right found stairs going down to another floor under the main Bar. Reena spoke as they descended, holding tightly to Hadder's arm. "Careful going down, Marlin. That Number 7 can do a number on your equilibrium."

"Where are we going?"

"To the living quarters. *Morning's Echo* is one of the few Bars in the Celebration Cluster that maintains living quarters, which is great if you don't feel like getting ready until you get here. Or if you make a new friend and can't wait to tear their clothes off." Reena released another giggle that Hadder found intoxicating, building on his foundation of Number 7.

At the bottom of the stairs, Hadder found that he had entered a spacious lounge area. There, he found plush white leather armchairs, expensive-looking rugs, full-length mirrors, and ornate side tables. Spread throughout were colorful drinks, smoking ashtrays, and unfamiliar board games. Several patrons were in the lounge, some merely relaxing with drink and smoke while others worked furiously at the mirrors, straightening here and curling there in an attempt to look their best. Those that noticed the new pair enter the room gave Reena a friendly nod and Hadder a curious glance before returning to their thoughts and endeavors.

Also in the room were two manikins, this time in the shapes of females, waiting patiently for instruction. Reena marched up to the nearest one. "Lemma, I need some clothes for this beautiful man." The manikin's white eyes showed no recognition nor betrayed any emotion, if it had any, merely turning on its heal and moving towards one of the many small hallways that spidered off from the lounge. It passed several closed doors before coming to one with a white hand insignia on its face. Standing silently before the door, the lemma manikin placed its own white hand on the door's matching mark. An electric blue line outlined the door momentarily before it slid to the side, allowing entrance.

Reena explained, "Throughout Station, doors that you can enter have white hand buttons on them. If the hand buttons are red, it means the room is currently occupied or off limits to residents."

Shuffling into the room, Hadder looked around to find that it looked like an impossibly fancy fast food restaurant. Maybe twenty feet into the room, a lucent counter ran from right to left, effectively cutting the space in half. The lemma manikin walked behind the impressive counter through a short break on the right side and waited patiently. After a few seconds, it pointed up.

Hadder looked above the manikin and watched as a screen running the wall's length came to life, showing images of men and women wearing a variety of clothing, much of which he had never seen or even imagined.

"Show me men's. More formal," said Reena, looking up as the filters took effect and narrowed down selections. "What's your style, Marlin? And don't tell me it's this t-shirt and jeans look. I mean, sure it has its place, but not here. And certainly not tonight. You're going to be the belle of the ball this Haela."

Hadder thought back to what the people in Station referred to as the Before, back to a life too-briefly full of joy and love, hugs and kisses, big smiles, and tiny laughs. In that life, Hadder wore suits to work, taking real pride in his appearance as a reflection of his contentment. He wanted to feel that way again, if only for a night.

"I'd like a suit, Reena."

She slapped her hands together. "Oh, I was hoping you'd say that. I was terrified you were gonna say khakis or a hoodie. Do you mind? I have a vision of something breathtaking but casual, perfect for this Haela. Also, there's a lot of materials and options here you've never seen before."

Hadder looked again at Reena's exotic outfit, "I believe you. Please have at it."

Reena marched up to the lemma manikin and began speaking too low for Hadder to overhear, motioning with her hands in an expression of her excitement. The manikin, as usual, stood unmoving. After several minutes passed, with Reena conferring with the digital board and making various selections, she returned to Hadder's side. "Ok, stand up straight, Marlin. Now turn to the side. Good, now turn around. Perfect. It should have all your measurements now. Let's head out while it works."

Reena began leading Hadder back into the hallway. Hadder turned briefly and saw the manikin start to move in a blur of motion, grabbing fabrics from behind the counter and taking them to the left-hand wall, against which he noticed a sewing station. There, it sat and began cutting cloth in a fast, measured pace. As the door slid shut behind him, he already began to hear the whirr of a sewing machine.

Once outside, Reena walked Hadder further down the hallway, stopping at a pair of large double doors, which slid open upon Reena's light touch. Inside was a large shower room, with nozzles of bright brass on the ceiling and back wall. Vented flooring gave off warm and inviting steam, and Hadder, for the first time, took note of the dirt and grime that stuck to his skin with dried sweat. Around three-quarters of the shower area, save the back wall, was an area set back from the sprayers that housed marble benches and open lockers of polished metal. No one else was in the community shower, for which Hadder was grateful. Although not a prude, he wasn't quite ready for a group cleansing.

Reena motioned him to the left. "You can get undressed over at the locker. I'll take those clothes."

"Where are you going to put them?"

"In the nearest fire, silly. These rags reek of the Before."

Hadder walked over and began to undress, feeling awkward about handing a beautiful girl his soiled, smelly garments. He stopped when down to his underwear and gave Reena a nervous look. She smiled knowingly. "I'll leave the rest to you," she said, turning back to the main doors. Just walk into the shower area and say *water*. When you're finished, say *water stop*. Say *air*, and you'll discover why no towels are provided. I'm going to dispose of these and check on your suit."

"But it's only been like a minute."

"Desires are met fast here in Station," Reena responded as the double doors slid closed again.

Hadder took a deep breath to calm himself. Although he had always done well with women, it had been a long time since he had allowed himself to be so close to one, especially in such intimate circumstances. After the accident, being around another woman had seemed tantamount to cheating, bringing with it guilt that tightened like a noose the closer they got. Therefore, he just stopped and resigned himself to a life alone.

But this wasn't then. This wasn't the Before. As far as he could tell, this wasn't even the Earth he knew. Maybe his vows didn't apply here; he certainly didn't feel them pressing on his chest the way he used to. Perhaps he was finally rid of their hold on his life.

Sliding his underwear off, Hadder stepped onto the community shower floor and was greeted by the warm mist. Moving closer to the center, he saw specks of color dancing in the steam, rainbows that not only touched his skin, but awoke something inside. Standing in the middle, Hadder said *water*, and gentle cascading waterfalls fell upon him. As the only bather, not only did the water from directly above him strike him, but liquid from other far away nozzles began to bend impossibly in the air, some at 90-degree angles, to touch his feet, legs, hips, and back. Hadder felt the glittered water open his pours, soften his skin, smooth age lines, tighten fat deposits, and thicken his hair.

Head down, letting the magical water wash away the past years, Hadder began to gently weep, not only in gratitude for this new life but in mourning for the life he was leaving behind, placing it firmly in the Before. Although in recent years the Before had given him nothing but pain and loss, he had grown to depend on that pain, to define himself by it. Without it, who was he?

Who was Marlin Hadder now?

"You're one of us now," Hadder heard softly behind him, a simple answer to his difficult question. Reena had entered the community shower and now stood before him, naked save her Light Crown, which continued its rotations and appeared even more enchanting as it cut through the water. She, too, had the prismatic water moving at strange angles to wash her. With half the water on Hadder and the other half on Reena, it looked like two crystalline arms pushing them together, needing them to connect under a glassy gaze. Reena reached up slowly to softly touch Hadder's cheek before cupping her hand behind his head and pulling it in for a sensual kiss. Her tongue darted into his mouth, and he tasted tropical chemistry as it flicked his own, sending shockwaves through his body as it shrank pupils and enlarged something else. Hadder nearly fell over from the sensation but was kept upright by Reena, who seemed to anticipate this reaction.

"What about Jonny VV," Hadder managed weakly, barely pulling the words from a foggy mind.

"This is Station, Marlin. We all belong to each other, but none to one. Relax."

And Hadder did relax as their lips met again, sending waves of ecstasy through his body, a mere precursor of the pleasures to come. Hadder fell out of time as his and Reena's bodies intertwined. At one point, he laid on the warm shower floor, Reena astride him as two jets of water met her back, a true angel nursing him back to health. In that warm embrace, Hadder drifted away from the Before forever, floating softly to land in Station's permanence.

"Welcome home," Reena whispered in his ear, and all went white.

————

HADDER CAME to completely dry on one of the side benches. He rose his head and saw Reena, already dressed, waiting near the front shower doors.

"How are you feeling?" she asked.

"Alive" was the only response he could formulate, and she laughed.

"I hope you don't mind; I took the liberty of having the system dry you while you slept."

"How long was I out?"

"Not long at all."

Hadder became suddenly embarrassed. "I'm so sorry, I shouldn't have passed out like that. I..."

Reena stopped him. "Happens to everyone the first time they take Awakening." She saw his confusion. "The chemical that was on my tongue. Better you experience it first with a friend, the stuff is going to be all around you tonight." Reena pointed to the nearest locker. "I already picked up your suit from the lemma. It's hanging up. There's a full-length mirror by the door here. I'll wait for you in the hall."

When she exited, Hadder tried to get up, but immediately fell back onto the bench laughing. His legs were jelly, and his heart was beating like a lab rat's, but he felt truly fantastic. Composing himself, he rose again, this time remaining upright, and moved over to the locker that held his new clothes.

Hanging in the locker was an eloquent single-breasted suit made of a strange sterling material that swam like quicksilver. Below the hanging suit, folded nicely, was a pair soft, form-fitting underwear and socks. As he dressed, Hadder marveled at the material used for everything. Light and airy, it felt as if he wore nothing at all. The pants and white button-up shirt stretched to accommodate his large form without being tight. The jacket was a perfect fit, hugging his shoulders but giving way easily as he moved. Soft, elegant cognac dress shoes and belt completed the look.

Moving towards the full-length mirror, Hadder was shocked by the man who stared back. The suit was as Reena said, fashionable but loose, skillfully tailored for a man who wanted to give the impression that he really didn't care to try hard. It was perfect.

But it wasn't just the clothes that had changed. The man who stood in the community shower had a light in his eyes, one Hadder thought to be extinguished long ago, never to be reignited. After straightening clothes that probably never needed smoothing, Hadder ran a hand through his wavy brown hair and left through the double doors, a smile plastered on his face that would take a putty knife to remove.

Reena, true to her word, waited in the hallway. She inhaled deeply as Hadder came into the light. "Well, well, I must say. I have really outdone myself with this one. You look amazing. The women are gonna hurt themselves falling over you."

Hadder tried to find the words to thank this magnificent creature. "Reena, I..."

Understanding flashed in her eyes, and she quickly grabbed his arm, pulling him back down the hall. "Not necessary and no time anyway. We're late, and they're waiting to meet you."

"Who is?"

"Everyone, silly."

Down the hall, they rushed through the lounge area, which was now empty save a single manikin, and up the stairs. They passed the landing to the ground floor and kept climbing, exiting at the top onto the second-floor mezzanine. People milled about along the entirety of the balcony, many looking towards Hadder when he stepped out. Jonny moved up quickly to greet them.

"Took your time, didn't you, love," stated Jonny without any undertones of anger.

"A Baptism was needed."

"Ahh, lucky you," said Jonny through a bright smile, and again, Hadder detected no jealousy in his new friend.

"And anyway," said Reena, "look what I've brought back."

"But by god, old chap, you do look incredible. Who could have known what was hidden under all that dirt and cotton?"

"I did," answered Reena, proud of her handiwork.

"Well, of course. But I knew all along you were in good hands, didn't I, Hadder? Come old boy, it's time to introduce you to the city. Don't worry, I can already see the concern on your face, no need to make a speech or open up the book of your life. This will merely save you a lot of time and confused looks later this Haela. Just trust me."

Jonny moved Hadder past the throngs that had gathered on the mezzanine and towards the pearl-like railing that protected revelers from nasty falls. As Hadder made his way to the front, his breath caught as he glimpsed the crowd that had gathered below. Arm across his shoulders, Jonny joined Hadder and touched a small indentation on the railing. His voice boomed across *Morning's Echo*, amplified by unseen speakers.

"Dear, dear residents, and friends. Silence for a moment, please." Jonny waited for a moment as the crowd quickly quieted. "You all know me by now."

In unison, the entire bar shot back, "Jonny VV!"

"That's right! Your recognition honors me. But you do not know this handsome gentleman to my left, for he is new to Station." Loud conversation rose up across the Bar, some excited, some worried. Jonny paused again, then continued. "Now, before you all start asking what this means, please note that Station did not sink into the desert. The drinks are still cool and effective." Jonny shot a smirk towards Hadder. "The showers are still hot and inviting. Nothing has changed. Except we have a new member of the family, a striking one at that! So, please, one and all, join me in welcoming our newest resident and family member - Marlin Hadder!" Applause started slowly but picked up steam. Within seconds, the entire Bar was a theater after a Shakespearean play, pushing Hadder back with the volume and enthusiasm of its welcome. Jonny held his hand up, calming the crowd. "Now that you know Hadder here, please be nice to him. We all know how wonderful but strange our fair city can be. Help him adjust. Help him forget the Before. Help him live again!"

With that, Jonny took two drinks from a glume manikin who had approached, handing one to Hadder. He lifted it to the audience. "*The Before is no more, we've all closed that door. To Station, our home, where new dreams are born.* Cheers! Cheers! And welcome!" With that, the audience exploded. Reena came over and kissed Jonny on the cheek. Hadder stamped down the sick feeling that briefly made an appearance in his stomach. Together, they embraced Hadder and moved him from the balcony. Those near on the mezzanine came up to shake Hadder's hand and clap Jonny VV on the back. As they paid their respects and spread back out, Hadder turned to face Jonny and Reena.

"What now?"

"Now, old chap? Well, now we party. Like only Station can."

Reena leaned back and belted out a scream of excitement, her Light Crown spinning faster than ever before. Although he didn't scream, Hadder's nerves began to shake in anticipation of what was to come, what sites he was to see in this new world on this first "night."

7

The next hour passed in a blur of greetings, welcomes, and congratulations mixed with the occasional uncomfortable glance or angry look, always from a face in the background that quickly vanished into the throng. Hadder was ushered by Jonny VV and Reena Song along the length of the mezzanine, hearing but failing to remember countless names. Faces melded together as did outfits, from the garish to the divine, all looking well-crafted.

Once the entirety of the mezzanine had been traversed, the celebrated trio marched back down the stairs to meet an even more extensive collection of residents, each wanting to either speak with or simply get a better look at Station's newest addition. Even more so than on the floor above, sheer numbers overwhelmed Hadder's ability to understand phrases shouted, comprehend questions asked, or later recall faces encountered.

Jonny and Reena tried to assist where possible, but soon all they could offer were embarrassed smiles and shrugs that said *this is the cost of celebrity*. As more and more faces entered the fray, Hadder's confusion and anxiety continued to mount. Everyone who approached was strangely attractive, just off the pages of Vogue or GQ, many with facial accents that would have been hard to describe in words. Now and then, on the edge of sight,

Hadder thought he spied more extreme anomalies. *Did that woman's eyelashes curl over her bald head? Did that man have two colorful birds holding up both sides of a long mustache? Could he really have seen a third eye on that individual who drifted in from the crowd?*

Just as Hadder began to fear that he would be overrun with attention, that his only escape would be to curl up in the fetal position on *Morning Echo's* clean floors, he was rescued by the piercing shrill of a whistle coming from the Bar's front doors. In unison, the congregation halted its carousing and turned to face the whistleblower. Standing in *Morning Echo's* opening doorway, the small man looked to have come directly from the mind of a steampunk author. He wore a heavily embroidered white trench coat, expertly fitted with a swallowtail cut, over a frilly black shirt with black slacks and knee-high black boots. His eyes seemed overlarge for his head, and stood out even more due to their gray hue, looking like two raging storms above a placid tanned face. Slicked back gray hair under a black top hat completed the look.

Once he knew he had the attention of the audience, the small man took the long silver whistle from between his pursed lips with a white-gloved hand and raised his other in a flourish. "Ladies and gentlemen, residents of all ages, seekers of happiness and lovers of Elevation; it is my honor to announce that *The Soiree Noire* is now open for your enjoyment. You are limited only by your imaginations, but please be kind to each other. Judgment will be commencing...NOW!"

Speech completed, he spun impressively on a heal and disappeared down *Echo's* front stairway. The crowd, momentarily quieted by his appearance, exploded in another release of pure elation and began to slowly filter out of the Bar, drinks being poured down throats on the way out, Hadder's trio already forgotten.

Jonny came back up to Hadder. "Don't worry, old chap, everyone always loses it when *The Soiree* opens. Now that they've all seen you expect more personal attention for a while."

"Who was that man?"

Reena answered. "That's Montgomery Walls, but everyone calls him

Monty the Mod. He and a few other self-selected purveyors of all things fashionable run *The Soiree Noire*. He can be a bit of a prick, but his parties are always the best. Right, Jonny?"

"Indeed, you're correct, my dear. And you're lucky to have run into us this past Solay, Hadder. Not just anyone can get into Monty's parties. Usually, you have to work your way up to his shindigs, prove that you're one of the glitterati. But he likes me and absolutely loves sweet Reena here, so we'll pull you in with us. Also, there's no way he could turn away our first new resident in forever."

The crowd continued its slow exit from *Morning's Echo* while some used the opportunity to take up seats at tables now unoccupied, meaning to spend more time at their current establishment. As the excitement began to die down, Hadder could feel his energy also begin to dwindle. From his long drive to the shit hole bar called Station, to his harrowing journey through the inter-dimensional tunnel and across the trackless desert, to his orientation to the city called Station and his escapade with the intoxicating Reena Song, to his introduction to some of Station's most prominent residents, Hadder had lived a lifetime in a few short hours with little rest. He could sense his body begin to sag under fatigue.

Jonny sensed his friend's failing stamina and put a hand to Hadder's face, concern marking his own. "You alright, old chap? You look completely drained. Think you have it in you to continue?"

"Go on ahead, Jonny," Reena intervened. "I can help him."

Jonny smiled. "What would we do without her? Wait for you both just outside."

As Jonny walked away, Reena knelt down and reached into one of her remarkable high-top sneakers, fingers revealing a hidden pocket in the tongue. She fumbled around for a bit before pulling out what looked to be lipstick in the shade of light blue. Removing the top, Reena expertly applied the glossy blue wax across her full lips. Without waiting for Hadder to comment, she once again pulled his head down for a passionate kiss, this time leaving her tongue out of the equation. As her lips rubbed vigorously against his own, Hadder could feel his entire body waking up, as if he had been submerged in a vial of B12. Color rushed back into Hadder's blanched face, and power returned to his arms and legs. The haze that had been preventing him from locating clear thoughts lifted as brain synapses fired.

They separated. "Better now, Marlin?"

"Yes, much, thanks. Me thanking you is becoming a habit."

Reena smiled sweetly. "I like it that way. Come on, Jonny is waiting for us." As she turned and started for the front doors, Hadder fought down the urge to yell, "I fucking love you" at the beautiful girl's back. He was happy he did, however, when a second later, Reena's shifting dress spelled out *Free Spirit*, reminding him that this girl was never meant for reservation by one person. Her anima was simply too much.

Disaster and embarrassment averted, Hadder followed Reena towards the entrance, a spring in his step like he had just risen from a week's worth of rest.

———

As promised, Jonny VV was waiting for them outside *Morning's Echo.* "Looking much improved, Hadder. Miss Reena works wonders, does she not?"

Hadder threw a thankful smile at Reena. "She certainly does." Reena curtsied in response.

"Then let us be on our way. It's obviously not far, but the gathered masses can proliferate. Luckily, Reena and I are regulars."

As they walked, Hadder noticed that true night, or Haela, had fallen over Station. Raising his eyes to the heavens, Hadder immediately understood how the city's evening had gotten its name. The Idol Moon, now half the size as during Solay and significantly less bright, was entirely encircled by a halo of light, an optical effect of the reduced emissions. Hadder quietly congratulation himself for uncovering another of Station's lesser mysteries.

Within minutes, *The Soiree Noire* appeared before them, the light-encased white building more striking now that full Haela had settled in. A thick mass of people had begun to form at the base of the Bar's elegant grand twin stairs that led up to its equally ornate double doors above. As residents mingled and conversed, a palpable buzz permeated the crowd, even affecting Hadder's two seasoned friends.

Just as Hadder was about to ask what everyone was waiting for, a disc that seemed to be made of pure light rose between the twin staircases, stopping when it was ten feet above the ground. On the conveyance stood Monty the Mod, whose top hat now shot a cascade of color from every angle, highlighting the small man's sharp features. Monty had traded in his silver whistle for equally shiny silver opera glasses with which he eagerly searched the crowd below.

When he spoke, his voice boomed from hidden speakers and was easily heard over the din of the crowd. "Lulu! What an interesting gown. Please enter. Is that you, Rafa? I don't know if I love it or hate it, but I am intrigued. Come on in. Bessa James, I know you are wearing the same thing you did just last week. Come back with something new, or don't come back at all! Benny and Sunrise, I love the matching ensemble. See you inside!"

This went on for a while before Monty's glasses fell upon Hadder's trio. "Jonny VV and Reena Song, two of my favorites. You both never fail to disappoint. Reena, I'll need to take a closer look at those shoes later. Both of you are free to join me this Haela. And by all means, bring that handsome, smartly-dressed friend of yours."

And with that, the crowd peacefully parted, allowing Hadder, Jonny, and Reena an unobstructed path to the stairway on the right. As they climbed, Monty the Mod continued his selection process. When they were eye-level with the diminutive doorman, Monty looked from his eyeglasses for a brief moment to shoot Hadder a curious look. Before Hadder could read into it, however, Monty returned the glasses to his face and berated a man in the crowd for his choice of footwear.

Reena spoke as they neared the top. "This is just part of Monty's show. He'll make his dramatic selections for an hour or so before tiring and turning it over to his personal manikin, who has a list of everyone allowed in. Almost everyone who's waiting downstairs is on the list; Monty just likes to give them shit. It's fun, but sometimes you just want to get in and get a fucking drink, you know?"

At the top of the stairs, an exceptionally tall glume manikin stood before the enormous open double doors, an ancient parchment scroll held in its hands that must have been Monty's treasured list. "Nice touch," commented Hadder as they passed under the lanky manikin's white gaze.

Moving into *The Soiree Noire*, Hadder's breath caught for the hundredth time that day. If the exterior of the Bar was beautiful, the interior was something no one word could aptly describe. The room they had entered was a colossus, with ceilings soaring high above and the back wall beyond view. The floor was a deep, warm crimson that briefly showed footprints in lighter red as one walked. The walls surrounding the room showed beautiful scenery that changed every few minutes. One minute, the room sat on the balcony of an Italian villa that overlooked Lake Como. Later, it would be at the center of the Roman Coliseum. The walls were not simple LED screens, however, as Hadder discovered upon closer inspection. They were something else entirely, creating images so clear and vibrant that one could almost feel breezes coming off the Mediterranean and smell the evergreens of Colorado's Rocky Mountains.

Globes of light floated throughout the room, providing illumination without impeding on ambiance. Comfortable leather chairs and couches could be found throughout the room, and Hadder watched in amazement as one shifted to make room for a third occupant as another melded to perfectly fit the form of the small woman who had recently sat.

Although there was no bar as far as Hadder could tell, manikins were positioned throughout the room, some waiting for a command and others carrying trays of colorful drinks. Jonny grabbed one manikin as it passed and took three beverages, all with a bright green tint.

"Here you go, my friends. Don't worry, Hadder, this is just a sweet starter drink to loosen our dancing hips. It's the Number 4 for future reference. So tell me, my new friend, what do you think of *The Soiree?*"

Hadder searched but was unable to come up with an appropriate metaphor. "It's amazing," he settled on.

"Indeed, but you haven't seen anything yet. Wait until the Haela truly gets going. Let's mingle."

Deeper into the Bar they walked as more of Monty's selections trickled in behind them. As before, residents greeted Jonny and Reena as they moved, some even including Hadder in their greetings.

They meandered through the ample space for several minutes before something caught Reena's eye, and she halted the group. "Over here, Jonny. Marlin needs to experience this." Reena led them to a large, chest-high circular table surrounded by leather-ensconced bar stools. Two other residents were already at the table, speaking together. Reena politely interrupted them. "Good Haela, Benny. Sunrise. Do you mind if we join you?"

The couple Hadder recognized from outside answered in the affirmative, and the three sat down across the table. As Monty mentioned, they wore matching outfits, his an electric blue tuxedo, and hers an electric blue column dress. In line with what Hadder had already observed, both were extremely attractive, with blue eyebrows, lashes, and, in Benny's case, goatee that paired with their attire. Sunrise spoke first, "We were just about to start. Hoping to beat the crowds."

"That's perfect," said Jonny. "As you both know, Hadder here is our newest resident, and Reena is eager to show him the Ophidian."

"Of course," Benny responded. "Please, Jonny, do the honors."

As Jonny's slender fingers slide along the table, Hadder noticed a square etching depicting a snake just off the table's center. Jonny's index finger hung over the engraving.

"Now, Hadder, promise me you're not going to freak out, old chap. I swear on Reena Song's life that nothing bad is going to happen. Do you trust me?"

A knot formed in Hadder's stomach. "Of course," he answered, hoping he sounded sincere.

With the answer he was looking for in hand, Jonny pressed his finger to the etching. Seconds passed, and a round opening appeared in the center of the table. Hadder held his breath, which came out in panicked pants moments later.

From the hole emerged a kaleidoscopic serpent, slithering on the table before the five residents. Hadder attempted to fall out of his chair but was held fast by Reena. "Trust, remember."

Hadder stamped down his innate instinct to run and sat before the snake. It moved gingerly around the table, taking note of each guest. With part of its body still in the table's hole, Hadder couldn't tell how large the creature was, nor did he care to find out. Having taken stock of guest arrangement, the serpent then rose up into the air, showing off a sizeable Cobra-like hood, and drifted towards Jonny.

Hadder could barely contain his panic as the Ophidian moved to within inches of Jonny's face and opened its dark maw. Instead of screaming in fear as Hadder would have done, however, Jonny fully opened his mouth. From the Ophidian's mouth, a yellow smoke poured forth, and Jonny inhaled deeply, holding it for a moment before releasing the vapor through his nose. Almost immediately, his features slackened, and a stupid grin dominated his face. "Next?"

Reena raised her hand and repeated the terrifying ceremony. "Your turn, Marlin."

Hadder froze as the Ophidian drifted from Reena and towards his face. Reptilian eyes bore a hole through his soul as Hadder stared down the snake's open mouth. Reena pinched his leg under the table, and Hadder opened his mouth and breathed in deeply as a rope of gas briefly tied man and Ophidian together. Hadder felt his pupils immediately dilate as the smoke poured down his throat and filled his lungs. Music that was previously barely detectable in the background pounded in his ears, waking up all of his senses.

Hadder opened his eyes, unsure of when he had closed them, and saw that the Ophidian had already slithered to Sunrise, presenting her with its ephemeral gift. Once Benny had completed his turn, the Ophidian slinked back into its hole, which closed soon after that. The five residents stood in unison on wobbly legs, each giggling in euphoria. Looking around, many new faces had entered *The Soiree Noire*, and the beginnings of a real celebration seemed to be present.

As usual, Reena was the first to break the silence. "Now, let's fucking party!"

———————

HADDER'S MIND buzzed like pre-cable Channel 3 after midnight, a mashup of colors and sounds. The remainder of the Haela, when recounted later, played like Pulp Fiction on acid, a series of haunting scenes and images loosely tied together under the umbrella of *The Soiree Noire*.

Hadder recalled more residents filing in as they floated through the Bar, the large room starting to reach that optimal occupancy level that maximized reveler experience. Reena laughed loudly when she caught Hadder staring mouth agape at an elegant Amazonian woman whose evening dress flashed translucent every few seconds, revealing a tanned athletic body underneath that appeared carved from smooth wood.

Hadder recalled that the party shifted dramatically every hour, with the walls depicting new locations that set the theme. One shift placed *The Soiree* in space, synthwave dance music blaring from invisible speakers. Holograms of comets, asteroid belts, stardust, planets, and suns careened through the main room. Many of the drinks taken from server manikins, especially the transparent and bubbly Number 3, induced psychedelic visions, causing Hadder to see long colorful trails behind each hologram, adding to the "space on drugs" vibe. Later, the entire party shifted to 1980's Times Square, scored by the best music of the decade. Madonna, Michael Jackson, and Guns N' Roses thrummed in Hadder's ears as the logos of Coke, Pepsi, and MTV floated above heads. The last shift Hadder could remember took everyone to Moscow's Red Square, where 90's Hip Hop complemented the cold Russian environment. Each theme transition renewed the room's festivities, a call to alter dance moves, trade-in dance partners, and try a new cocktail or two.

Hadder recalled fleeting meetings with strangers that were to become his makeshift family. While everyone he spoke with was beautiful or handsome, a few stood out and fought through his drug-addled brain to find permanent residence in his memory. A young black man named McKintosh Reed had eyes that perpetually shifted colors and dreadlocks that moved of their own accord like a nest of snakes. He used these to great effect as they were adept at snagging dancing women and pulling them towards their owner's beckoning arms and thrusting hips.

Yasmin Dash drifted down from *The Soiree's* high beams on white wings that sent white dust into the air behind her. Wearing only a white cropped halter top and white shorts, she stole the attention of the entire party as she glided down on undetectable currents, circling the party many times to ensure that all could admire her milky six-pack abs and taught legs. As she executed a perfect landing onto the shoulders and back of a waiting manikin, Hadder commented at the quality of the prosthetic wings, to which Reena laughed and said something that Hadder was unable to make out over the congratulatory shouts. Yasmin and Hadder shared a moment late in the Haela as her wings pulled him in painfully for a deep kiss that resulted in a fast-dissolving pill being deposited on his tongue. For the next fifteen minutes, Hadder could only lay on one of the leather couches as the world melted around him, Reena's fingers combing his hair his only tether to reality.

Hadder recalled Monty the Mod making the rounds, the Ophidian draped over his shoulders like an accessory. He danced from one group to the next, offering each the Ophidian and throwing dark looks at those who turned down his gift. Eventually, Monty sauntered over to Hadder's trio as they took a break from dancing. He nodded to Reena and Jonny in turn but spoke to Hadder. "So, I've been expectantly waiting all party, young man, for you to find me, introduce yourself, and maybe pay your respects. But I can't wait any longer as I'll soon be completely out of my mind, and I want to remember this meeting."

Hadder immediately felt embarrassed for his lack of party etiquette and tried to formulate an appropriate apology through his haze. "I'm so sorry, Mister...the Mod. I thought you'd be busy managing the party, and I didn't know where you were, and there's so much to take in, and I don't know what this stuff is I'm drinking now and..." Words spilled from Hadder's mouth, launched and accelerated by the unique combination of a dozen chemical compounds. He grew more flustered before Monty, Reena, and Jonny all fell into fits of laughter.

Monty turned to Jonny and Reena. "Oh, he's adorable. Wanting to be a real gentleman in such a state; that shows true class." Back to Hadder, "Don't worry, my dear boy, I'm just playing with you. As you know, I'm Montgomery Walls. But that's so bourgeoisie, please call me Monty, leave the "Mister" with that old devil Rott. And you are?"

"I'm Hadder, Marlin Hadder."

"A real pleasure to meet you, Hadder." Monty motioned Hadder in for a hug, but when Hadder obliged, Monty aggressively grabbed ahold of Hadder's head and angrily whispered in his ear, "Are you the Harbinger of the Fall?! Is the Last Judgement upon us already?! Goddammit, tell Rott I'm not ready!"

Before Hadder could even register what was being said to him, Monty had separated, and the Ophidian was in Hadder's face, billowing smoke blinding him while infiltrating his nose and lungs. Hadder closed his eyes before the torrent of smoke. When he opened them, gone was the Ophidian, and Monty the Mod could be seen waltzing his way to another group of residents.

Jonny's arm on Hadder's shoulder startled him. "Don't worry, old chap. Monty's a funny one. Been here as long as anyone, they say. Your appearance probably just stirred up some old superstitions. Have you met Stevie Coolota? You have *got* to see his third eye; it moves independently of the others."

Finally, Hadder recalled the specialty rooms off of *The Soiree Noire's* main chamber. As Haela deepened and the party began to thin, Hadder noticed residents pairing off or grouping together and moving towards the back of the main space. Along the back wall, almost imperceptible doors led to corridors that took partygoers to a series of more private rooms. Hadder had held out hope that Reena would take him to one but was crestfallen when he saw her heading through one door with several other striking women. Just before passing through, Reena looked back and saw the smoke of disappointment coiling off Hadder. She ran back and threw herself into him, planting another Sweet Tart kiss on his lips. "Sorry, Marlin, my love, but you're reserved for the evening. Jonny and I will find you tomorrow. Have fun."

The last bit came out in a giggle as she pointed towards a couch on which sat two women who had captured Hadder's attention earlier in the Haela. They stood up in unison and sashayed towards Hadder as Reena walked away. The woman on the left spoke first. "I'm Helen, this is Nestra. We've wanted to properly meet you, Marlin Hadder. I'm glad we now get the opportunity." Hadder swallowed hard, hoping his nervousness would disappear alongside his mounting saliva. Helen and Nestra were tall and lean like supermodels, and both wore red form-fitting evening gowns that left little to the imagination. That, however, was where traditional comparisons ended. Each woman sported cat eyes, Helen's emerald green, and Nestra's bright orange, and had long, sharp nails that glowed white. Even stranger, though, were the full-body tattoos that covered their skin. Helen was covered in leopard spots while Nestra sported white zebra stripes that stood out against her ebony skin.

Before Hadder could speak, each took hold of one of his arms and led him to the leftmost door on the back wall. They walked in silence, through the door and down a short corridor that ended in a small room with padded leather benches and clothing hooks. Past the changing room was a door on which sat a brightly lit spaceman symbol. "A little help, Hadder?" they asked, turning their backs to Marlin. He steadied his hands and prayed that his fingers wouldn't shake as he unzipped their gowns. Like synchronized swimmers, Helen and Nestra then slid the spaghetti straps of their dresses off their shoulders and let the red material fall to the floor, eventually hanging their clothes on the hooks provided.

Hadder's heart threatened to pound a hole in his chest as he stood before the nude, feline-like women. "We'll wait for you inside. Don't take too long," said Nestra. She fingered his silver suit. "And while this suit is hot, leave it out here." With that, both women walked over and opened the spaceman door. It was dim inside, and Hadder couldn't make out much before the door closed behind Helen and Nestra.

Hadder quickly undressed, carefully hanging up his suit jacket and attentively folding his pants and shirt. Pausing at his underwear, he ultimately said *fuck it* and stripped them off as well, leaving them atop his pants. Having traded one suit for another, Hadder opened the spaceman door and moved through with haste before he lost his nerve.

One step inside the room and Hadder's world turned upside down.

———

HADDER'S FOOT, instead of feeling the hard ground beneath it, found only open space as he stepped down. With nothing there, he careened forward, head over heels, spinning into the room. Frantically flailing about momentarily, Hadder was eventually able to grasp something bolted onto the ceiling or floor and steadied himself to look around.

Hadder found himself in a medium-sized room, lit only by blacklight and pulsing neon, with soft leather cushions, mattresses, and chairs mounted to the ceiling, floor, and all four walls. Floating there naked in zero gravity, Hadder took a moment to calm his nerves and acclimate himself to the experience.

"How do you like it, Hadder?" he heard Helen say from across the room. Looking over, he finally found her lounging with Nestra on a couch on the ceiling, both sitting casually and giggling at his ineptitude.

"It's different, that's for sure."

"It's the best way to meet someone new. Don't you agree, Nestra?"

"For sure, Helen. Hadder, are you coming over here?"

Hadder floundered along the lower part of the wall. The girls laughed again.

"Maybe it's best if we go to him, Nestra."

"I think you're right, Helen."

Together, like aerial gymnasts, the women pushed off and easily spun towards Hadder like twin missiles topped with burning feline eyes. Nestra's white stripes and Helen's leopard spots glowed fiercely under the blacklight. Their nude bodies struck Hadder in a warm embrace, and the three eschewed speaking for passionate three-way kisses. Helen took her mouth from Nestra's neck to shout, "Play Diamond Cafe!" and the room filled with the musician's unique blend of synth-pop RnB, elevating the experience.

At one point, Nestra gave Hadder a strong push, sending him careening across the room. Helen gave chase, catching Hadder and pinning him to one of the ceilings many mattresses. Although they were in zero gravity, the ceiling and walls provided just enough pull to keep one pressed against it. In this way, Helen was able to mount Hadder, her feline eyes hovering in front of his own as she allowed him to enter her. Hadder breathed in deeply as Helen moved back and forth in rhythm with the music.

In short order, they were joined on the ceiling by Nestra, who gently tongued Hadder's nipples before digging her pulsating nails into his taut stomach, drawing blood. Hadder almost cried out, almost cursed at Nestra, before a feeling a pure euphoria cascaded over his body, turning him into a quivering mess and scrambling his brain, turning him from man to beast, matching the disposition of his companions.

From the ceiling, they went to the wall, where there was a variety of leather-wrapped bars and seats that facilitated an unlimited number of sexual positions for a creative trio. Every now and then, Helen or Nestra would stick Hadder with their medicinal nails, sending him into another head spiral. Bodies intertwined against leather and in open space. Lights flashed, and feline eyes sparkled. Melodic soundtracks gave order to chaos. In that dark room with those two strange women, Marlin Hadder lost himself in a medley of mouths and space and breasts and music.

Later, entirely spent, the three gently spun in the air, their bodies' internal humming holding the three together like magnets, allowing them to turn as one, sharing an experience like no other. As ceiling, wall, and floor slowly rotated past, Hadder sighed deeply, understanding that he had just enjoyed the third-best day of his life.

8

Hadder woke with a start, taken aback by his rather unexceptional surroundings. He was lying atop a comfortable bed, fully clothed, failing to have made it inside the covers. Looking around, the room was basic but clean - just a bed, a nightstand, a closet, a full-length mirror, and a bathroom. On the nightstand sat an unusual clock that was without numerals, instead using an image depicting the Idol Moon that shrank and expanded to denote the time. If Hadder was reading it correctly, it appeared to be near the middle of the next Solay - Station's noon.

Hadder swung his feet to the floor and was struck by the sensation of gravity weighing him down, a now-foreign feeling thanks to his late-night escapades. Given the number of chemicals he had imbibed the previous Haela, he was pleasantly surprised that his headache was minimal, and his stomach, while terribly empty, wasn't trying to torture its inconsiderate owner.

Hadder was, however, painfully dehydrated, and stumbled to the bathroom to rectify the situation. After consuming a liter of water, Hadder stared at himself in the mirror. Gone were the lovemaking wounds caused by Helen and Nestra; no trace at all was left of their surgical nails. Glad to be rid of last

Haela's evidence, Hadder walked into the shower, a miniature version of the community shower he had shared with the lovely Reena Song. "Water," said Hadder, and jets attacked him from all angles as steam rose from the bottom. While washing off the previous Haela's effects would have been sufficient, Hadder felt something more in the shower. As he breathed in deeply, the rising steam felt slightly narcotic, leaving behind an enjoyable body hum reminiscent of those pills he found solace in during the Before.

"Water stop," Hadder said to the room. Ready to get out but seeing no towels, Hadder remembered what Reena had told him. "Air," he demanded, and a cyclone of warm air encircled his naked form, drying him in seconds.

Back out in the main bedroom, Hadder had no choice but to put his silver suit back on. Fearing it would be severely soiled, Hadder was happy to discover that it remained perfectly pressed and still smelled like fresh lilac, another hidden benefit of Station's magnificent textiles.

Checking around the room, Hadder was reminded how little he had, literally just the clothes on his back. He exited his temporary home and was relieved to find that he had stepped into a hallway that looked familiar. Once again in the bowels of *Morning's Echo*, Hadder made his way back towards the upper level, trying to retrace the steps taken by him and Reena on a previous trip. He knew he was on the right track when he passed the community bathroom's double doors. Unable to wrangle his curiosity, Hadder peaked in and found two couples locked in a singular embrace under the magical torrents of water. Still shy compared to Station's veterans, Hadder backed out to give the couples privacy.

As he continued down the hall, Hadder recognized the room where Reena procured his suit and stepped in. Luckily, a lemma manikin was there already, waiting patiently behind the counter, its milky eyes staring at nothing while seeing everything. Hadder stood before the lemma uncertainly. "I'd like some clothes, please." The lemma pointed above, and Hadder watched as the screen blinked to show an array of men's clothing, a vast selection that overwhelmed him.

"Just some gray pants, black t-shirt, boxer briefs, and socks, please." The memory of Reena's impressive shoes inspired him. "And high tops, maybe whose designs fluctuate between black and white as I walk?" Marlin Hadder was no fashionista, but he was damn-well going to try.

The lemma stared at Hadder for several seconds before turning and becoming a tornado of labor. Fabrics flew in its hands, scissors moving at blinding speeds, and the sewing machine was barely able to keep up with its user. Hadder waited patiently, mesmerized by the efforts of the wind-up servant, and in 10 short minutes, his entire ensemble was ready. Seeing no point of modesty before the manikin, Hadder changed in the room. Once again, he was astonished by the craftsmanship exhibited in the clothing and the quality of the materials used. The light gray pants were soft and stretchy while looking expensive and tailored. The black t-shirt was a perfect fit, not tight nor loose. The high tops, however, stole the show. They were black and white, similar to Jordan 1s, and the colorways alternated as Hadder moved.

More comfortable in his new digs, Hadder left the manikin clothier and once again made his way towards the *Echo's* first floor. Eventually, Hadder returned to the lounge area, where several residents were back meandering, some playing unknown board games and others only smoking and sipping on drinks.

As Hadder passed through, a couple greeted him. Unable to recall their names, Hadder waved dumbly and continued towards the stairs, taking them two at a time when he reached them, growing desperate for fresh air. Pushing his way through the stairwell's doors, Hadder was greeted by two familiar faces as he entered the main floor of *Morning's Echo*.

Jonny VV and Reena Song sat at a nearby table, drinks in hand, smiling widely. Jonny slammed his palm onto the table. "I told you he'd end up here, Reena. Never doubt my superior intuition."

Reena smiled sweetly. "How are you doing, Marlin? Fun night, I assume?"

Jonny rose and walked to Hadder. He began to playfully look over his new friend. "Let's check you out, old chap. What did those awful creatures do to you last Haela? No permanent damage, I hope."

"Leave him be, Jonny," Reena jokingly reprimanded. Her eyes lit up. "Oh my, look at that new outfit. And those wonderful kicks. Do they? Oh, they sure do shift as you walk. Well done."

Hadder blushed at the compliment. "When in Rome, you know?"

Jonny responded, "I do know. And just like Rome, Station has excellent food. You must be famished."

"Poor thing hasn't eaten in days, Jonny."

"Well, not food, anyways, dear Reena."

"Oh, Jonny, don't be vulgar."

Hadder's stomach bellowed at the word food, forcing him to cut into his friends' banter. "I'm starving. Lead, and I'll follow."

Jonny quickly finished his drink. "Well, that settles it. Dine, we shall! Let us make haste to *The Medici*."

Hadder followed Jonny and Reena across *Morning's Echo*, seeing the Bar with new eyes framed by lenses forged from the activities of the past two dozen hours. As they stepped out into the city called Station, Hadder could only imagine what this new Solay would bring.

————

THE CELEBRATION CLUSTER was quiet in the relative brightness of the Solay. Hadder walked silently beside the chatty Reena and Jonny, who were exchanging notes from late-night *Soiree* engagements. Both had changed into new, equally exciting outfits.

Reena was wearing transparent haram pants whose shower-glass textured showed the hint of tight boy shorts underneath. Her shoes were simple, clear sandals that showed off manicured toes. A tight-fitting tube top finished off the look. On the tube top, a moving graphic image of a nude girl dancing repeated on a loop. Her short pink hair was done up in pigtails, and her Light Crown continued to circle her head.

Jonny VV was donning bright red pants over white boots and a white silk hoodie under a black vest. On the back of the garment, a red dragon flew through the black sky, every now and then breathing holographic red and orange breath at anyone bold enough to stare. Hadder laughed lightly, real-izing that this was casual wear for Reena and Jonny.

Taking a moment to get his bearings, Hadder realized that they were taking one of the major thoroughfares that fed into the Celebration Cluster's western side. Heading west while making small talk, Hadder again marveled at the sights that assaulted him. The roadway on which they walked was a busy one, so Hadder was able to catch glimpses of many more of Station's residents.

Unsurprisingly, they all retained an air of attractiveness, even those that looked bored to death. While not all had Jonny and Reena's continual drive for cutting-edge fashion, everyone seemed well-dressed, and most had some unique quality that marked them as an individual. One woman's hair stood straight up, nearly reaching the bulb-like fruit of the Monarch Trees. Another went the other way, shaving her head and allowing small implants above each ear to beam holographic hair onto her bald pate. As Hadder watched, she went from green half-shaved bob to blue mohawk in less than 10 meters. One man who passed had knees that bent in the opposite direction, tight shorts accentuating the irregularity, while another had skin that was decorated like a checkerboard, reminding Hadder of Helen and Nestra's modified dermis.

Jonny and Reena took no notice as they walked, leaving Hadder with his questions and childish wonder. A short time later, the Monarch Trees ceased on their right, and a large brick building came into view, simple but with impressive classical stonework. A fountain in the front of the building demanded Hadder's attention as he passed. A nude marble man scooped water from the basin into an ornate pot and turned counter-clockwise, pouring the liquid into the open, waiting mouths of marble heads that lined the circumference of the fountain. Bowl emptied, the decorative man bent low and repeated. Hadder followed his friends past the fountain, shivering as he felt its cold gaze penetrate his thin shirt and send an icy shard into his heart.

Exhaling as he entered *The Medici*, Hadder became aware that he had been holding his breath as he walked through the building's courtyard.

As usual, Jonny stole Hadder from his dark thoughts. "Welcome to *The Medici*, old chap. You can order food from almost any manikin in Station, but nothing quite matches the sheer options and ambiance that this place provides. Isn't that right, Reena, love?"

"He's gonna love it. Come on, I'm starving."

Crossing under the archway that framed *The Medici's* large front doors, Hadder entered an impressive hall, the center of which was filled with long dining tables and a smattering of more personal round tables. The hall's sides registered like any cafeteria in the Before, counter upon counter of food with manikins attending each station.

Starting on their left, they grabbed crystalline trays from the corner and began to investigate the offerings. Holding onto the tray at first, Hadder soon saw that this was unnecessary, as Jonny and Reena had released theirs, which glided effortlessly in front of their two users, shifting to accommodate their movements.

Hadder was floored by the quantity and apparent quality of the food provided. Rare prime rib sat across from lobster bisque, which lay only two dishes away from whole roasted chicken. Hadder's stomach roared to life, reminding him loudly that it had been more than a day since he had eaten, and years since he had eaten properly.

Reena took half a roasted chicken alongside seasoned rice, asparagus, and a beautiful fruit medley, comprised of several fruits he did not recognize. Jonny went a heartier route, selecting a cream pasta topped with a cornucopia of seafood. Hadder's appetite demanded variety, so he piled a sirloin steak, French fries, and cream spinach alongside a lobster tail, clam chowder, and mini creme brûlée. No one seemed put off by his gluttony.

Despite *The Medici's* general fullness, Jonny, Reena, and Hadder were able to secure a personal table in the corner, each of them receiving greetings from around the hall as they made towards their seats. As they sat, Jonny commented, "You were a big hit last night, Hadder, old chap." He leaned conspiratorially. "There's good buzz surrounding you, which should swell your prospects."

Hadder screwed his face in confusion. "Prospects for what?"

Jonny fell back, no longer in tryst-mode. "For having fun, next-level fun, old boy! People are gonna want to spend time with you - people of repute, with access to some of Station's more restricted events."

"I don't understand. I didn't do anything spectacular last night."

Reena put her hand on his own, tried to explain. "Station is a crazy place, Hadder. Beautiful and exhilarating and orgasmic - yes. But it's also crazy, especially given the makeup of its residency."

"Current company excluded I'll assume, love," cut in Jonny. Reena ignored him and continued.

"None of us would have blamed you if you had lost it last night."

"Lost it, how?"

"I don't know. Maybe throw up all over yourself. I mean, these aren't run of the mill drugs we're doing here. Maybe act like a madman, trying to fight some and fuck others. Maybe run down the thoroughfare screaming, curling up in the fetal position at the bottom of a Monarch Tree. But you didn't do any of those things. You handled yourself but still gave in completely to the experience. That took a lot of us a long time to accomplish."

Jonny took it from there. "People noticed, Hadder. It didn't look it, but everyone at *The Soiree* had their eye on you, waiting for reactions, hoping to judge a misstep and declare you a square or a lush or a nutter or a Weep or even a spy for Rott. But you didn't give it to them, did you, old chap. You had a damn fine showing, and lord knows Reena and I didn't make it easy on you."

"Deep end of the pool and all that," said Reena.

"Anyway, there's good buzz among those who matter that there's a new resident worth knowing. You must have had a good showing with Helen and Nestra as well, you old dog! They've been singing your praises since early this Solay."

Hadder felt the blood rush to his face and looked embarrassedly at Reena, who smiled like only she should could, silently letting him know that not only was she not bothered by his time with other women, but she was legitimately happy for him.

They ate in peace for the next several minutes before the questions that had been mounting in Hadder could no longer go unasked. "About Helen and Nestra, and all the other residents I see. How does everyone look so perfect or get these body modifications? Honestly, it looks like most of Station has altered itself. How?"

Jonny stopped eating, but Reena continued to pick at her chicken. "Well, there it is! We've been waiting for you to ask us about this, old chap, and by god did you make it a long time. See! This is why people like you, even when you have no clue what's going on, you don't let that deter you. You keep going forward. That's a very rare trait, and one that is truly valued in Station."

"Thanks. But to my question?"

"Of course, of course. Mister Albany Rott, our mysterious benefactor, in his quest to make Station a true Xanadu, established Elevation Centers around the city. At these...clinics, if you will, cosmetic operations only limited by the imagination can be performed by highly skilled manikins using technology never seen in the Before."

"But why?"

Jonny struggled with a response, so Reena answered for him. "Remember, Marlin, why we're all here. We either hated where we were in the Before, or we hated who we were in the Before. For some people, the change in scenery is enough. For many others, the person in the mirror also needs to change, or the same baggage that plagued them in the Before will continue to weigh them down here."

Jonny added, "Station is about eliminating barriers to happiness, Hadder. Job got you down? Nobody works in Station. Family responsibility killing you? There is no family nor responsibility in Station. Unhappy with the way you look? Elevations will fix whatever you dislike about yourself. Feeling unable to truly express yourself? In Station, any image you want to project can be made real, no matter how bizarre or extreme."

"So, are there no limits to what can be done? I met a woman with wings, a man with three eyes, and had sex with two cat women. Is nothing off-limits or beyond the clinics' abilities?"

"I'm not sure there's anything beyond their abilities. We've seen some pretty extreme Elevations, haven't we, love? But there is one rule that's been in effect for a while."

"And what's that?"

Jonny and Reena looked at each other uncomfortably. "*No Elevations are to be executed that would be used as weapons or to harm another,*" recited Reena.

"Who would want to hurt people with Elevations?"

Jonny grimaced but responded. "You know, Hadder, some people are always going to want to destroy rather than build. Station gives them tools to better themselves, and all they see are engines of destruction. Life is no longer about living to them; it's about crushing the world that so deeply wounded them. Station's clinics, while extraordinary, don't have the technology to heal those scars."

Reena interjected. "Before the One Rule was in place, many got Elevations and used them to hurt others. They were eventually banished across the Skirt, which was created as a makeshift border, and the One Rule was created."

"And, thus, problem solved, old chap! Let those ruinous twats shadowbox in misery on the other side of the Skirt while we live, truly live, over here!"

Hadder thought for a moment. "I could barely make out the Skirt when I was on the Perch with Miles. I didn't see any walls or fences, just a swath of open land. What's to keep those from across the Skirt..."

"Risers," stated Jonny. "They're called Risers as we've banished them to Station's eastern side."

"Well, what's to keep the Risers from just walking over?"

"That's the Caesars' job, old chap."

The image of a colossus with blue skin towering over him flashed across Hadder's mind. "Those giant freaks?" a shocked Hadder asked.

Reena giggled. "I see Marlin has met a Caesar. Don't worry, they're here for our protection. Mister Rott created them, first merely to act as Station's police force. You know, just keep the true wildings in check or break up the odd fracas. Now, they're not only responsible for tossing serial offenders over to the Risers, but they also guard the Skirt, making sure no one crosses it without proper authority. Without them, Marlin, our lifestyles wouldn't be possible."

"Trust me, old chap, despite their imposing appearances, they're a top-notch crew to have around should shit go sideways."

"Are they manikins?"

"Oh no," answered Reena. "No one knows where they came from or how Mister Rott created them. But the Caesars have minds of their own and can be quite sharp when needed. Not automatons like the manikins."

"So, they have souls?"

"I didn't say that."

Another thought struck Hadder. "Miles said there are eleven Caesars."

"That's right," agreed Jonny.

"But there were originally twelve. What happened to the Caesar that's no longer here?"

Jonny and Reena shared another fearful look. Reena looked down at the remnants of her chicken. Jonny mustered the courage to answer. "His name was Claud, probably the most personable of the Caesars. He was found at the edge of the Lethe River, his heart ripped from his giant chest. There are rumors of all kinds, of course, but most believe it was some disagreement between Caesars that led to battle. If you've seen a Caesar pissed off, then you'd understand the validity of this theory."

Reena looked up finally. "Can we change the subject, please? I get sad when I think about what happened to poor Claud."

"Of course, sweet Reena. Well, Hadder, old chap, I think that's enough question-answer for now. More things will be revealed in due course and through experience, not mere explanation." Jonny rose from his seat, showing that it was time to leave. A quartet of men who looked exactly like The Beatles was waiting patiently for Hadder's trio to free up the table. Hadder hadn't taken two steps before a glume manikin moved in quickly to clear and wipe down the table for the new guests.

The three friends stepped out into the relative warmth of the large Idol

Moon, Hadder keeping his eyes from the unnerving animated fountain. "So what do we do now?" asked Hadder to no one in particular.

Jonny moved and put his arms around both Reena and Hadder. "Now? Now we do whatever we want. First things first, let's get a proper drink. I think *Steam Dreams* should do nicely. Reena?"

Reena nodded in agreement.

"No, I mean, what do we *do* here, Jonny?"

"You're going to have to let that go, Hadder. The idea that the day has to have purpose and structure was left in the Before. We can do anything, everything, or nothing. No one will judge us in any case. Right now, dear Reena Song and I usually meet for a drink to clear the head, laugh about the previous Haela, and plan."

"Plan what?"

Jonny laughed as they began to walk together. "Plan the next Haela, of course. *Where will we go? What do we want to wear? Who do we want to be?*

And most importantly, *who do we want to go with?* And lucky for you, Hadder, that last question has already been answered, old chap. You want to know what now? Now we do our best to make this next Haela the best one ever!"

"And get ready to fucking party again!" yelled Reena into the Solay night air.

"Well said, my dear," said Jonny VV, a big smile dominating his face. Feeling the excitement of his two friends as they walked, Hadder couldn't help but feel eager for the next Haela. If this was to be Marlin Hadder's new lot in life, spending the day to maximize the night, so be it.

The Before was totally bereft of joy. Hadder was going to make damn sure that his time in Station would be defined by non-stop euphoria. His revenge on a world that so brutally forced him out.

9

The next few weeks passed in a blur. Or was it months? Days flew by faster than Hadder could comprehend, powered by strong drink and other chemically enhanced substances. Solay slid into Haela, which torpedoed back into Solay with no end to the cycle insight.

Solays were spent recovering from the previous Haela's festivities, assisted by copious amounts of Number 1, aka the Cure. This elixir was standard across all Bars, so Jonny, Reena, Hadder, and a rotating cast of characters would meet up at any number of places around mid-Solay to lick their wounds and exchange stories.

Not all Bars, especially those in the Celebration Cluster, were open during Solay, so the group often traveled across western Station in search of that Solay's watering hole. This presented Hadder with opportunities to explore Station, visiting other clusters, and observing how those outside the Celebration Cluster carved out lives in Station.

Bored one day, Hadder's usual trio dragged new friend Goldie, a twenty-something who only wore gold-colored clothing, stating that the gear, coupled with his extensive collection of gold jewelry and bleached hair, made his tan skin sing, to the Weep. Thinking the trip a gaff to kill time, the quartet left the Cluster soon after arriving, hearts a little heavier from the sob stories they were inundated with upon arrival.

Drinking away the Solay in the New Age Cluster, however, turned out to be good fun. While the residents there didn't use Elevations much to improve their looks, the crystals and gemstones that most had implanted across their faces and bodies certainly created an interesting effect. While neither Jonny, Reena, nor Hadder thought much of the philosophies and practices of the Cluster residents, their passion for life was contagious, and everyone always left the Cluster a bit happier and a great deal higher.

The Gaming Cluster was always a favorite, a group of buildings where residents congregated to play traditional sports like basketball and tennis while also trying out Station-only creations like Moonball and Space Discus. Drinking games also permeated the Cluster, with extensive variations of Beer Pong, Flip Cup, and Quarters. For many residents, a Solay in the Gaming Cluster assured that the Haela would be spent passed out in the nearest living quarters.

When sufficient Number 1 had been consumed to heal all wounds, the trio would begin discussing the upcoming Haela. Where were they going to go? Who did they want to meet? What were the appropriate clothes for the evening?

While Jonny VV and Reena Song created entirely new ensembles for each Haela, Hadder reserved this for only specific parties and occasions. Exceedingly comfortable in his gray pants, black shirt, and high tops, Hadder would often get a light jacket made, designed by Reena, to switch up his look, sometimes copping a new pair of shoes to match the top.

If Solays were for recovery, creation, and relaxation, Haelas were only for one thing - pushing the limits of revelry, into and past decadence. Some Haelas saw a return to *The Soiree Noire*, where no two nights were the same as party themes never repeated. While Hadder no longer needed to be with Jonny and Reena to catch Monty's eye and gain invitation, the Mod continued to throw suspicious looks Hadder's way like darts.

At *The Legged Fish*, the Bar's interior was built to look like one long beach line, complete with an artificial ocean, allowing everyone to show off their Elevated physiques in small bathing suits. Hadder mentioned his concern for drugged-out residents drowning in the false sea and was blown away when Reena told him that it was not water, but a water-like substitute that allowed for breathing, that filled the Bar. For the remainder of the Haela, Hadder was under the machine-induced waves, gliding with groups of residents. Together, they investigated iridescent coral reefs that hummed with Station life, including bright seahorses, glowing schools of purplish fish, and peaceful eels whose gentle bites sent pulses racing faster than the purest cocaine. Several bars were anchored to the fake ocean's floor, with pinkish dolphins more than happy to whisk residents from one counter to another, where long tubes crewed by manikins were presented to serve underwater beverages.

Other Bars were less distinct, offering experiences that ran together with countless others. The places, however, were only one element of the Haela. Alongside the drugs that were consumed, the residents that one met and spent time with defined the evening. Several Haelas found Hadder waking up next to Reena Song, her soft skin hugging his own like a life vest. Upon rising, Reena never made the encounters awkward, playfully getting dressed and stating where to meet later before quietly exiting their short-term living quarters.

Jonny VV's assertion that Hadder would be a wanted man after his initial successful Haela proved prophetic. Each Haela, regardless of Bar or Cluster, Hadder was bombarded with offers of exotic narcotics, late-Haela trysts, and exclusive experiences. Invite-only parties at enigmatic Bars ratcheted up the drug use and introduced Hadder to even more extreme residents with insatiable appetites.

Helen and Nestra guided Hadder to a Bar called *The Gloaming*, where naked residents paraded around in pitch blackness, with only psychoactive, glow-in-the-dark stickers placed between partygoers' eyes to guide hands, mouths, and tongues. Benny took Hadder to *Gearworks*, where the floors, walls, and ceilings twisted and turned at a deliberate pace, intensifying any visuals the resident was enjoying.

While each Haela brought unique experiences with distinct residents and increasing chemical usage, Hadder began recognizing diminishing returns in terms of enjoyment. Orgies, even with the perfectly Elevated bodies, specially-designed love rooms, and intensely sexual drugs, became more and more humdrum. Creating a new costume for the evening and helping others with theirs became a chore. In this land where anything was possible and wildest dreams could be made real, Marlin Hadder was growing bored.

As he seemed to be chasing the dragon, that first perfect night at *The Soiree Noire*, Hadder concluded that the best course of action was to simply visit the dragon's lair. As Jonny and Reena had tried to dissuade him several times, Hadder decided not to tell them about his plans for the upcoming Haela. That he was finally going to attend *Inferno*.

———

HADDER STOOD OUTSIDE OF *INFERNO*, a belly full of Number 6 simultaneously calming his nerves and lending courage to his spirit. Full Haela had set in some time ago, and still, residents were just beginning to trickle into the imposing building. Hadder watched silently as some of Station's most extreme residents made their way through the blood-red wooden doors of the Bar. Francis Starr and her six breasts glided in alongside Shiva El, also known as Third-Eye Eliot. Helen and Nestra led six others into *Inferno*, a group of men and women that had latched on to the magnetic duo and had Elevated their bodies in similar fashions, now looking as much sexy animal as human.

Mustering his courage, Hadder made his way to *Inferno's* front door, where he was forced to jump back, startled, as a body fell from the thick layer of vines that covered the building. It stopped to hang mid-air, supported by the vines. The legs of the stranger dangled in front of the entranceway. Looking up, Hadder saw an old woman, skin pulled tight from multiple Elevations, wearing a red jumper with flames that danced within the material. She was hanging from the rose vines, the thorns cutting into her arms and sending droplets of blood down her aged skin to splatter on the ground before Hadder. Her ancient white hair floated in the Haela air as if underwater, and her eyes blazed like blue fires.

She pointed a bony finger at Hadder. Others had stopped to stare at the commotion. "You. I don't know you. What makes you think you can handle *Inferno?*"

Hadder opened his mouth to form a response, but nothing came out. Having no idea what was lurking in that crimson building, how could he be sure that he could maintain within its walls? Just as Hadder was about to shrug dumbly, a savior slithered its way around Hadder's neck and waist. He panicked for a moment before realizing that McKintosh Reed and his magical dreadlocks had joined him.

Reed spoke for him. "Hey Jackie, you old sea hag! This is Marlin Hadder, the newest resident. I've partied with the man countless times and can vouch for him. Let us in before I rip you out of those goddam vines and toss you in the Lethe River."

Hadder now remembered the name bandied about various parties - Jackie Crone, one of Station's original residents. Jackie stared at Reed for a moment with those fiery blue eyes before speaking. "It's on you, McKintosh Reed. If he's not ready, there will be a price to pay."

Reed waved Jackie away and whisked Hadder under her dangling legs and into *Inferno.* "Thanks, Reed," managed Hadder as they crossed the threshold into the Bar. Surveying the first floor, Hadder thought that *Inferno* seemed very much like every other bar. Residents milled about making light conversation and floating from one group to another. "Seems fairly normal, Reed. I mean for Station standards."

Reed laughed. "This is just the first floor, man. This here is just to prime you for the trip up. Has anyone told you how it works?"

Given the inconspicuous nature of his trip, Hadder had failed to inquire about the particulars of the notorious Bar. He had spent a Haela getting wasted under the ocean, after all. How could this possibly top that? "No, but I'd appreciate it if you filled me in."

Reed led the two of them over towards a manikin-serviced counter and started to explain. "So, there are nine floors, of which this is obviously one.

You spend a requisite amount of time on each floor before you're allowed to continue on to the next. During this time, you can't simply be a wallflower. You have to actively participate in whatever is happening on that floor. Once at the top floor, there is an exit that will take you straight down to the bottom."

"I don't understand. If I'm not having a good time, can't I simply leave?"

Reed faced him and delivered a stern look. "Not a good idea, Hadder. Jackie Crone holds the hidden strings that control the Celebration Cluster, and maybe other areas of Station, for all we know. Some say she converses with the man himself - Mister Rott. To not finish *Inferno* is considered a slap in the face to her. She'll go out of her way to make Station less than inviting for you. Bars you used to enjoy will be closed off from you. People you thought friends will stop speaking with you. Station can be a lonely place once you're on Jackie Crone's shit list. Might as well go stay in the fucking Weeps."

Hadder's Number 6 was no longer working as anxiety set in. "Shit, Reed, I guess I should have researched this thing more."

Reed threw Hadder a sympathetic nod. "Well, you're in here now, so I suggest you make the best of it. Lots of people really enjoy the experience. I couldn't do it every Haela, but I need it once in a while to shock my system and renormalize."

"So what do we do on this level? Just sit around and drink?"

Reed motioned the manikin behind the counter. "Drink? Yes. Two Number 7s, manikin!"

Hadder was confused. "You don't think Number 7 is a bit mild for the Haela in store for us?"

Reed waited for the glume manikin to bring the drinks before he responded. "No, Hadder, this calming elixir is exactly what we need right now. Drink it down. Fast." They both emptied their glasses in one tilt back. "Another," ordered Reed, and they repeated the process. Hadder could feel the narcotic beverage lowering his heart rate and slowing his breathing. "And now, Hadder, you're going to have to trust me. Do you trust me?" Hadder nodded in affirmation. "Then, please give me your forearm."

Hadder removed his pattern-shifting green and black camouflage jacket and presented McKintosh Reed with his bare forearm. Reed flagged down a lemma manikin that was carrying a silver tray and held up two fingers. The female-form manikin with white cornrows approached and placed a palm-down cupped hand over Hadder's forearm. When it removed its hand, what was left on Hadder was a small wormlike creature that pulsed a deep red. As it painlessly began to burrow into Hadder's flesh, he moved to pull it out but was restrained by several of Reed's dreadlocks.

"Let it do its thing, Hadder. You have to take the Slink to move to the next floor."

Hadder, no longer fighting Reed's impossibly powerful hair, just stared in horror as the four-inch Slink sunk into his forearm, remaining just below the skin, pulsing like Station's most uncomplicated tattoo design. As Hadder gently rubbed his fingers over the embedded Slink, Reed had his own Slink inserted by the manikin.

"Reed," Hadder asked nervously, "what the hell does this thing do?"

Reed silently ordered two more Number 7s as he explained. "The Slink is a long-lasting, multi-effect drug. As the creature slowly disintegrates in the body, it releases several combinations of toxins that will have intense effects on its host. The breakdown of the Slink tends to coincide with advances up *Inferno*. Thus, it will have varying impacts from level to level."

"This is insane, Reed."

Reed let out a crazed laugh. "I know, right! This is the height of the Station experience, Hadder, except for maybe those nutters at *Biomass*. Listen, you seriously have to just try to enjoy each floor, regardless of what's going on there. Disgust can lead to panic, which can lead to a swift kick out of here and into Station purgatory. Here, have another Number 7."

Several Number 7s and a Number 9 later and Hadder had more or less forgotten about the alien entity slowly dying in his arm. Hadder and Reed made their way around *Inferno's* first level, renewing acquaintances with Helen and Nestra, and making new friends such as Penny Wonder, a middle-aged woman who had Elevated herself to appear as a young teenager.

Wearing a Japanese schoolgirl outfit and pink-tipped pigtails, Hadder was unsurprised by Penny's popularity among a gross subset of Station residents.

As their time on the first floor continued, Hadder began to see a definite shift in the party as conversations became ear-blown whispers and caressing hands conveyed more than speaking mouths. Within himself, Hadder also felt a change as his face flushed, body tingled, and lips hungered for the skin of another.

As Hadder made his way towards one of Helen and Nestra's newest followers, a light-skinned Asian woman with golden scales tattooed on her upper thighs, lower arms, and chest, he was grabbed by the cornrowed lemma. It pointed to the single door at the far end of the level, opposite from the main entrance doors.

Reed leaned in from behind. "That's our cue to move up, Hadder. God, I wish we could stay at this next level forever." Saying nothing more, he ushered Hadder through the back door and up a flight of stairs to a landing on the second floor. Checking his breath and smoothing down his black on black ensemble, Reed took a deep breath and knocked on the door to the next level. It opened silently, and they entered.

THE SECOND FLOOR of *Inferno* was a dimly lit open space furnished heavily with comfortable-looking couches, corner-beds, swings, tables, and love seats. Hadder's mind buzzed loudly, and his testicles felt heavy as they swole uncomfortably. He looked to his forearm and saw that the Slink had increased its pulsing, sending alien chemicals flowing into his bloodstream. *Inferno's* second level was relatively full, and it didn't take Hadder long to understand the purpose of this floor - fucking.

Everywhere that Hadder looked, couples and groups littered the room in sexual ecstasy. Clothes that were hastily removed and ignominiously cast aside were collected and politely folded by wandering manikins doubling as both servers and maids.

Reed clapped Hadder loudly on the shoulder. He had a crazed glint in his color-shifting eyes, evidence that his Slink was also working its magic. "Looks like I've got some work to do. See you on level three." And with that, McKintosh Reed began walking towards the back corner of the room, where a small army had congregated on an oversized bed to share each other's bodies.

Hadder, although overwhelmed by the sheer quantity of sexual activities playing out before him, was unable to sit idly by and simply gawk. Beyond what Reed had told him about being an "active participant," the Slink's enigmatic releases had ignited a lust in him that would have to be satiated lest he risks his eyeballs exploding within their sockets from unreleased internal pressure.

Letting his clothes drop to the floor, Hadder dove into the mass of flesh and sweat and lubricants. And for a while, he lost himself to the experience.

———

UNCOUNTED TIME LATER, Marlin Hadder and McKintosh Reed sat with their backs against the wall, attempting to catch their breaths. Both were surprisingly dry, having wrung out every bit of bodily liquid. Others joined them along the wall while many continued the show, including those residents that were still just entering the second floor.

Manikins walked past with armloads of clothes, handing folded stacks to their matching owners. Hadder and Reed both received their clothing, and Reed began dressing. "Looks like we're done on this floor, Hadder."

Hadder sighed deeply. "That's too bad, but probably for the best. I really need to refuel. I've never felt so hungry."

Reed helped Hadder to his feet. "You're in luck. Get dressed and let's move on up."

Hadder dressed quickly, but not fast enough for his stomach's liking. It growled fiercely, threatening pain should he dally any longer. The Slink throbbed dully, noticeably smaller and taking on a brownish hue.

Together, Hadder and Reed made their way up the stairs leading to *Inferno's* third level, a banquet hall with rows of long tables and ornate, tall-backed chairs. Many diners were already seated and eating, so Hadder and Reed found two seats near the end of one of the large tables. Hadder's hunger had grown to the point that his head was spinning, causing him to fall into his chair unceremoniously.

As soon as Hadder and Reed were seated, a lemma manikin approached and deposited plates of food before them. The meat on the plates was unrecognizable, perhaps something of the propriety variety from Station's organism-rich gardens, but Hadder didn't care, couldn't care. He dug in with both hands, shoveling fistfuls of mystery meat into his mouth.

As Hadder and Reed finished plates, more were brought, each more exotic than the ones served before. A turtle shell filled with fried glowing insects was scooped clean. Strange vegetable medleys were presented in the cupped dismembered hands of mysterious beasts. Thin, flavorful soups swam with sea monkey creatures that were swallowed whole.

Everything was consumed without question or concern regarding the nature of the food. Eventually, empty plates were taken up, and no more were delivered. Hadder leaned back in his chair and took a deep breath, glad to be done with the curious heavy meal. Hadder's stomach had finally fallen silent, but his mind continued to spin dangerously out of control.

Thinking this floor concluded, Hadder began to rise but was restrained by Reed's autonomous dreadlocks on his shoulder. "One more," was all that Reed said.

Four hidden doors along the left and righthand walls opened simultaneously, and wheeled tables being pushed by glume manikins exited from each. The wheeled tables were positioned so that each covered roughly one-quarter of the diners. On each table, Hadder was surprised to see a nude lemma manikin, milky eyes staring blankly at the ceiling's swirling frescos. From somewhere in their black skin suits, each of the glume manikins pulled out a scalpel and a carving knife. Hadder's full stomach teased a complete emptying.

Unable to conceal the panic in his voice, Hadder said, "Reed, what's this about?"

"This is where shit gets pretty intense, Hadder. I'm sorry, man, but there's only forward now. Don't hold on too tight."

Hadder watched in horror, mouth agape, as the glume manikins cut open their lemma counterparts in unison like synchronized swimmers. From Hadder's seat, he could see the gruesome show in its entirety, one poor lemma being only feet away. The lemma's sternum was sliced open, and its chest cavity was opened with a brutal pull by the butcher manikin.

Given the tick-tock nature of the manikins, Hadder had assumed their internal workings consisted of gears, pistons, and springs. But from his vantage point, it appeared that the lemma's innards very much mirrored those of his own, adding to his discomfort. One significant difference, however, was that where the heart would typically be found, the lemma had a banana-shaped organ that glowed a violent blue. The butcher reached into the gaping hole and viciously ripped out the blue organ, placing it on its table next to the body. The lemma had no reaction.

The butcher glume then used its carving knife to skillfully portion the blue heart, placing one piece in the center of each fresh plate that was procured from a hidden shelf under the table. Other service manikins rushed forward to pick up the final dishes and deliver them to waiting residents. One was placed in front of Hadder, and another was given to Reed.

"Try not to think about it, Hadder," was all the advice that Reed could muster. Before Hadder could respond, Reed plucked the heart from his plate, deposited it into his mouth, and began chewing loudly.

Don't think about it. Don't think about it. Don't think about it. The mantra repeated in Hadder's mind as he scooped up the jiggly blue muscle and placed it on his tongue. Closing his eyes, he chewed slowly and was pleasantly surprised that the heart had both the texture and flavor of an oversized gummy bear. He chewed just enough to swallow, then opened his eyes.

Only to stare directly into the white eyes of the dissected lemma, who had turned its head on the table to look directly at Hadder, throwing silent accusation. Hadder dropped his head in abashed guilt, reminded of Harlan Ellison's "I Have No Mouth, and I Must Scream," only raising it when Reed gripped him under his arms.

"Let's go, Hadder. Time for the next floor. And you may want to prep yourself."

"For what?"

"That thing we just ate packs a real wallop. Everyone is kinda on their own from here; best of luck to you."

With those unhelpful words, McKintosh Reed walked towards the back of *Inferno* level three and up the next set of stairs leading deeper into mania. Hadder started to follow, then stopped and took one last look at the lemma he had just eaten. The marble eyes continued to stare at Hadder but were now joined by a devilish smirk that cut into the human's own heart, forcing him to trip on his way out.

The Slink throbbed painfully under his skin. And then Marlin Hadder's mind detonated.

———

THE MANIKIN HEART ruined Hadder's brain for the next terrifying hours. *Inferno's* fourth floor was a sight for the eyes that threatened to burn Hadder's ocular nerves. The entire main room was made of gold, from the heavily decorated columns to the side counters that offered potent drinks in crystal goblets.

The combination of manikin heart, decomposing Slink, and a cornucopia of smoke and drink left Marlin Hadder a mess of a person, which paired perfectly with level four's other residents who were equally stoned. Most of his time was spent on the large dance floor, a crystal floor that sparkled with inlaid diamonds and played games with the overhead rainbow light.

Gilded pipes that contained intense smoke were passed around as were baroque crowns that, when placed on the head, sent waves of euphoria directly into the brain. One such crown, with green emeralds encircling the band, was placed on Hadder's head by a woman with an elongated neck reminiscent of a swan. Shockwaves thundered through Hadder's body, forcing him to the floor as residents danced like feral beasts around him.

Surrounded by crazed mirth, Hadder convulsed and came in his pants before darkness overtook him, the laughs above raining down like a summer heat storm.

————

WHILE DARKNESS HAD INDEED enveloped Marlin Hadder, lose consciousness he did not. Hadder's body began moving on autopilot, the kernel of being that was Marlin Hadder reassigned to the back of the theater, a mere viewer of the unfolding Haela. Much was observed, but only bits and pieces could later be recollected.

The fifth floor was a marketplace of pain, where residents took turns gleefully doling out and receiving lashings from light whips that shattered nerves and locked up jaws but caused no permanent damage. As the Slink continued its descent into nothingness, the pain transformed somewhere in the body, resulting in the perception of some twisted pleasure from the agony. Laughs, screams, moans, and wails melded into a symphony as arms pumped until they were spent, voice boxes eventually falling silent under strain.

Level six was a return to the more mundane party atmosphere if that party was wrapped in religious idols and symbology. A large cross dominated the room, from which a red liquid flowed to be ladled by manikins into roughly hewn wooden cups. Stars of David were tiled into the floor to be stepped on, and pages of the Koran were distributed to wipe excess drink from mouths.

Level seven was an all-white room, devoid of any furniture, counters, or entertainment. Residents were given bright ponchos upon entrance, which they promptly donned over their Celebration Cluster couture. As the residents formed a perimeter around the room, five manikins - two glumes and three lemmas - marched in to stand in the middle of the circle. The hiss of gas could be heard in the relative quietness, and Hadder could palpably feel the Slink's pulsing responses to the new stimulant.

Without warning, one of the residents, a tall Latina with the top of her head shaved, moved forward and scratched the face of the nearest glume, her sharp nails painting long lines of blood. As if this was a call to action, another resident, this time one of Helen and Nestra's lackeys, rammed her elbow into the face of a flat-topped lemma, sending a wet cracking sound to echo across the room.

From there, all hell broke loose, and sanity was lost.

Residents ran forward to pummel the defenseless manikins. Hands tore off ears, gouged out eyes, and ripped out hair. Teeth removed chunks of manikin flesh. Fists shattered jaws while feet caved in chests.

Hadder initially stood by, transfixed by the horror show that was unfolding. But as the Slink continued its dissolution, it dragged Hadder into his own descent into madness. An inexplicable rage began to build deep within Hadder, one that refused to stay quiet and demanded action to satiate its desire.

One of the glume manikins, already battered beyond recognition, stumbled into Hadder. Relinquishing control of his body to the Slink, Hadder made a claw of his hand and snatched the throat from the feeble automaton. Blood sprayed like a geyser, baptizing Hadder and those around him in gore. Other residents quickly joined Hadder, and together they ripped the manikin apart, separating arm from shoulder, leg from hip, and head from neck, a callback to the sick games that children played with helpless insects.

The orgy of violence raged on for some time until red mist hung heavy in the air, and only small mounds of viscera marked locations where the five manikins once stood. Shaking residents stood under masks of red, the final bit of dangerous adrenaline leaving their systems. Without laughter, or high-fives, or words, the group removed their now crimson mantles in silence and shuffled towards the stairwell, all wishing they could leave the remainder of their Slinks behind.

As Hadder ascended to *Inferno's* eighth floor, exhaustion was now added to his growing list of sensitivities, magnifying the effects of all else that was in his system, especially the cursed Slink. Level eight had small stages peppered throughout its main chamber, with seating surrounding each. As residents randomly arranged themselves at stages, nude lemma manikins began to populate the platforms.

These, however, were not typical lemma manikins. Beyond having actual mouths that were framed by pouty lips, the manikins were the idealized images of female perfection. Impossibly slim waists sat upon impressive hips. Oversized breasts hung high in direct opposition to gravity, while round asses bounced quickly on thin, athletic frames.

Drinks were served, and the Slink continued its work, replacing the bloodlust of the previous floor with a sexual lust that harkened back to the Bar's second level a lifetime ago. As testicles and nipples swelled, the manikins began provocative dances that were part cabaret, part Cirque du Soleil, and part porn shoot. Residents, male and female alike, reached lustily for the manikins, only to be slapped away. Once the choreographed portion of the show had finished, the manikins twirled through the crowd. One stopped to dance on the one lap of one male resident. Another straddled a female resident, covering her in passionate kisses as it placed its perfectly crafted bare feet in the faces of the men to each side.

Cocks throbbed, and clitorises ballooned, but no sexual releases were to be found on the eighth floor. Hadder drifted in and out of coherence, heightened sexual desire turning his cognizance on and off like a light switch. He tried to dampen the carnal urges with strong drinks, but the beverages that were served only added to his arousal.

Just as Hadder thought he could take no more, that he would be forced to assault one of the manikins or publicly pleasure himself, the intoxicating manikin dancers filed back into side rooms. Once safely packed away, the group was ushered towards the back stairwell, everyone noticeably stiffer than when they entered the floor.

———

THE FINAL STORY of *Inferno* appeared at first glance a welcome change of pace from the gauntlet through which Hadder had just walked. White curtained beds were organized in neat rows that filled the room. Servant manikins led residents one by one to beds, drawing the curtains closed as each resident settled onto their mattress.

Hadder laid back against plush cushions after the manikin left him alone behind the elegant drapery. His foot shook anxiously, still reeling from his unanswered call for sexual release. Looking at his forearm, Hadder felt a momentary sense of comfort in seeing that the Slink had all but disappeared. Despite his head spinning uncontrollably and his brain unable to decipher real from imagined, Hadder took pleasure in the one idea he knew to be true - it was almost over.

A figure could be seen moving just outside of Hadder's makeshift room; a female finger caressed the edges of the bed curtains. Hadder grew excited, anticipating a final satisfaction after endless longing. He was ready for what-ever came through that curtain, confident that he could handle it given his time in Station. Satisfied that no manner of creature that appeared before his bed would break him more than he had already been broken. Confident that he would take his satisfaction and be done with this fucked up place, stronger for having survived it.

Marlin Hadder was wrong on all accounts.

As the curtains slowly parted, Hadder ran the gamut of emotions, from disbelief to confusion to fear to, worst of all, hope. Emily moved gracefully onto the bed, looking as youthful and full of life as she did on their wedding day, her curly auburn hair framing her pink freckled face. Her light brown eyes, soft and gentle, locked onto his own, reminding Hadder of a life long lost.

From somewhere deep, Hadder's inner mind fought with the story his eyes were telling, screaming that a great betrayal was being executed. But Hadder's bruised heart muted that distant voice, backed by a Haela's worth of chemicals and leveraging a damaged brain that was functioning at minimal capacity.

Emily crawled up the bed to lay on top of Hadder, her hands cupping his face and wiping away twin rivers that now ran down his cheeks. Her face pressed against his own, Hadder closed his eyes tightly as the last image he had of her flashed across his vision. He could barely see her eyes through a veil of red. She wore a crown of brain matter but somehow kept moving, crawling through broken glass and over rough concrete, doing everything possible to get to the small hand that poked out from beneath the twisted metal.

Hadder opened his eyes, and there she was again. Face clean and serene, clear of the terror and desperation that soiled his last look at her. Hadder trembled beneath Emily, working hard to put words to his thoughts and even harder to vocalize those feelings. "Emily, it is really you? I thought I had lost you, sweetheart. I'm so sorry. I'm so sorry, honey."

Heaving sobs overtook Hadder, and he may have remained like that forever, caught in a loop of pity, had Emily not extinguished that despair with a passionate kiss that stole his breath and forced him back to the present. "It's ok," she said. "I'm here. I'm here with you, Marlin. I've missed you so much. Be with me."

They fell into each other again, paired souls that were brutally separated had found each other in absolute darkness, against all the odds. Grief, love, exhaustion, longing, loneliness, and drugs commingled to create a sexual frenzy between two star-crossed lovers. They didn't bother with clothes; Emily pulled down Hadder's pants, and Hadder pulled up Emily's floral dress, two sets of hands shaking with impatience.

Hadder slipped inside Emily, and his pupils shrank to pinholes. He was immediately transported to a previous, better life. Everything flooded back as she moved back and forth on top of him. A drunken kiss at a party that neither were supposed to attend; a beautiful secret wedding on a small island; shopping for little dresses; playfully arguing over names; selecting photos for scrapbooks; family walks at sunset during Autumn months.

Hadder looked up at the love of his life and knew that he was brought to Station for this very moment.

They continued their lovemaking, and their curtained bed might as well have been another world rotating another star in another galaxy. The two lovers were their own universe, alpha and omega. Marlin Hadder never wanted it to end.

As Hadder grew close to climax, he reached up to caress his wife's beautiful face. Emily took his hand and kissed his palm before placing it back on his chest. She then reached up and touched her own face, grabbing herself just under the chin. In one swift, violent motion, she ripped the flesh from her face to reveal a demon underneath.

Hadder's eyes went wide, and his heart sank as he recognized Jackie Crone straddling him, her angry blue eyes carving permanent trenches into his soul. Hadder's heart broke again, and even the small bit of sanity he had clung to all night abandoned him. Jackie Crone sensed his frozen anguish and smiled wickedly, riding Hadder harder until she came powerfully, soaking his groin and the bedsheets below in thick mucus. She kept thrusting Hadder deep inside her as he laid there a catatonic mess. Eventually, he came, the sad involuntary reaction of a shattered man.

Jackie Crone stood by Hadder's bedside, stroking his grief-stricken face. She leaned in towards his ear, her oily white hair and too-tight skin stirring his stomach. "Welcome to *Inferno*, new boy. Nothing ends. Tell Rott that you change nothing."

If Hadder had any control of his bodily functions, he would have retched in the bitch's face. Jackie moved away, gave one last toothy smile, and disappeared, leaving the curtain open behind her. Raising his head, Hadder could see other residents exiting their beds, most in either a daze or a desperate flight. Hadder's tattered mind and body elected the latter as he pulled up his sticky pants and hobbled towards the exit - *Inferno's* final door that would take him to the ground level.

THE ELEVATOR down was shared by three other residents, each silently dealing with their own personal hells. After a long descent, the doors opened directly to the outside of the Bar. The residents fell out one by one; two stumbled away in the pre-Solay haze while the third fell to the ground and held her head in her hands.

A cool breeze brushed Hadder's face, the phantom touch of his dead wife, and Hadder's mind lurched. He had lost everything a second time, and it was too much to bear. While the Slink was gone from his forearm, Hadder could still feel it coursing through his body, playing tricks on his eyes, pulling strings on his nerves, and squeezing adrenaline glands.

With no idea of where to go, what to do, or how to terminate the Slink's hold, Hadder began to run. He speedily lumbered along, utilizing movements that looked and felt half toddler, half drunkard. On and on Hadder ran, past quiet Bars and down dim thoroughfares, ghosts chasing him, hot on his heels. Despite the streets being empty as Haela slowly surrendered to Solay, Hadder fell as much as he ran, his mind no longer having mastery over his flailing limbs. His drug-clogged, ruined heart pounded in his chest, and his breathing resembled an asthma attack. But still, he ran.

After numerous twists and turns, Hadder was spat out of a small pathway and limped into a sizeable open avenue of unseemly asphalt. Looking left and right, Hadder could see that a swath of emptiness ran endlessly in either direction. Excessively bright lights hung from ugly metal poles that dotted both sides of the swath, in stark contrast to the beauty of Station.

Hadder shuffled forward, grief no longer enough to drive him. His brain sizzled as circuitry shorted, and synapses refused to fire. Hadder fell to his knees and began to crawl across the strip of concrete. In the dark recesses of his mind, Hadder recalled conversations with Miles and Jonny, something about a division of Station. Unable to switch gears; however, he continued to crawl, eventually reaching the other side of the divide, feeling an end to the cold asphalt and discovering the soft grass that dwelled just beyond.

A muddled idea coalesced within Hadder, telling him that he had reached some invisible goal. That was all the motivation he needed as he fell onto his back, staring up at the Idol Moon stuck between phases. Hadder's eyes grew heavy as exhaustion finally won the war over drugs and heartache. Closing them, his other senses immediately elevated. He smelled the burnt fruit smell of pollen on air currents and the musk of fertile soil that fed countless plant varietals. He heard the buzzing of glowing insects as they passed above on their way to pre-Solay trysts with open flowers. He listened to the gentle breeze that shuffled the grass beneath his head and footsteps in the distance growing closer.

Hadder's eyes rocketed open. Why did he hear footsteps growing closer? Unable to move anything below the neck, Hadder turned his head to the right and squinted. In the distance, a shadowed figure made its way towards Hadder at a fast walk that transitioned into a deliberate jog. As it drew closer, the shadows fell back to reveal the being that was now racing towards Hadder. While human, it was a twisted thing that seemed to have as much in common with a chimpanzee, elongated arms on a muscled frame supported by sturdy bowed legs. Its skin had a grayish hue, and it wore another's human face over its own, secured to its bald, deeply scarred head by black leather. As it ran, it held its long right arm out, and Hadder blinked as the brightening Idol Moon's rays caught the metal blade running the length of the creature's forearm, springing directly from the fiend's flesh.

Everything moved in slow motion as Hadder, unable to move, took in every detail of the terrifying but fascinating warped human that was closing the distance. Under the mask of flesh, Hadder could see a malicious grin punctuated by sharpened teeth, all the proof he needed that these were the last moments of his life. Tired, detached, and immobilized, Hadder looked away from the racing murderer to stare again at the Idol Moon, one last picture of beauty before the end. He closed his eyes once more, hearing the footsteps draw closer until they were upon him. Hadder could sense the weaponized arm pull back for a killing stroke. He welcomed it.

At what should have been the moment of impact, Hadder was yanked back by something with enormous strength. A wet slapping sound echoed off the concrete, followed by a weak scream and a scramble. "Get back, Riser! This one's not for you!" The voice was that of an elemental straight from the pit of an active volcano. The twisted man screamed something in return, an awful high-pitched thing, but Hadder was sinking deeper into unconsciousness and unable to understand his words.

The last thing Hadder remembered was being hefted into the air, thrown over a giant shoulder that felt like a skin-wrapped mountain. His savior's booming words chased after him as he dove headlong into oblivion. "Message from Mister Albany Rott. You're not to die. Not yet, anyway."

10

H adder opened his eyes slowly, fearing that he ran from one nightmare only to plunge into another. Hidden lights dimly lit the room in which he resided, typical Station living quarters, comfortable but sparsely furnished. Someone had removed and laundered Hadder's clothes, which were folded nicely on a chair by the front door. Looking at the Moon Clock, Hadder saw that it was already deep into Haela; he had slept away the Solay.

Although he was safe, an ember of anxiety continued to burn in the pit of Hadder's stomach like the morning of dread following a blackout. Whether it was the remnants of the damage inflicted by Jackie Crone's betrayal, residual effects of the dark drugs he had consumed, or knowledge of the knife-armed subhuman that shared Station with him, Hadder was unsure. Most likely, it was the rank combination of all three that had him on the right side of hysteria.

After a long, dangerously hot shower where he tried to wash off both dirt and the memory of Jackie Crone's body atop his, Hadder dressed hesitantly. Although his clothes had been thoroughly cleaned, his mind superimposed Jackie's thick juices onto his pants and underwear, making him wince. He quickly removed them.

Next to the front door, Hadder found the service button and pressed it. Less than a minute later, Hadder answered a polite knock at the door completely nude and ushered the glume manikin inside. Holding up his old clothes for the manikin to take, Hadder requested the same material and cut, but he wanted all black everything, including the jacket, thinking it best that his clothes matched his mood. Before he left, Hadder also asked that food be brought to the room, anything would do. The manikin, docile as always, simply nodded almost imperceptibly, turned, and left.

Hadder collapsed back on the bed, trying to understand this new life and what he wanted from it. The *Inferno* experience was forcing him to reevaluate everything. His time in the Celebration Cluster was eye-opening and exciting, no doubt, but it was growing more evident by the day that it wasn't enough. He enjoyed his time with Jonny VV, and Reena Song was the closest he'd come to meeting an actual angel, but they and everyone else in the Celebration scene was caught in a loop, an endless gif of clothes, drugs, and sex. Despite the time he had spent with Jonny and Reena, heady with narcotics or, in Reena's case, laying together deep into Solays, he knew very little about his close friends. Any conversations that began to tilt into the Before were redirected or outright ignored. Everyone in the Celebration Cluster seemed to suffer from this same malady, an inability to talk about their past. Initially, Hadder didn't think that this would bother him, that he could adapt and follow suit.

Marlin Hadder was wrong. All the drugs and sex in Station weren't enough to keep his mind from drifting backward. And truth be told, he didn't want to burn the past from his soul. It was too dear to him.

Beyond many residents' reluctance to honestly share anything more than their bodies, Hadder had also stumbled upon another taboo topic in Station. While his mind was too shattered to grasp where he had ended up the previous Haela, upon reflection, Hadder recalled Miles's brief introduction to the city and had reached a conclusion. He had wandered across the Skirt, and, in doing so, had encountered one of Station's more twisted citizens. Whispers of the division floated through parties, and talk of Risers was accidentally overheard late into Haelas when tongues had been greased by drink and smoke. Now, with the image of a bladed beast bearing down on him permanently etched into his brain, Hadder understood that something much more sinister was going on in Station. Something that everyone knew about but refused to discuss, as if giving voice to concerns would make them real.

Hadder was pulled from his dark thoughts by the returning manikin who had new clothes draped across one arm and was balancing a large bowl of stew on a tray with the other. Hadder took the clothes and food with shy words of thanks, still uncomfortable speaking with Station's caretakers. Before the manikin turned to go, it reached behind its back to pull out Hadder's old clothing, once again folded and tied into a neat package. It held out the bundle.

"Burn those," was all Hadder said as he showed the manikin out. As always in Station, the stew was delicious, and the clothes were a perfect fit. Regardless of his severe questions about the city, Hadder couldn't deny that it offered many enjoyable benefits.

The food and fresh clothes calmed his nerves and evaporated the gloom residing in his head better than any pill or chemically-laced drink. Now with only depressing thoughts and unnerving questions plaguing him, Hadder exited the living quarters, grateful for their existence. The halls were similar to those found in countless other Bar sub-levels, so he quickly found his way through them and up to the Bar's main floor.

Entering the main bar area, Hadder was thankful for what he found and even more grateful for what he didn't see. The last thing he wanted to walk into was another costumed party filled with frolicking zombies offering mind-numbing concoctions. Luckily, Hadder discovered that he was in an unfamiliar Bar, one that was, for the moment, peaceful. It resembled many of the bars that Hadder had frequented in the Before, with a long mahogany counter running the length of one far side with bar stools, three of which were occupied by residents, and tables with chairs dominating the remainder of the space. Muted lo-fi hip hop filled the room, adding to the relaxing environment.

Hadder took a seat at the bar and ordered a Number 7, the kindest drink he could think of, from the glume manikin operating the counter. After a few sips from the glass, feeling its soft effects, Hadder turned to the nearest resident, an older gentleman with salt and pepper hair wearing simple blue jeans, a flannel shirt, and boots. Hadder cracked a smile before speaking, the man's modest garb tickling something in Hadder's past that he dearly missed. "Excuse me, what Bar is this? I was kinda out of it when I got here."

The man chuckled, the act making his thick beard dance and turned to Hadder. "You weren't out of it; you were delirious. And dangerously dehydrated to boot. We had a manikin give you an IV while you slept it off. You were lucky Cal got you here when he did."

Hadder's face flushed with embarrassment. Although Station was a haven for the out of control, Hadder still prided himself on being able to take care of himself at all times. "I'm sorry about all that. Thanks for helping me; I really appreciate it. Is this Cal in here? I'd like to thank him as well."

"Cal doesn't need thanking. It's his job." Hadder's confused look forced the man to continue. "Cal's one of the Caesars. Told me he found you fucking around down by the Skirt, out of your mind. You're blessed that he found you in time."

Hadder had an inkling of the answer but pressed anyway. "In time for what?"

The man turned back to his beer. "Never mind."

"I'm sorry; I didn't get your name to properly thank you. I'm Marlin. Marlin Hadder."

The man's eyes remained forward. "Name's Glen. No need to thank me, either, Hadder. But tell me, what got you in such a state? I mean, there's messed up, and there's what you were. That wasn't just a man drunk on chemicals that I saw. That was a man with a broken spirit." Glen turned back to Hadder, his dark eyes swirling like a thunderstorm. "What broke your spirit, son?"

Glen's eyes bore holes into Hadder, but he refused to look away. "I visited *Inferno*. It's a Bar in..."

"I know what *Inferno* is," interrupted Glen. He spat on the floor after saying the name of the Bar. "What were you trying to accomplish by entering that foul establishment?"

"Accomplish?"

"People only go to *Inferno* for three reasons. One, to lobotomize themselves, keep any real thoughts or feelings from disturbing their endless summer. Two, to actually feel something. They've done so much fucking and drinking that only the most extreme can blow their hair back. You know what we called those people in the Before? Fucking serial killers. And three, to briefly remember the past, but only to curse it and bury it deeper. Which of those fits you, son?"

Hadder pondered Glen's question and couldn't deny the truth of the options he presented. "I think it was number two, but looking back, it may have been all three. I made a big mistake."

The storms raging in Glen's eye calmed as he detected the truth and melancholy behind Hadder's response. "You know, a trip to *Inferno*" - another spit - "proves an inflection point for many residents. From there, you either sink lower into Station's muck, or you decide that there's more to living than forgetting."

"Did you ever go to *Inferno*, Glen?"

A deep sigh. A disturbing flashback. "Long time ago. Last time I ever set foot in the Celebration Cluster." Glen shook the memory loose. "Look, kid, if you're trying to forget, there's less destructive ways to do so. Why don't you go check out the Lethe River? This Bar is called *Cranesman*; it's a fair way northwest of the Celebration Cluster. When you walk out the front door, take the small path to the left and stay straight. It'll spit you right out onto the Lethe's banks."

"Thanks, Glen. I'll do that." Hadder took the rest of his drink down in a gulp and stood. He took another moment to enjoy the ambiance of *Cranesman*. "You know, I really like this Bar. I've missed places like this. And the conversations that they bring."

"Thanks, I had it built myself. I modeled it after a place that was special to me in the Before."

"You can have Bars built? How?"

"You gotta petition Mister Rott. A simple form, really. But it was a lot easier back in the day when there was open land everywhere. I had this built away from everything else, my own selfish sanctuary. Now there's six other Bars within five minutes. Just as well, I ain't running from anything anymore."

"Well, I'm glad you got it made, regardless of the reasons."

Glen stood and shook Hadder's hand, a firm thing that reminded Hadder of a life almost buried. "You're welcome at *Cranesman* anytime. I know it's empty now, but this is more of a Solay Bar. I was just waiting for you to rise to make sure you were okay."

Hadder nodded his sincere appreciation and walked to the entrance. At the door, he stopped and turned back to Glen. He raised his finger to the ceiling. "Lo-fi hip hop?"

Glen smiled. "I died. But I ain't dead. This old dog keeps up with the times."

Hadder laughed as he turned back and exited. Walking out into the deep Haela, Hadder smiled. He had met plenty of residents that he liked, but Hadder finally met someone he could relate to.

———

HADDER FOLLOWED Glen's instructions and took the small path to the left, staying straight as it cut through lush gardens and split off to either side. Hadder rediscovered Haela plant and animal life as he walked, soaking in the animated leaves, glowing insects, and multi-colored creatures of Station's night.

Before long, true to Glen's word, Hadder left the life-filled gardens behind and stood on the bank of a large river that cut through the city like a scythe. The river was several hundred feet across, and its currents moved swiftly. As Hadder approached the water's edge, he discovered the real magic of the river. Below its surface, ropes of prismatic light danced and swirled, exposing the river's frightening depth. The Lethe's expanse gave off a gentle indigo light, bathing its banks in a glossy shine that created a calming atmosphere.

Looking down the bank, Hadder noticed that benches had been placed every fifty feet or so. He took one, spotting a silhouetted figure on the other nearest seat. Leaning forward, Hadder stared deep into the churning waters, watching the swirling colors dance and pulse. Within a few short minutes, Hadder's heartbeat had aligned with the Lethe's vibration, and Hadder fell into a trance.

His mind followed the twisting chromatic ropes beneath the surface and dove deep, passing blue-glowing lantern fish and stingrays whose barbed tails left trails of color crisscrossing the water. Down the river, Hadder's mind leaped, pulled by the current and driven by his own desire to lose himself. Hadder closed his eyes but still saw everything, the ropes of light soaring past his body and turning on a dime to strike his chest, entering powerfully and warming his heart. Hadder sucked in air as he felt the Lethe's energy flowing into his soul, repairing some of the damage caused by *Inferno* and Jackie Crone.

Hadder relinquished all control to the Lethe as it drove him deeper, farther, faster, only to return him to his seat on the bench sometime later. Feeling reinvigorated, Hadder opened his eyes and almost jumped out of his chair, startled to find someone standing in front of him.

She laughed softly, honeysuckle on a summer breeze. "I'm so sorry to have frightened you." Hadder looked around, found that the bench closest to him was now empty. She continued, "We seem to be the only ones out here. Do you mind if I join you?"

Hadder weakly motioned towards the empty seat. As she sat, the light from the Lethe kissed her face and gave Hadder a view of true beauty. The woman had long silver-blonde hair pulled back into a loose ponytail and cognac eyes that made Hadder want to build a home where they would live their shared days out in happiness. As Hadder's mind raced with something witty to say, the woman simply sat in silence, looking into the enchanted water. After some time, Hadder gave up on his creative writing assignment and simply relished sitting quietly with the mysterious woman.

Several minutes later, she finally broke the silence. "You trying to forget?"

"What do you mean?"

"The is the Lethe River, where you can supposedly forget that which hurts you. A lot of residents come here when the Before starts seeping back into their lives. They stare and stare. And stare. Let their minds go blank and wash away unwanted memories. It takes them downstream and out of the city. Then they get up with a clean slate and go back to their lives of diversion. Is that what you're doing here?"

"I don't really know what I'm doing here. But I don't think that's it. I like staring into the river. And while the idea of stripping away those memories that hurt so much sounds nice, I don't think that's what I want." The words poured out of Hadder, aimed at a woman he didn't know, but with whom he wanted to share everything. "Those memories hurt so much because of how essential they are to who I am. Do they often bring me sadness? Yes. Hell, they brought me to this city, didn't they? But after months of burying them, I see now that they also bring me joy that no short-term fix can provide. No matter how drunk I am or hot she is." The woman laughed at this. "No, I think I need to keep them, cradle them. Somehow make them a part of me without allowing them to destroy me. I failed at this in the Before. I'd like to try again here. But I don't know how."

The woman stayed silent for a long time, digesting Hadder's monologue. Instead of responding to Hadder's existential contemplations, she sat, sharing the musical sounds of the Lethe's current. Hadder grew anxious, wondering if opening his heart to a stranger that he fancied was the best approach.

"My name's Lilly. Lilly Sistine."

"Pretty name."

"Thanks, but it's not my real name. I mean not the one I had in the Before. That takes some of the shine off it, I think."

"I'm Marlin. Marlin Hadder."

"Interesting name. You come up with that yourself?"

"Real name, no gimmick."

Still staring ahead, Lilly placed her hand on Hadder's leg, an action of comfort and friendship rather than sexual strategy. "It's nice to meet you, Marlin Hadder, no gimmick. You're gonna be ok. I like you already, and I'm going to help you."

Hadder's face split in two from the goofy smile that crash-landed there, and he was thankful that they were both still looking towards the Lethe. "I would like that."

"Me too. But let's enjoy the Lethe for a bit longer. Lost people come here to forget. Found people come here to remember."

Hadder liked that.

———

HADDER AND LILLY sat for a while, enjoying the sounds of the Lethe and each other's quiet company. Suddenly, Lilly slapped Hadder on the thigh and stood up, motioning him to do the same. "It's getting late, Marlin. And you look like you've been through a shit storm recently. Let's get some sleep."

"You don't sleep during the Solay like everyone else?"

"Everyone else isn't the Celebration Cluster, you know. There's a lot of us who try to live more normal, fulfilling lives here. You want to give it a shot?"

Hadder was unable to deny that although he had woken from a long slumber a few short hours ago, he was already exhausted, weighed down heavily with thought and worry. He rose and followed Lilly away from the Lethe, silently thanking it for not only its cathartic effects but for bringing him together with this lovely woman. Lilly wore faded blue jeans that hugged her long, fit legs, a tight gray tank top, and weathered black boots. Her outfit was a far cry from the varied material, multimedia, stream of consciousness ensembles that those in the Celebration Cluster worked so hard to create. And Hadder loved it.

As they walked, Lilly spoke. "I usually stay at *The Royal Jelly* and have permanent living quarters there. But I'm tired, and you look like the living dead. Or at least someone who works with the dead." Hadder looked down at his black on black clothing and shrugged shyly. "Anyways, you mind if we just crash at *Cranesman*? It's the closest bar, and I'm friends with the proprietor."

"Yeah, I know it. I ended up there last Haela. Or maybe it was Solay. Anyways, I met Glen already. Happy to go back there."

"Good, then it's settled."

They came upon *Cranesman* a few minutes later and entered the modest building. Now late into Haela, Glen was gone, and only one resident remained at the counter, fast asleep on the hardwood. Lilly kicked the small man's bar stool as they walked past, and he lifted his head. "Get to the living quarters, Squeak. The ghosts won't follow you to your bed."

"Ok, Lilly," was all that the small man weakly offered.

Hadder trailed as Lilly led him back down to the Bar's sub-level and its living quarters. Walking down several halls, she finally stopped at a door and pressed her hand to the glowing white mark on the wall to the right. The door slid open, unveiling a room identical to the one in which Hadder had awoken. For all he knew, it may have been the very same room. Lilly gently pushed Hadder inside. He walked forward to the room's center and turned around, confused when Lilly remained at the doorway. "When we sleep isn't the only difference here compared to the Celebration Cluster."

Hadder's stomach clinched in embarrassment. "Oh, I didn't mean to..."

Lilly chuckled, holding up her palm to shush the stammering Hadder. "It's quite alright. I get it. But let's just get to know each other first. We have nothing but time here." Hadder offered a grateful nod. "I'm gonna stay next door. Buzz me if you need anything. I usually get up within the first hour or so of Solay. You want me to come to wake you?"

"I barely remember what early Solay looks like. Yes, please wake me."

"Dreams are rarely sweet in Station, so I always say, 'have a restful time.' So, have a restful time, Marlin Hadder."

"You, too, Lilly Sistine."

With that, the door slid shut, leaving Hadder alone with his thoughts. These thoughts, however, were much brighter than those he started his shortened day with. Images of Jackie Crone and twisted killing machines were replaced by visions of Lilly Sistine's cognac eyes staring at him from the pillow next to his and her silver-blonde hair tickling his face as they danced closely to Motown music.

Hadder sat down slowly on the bed and laughed to himself. In his months at Station, this was the first instance when he had spent time with a woman only to end up alone. But Hadder didn't mind. For the first time in a while, warm anxiousness had appeared in his stomach, promising something special in the Solay to come.

Hadder laid down and closed his eyes. Jackie Crone didn't caress him in the darkness, and no scythe arms swung his way in the pitch black. Hadder didn't have sweet dreams. But he rested.

11

Hadder was ripped from a deep, restful slumber by a knock at his door. Looking over at the Moon Clock through bleary eyes, Hadder saw that Lilly had kept her word, coming to get him a couple of hours into Solay. Despite being in deep REM sleep moments earlier, Hadder quickly shook off his tiredness, the possibility of an entire Solay spent with Lilly Sistine sweeping away all cobwebs.

Opening the door, Hadder's breath caught as he saw Lilly again for the first time. He exhaled in relief as the fear that last Haela was a construct - that his sadness, worry, exhaustion, and confusion had made him build this woman into more than she was - dissipated into nothing. Lilly was all that he remembered and more. She now wore worn gray jeans, a white tube top, and a weathered jean jacket. Her hair fell past her shoulders like a blonde-silver waterfall, and she displayed a silver choker crafted in the shape of a snake eating its own tail. The snake slowly consumed more of its tail, which continued to grow from the back of its head, giving the piece an entrancing quality. Black Converse sneakers topped it off, with white graphics that moved of their own accord like shoe anime.

"Something the matter, Marlin."

"No, you just look great. Cool clothes."

"Just because we don't live like your friends in the Celebration Cluster doesn't mean we don't take advantage of the custom clothing here."

"I can see that."

"Well, get cleaned up, and I'll meet you upstairs. No rush, but don't keep me waiting either. There's a lot I want to show you today."

"I'll get moving. Thanks for coming to get me."

"No problem. See you up top." Hadder thought he noticed Lilly's eyes drop and look over Hadder's underwear-clad body as the door was closing. At least he hoped that was what he saw.

Hadder showered quickly and dressed, frowning in the mirror at his funeral director's clothing. On his way to *Cranesman's* main level, Hadder found a lemma manikin on its way to complete some trivial task and asked to go to a garment room. He waited patiently as the lemma manikin sewed gray pants and a white t-shirt. After thinking it over, Hadder also ordered a light black jacket with the back showing an animated grey Ophidian blowing smoke. Finally, he had his black and white high tops remade. Lilly Sistine was right, it would be a shame not to take advantage of Station's more enjoyable perks.

Suited for the oncoming Solay, Hadder took the steps up to the bar level two at a time, crashing through the doors with excitement. Glenn and Lilly sat together at the counter, talking and sipping on orange drinks. They stopped their conversation as Hadder approached.

"There he is," said Glen cheerfully.

"Nice threads," added Lilly, spinning Hadder around while admiring his clothes. "Care for something to drink?"

Hadder stared at their drinks. "What are those? Number 3s?"

Glen and Lilly laughed in unison. "It's just orange juice, Marlin. We don't need to get high first thing in the Solay here."

"Plenty of stuff out there to get you high naturally," added Glen, nodding his head towards the Bar's front door.

"Sorry, habit, I suppose," replied Hadder. "Sure, I'll have some."

Lilly handed him her drink. "Here, just finish mine. I want to get going."

She picked up a brown paper bag from the counter. "Glen was kind enough to make us some breakfast-to-go."

Hadder looked at Glen with confusion. "You cooked? Why?"

Glen shrugged. "I cooked breakfast for my family every day in the Before. Why not do it for my young friends here in Station? There's a joy to be found in the little things, Hadder. The regular things that those in the Celebration Cluster take for tedium can bring great pleasure. Remember that."

"I will," said Hadder as Lilly dragged him away and towards the Bar entrance.

"Oh, thank you, wise sage Glen. There will be odes to your timeless words," said Lilly jokingly, tussling Glen's hair as she passed.

"You two kids enjoy yourselves! Plenty to see in Station! The raw materials are here to mold your own utopia!" Glen's words chased after them as they exited *Cranesman*.

Hadder shielded his eyes against the full Idol Moon. Lilly laughed. "Geez, it has been a while since you've been out this early."

"Where to?" asked Hadder as his eyes adjusted to the brightness of Station's other night.

"Leave that to me," said Lilly, grabbing his arm.

———

LILLY LED Hadder west and then north, taking a twisting series of garden paths. As they walked, she pointed out interesting aspects of Station's natural environment. They watched in silence as a small bunny rabbit stood on hind legs the length of a human's to reach the bright red berries of a tall plant bordering their path. When it had its fill, the legs folded down like an accordion, leaving a normal-sized rabbit to hop away into the garden. A rather unimpressive tree with a large hollow, small branches, and sickly yellow leaves sang "Ave Maria" from its opening when Lilly tickled its bark with her black fingernails.

Not long after turning north, they came upon an ornate bridge crossing the Lethe River. While the foundation of the bridge was white marble, the railings were pure crystal, granting pedestrians an exhilarating feeling of exposure as they crossed the hypnotizing waterway. Lilly informed Hadder that there were several bridges over the river; this one was the Bridge Gab'Riel.

After leaving the bridge behind, Lilly continued to traverse various garden paths, traveling in a generally north-easterly direction. This far north in Station, the gardens were tall and thick, and Hadder was utterly lost within minutes. Should Lilly abandon him now, he thought, his bones would become a permanent part of the complex ecosystem.

"We're almost there," said Lilly as they passed an onyx statue jutting out from the garden in the shape of a man kneeling down with fists raised, frozen in a scream as if he were cursing the heavens. Just minutes later, their small path emptied into a large clearing, and Lilly threw her arm around Hadder. "This, Marlin, is the Samsara. It's my absolute favorite thing in Station. Except for some of the wonderful people, of course."

Hadder looked around, taking it all in. If this was Lilly Sistine's favorite place, it must be truly magical, and he wanted to appreciate it fully. The border of the clearing was simply manicured grass, green and vibrant. Dominating the open space, however, was a large circle of silky white sand, perfectly combed as if it were a Japanese art exhibit. In the center of the circle sat the most giant tree Hadder had seen in Station, dwarfing the Monarch trees that lined main thoroughfares. This was the Samsara.

While enormous, the Samsara appeared dead, its black bark looking like it had been pulled from the fires of hell and its bare branches looking like they hadn't given life to leaves or blossoms since Christ himself walked the earth. Despite its cadaverous presentation, however, the Samsara stood in dark contrast to the white sand that surrounded it like a loyal proselyte, creating a wholly moving image.

"Impressive," was all that Hadder could say. "Very impressive."

"Oh, it gets better. Come on, I'm hungry."

Lilly led Hadder forward and dropped Indian-style on the soft grass. She patted the carpet of green. "Join me. Please."

Hadder did as he was told, and was surprised by the soft, spongy quality of the ground that made for an excessively comfortable seat. Lilly opened the brown paper bag and took out two round sandwiches that had been carefully wrapped in wax paper. She handed one to Hadder and tore open the other. Hadder followed suit and found that Glen had made them bacon, egg, and cheese biscuits. Taking a bite, Hadder's eyes widened at the quality of the sandwich, equaling that of anything any manikin ever provided. "Wow, this is pretty damn good."

Lilly nodded vigorously in agreement. "I know, right? I think Glen makes the biscuits from scratch."

"What's his deal," Hadder asked between bites. "I mean, he seems so together, nothing like the others I've met here. How does he end up in a place like this?" Lilly remained silent for a moment, enjoying her biscuit, and Hadder took this to mean that he had overstepped, something he had done routinely in the Celebration Cluster. "Sorry I shouldn't have asked. It's none of my business, I know."

"No, no, it's quite alright, Marlin. We aren't like those residents who try to act like the Before didn't exist. We often talk about the Before and what we miss about it. We also talk about what drove us here and how we can learn from the low points in our lives. In Glen's case, you're right; he is pretty normal. Had a wife and two grown daughters that he loved very much. He was a tower crane operator, and a good one, nearing retirement, I think. He was working on a new skyscraper in the city, I forget which one, and conditions got bad as a storm moved in. He kept pushing as the winds picked up. Thought he could handle it and keep the project on schedule. Anyways, a huge gust comes along like a rogue wave and sends his load spinning hundreds of feet in the air. He tried to regain control, but one of the clips snapped under stress, and some items came loose and fell to the ground. A mother pushing her baby was struck and died instantly. The courts ultimately found him not liable, just a sad accident, but he never forgave himself. I guess you can figure out the rest. He was one of the original residents of Station, known as Keys. Most of the Keys have gone completely bonkers in their time here; I think you've met a few. But Glen remains Glen, a sweet guy who couldn't recover from one bad day at work. You done with that?"

Hadder, absorbed in Glen's story, looked down to see that he had finished his breakfast sandwich. He handed the wax paper to Lilly, who added it to her own and balled it up with the brown paper bag. "Check this out," she said as she threw the ball of trash onto the Samsara's white sand. Hadder watched in amazement as the refuse disintegrated and disappeared before his eyes, hundreds of years being played out in seconds. "Cool, huh?"

"Very."

Lilly looked at Hadder as if waiting for something. "So you want to share your story, Marlin? It's just me here."

Hadder stared at the Samsara, wondering how he could escape this conversation, wondering if he really wanted to. He had worked hard over the past few months not to think about the family that was stolen from him, attempting to whitewash a beautiful painting that stirred up uncomfortable emotions. "I don't know if I can, Lilly." Tears began to well up in Hadder's eyes. He looked away in embarrassment.

Lilly continued to stare forward, offering Hadder privacy even in their closeness. "You don't have to tell me, Marlin. You can tell the Samsara."

Hadder didn't understand, but he focused on the Samsara, nonetheless. Its bare black branches remained unmoving, twisted arms that looked to provide little comfort and even less understanding. Still, he stared, narrowing his vision to the tree's dark trunk, allowing himself to shrink down, become ethereal, penetrating the antique bark and boring deep inside the cold wood. Hadder's world went black as he swam within the Samsara, endless tunnels of lifelessness, vast expanses of nothing.

Just as he turned to exit, another impotent experiment exhausted, he spotted a flicker of light in the shadowed distance. Hadder willed himself forward, squeezing through idle veins and hardened pulp, eventually coming upon the Speck of light, the last crumb of a once vibrant life. Although minuscule, the Speck gave off tremendous warmth, and Hadder moved closer to gain a reprieve from the miserable cold of death. Soon, the Speck took up Hadder's entire field of vision, so close they were, and he could feel its energy pulsing, pulling, and pushing, locking him in its orbit.

"Share," it said to him, the singular word echoing in his head, each reverberation growing louder and stronger. Hadder continued to orbit the light, rotation speed increasing, warming then comforting. As he spun, layers flew off of him into the dark beyond, unneeded armor in this sanctuary. Stripped clean with nowhere else to hide, Hadder invited the light in.

And let go.

Hadder spoke of his troubled years as a young man, drugs and violence preventing any kind of personal growth. He spoke of his parents, their heartbreak in witnessing the failures of their only child. Hadder spoke of Mom's cancer that ate away at her over two years, leaving her a shell before taking that, as well. He spoke of Dad's inability to cope, how he literally wasted away without her, joining her eighteen months later. Hadder spoke of meeting Emily while bouncing one night, her soft eyes cutting through the booze and pills to touch his heart. He spoke of how he became a better man for her, the bottles of pills discarded, and the alcohol put back on the shelf. Hadder spoke of going back to school, earning his Master's, and landing with a respectable outfit. He spoke of the angel that they brought into the world together, how she taught him more about true love and responsibility without being able to say a word. He spoke of the suffocating guilt he felt for acting too slow, for becoming the man his parents wanted him to be when it was too late for them to take pleasure in it.

He spoke of the accident that stole everything, that second that he glanced back to check on baby Mia. That second that may have allowed him to see the truck out of the corner of his eye, a small reaction that may have changed everything.

And Hadder spoke of how he found himself alone in a sea of despair, how he wasn't much for friends because he had poured everything into his two girls. He spoke of how he treaded water for as long as he could, but the ocean of loss proved too vast. He spoke of how he ultimately ended up exactly as his parents knew him, how he wasn't worthy of the world and how it didn't deserve his toxic presence.

Tale of woe complete, Hadder's rotations around the Speck halted. The pulsing light began to swell, encompassing Hadder in energy that warmed his soul and greased his smile. Safely bathed in the Speck's light, Hadder could feel the grief, anxiety, guilt, and anger drain from him through infinite pinholes. Soon after, he drifted in the luminescence, emptied but not empty, a man with loss who was no longer lost.

"Thank you for sharing," boomed the Speck, voice emanating from everywhere all at once. "Now live."

On that cue, Hadder was thrust violently from the Speck's light, watching as it disappeared from sight, leaving Hadder in the dark once more. Until he opened his wet eyes.

The Samsara was before him once more, sitting silently on its foundation of white sand. Hadder was lying on the soft grass, his head cradled in Lilly's lap as she stroked his hair. Sitting up, he noticed the wet spots on Lilly's jeans and offered an abashed apology, which she waved away. While Hadder recovered from what must have been heaving sobs, Lilly sat patiently, silence the greatest gift she could have given him.

"Was I talking out loud that whole time," he asked, unsure of what had just transpired.

Lilly smiled sweetly. "Yes, but I only listened to most of it. I'm sorry for what happened to you, Marlin. I truly am. How do you feel?"

Hadder took a moment to evaluate. "Better. Much better." He took a deep, shaky breath, let it out slowly. "How about you, Lilly? What's your story?"

"Later, Marlin. Time for that later." She put her arm around Hadder's shoulder's, pointed at the Samsara. "Look at what you've done."

Hadder looked on in astonishment as the Samsara began to change. Its expired coat slowly turned from black to brown to beige to white, matching the sand found beneath it. The Samsara's decrepit arms grew thick and durable, giving birth to large blossoms that ran the spectrum of colors. Hadder's eyes went wide at the metamorphosis, from the remnants of what was to the pinnacle of what was possible. Lilly held him tight as the Samsara towered over them, vibrant and healthy, its brightness warming the entire courtyard and stealing residual negativities from his mind.

A breeze entered the courtyard, and the Samsara danced at its introduction, its large blossoms moving to and fro in time with a muted melody. The breeze became a wind that whipped through the courtyard in a counter-clockwise direction. Blossom petals leaped from their perch to join the wind, riding its circular currents. More and more fell until a cyclone of color surrounded the Samsara and filled the air, raining color upon Hadder and Lilly.

Hadder stood, and Lilly joined him, transfixed by the scene playing out around them, grateful to be background characters in a living Van Gogh painting. Petals tickled their faces, many sticking to Hadder's tear-slicked cheeks, and he laughed loudly, an honest sound that came from a place just recently rediscovered.

Lilly, her face a chromatic work of art, cupped Hadder's face with her hands and brought him in for a kiss as they stood in the blossom storm. It wasn't a deep, passionate kiss like Reena's, but rather the warm, comforting kind that Hadder had thought off-limits to a wretch like him.

As they separated, the wind died down, and the storm of petals became a gentle snowfall, scraps of color falling to the green grass and white sand, only to disappear seconds later. The Samsara, its show concluded, darkened again, shedding its last remaining blossoms as it thinned. Minutes passed, and it stood dark once more, an inkblot on the white canvass.

"Well, what do think, Marlin," asked Lilly, one arm still over Marlin's shoulders.

"I think I'm ready to see the rest of your world. All of it."

"You sure? You might not want to leave."

"I'm counting on it."

12

L illy Sistine led Hadder across the Bridge Gab'Riel once more and due south along one of the more significant thoroughfares that Hadder had seen. Just off the street and down a medium-sized garden path, they eventually passed into a large clearing. To the left, a group of residents was playing volleyball, enjoying the fresh air and heatless light of the Solay. To the right, a man with four arms played a double-neck guitar for an enthralled audience that surrounded him on the grass. In the center of the clearing stood a large three-story wooden Bar bordered by a lush, manicured garden on its sides and back. Five steps led up to an impressive porch and the main entrance, which were below an overhang that was supported by four wooden columns. Although the building looked to be an antique theater, the front overhang was trimmed with yellow neon, and the words *The Royal Jelly* were spelled out in matching neon of vibrant blue. The Bar was unlike anything Hadder had encountered in Station to date.

Lilly stopped on the small footpath that led up the Bar and extended both arms towards the building, cracking a smile that lit up her face and melted Hadder's weakened heart. "This is my home, Marlin. This is *The Royal Jelly*. Come on!"

Taking Hadder's hand, Lilly pulled him towards the Bar. Twin golden bees, standing on opposite sides of the footpath just before the stairs and standing at twice Hadder's height, welcomed them. As they neared, the statues' golden wings began to slowly flutter, reflecting the Solay's rays in small explosions of brilliant light. Up the stairs they went, and through the large double doors.

Hadder walked into a warm, open space that was lit with what almost seemed to be natural sunlight, and he was besieged by Sunday morning memories that almost caused him to trip. He moved forward, investigating this place that obviously meant so much to Lilly. On each side were comfortable seating areas, many of which were presently home to residents, wrapped in dark leather that begged for someone to enjoy them. Beyond the sitting areas, centered in the room, was a small bar that looked mightily stocked, carrying much more than Station's standard numbered offerings. Stairs descended on both sides of the small bar to another level, where another small bar backed into the one above it, creating an interesting dual-level effect. The second mini-level also contained numerous seating areas in addition to a long counter that looked down to the last lower level. Several more residents occupied this bench, engaged in quiet conversations over cold drinks.

The final level, reached via cascading steps on either side of the second mini-level, was the money shot. An enormous dance floor dominated the majority of the space, with cozy booths lining both sides and couches acting as backstops. As Hadder slowly raised his eyes, however, he saw what really separated *The Royal Jelly* from other Bars. A magnificent stage stood six feet above the dance floor, ornate wood trim work present to enhance and legitimize any performance. Looking up and around, Hadder saw that the second and third main floors were comprised of balconies that overlooked both the stage and revelers beneath.

"So, what do you think," Hadder heard Lilly ask him from behind.

"It's great," replied Hadder honestly. There was a warmth to the Bar, similar to *Cranesman* on a much larger scale. "What kind of shows get put on here?"

Lilly joined him to more closely admire the stage. "Anything, really.

Obviously music concerts, but we also have plays, dance performances, talent showcases, whatever. If a resident wants to do something, is in good standing with Royal, and is willing to take it seriously, the stage is theirs. Which reminds me, you need to meet Royal. This way."

Lilly returned Hadder to the ground level and guided him to the first bar facing the main entrance. Sitting at the bar, holding a half-empty glass of amber liquid, was a distinguished-looking man in his late fifties or early sixties. He had a full head of thick silver hair that grazed his shoulders and a matching mustache that marked him as a man's man. Although thin, sinewy muscles could be easily made out beneath bell-bottomed jeans and white t-shirt. With leather bracelets and an army of charms and trinkets around his neck, the man looked to be playing the role of aging rock star between gigs.

"Marlin Hadder, please meet Royal Winters, proprietor of this lovely establishment and one of the original Keys of Station."

"Don't lump me in with those other human wraiths. What're drinking?" was Royal's informal introduction.

"I'll have whatever you're having. What is that, a Number 8?"

"It's beer, Marlin Hadder. Just beer."

Hadder chuckled nervously as Royal's blue eyes took him in, the weight of his judgment making it hard to relax. "Sorry, it's just I haven't even seen a beer in ages. That sounds perfect, thanks."

Instead of summoning a manikin, Royal rose and jumped the counter of the bar, snatching up a glass with a trained hand and filling it from a tap.

Royal spoke as he poured. "You know, extremeness has its place, is a necessary component to many things - entertainment, revolution, art, to name a few." He handed the beer to Hadder. "But I don't want or need it first thing in the fucking Solay. Most Solays, I don't need it at all. Often, I just want a fucking beer. Now don't get me wrong, I, too, dabble in Station's various concoctions, they can really hit the spot on occasion. But for my money, nothing says friends, family, good conversation, honest art, and toe-tapping music like the originals - beer, whiskey, tequila, vodka."

"Oh Royal, you do like your speeches," said Lilly, who had lowered herself into the closest seating area. "I'll take one as well. Please."

Royal continued as he fulfilled Lilly's request. "I don't see any wild Elevations on you, Hadder. Frightened of a little change, are we?"

Hadder thought about it as he drank. The cold beer went down smoothly, and Hadder smiled admiringly at the glass; he had forgotten how refreshing and straightforward beer could be. "It's not that. I guess it's just something I haven't really given much thought to. There's a lot of things in my life I wanted different. An Elevation wouldn't address any of those things."

Royal hopped back over the bar. He cuffed Hadder behind the neck in a fatherly manner. "Fucking A. That tells me that you were running from something that happened to you, but not yourself. That's good. There may be hope for you yet." He released Hadder and moved to join Lilly, taking the armchair across from her. "And you've found the most captivating woman in Station, so bonus points for you, new boy."

Hadder looked to the empty bar before sitting down in the love seat next to Lilly. "Where's your manikin, Royal?"

"I got a few roaming around here somewhere, probably cleaning up after fixed guests like Lilly here."

"But none are handling the bar."

Royal gave a stern look. "That's my job. Some of us are uncomfortable doing nothing all day. I like the work, I like the camaraderie, and I like all the gossip I receive. I might get one of the manikins to help out if we get too busy, or I gotta take a dump or play, but for the most part, it's just me and whoever else wants to man the bars. I mean, who really wants to be waited on by a wind-up toy? Fucking impersonal if you ask me."

"So no other Elevations for you beyond the obvious ones?"

"What obvious ones," Royal asked, sounding offending.

"That thick head of hair and that beautiful mustache, Royal. That ain't normal."

Royal laughed. "You sonavabitch, my daddy gave me these, not some dead-eyed sex doll with a scalpel. Lilly, get this fucking guy out of my bar!" They all shared in a laugh. "You're alright, Hadder. But hell, if Lilly's bringing you to me, then I already knew that. But seriously, for a new resident, you're ok in my book."

"Wish your fellow Keys felt the same way."

"Some of them gave you a hard time?"

"Mostly just hard looks and words. But some worse things, too."

"I'm not surprised. Your appearance here could mean a lot of things, many of which are unappealing to those decrepit psychopaths who are more Elevation than human at this point."

"What possibly could I mean for them, though?"

Royal shrugged. "An end to the status quo. An end to their fiefdoms. Hell, maybe an end to whole goddam city."

Hadder was lost as to how his arrival could usher in such change, but he accepted it blindly and pushed on. "And this doesn't scare you, Royal."

"Nothing scares me anymore. All of us here have lived two lives, and that's one more than everyone else gets, and two more than many of us deserve. You being here portents something, but that something is out of your control. Chess pieces are being moved by the Gods, Hadder. Let's just enjoy the board while we're here."

"Cheers to that," Lilly and Hadder said together.

"More beers. And some goddam music! Where are my manners?"

―――――

IN RESPONSE to Royal's request, Hadder filled both Lilly and Royal in on his escapades of the last months, coyly leaving out most of his sexual activities given Lilly's presence. Lilly nodded her head in understanding through most of it, stating that most everyone goes through a "kid in a candy store" phase upon arrival. "Some find their way out it," she said, "Many don't."

Lilly reacted much differently than expected when Hadder shared who he had been with most of that time. "Oh, I love Reena Song so much. It's a shame she can't get out of that party rut. She was a nurse, you know? Like a really quality one. She worked in the burn unit of a major hospital. Poor thing saw so much pain and suffering, remaining strong. But when a foster mom soaked her three mentally ill children in a tub of gasoline before lighting them on fire, something broke inside her. She stayed with those children around the clock, listening to their confused little wails and cries, watching as one by one each succumbed to their burns after ten lives' worth of pain. Many Solays I held her head in my lap as she cried. I hope she finds something other than sex and drugs that will keep the specter of those kids from haunting her, I really do."

Royal grew especially angry after hearing of Hadder's visit to *Inferno*. "Your friends should have made sure you stayed away from there!" Royal said, shaking his head in anger. When Hadder spoke about Jackie Crone and her wicked deception, Royal spat on the ground, echoing Glen's reaction to the vile woman. Royal thought on the story for a moment before providing his take. "Just as I thought, your existence has the Keys really shaken. Fear is a powerful weapon, and Jackie Crone wields it like a samurai. They want you scared of the Before, terrified of the pain that it can bring you, hoping that you seek refuge in the endless cycle of the Celebration Cluster. But it sounds like her plan backfired, drove you from that murky world, made you realize something of critical importance. That says a lot about you, Hadder."

Lilly added, "You wanted desperately to share, Marlin. To mourn and cope and move forward. You can't do that in the Celebration Cluster. Everyone is too busy hiding."

The rest of the Solay passed by in a blink, as is often the case when good company engages in enjoyable conversation eased by classic alcohol. They went outside, beers in hand, to sit in the clearing, basking in the light of the Solay as they spoke about music, movies, love, and loss. Hadder was struck by how easily both Royal and Lilly spoke of the Before, comfortably inserting pieces of their previous lives into the talks. Royal often referenced his wife, who had died of brain cancer, leaving a hole that the studio musician filled with heroin. Lilly joked about her struggling singing career, becoming serious when speaking of her mother's overbearing control over her young life, a mother who saw her own fame and fortune reflected in the eyes of her innocent child.

As Solay began to near Haela, Hadder noticed more and more residents beginning to enter *The Royal Jelly*. Royal saw this, too, and rose from soft grass. "I better get in there, y'all. It looks like we got some thirsty residents this evening. Pleasure speaking with you, Hadder. I don't know what your being here means, but I know I'm happy for the new company. See you both in there."

Lilly and Hadder watched Royal walk back into the establishment that partially bore his name. "Good guy, huh," prompted Lilly.

"Yeah, he is. What's going on at the Bar? Residents have been piling in for the last hour or so."

"What's going on? Music, Hadder. Music is what's going on. Get up, lazybones. I'm calling first dance right now."

Lilly pulled Hadder up quickly, showcasing impressive strength for one so small. Hand-in-hand, they joined the throng of residents gleefully passing between *The Royal Jelly's* golden guardian bees, happy to be entering a world where drugs, alcohol, and sex took a backseat to the fellowship of music.

———

HOURS LATER, *The Royal Jelly* was a hive of activity and music. Every seat in the house was taken, but that didn't stop groups from welcoming others over, sharing in old school beer and smoke. Royal was a whirlwind, dishing out drinks, stories, and advice in equal parts. Although all the residents here were also reasonably attractive, they didn't have the overwrought look of the Celebration Cluster regulars, those that always did too much, those that always acted extra. Hadder felt relaxed in an environment where everyone's raison d'etre was not to one-up the person next to you, but to share real stories with real friends.

While most residents in *The Royal Jelly* had gone subtle with Elevations, extreme exceptions were as readily accepted by the group as a kooky aunt. Lilly pointed out one young man, pale and slight, with an abnormal bulge in his slim khaki pants. "Poor Theo. The boy went and Elevated his junk to a ridiculous level. Little did he know that most girls here Elevate their love boxes, as well - making them smaller. Now the guy just walks with a loaded shotgun and nowhere to shoot it."

"Why doesn't he just get it reversed? It seems like they can do anything at the Elevation Centers."

"He could. But everyone calls him Theo the Cock now, sometimes just The Cock. I think he likes that."

Residents like Theo were seen now and then, escapees from the dangerous Elevation addiction. A woman with obviously extended legs danced erotically in a booth by the stage. A short man with impossibly inflated muscles tried to join her, but his oversized frame prevented him from moving correctly. He ended up merely flailing his arms next to her, frightening everyone around. Lilly and Hadder laughed at the comical scene.

Lilly mentioned that many residents who found their way to this sanctuary had some of their more apparent Elevations reverted, having grown more comfortable in the skin in which they arrived at the city.

Hadder was digesting this information, looking over the crowd, when there was a change in the musical acts. An excellent band that sounded exactly like The Doors, complete with its own Jim Morrison clone, was exiting the stage, and a lone figure was approaching the microphone as musicians in the background traded out instruments. Hadder's eyes widened in recognition as he saw Miles move to the forefront of the stage. "Holy shit, that's Miles!"

"You know Miles," asked Lilly.

"Yeah, I guess he was sent to orientate me to the city. Show me the ropes."

"I can't imagine a worse choice for that."

"Yeah, he was pretty shit."

"Well, he's not shit at this. Listen."

Hadder knew something special was coming when the crowd, comprised of hundreds of intense conversations, joyous invitations, and loud expressions of gaiety, immediately went silent as Miles took the mic. Miles quietly thanked everyone before he began. Before he sent Hadder back to his childhood.

Miles started with a heart-wrenching take on Sam Cooke's "A Change is Gonna Come," following that with Otis Redding's "Try a Little Tenderness," and concluding with "Georgia on My Mind" by Ray Charles. Hadder stood transfixed, teleported back to when he was a child, his mother cleaning the house as this same music played in the background, filling the home with warmth and affection.

Lilly saw the music's effect on Hadder and put her arm around his shoulders. "There is one area where they don't skimp on the Elevations here," she whispered, respectful of the extraordinary performance taking place. "When it comes to music and performing, we'll do whatever it takes to reach the next level. Miles was an exceptional musician in the Before. Now, he's a god."

Hadder couldn't disagree, losing himself in Miles's powerful voice and exceptional showmanship. Gone was the distant, unsociable man that he met so many Solays ago, replaced by a person who held the emotions of a thousand residents in the palm of his hands. Hadder sipped his beer, closed his eyes, and relinquished himself to the music, opening them only after "Georgia," adding his applause to the appreciative whistles and screams of the rest of the audience.

As he clapped, Hadder looked around but saw no sign of Lilly. Just as he was about to return to Royal for another drink, perhaps something with a bit more kick, Hadder spotted her walking from behind the stage curtain to join Miles, a second microphone in her hand. If the crowd had been loud before, it absolutely exploded at the sight of Lilly Sistine taking the stage. With a small, familiar nod to Miles, the musicians began again, and she and Miles broke into "Endless Love," another song that reminded Hadder of a simpler time. For the next four minutes, "Endless Love" no longer belonged to Diana Ross and Lionel Ritchie, but was in the ownership of Lilly Sistine and Miles, who injected the song with a steroid cocktail before releasing it onto an enraptured group of residents.

Lilly sought Hadder out in the crowd and smiled as she sang, and from that moment on, they were the only two people in the Bar, her serenade making him smile dumbly like a dog who was getting his belly rubbed. Two days in and Hadder knew, was as sure as that morning in the hospital when he held that little bundle and stared into wide eyes trying to come to grips with the world. Hadder knew he was in love.

Lilly and Miles finished their duet to more raucous applause, and Miles exited the stage, leaving Lilly alone. Lilly Sistine didn't just continue the show, she intensified it, showing incredible range as she bounced from Tina Turner's "What's Love Got to Do with It" to Cyndi Lauper's "Time After Time" to Madonna's "Live to Tell." By the time Lilly concluded with Whitney Houston's "I Have Nothing," Hadder was drunk, partially from the Number 9 he had ordered, but mainly from the whirlwind feelings of love, admiration, and respect for Lilly Sistine that he was trying unsuccessfully to wrangle.

She found Hadder on the entrance level, away from the stage, sitting alone on a leather love seat. "Well," she asked, falling into place next to him, cigarette dangling between her thin fingers.

"It was the most incredible thing I've ever heard." He felt stupid as the words fell out, unable to fully express the complex emotions he was experiencing.

"Thanks," she said between puffs, putting the cigarette to Hadder's lips when she finished. "But it's all bullshit, you know. I've had three Elevations on my vocal cords. But it's not like I'm trying to take credit for something; I just love singing and having fun. Miss Turner doesn't ever have to worry about me."

"It's not bullshit, Lilly. You're amazing."

She waved him away, not understanding the depth of his meaning. "What's that, a Number 9? I could use one of those."

The following hours were among the most fun that Hadder could remember. Lilly and Hadder bounced between groups, engaging in conversations that traversed topics, many touching on the Before, including friends and families from those previous lives. While Royal and a few volunteer residents handled the bars, manikins walked around offering food on trays, the perfect complement to good drink and better company.

Lilly and Hadder grew closer as the Haela deepened, her hand on his thigh here, his hand brushing hair behind her ear there. Group conversations slowly deteriorated into just the two of them, speaking almost nose to nose to hear each other over the background noise. Speaking naturally transitioned into dancing, Hadder twirling Lilly as a synthwave band played on stage, the singer killing saxophone solos when not belting out lively lyrics. Hadder and Lilly spun together, the world outside of them becoming an insignificant blur.

When the music finally stopped, Hadder and Lilly held each other, trying to catch their breaths through laughter. Miles retook the stage, and they held each other tighter, laughter fading away into deep penetrating stares that said more than any essay ever could. Miles broke into "These Arms of Mine," and foreheads touched as hips began to sway to the timeless song.

Whether Hadder moved first or Lilly initiated would be playfully debated in the weeks to come, but two lips found each other nonetheless, passing grazes becoming shy introductions before long-awaited embraces. As Miles began "Nothing Compares 2 U," Lilly led Hadder through the dance floor, ignoring the shouts of friends, up to the entrance level, and through a small door to the right. Hadder looked back as the door closed and saw Royal nodding in acknowledgment, an ironic callback to Purple Rain.

Stairs rose to the upper balcony levels and fell to the living quarters. Lilly guided Hadder down in a brisk, silent walk. Down halls they hurried, finally stopping a door with a red hand next to it. She placed her hand on the mark, and the door slid open, revealing a room very different from most living quarters.

While most rooms were comfortable but impersonal, the perfect spaces for those always on the move, wanting to forget who they were, Lilly's place was reminiscent of the Before. Posters lined the walls, depicting everyone from *Berlin* to *Blondie* to Chuck Berry. Clothes were thrown over chairs, and little mementos littered the desk and dressers.

Lilly moved Hadder to the bed and went to the corner, where she dropped the needle on an antique record player. As she returned, Sade began to play, and no words were necessary. They collapsed into each other, both suffocating, needing the air that only the other could provide. Clothes fell away, bodies were explored, and secrets were discovered in a world of sweat, laughter, heat, and gasps.

Eons later, when they came together, the fusion of two souls released a burst of energy, causing the record to skip as they both dropped onto the bed in a single heap, working hard to appease their air-deprived lungs, born again in the fires of passion and a love both felt lost to them forever.

———

THEY LAID TOGETHER on the bed, sharing a cigarette, afraid that if they succumbed to sleep, the other would disappear like a mirage. Hadder stroked Lilly's head gently, keeping beat with the Sade soundtrack.

A thought struck him. "We all listen to Sade when we make love. What does Sade listen to when she makes love? You think she listens to herself?"

Lilly laughed, then thought for a moment. "I think she listens to covers of her own songs, that way it's not weird. Otherwise, it'd be like jacking off to your own picture."

"That makes sense," he conceded before moving on. "What should we do tomorrow?"

"What would you like to do?"

"As long as you're with me, I'll be happy doing anything."

"I'm not going anywhere, Marlin."

Anxiety crept into Hadder's stomach, the plague of anyone who has endured real loss, screaming that this could all come crashing down in an instant, that another blow would be the last. "You promise?"

Lilly looked up, her cognac eyes holding his own, making it impossible for him to look away. "I promise." She dropped back into Hadder's lap and was sleeping soundly minutes later. Hadder kissed the top of Lilly's head, stroked her tanned arms, and looked around, shocked at where his life had taken him. In the throes of drugs in the Celebration Cluster, Hadder had found a new life in the city called Station. But now, here in *The Royal Jelly*, in this room that perfectly reflected its occupant, with this woman whose capacity for love and understanding was beyond anything he thought possible, Hadder found a true home.

He wept softly, not wanting to disturb Lilly. Most were lucky to find one home in a lifetime. Who was he to be gifted two times? What was the price?

He pushed these thoughts away angrily, handed the reigns to Sade, and slid down to join Lilly in sleep, where they met again in all-new adventures.

13

The following months were among the best Marlin Hadder had ever known, his life in the Before becoming a barely visible shoreline as he sailed further and deeper into this new voyage. He spent almost every moment of every day with Lilly Sistine, their time together in no way mirroring his initial months with Jonny VV and Reena Song. With Jonny and Reena, life was a broken record, the degradation of a song once loved, having grown impotent through ceaseless repetition.

For Lilly Sistine, life was never meant to be defined by a single song but was instead an ever-changing compilation of varying genres, decades, and artists. One day they organized a resident volleyball tournament outside *The Royal*, with Stretch Reese, a resident who had significantly Elevated his height to shed the effects of ridicule experienced in the Before, dominating the competition. The joy on the young man's face as he hoisted the makeshift MVP trophy warmed a place in Hadder's heart long dormant, the place that allowed him to feel happy for another's triumph despite his own losses.

Another day, Lilly and Hadder dedicated most of the Solay collaborating to pen a song, recruiting the assistance of Billy Crossroads, the two-armed guitar virtuoso, to play an impromptu one-song concert just as Haela settled onto the city. Hadder, unable to sing, kept the beat on bongos borrowed from Royal as the real musicians of the trio wowed a small audience of residents.

Still another day, Lilly and Hadder took a walk around Station, spending the day enjoying the city's distinct bioactivity and lush gardens before setting up a picnic outside of the one the Elevation Centers that sat against Station's western wall. They sat and talked, stories from today easily mingling with tales of the Before, even when they touched on less than happy times. As they spoke, residents would enter the Elevation Center, and Lilly and Hadder would predict what kind of Elevation would appear upon exit. They laughed genuinely as a tall, skinny blonde woman, who Hadder thought would walk out with double Ds, left the center as a medium-sized, muscled man, still donning the daisy dukes and crop top that she, now he, came with.

Between the Elevation guessing game, Hadder engaged in another pastime - learning of Lilly's past. Although he had only gathered bits and pieces, not wanting to pry, Hadder learned that Lilly's mom wanted nothing more than to have a pop star daughter. She paraded the young girl from pseudo-producer to unscrupulous record executive, willing to turn a blind eye when they wanted things other than money in exchange for studio time or the empty promise of an industry contact.

In return, Hadder spoke of his daughter Mia in response to Lilly's countless questions. Hadder detected a sadness in Lilly when she asked about Mia, understanding that this void in her would never be filled, not by Hadder nor music nor strong drink, as conception was something that didn't happen within Station's walls. Despite the pain of the topic, straight blades in his heart that cut more with each beat, Hadder did his best to share everything about Mia with Lilly. And while he died a little recounting each story about his baby girl, he was always resurrected in soft Lilly's arms minutes later.

In addition to daily activities, Lilly and Hadder also took on larger projects. One week, they oversaw the construction of an enormous fire pit behind *The Royal Jelly*, made especially for those who treasured the outdoors or enjoyed hanging out deep into the Haela. Although manikins did the majority of the labor, working at speeds that no human could match,

Lilly and Hadder felt alive getting their hands dirty, the cuts on their hands leaving their blood to mix with the stone, making them truly a part of the beloved hangout.

Another week, Lilly and Hadder produced a stage production of "Glengarry Glen Ross," even getting curmudgeonly Glen to play the role of Shelley Levene. With a small but eclectic, Elevated cast, and backed by set-pieces crafted by manikin workers, the performance played to a packed house that showered Lilly and Hadder with applause at its conclusion. Later that night, Lilly and Hadder were inundated with requests for future plays and comments regarding how so-and-so would be perfect for playing the role of such-and-such. Lilly and Hadder sat together once the crowd around them had died down, sharing the moment and a Number 7. "You available next month," asked Lilly, staring intensely at Hadder.

"I'll have to check my schedule, but I can probably move some things around."

"Well, don't put anything off on my account. I know time is money."

"This is true. But perhaps if I got some sort of downpayment, I could reserve some time for your endeavor."

Lilly climbed up to straddle Hadder, putting foreheads together the way they always did. "How's this for a downpayment." She kissed him deeply, the remainder of *The Royal Jelly* fading away into the recesses. They separated and laughed.

"Acceptable."

————

WHILE THOSE WHO frequented *The Royal Jelly* and its surrounding Bars, a Cluster loosely defined as The Commons, had done admirably in adjusting to Station, there were always moments when Hadder was reminded that the city's people were a broken bunch. Some were simply fixed better than others. Hadder would sometimes wake to find Lilly sobbing in the shower, the water hot enough to scald. Royal would spend all Solay and most of the Haela ensuring that others were able to be themselves and escape into a good time, only to end up drinking alone in a booth at Haela's end, powering through joints as he stared blankly at the wall. Even Glen, generally a rock, was found one day digging a large hole for no reason, his hands showing open wounds from his furious efforts.

Hadder asked Royal about this one day as they sat alone on the steps of *The Royal Jelly*, enjoying beers early in the Solay. Royal sighed deeply before responding. "We all do our best here, Hadder. Some, like those lost souls that stick to the Celebration Cluster, cope by running, thinking the past will never catch up to them if they never stop moving, never stop diverting their attentions from how they ended up in Station. Some endlessly mourn, like those sad bastards in the Weep. They've grieved and cried so much, they're afraid of what they'll find if they stop. Scared that there'll be nothing left once the anguish is left behind. Then you have us who try to heal. We talk about the Before, how we came to be in Station. We try to own up to our mistakes, try to offer consolation to those dealt bad hands, try to improve. But even the faintest scars itch once in a while. You try to scratch it without drawing blood and then move on. None of us will ever be normal, Hadder, even that beautiful creature you're with. But we can strive to be the best versions of ourselves, and hope that that's enough."

Hadder thought for a moment. "It's enough for me, Royal. But I don't know about some of the others, Lilly included."

"Well, you ain't been here that long, have you? The longer you're here, the mind starts to drift over the city's walls, to the bigger world, and its endless opportunities to ply what's been gained from Station."

"What are you saying, Royal?"

"I'm saying lots of people, including myself, become institutionalized, accept their lot here. But many others refuse, feel like they've done their time, have been rehabilitated, and now want another shot."

"You make Station sound like prison."

"Isn't it? Just because we're free to do what we want and enjoy ourselves, that doesn't change the fact that happy, sad, content, or angry, we're confined within these oversized walls."

"You think some want to sneak out of Station?"

"Sneak out? No, Hadder, they don't want to sneak out. They want to break out, tear the walls down. They want to see Station laid to rubble."

"There you two gossiping gals are," said Lilly from behind, preventing Hadder from further follow-up questions. She dropped a breakfast sandwich in each of their hands. "So, what are we talking about?"

Royal forced a smile. "Hadder's thinking of getting that scar on his forehead removed."

"The one you got from kickboxing? No, I love that one." Lilly grabbed Hadder's head and kissed his forehead. "Don't do that, Marlin. I love your scar."

Hadder simply nodded, wishing he could say the same back to her.

———

HADDER SAT DRINKING with Jess Dangles, a well-adjusted young woman whose strange Elevation was four ears on each side of her shaved head that provided real estate for her strange addiction - earrings that sung like chimes and glittered like bouquets of starlight when she moved her head side to side. Despite her unique look, Jess was a reasonably normal, personable addition to the Commons, having recently grown tired of the Celebration Cluster.

Lilly ran into *Cranesman* and immediately addressed Jess. "Did you tell him yet?"

"No," answered Jess, "I thought it best that I let you bring it up."

"Bring what up," asked Hadder.

"There's a party this Haela, Marlin. I want to go."

Hadder shot Lilly a confused look. "Of course we can go, what's the issue?"

Lilly looked to Jess and back to Hadder. "It's in the Celebration Cluster. At *The Soiree Noire*, to be exact."

Hadder could feel his face scrunching as if he had just smelled something foul. Lilly responded to the look. "Listen, I know you had a rotten time in the Celebration Cluster last time you were there, and I know you're not crazy about Monty, but this is gonna be the party to end all parties."

"What is it?"

Lilly smiled. "It's a Blade Runner party."

"Your favorite movie."

"That's right, so you know I have to be there. Come with me, please, please, please."

Hadder leaned forward and kissed Lilly. "Anything for you. Plus, it'll be good to see Jonny VV and Reena Song again. I've always felt bad for how I disappeared on them."

"See! Two great reasons to go! Ok, you two enjoy your drinks, I gotta run."

"Where are you going," asked Hadder to the back of Lilly, who was already quickly making her way towards the Bar entrance. "To get my outfit made, silly," she said over her shoulder. "Don't worry, I'll get yours made, too."

"Nothing too tight!"

Lilly turned around in the doorway, a shadowy figure against the Solay backdrop. *"I've seen things you people wouldn't believe. Attack ships on fire off the shoulder of Orion. I watched c-beams glitter in the dark near the Tannhuser Gate. All those moments will be lost in time, like tears in rain.* You'll wear what I get you, Marlin Hadder." And with that, she was gone.

Jess looked to Hadder. "You're going to have your hands full with that one tonight."

Hadder smiled. "Looking forward to it."

14

The butterflies in Hadder's stomach stirred as he set foot in the Celebration Cluster, arm-in-arm with Lilly Sistine. Those same butterflies began to flutter and fly as he spotted the red monolith that was *Inferno* in the near distance. A storm from deep within Hadder started to form, that old Rage that he had spent years clamping down, fighting to maintain control. Even after losing his family, while he had succumbed to grief and self-hate, he had kept the Rage at bay. Now, looking at *Inferno*, Hadder pictured Jackie Crone's too-pulled face and yellowing body hanging like a twisted marionette above the entrance. That old feeling rushed to the surface and threatened to demand action before he took a deep breath and squeezed Lilly's hand, reminding himself of what he had and what he could lose.

"Ouch, Marlin, too tight," exclaimed Lilly.

"Sorry. Shall we?"

As they moved together towards *The Soiree Noire*, Hadder once again marveled at how the Celebration Cluster came to life at Haela. With the glowing blossoms, explosions of color, and electricity in the air, Hadder quickly saw how he lost himself in this world of excess. He even considered that perhaps his time here was necessary to strip away the baggage of the Before, leaving him naked to receive Station's more profound gifts.

Hadder's trench coat, a key component of his Rick Deckard outfit, danced on a small breeze as he walked. Lilly's meticulously pinned hair, matching Rachael's perfectly symmetrical updo, refused to do the same as she marched in her custom black suit with broad shoulders. Nearing *The Soiree Noire*, Hadder could see that a crowd was just beginning to form outside with no sign of Monty the Mod on his floating pedestal. Waiting patiently among the milling crowd, Hadder recognized countless faces, many of whose names escaped him. Several shouted greetings to him while many others simply nodded in welcome. Hadder held Lilly tight, uncomfortable around the sheer numbers of extreme Elevations that surrounded him.

"Marlin? Oh my god, Marlin?"

Hadder turned around at the familiar voice to find Reena Song walking up with Jonny VV. Reena, stylish as always, was dressed as Darryl Hannah's Pris, with the added touch of her ever-present light crown, while Jonny VV was the spitting image of Edward James Olmos's Gaff, complete with the fedora and mustache-soul patch combo. Reena hit Jonny playfully on the chest. "See! I told you he'd come back!"

Hadder's heart swelled as he embraced his two friends. He fought back a grimace as his guilt for leaving them without explanation or goodbye weighed heavily. Reena kissed him on the lips as they separated, and, for a moment, Hadder worried about Lilly's reaction. He soon saw that his fears were mislaid.

"And who's this you're with? Oh my god, is that you, Lilly!?! Jonny! It's Lilly Sistine, maybe my favorite person in the world!"

"It's awesome to see you, too, Reena. I've really missed you." The two women embraced, and Hadder felt vindicated when they, too, shared a kiss before separating.

Jonny VV shuffled up to Hadder. "Good to see you, old chap. I do say, it looks like you've been busy since your departure. Well done, old boy."

Reena returned to face Hadder. "Marlin, I heard that you had a tough time at *Inferno*. I'm so sorry. I feel terrible. We would have tried to stop you if you had told us your plans. That place is horrible; I have no idea why it's in the Celebration Cluster."

"It's ok, Reena. My fault completely." He looked at Lilly. "But I think it all worked out in the end."

Reena followed Hadder's eyes to Lilly and smiled. Seconds later, she slammed her hands together in excitement. "Holy shit! My two favorite people are an item. Jonny is this not the greatest thing ever!"

"It's a real scene, love."

Reena put her arms around both Lilly and Hadder, pulled them in tight against her tiny frame. "This is gonna be the best Haela. I've missed you both so much. Let's never stay away from each other this long again." Hadder and Lilly shared a look that agreed with Reena, that said their lives would indeed be richer if this charming woman were a more substantial part of them. Maybe Reena couldn't talk about the Before, perhaps she needed to continue running from the past, but that didn't mean she didn't bring other invaluable things to the table like empathy, love, passion, and unencumbered joy. Things of which Lilly and Hadder always had more use.

Just then, a burst of light issued from in front of the Bar as Monty the Mod made his appearance on his magical disc, floating above his attentive audience. Appropriately, Monty was cloaked in the garb of Eldon Tyrell, his shining square glasses bathing the crowd in soft silver light. Monty carefully perused the group and began calling out individuals, applauding some and insulting others for their costume selections.

Reena, already too excited to stand still, couldn't keep quiet. "Monty, you old cadaver, let us in," she yelled above the throng. "It's me and Jonny VV, with a resurrected Marlin Hadder and Lilly Sistine! There is no party without us!"

Monty's rimmed eyes swung Hadder's way. "Marlin Hadder! You sure you wouldn't rather visit *Inferno*? Jackie Crone says she misses you!" Hadder almost responded, but was stopped by Reena's soft hand gripping his neck. He remained silent. "And Lilly Sistine! I thought you too good for us. But maybe not tonight, huh?"

Jonny VV had had enough. "Monty, you old dog, too much talk! Either let us in, or we'll be happy to make another party the event of the Haela!"

To his credit, Monty laughed off Jonny's threat. "Oh, Jonny VV, too posh for a little barbed banter? Your concerns are unfounded, and threats unnecessary. How could I not let you all in dressed as you are? Entree, s'il vous plait."

Jonny VV joined Reena, Lilly, and Hadder as the four, connected by arms and shoulders, made their way into *The Soiree Noire*. Hadder's chest pounded with excitement and delight, his three good friends together at last, determined to make this Haela one impossible to forget.

———

THE BLADE RUNNER party did not disappoint, and Hadder had to admit that Monty had really outdone himself. The magical walls depicted Ridley Scott's vision of future Los Angeles, dropping the partygoers amid dystopia. Holographic advertisements appeared and disappeared throughout the party, large images that bent down to touch, then pass through, residents. Manikins walked around, as usual, serving an assortment of mind-altering beverages, oblivious to their close relation to the movie's replicants. Most jarring, however, was the rain. In line with the dark theme, the party was caught in a perpetual rainstorm, with holographic water falling from the ceiling only to disappear as it touched the crimson floors. Hadder and Lilly were so mesmerized by the effect that they actually held their hands out, their minds telling them that they should be soaking wet, only to find themselves as warm and dry as when they entered.

The residents of the Celebration Cluster also did not disappoint. In addition to the myriad of Deckards and Rachaels, various Roy Battys, Zhoras, and J.F. Sebastians, among other characters, paraded around the party. True to the individualistic nature of the Cluster, many residents chose not to be characters at all but created their own costumes that aligned with the movie's unique look and feel. This gave the party an authentic feel, a shared belief that everyone was dancing on the bones of a dead future, that all of them must make now the best for tomorrow is promised to be shit.

The four friends hung out and drank, Number 9s going down like water, lubricating hips that began to sway to a combination of Vangelis and synthwave. A Zhora with glowing purple eyes sauntered up to the quartet, a snake draped over her shoulder and hugging her naked glittered body. Hadder thought the snake a prop to complete the woman's costume, but upon closer inspection saw that it really was the Ophidian, its hooded head offering next-level revelry.

Hadder looked to Reena, who looked to Jonny, who looked to Lilly, and all four quickly reached silent consensus, Lilly leaning forward first to accept the serpent's smoky offering. In order, eyes glazed over, goofy smiles pasted onto faces, and laughs were injected into all sentences. As the Zhora moved on to the next group, the four hugged as one, the real party just beginning.

———

DANCING DOMINATED the next few hours, Reena with Hadder, Lilly with Jonny, Lilly with Reena, and even Jonny with Hadder to much laughter. At some point, Jonny VV caught the eye of a tall, dark woman in a white Grace Jones suit and faded into the crowd to join her.

The now-trio, legs aching from constant movement, took seats on one of the large leather couches, grabbing more drinks from a serving manikin on the way. As the three sat drinking, heads spinning and hearts racing, The Weeknd's "Tears in the Rain" started to play, Lilly and Hadder's favorite song. As the Ophidian's gift continued its journey through their systems, Lilly began to massage Hadder's shoulders as Reena's hand found his thigh. Soon, Lilly's lips found his neck and Hadder shuddered from the sensation. He turned, meeting her lips with his own, and both gave in to what the music demanded. As they kissed, a form slid atop Hadder to rest straddling both Lilly and him. Hands rubbed both Hadder's and Lilly's head as they lost themselves in each other.

Then there were three sets of lips, the electricity between them building to a crescendo as tongues came out to explore. Reena writhed on top of Hadder as she passionately kissed Lilly, who clawed at the back of Hadder's head as he watched the provocative scene. In that moment, three close friends became closer, losing themselves in each other, all bullshit gone, with just a sincere appreciation of enjoying this moment together, understanding that nothing lasts.

They separated as the song ended, breathless laughs a testament to the intensity of their embrace. Reena leaned in to be heard over the music. "It should always be like this. Here's to us never being apart too long again." The three raised their glasses and finished their drinks, feeling complete in each other's company.

"Never again," Hadder agreed.

————

More drinks, more smoke, and more dancing followed. Lilly and Reena moved off to use the bathroom, leaving Hadder alone on the dance floor, which now encompassed the entirety of the bar. Darksynth boomed over the hidden speakers, mirroring the ferocity of the drug-fueled dancers.

Hadder danced with anyone and everyone, got sandwiched between Helen and Nestra, and even got close with Yasmin Dash, who had her wings tucked in neatly to avoid hitting others in the crowd. Lightning crept into the party, as well, incrementally lighting up the cavernous room as the bass hit. Letting loose in the artificial rain, sharing an experience with these strange creatures, Hadder couldn't help but smile, a genuine and telling thing.

Then it disappeared.

As holographic lightning struck the party, Hadder saw over the sea of faces, his eyes drawn to a hooded figure. Although the top half of the man's face was shrouded in shadow, the bottom-half revealed an unmistakable sneer, a hatred that stood in stark contrast to the joyousness around it. As if feeling Hadder's eyes on him, the hood moved to face Hadder, the sneer transforming into a wicked smile. And then he was gone.

As lightning faded, the party was momentarily lost to darkness as Hadder's eyes adjusted. Once clear, he searched again, looking to locate the fiend hiding in their midst, to no avail. Hadder fought his way through the dancing crowd, eyes up and searching, but found nothing.

Eventually, he gave up, tried telling himself that it was all in his head, a figment of his imagination created by too much drink and smoke. He relaxed and danced again. He was almost himself once more.

And then a scream cut through the party, freezing everyone in place.

————

MORE SCREAMS FOLLOWED, ripped from the depths of those delivering them. The party came to a standstill as the music stopped and the lights were turned up.

Anxiety pelted Hadder from all angles, that feeling of knowing that something is terribly wrong, that your life is inevitably changed for the worse. A feeling that Hadder knew all too well.

Hadder raced through the crowd, pushing residents aside roughly, rushing towards the source of the cries. As he neared the back wall of the Bar, he encountered a semicircle of shocked observers and tore through the line. He stumbled as he passed through, his legs failing him as the scene he came upon assaulted his senses and shattered his heart.

Sitting against the wall, her pristine costume soiled by gore, was Reena Song. Her beautiful head no longer sat on her swanlike neck but had been laid on her lap, eyes still open in a look of absolute horror, her beloved light crown rotating above her, but slowly now, as if it too was in mourning.

A figure crashed into the catatonic Hadder. "Oh no, Marlin, why," shouted Lilly into his shoulder, burying her face in him as to escape the vile imagery around them.

Hadder stood, holding a shaking Lilly Sistine, staring at a torn apart Reena Song, the angel that Station and, especially, the Celebration Cluster didn't deserve. Her loss shattered something inside of Hadder, the last levee that had been keeping an ocean of anger at bay. The growing pain of her death brought his other losses back to the surface in a torrent.

As the crowd continued to stare at poor Reena Song, the rain continued to fall in *The Soiree Noire*. And although they all remained dry, an icy cold had fallen, soaking Hadder to the bones. And Hadder knew what that meant.

The love affair with Station had ended. His new home would no longer feel like home.

PART II

A DESIRE CALLED REVENGE

15

For two Solays and two Haelas, Hadder sat in the living quarters he shared with Lilly Sistine, lights dimmed when not off. Lilly came and went, bringing him food he barely touched and playing music he barely heard. And although he appeared unmoving, a battle was being waged inside him.

As long as Marlin Hadder could remember, there was a Rage within, making unspeakable demands. Hadder had employed numerous strategies over the years to keep the Rage at arm's length. As a youth, he used sports to drain himself of the energy required to sustain the Rage. As an angry young man, he used combat training to leech the Rage out lest it reach critical levels, first boxing then Muay Thai then Brazilian jiu-jitsu. As an adult, the love of and for his family overwhelmed the Rage, pushed it down into a small corner of his being where it had no real power. As a widower, grief and self-hate stole his will to act, extinguished the life-force need by the Rage to thrive. As a Station resident, first drugs, then friendship, then love and, finally, a sense of home would not allow the Rage to take hold.

That sense of home was now gone, had been severed just like poor Reena Song's head. And now all that remained was the Rage. And it had new demands. And it would no longer be silenced.

———

"We need to talk."

Royal could tell from Hadder's tone that he was serious, maybe danger-ously so. He felt a change in his friend, that person who seemed to bend so much like bamboo, quickly adapting to environments and willing to go along with whatever the situation called for. The man that stood before him no longer seemed bamboo. He seemed iron.

Royal motioned towards one of the side booths at *The Royal Jelly*. Solay had just broken over the city, so the Bar was empty save a few manikins cleaning up from a concert the Haela before. As they sat, Royal felt compelled to offer his condolences. Although he, too, was Reena Song's friend, hell everyone was Reena Song's friend, he imagined that Hadder and Reena were more than friends, but less than a couple. "Hadder, I haven't gotten a chance to see you since it happened, so let me just say, I'm so sorry about Reena. She was one of the good ones. One of the best of us."

"I want to know who did it."

Royal sank back a little in the booth at the look in Hadder's eyes, a barely controlled mania that he had never seen in his usually stoic companion. "No one knows, Hadder. It could have been anyone. Maybe just a resident tweaked out on some drugs he couldn't handle. God knows they take enough shit in the Celebration Cluster to make anyone lose their minds."

"No."

"What do you mean, no?"

"This wasn't just some fucked up resident. I saw him. It was dark, and I didn't get a good look at his face because he was wearing a hood. But I saw him, evil-looking fuck with only bad intentions swimming through his head, not party drugs."

"What are you getting at, Hadder?"

"I didn't tell you this before, haven't told anyone. Just before the Caesar found me, when I had lost my mind and was lying half-dead on the Skirt, I saw something."

"What did you see?"

"Some twisted creature came out of the Haela, Elevated to all hell, with long razors implanted along its forearms. It came at me. The Caesar Cal got there first, fought it off. But not before I saw its face, its wicked smile as it had me in its sights, in line for a killing blow. I saw that same smile at *The Soiree Noire*. On the man that butchered Reena Song."

Royal remained silent, unsure of what to say next, scared that the wrong thing could set off this new unpredictable man who sat across from him. "What do you want to know?"

"The Skirt. What is it? What's on the other side? The man who killed Reena is there. I demand retribution."

"What kind of retribution did you have in mind, Hadder?"

"The ugly kind. The messy kind."

"What exactly do you need to know?"

"Everything."

———

Royal went to the bar and retrieved two beers before beginning. Hadder declined his drink, another bad sign. Royal took half his down in one gulp, then started.

"Station is supposed to take away all those things that become obstacles to one's happiness. Hated your job? Nobody works in Station. Were always stressed about money? Everything's free in Station. Didn't like the way you looked? Elevations can make the person on the outside mirror what you feel on the inside. Couldn't handle the weight of responsibility? There is none in Station.

"Unfortunately, Station itself can't fix what's wrong with us on the inside. And in some ways, it makes things worse. In the Before, life is busy, often leaving little time to really reflect, allowing one to get by on inertia. But here in Station, with nothing to do but think, there's two ways to go. One, you start to fix that shit that's been eating away at you for years. You and Lilly are good examples of this. The shit is never gone, but we can clean a lot of it up. Two, with no distractions and the only direction to go being inward, stuff can go sideways real fast. Some people refuse to clean up the shit; instead, they feed it with chemicals and hatred and guilt and pity, expediting the eating away process. Next thing you know, nothing's left, nothing human anyway. Those poor bastards in the Weep are one example. Those across the Skirt are another.

"For years, who knows how long for sure, there was no Skirt. All of Station was just random Bars, some clustered together, as you see on this side - the Setting. But as some were driven to Station by melancholy, guilt, or fear, others were driven here by anger. They continued to act out, showcase violent tendencies. The Caesars would lock them up temporarily to cool down, but they would come out just as white-hot. All they knew was anger, all they wanted to do was inflict pain onto others.

"Regardless, things were still manageable at that point. That is until this group of residents, we called them Seethers, found Elevations. They started ordering weaponized Elevations. Metal knuckles and hands. Blade inserts like your twisted friend. Muscle implants that increased strength and speed. If they thought they could hurt someone with it, they got it. Things that were once manageable spiraled out of control.

"Mister Rott has always maintained a laissez-faire approach to the governing of Station. But the situation quickly grew out of hand. The Caesars couldn't be everywhere at once, and day by day, more residents turned to Seethers, underwent Combat Elevations. Eventually, Mister Rott decided that the two groups had to be separated, and if the Seethers thought that continual fighting made them happy, so be it.

"Mister Rott gave a speech, one of the few he's ever delivered, and declared that the eastern third of Station would now be home to those who wanted complete autonomy. In the East, there were no restrictions on Elevations. In the West, no Elevation could be executed for the sole purpose of harming another. What he really meant was that the fucking Seethers were gonna be sent packing East and if they wanted to kill each other, godspeed. Then, out of nowhere, in that deepest of darkness between Haela and Solay, the Skirt appeared, and the Caesars went on a mission to round up Seethers and move them East.

"Most of the Seethers went willingly, more than happy to relocate to what would become a theater of pain. But others, of course, fought just for the sake of fighting. It took seven Solays and seven Haelas, but almost all the Seethers were eventually moved. As western Station was now known as the Setting and eastern Station the Rising, the term Seether fell to the wayside, and they became the Risers. The Caesars now mainly patrol the Skirt, making sure Risers don't cross into our world, and drunken residents like yourself don't fall into theirs."

Hadder sat engrossed in the tale, his Rage momentarily quieted. Perhaps it, too, was intrigued. "But what do they do over there, Royal?"

Royal finished his beer and shrugged. "Beats the shit out of me. There's two Elevation Centers over there, with no rules to speak of. I'm sure all those angry freaks are Elevated to the hilt; they may be more Elevation than human at this point."

"But what do they do? How is there even a semblance of civilization over there?"

"Well, limited information comes across the Skirt, but from what I've heard, most spend their time like a lot of residents on this side. They drink, they smoke, they fuck, and they dance. Then they wage war. Apparently, groups of residents started cliquing up at certain Bars. They spend all Solay getting wasted, then launch all-out assaults on other Bars. Sometimes they just arrange battles between Bars in open fields, like it was the goddam Dark Ages.

Anyways, I heard it's a wasteland over there now. Lots of Bars have been leveled or looted."

"Hell on Earth, huh?"

"Hell on Station."

"The man who killed Reena Song is over there. I have to go."

Now it was Royal's turn to lose his cool. "Didn't you hear a goddam word I just said to you! There's an army of killers over there, half men, half weapons. And you don't even know who you're looking for. Great! A fucking twisted fellow with long blades on his forearms. Do you know how many Risers could fit that description? Cause I sure as fuck don't. You'd be looking for a needle in a haystack of needles, and all the needles are tipped with poison. And as you're looking, dark creatures are hurling spears at your back. Do you understand what I'm saying, Hadder!"

Hadder had never seen such anger come from Royal and appreciated it from his friend. Despite now viewing the world through Rage-tinted glasses, Hadder could still recognize when someone was acting kind. "I do understand, Royal."

Royal, exhaled, deflated into the booth, exhausted but content that he got through to Hadder.

"You're saying I need to know who I'm looking for before I go over."

Royal jolted up, back straight. "That's not what I'm saying at all! I'm saying that crossing the Skirt is suicide! That I'll lose two good friends instead of one, you stupid bastard!"

Hadder held up a hand to calm his friend. "I understand, Royal. And I appreciate your concern and your friendship. But I'm going, and you can either watch me go over there blind, or you can help me get some intel before I go."

Hadder's words, tone, and demeanor left no room for negotiation. Royal looked again at the man with whom he shared a booth. Royal stared into the man's eyes and was frightened by what he saw. Gone was the Marlin Hadder that he knew. The man he saw looked the same, sounded the same, and dressed the same, but was much different from the man he met and shared so many pleasant times with. Where there was always a deep sadness within Hadder's eyes, there was now ice, a cold rage that refused to veer from its chosen path of destruction.

"Very little, if any, gossip comes over from the Rising. And that which does rarely travels beyond an ear or two. Information about the Rising is a valuable commodity, one that those in the know hold close to their chests."

"And who's in the know? I need a name."

Royal hesitated, wanting nothing more than to remove himself from the booth, to do anything rather than deliver the name he was about to give. Hadder grew impatient. "Royal Winters, I need a name!"

Royal's head went back at Hadder's voice, such power there was in his demand. "Lester Midnight. He's one of the original Keys. He runs *Lester Midnight's Biomass* on the far western edge of the city. If anyone knows anything, he will."

Hadder's crazed eyes softened. "Thank you, my friend." He got up to leave. Royal grabbed his arm.

"Hadder, you have to know, *Biomass* is a real freak show, the most extreme Elevations on this side of the Skirt. And Lester Midnight is the biggest freak of all of them. And the place is invite-only, so you may have trouble getting in."

"Oh, I'll get in, don't worry about that."

"But once you do, Hadder, you have to be careful. Monsters aren't only found in the Rising. *Biomass* is swimming with them."

"Then, I'll fit right in."

———

HADDER'S FACE warmed where Lilly had struck him. She stood across from him defiantly, fists clenched at her sides. "Why?"

Hadder said simply, "She was our friend."

"No, she was *my* friend, Marlin. But I'm not going to die for her. What was she to you? Did you love her?"

"I loved her just as I love Royal, not as I love you."

"Then, why? I need a better answer."

Hadder sighed, tried to find the words. He wasn't ready to share the truth of himself, of the Rage that had laid dormant, now awakened by a terrible act. "I was finally happy, Lilly. Here, with you. You, Royal, Glen, and everyone else had made a home for me here, the first I've had in a long time. That home was broken in two the other Haela, and it won't feel like home again as long as the man who killed Reena Song is out there. If he was able to get into *The Soiree* unseen, what's to stop him from getting into *Cranesman*? Into *The Royal*?"

"Marlin, the Caesars are on high alert now. They won't let anyone else through."

"I can't take that chance."

"So, instead, you'll take the chance of killing yourself?"

"I've done it once."

"We've all done it once. You're not special."

"I'm sorry, Lilly. I understand your concern. And your anger. I really do. But I can't relax here, can't be the man you fell in love with again until this is taken care of."

Lilly fought back tears, but one escaped to fall gently down her soft cheek, sending a shard of glass through Hadder's heart. She stared at him through water-logged eyes. "What if it had been me, Marlin. Would you be so gung-ho about marching into the heart of darkness if it was me lying on the ground bleeding?

Hadder put his hands on Lilly's shoulders, kissed her forehead. "You? If it were you who was gone, dear Lilly, I would burn down the whole fucking city."

————

"I KNEW HIM, YOU KNOW?"

"Lester Midnight?"

"Yeah, back when he was Lester Minnot. The original batch of us wasn't huge, so all the Keys know each other to some extent. He was always odd, a disgruntled artist. In the Before, he did all kinds of weird installations and performance art. Shock art is what I would call it. He couldn't deal with the fact that the general public refused to acknowledge his unique brilliance and ended up in Station. Here, when he discovered Elevations, he was convinced that he'd been given a new palette and discovered his new medium - the human body. *Biomass* is his living gallery, where the most extremely Elevated residents of the Setting go to pay their respects and gain inspiration for future enhancements. He's treated like a god there, as if he didn't have a god complex to begin with. Nowadays, he straddles the border of complete insanity, a fucking Willie Wonka of flesh. You can't go in there with bad intentions, Hadder. He has too many followers that will throw themselves in front of you."

"This is the Setting. That means all those extreme Elevations aren't weaponized, right? Everything's just for looks?"

"That's right."

"Then, I'm not worried."

Royal shook his head, still in disbelief at this friend's dramatic turn. "I'm saying, there might be another way. One that leaves fewer bruises. They're not gonna want to let you in. I mean, you're basically going to a hardcore tattoo festival with no tattoos. You're gonna look like a fucking tourist. They're notorious pricks at the door at *Biomass*; they make Monty the Mod look like a Walmart greeter. When you get to the door, tell them that one of the Keys, Royal Winters, sent you. That you're someone Royal thinks Lester should meet - a fellow artiste. Knowing Lester, his curiosity and competitiveness will get the better of him. He'll have to see this new artist, if for no other reason than to shit on you and convince himself that you're not on his level. But at least you'll get a face-to-face."

"Sounds good, Royal. I'll give it a try."

"But it's no guarantee, Hadder. Lester and I were never the best of friends, I hated the little shit, truth be told. But I've never sent anyone to him before, so this should pique his interest."

"If this doesn't work, I have a plan b."

"And what's that?"

"Punch a hole in anyone that gets in my way."

Royal snickered, a sound full of the weight of exasperation. "Fine, but at least put something different on before you go. *Biomass* is full of loonies, but they're loonies who think of themselves as members of the glitterati. You'll do better if you don't look like a fucking dick at a cunt party."

Hadder laughed heartily at the analogy but stopped when he saw that Royal wasn't laughing with him.

16

Hadder stood a hundred yards away from *Lester Midnight's Biomass*, a garish building ripped straight from the mind of Salvatore Dali. Looking like a museum that had a blowtorch taken to it, it resembled a Frank Gehry construct, if only Frank Gehry had no taste and a head full of acid.

Assuming that those who frequented *Biomass* shied away from the harsh reality of Solay, Hadder had waited until deep Haela to make his way to the Bar. Residents continually approached the entrance, with many getting turned away by whoever was handling the door. Even from this distance, Hadder could make out the extreme Elevations of residents trying to gain entry.

One man's head had been stretched and elongated, resembling an ancient Scythian or one of those firsthand renderings of alien abductors. The woman he came with had a similar Elevation, with a neck that had been stretched, a callback to the National Geographic videos Hadder had seen on several indigenous tribes in Myanmar.

Hadder took a deep breath, cracked his knuckles, and moved towards *Biomass*, his custom blood red tuxedo shifting silently with him. As he approached the main door, Hadder saw that two men guarded the entryway, one checking guest lists and the other acting as muscle. The man making decisions looked to be a tall skeleton covered in skin, as if he had been pulled directly from King Tut's tomb, all the water drained from his body and just enough muscle to support the overall structure. The creature wore a schoolboy outfit to complete the look and showcase his veiny legs. The man that stood behind him, however, was the complete opposite. Thickly muscled, he wore the traditional black suit of a bouncer, one that Hadder had worn many times in his youth. Down his head was a mohawk of thick bone that escaped the confines of flesh to peer up towards the heavens. Hadder took note of that potential danger as he stepped to the forefront.

"Name," asked the mummified man, looking Hadder up and down with disdain.

"Marlin Hadder."

As he flipped through his pages of names, Hadder held the larger man's stare. "That bone hawk looks awfully close to a weapon, friend. I thought those were outlawed in the Setting."

The big man shook head. "Just for looks. The girls fucking love to pet it."

"But if it came to it..." prompted Hadder.

The big man smiled. "Yeah, if it came to it." Good to know, thought Hadder.

The mummy concluded his search. "Not on the list. Fuck off and fuck you for wasting my time." The skeleton stunk of chemicals, and his voice wheezed like that of someone in the throes of emphysema.

Hadder smiled patiently, like an adult dealing with an unruly child. "Please tell Lester Midnight that Royal Winters, a fellow Key, sent me. He knows they haven't spoken in some time, but he thinks that Mr. Midnight would like to meet me, a fellow artiste."

The talking bones snickered. "Take a look here, Gondo, a fellow *artiste*. But he don't look like any *artiste*. He looks like a fucking lame." The skeleton moved close to Hadder, standing a head taller, invading his space, looking down at him with disgust. "And let me tell you something, plain man, Lester Midnight is the only *artiste* in Station; he has no fellow. Now, fuck off before I have Gondo here make that boring face of yours match your outfit."

Hadder didn't move.

The skeleton tried to smile, said over his shoulder, "Gondo, please take this plain man and..."

He didn't get a chance to finish his order as Hadder executed a perfect Muay Thai leg kick to the creature. With no mass to cushion the blow, Hadder's shin shattered the mummy's leg, almost passing clean through, only to be stopped by a few shreds of dried skin. The skeleton crumbled in a heap, screaming like a banshee that had been lit on fire. Hadder backed up quickly, readying himself for a series of blows from Gondo. Seconds later, he realized that those blows weren't coming.

Gondo looked down at the squealing man and chuckled. "Shut up you worthless sketch of a man! You have no respect for the city's history." He looked to Hadder. "Truth be told, I've wanted to do that for a long time. It was almost as satisfying to watch it, though. If Royal Winters sent you, go on in. I'll have someone send word to Lester for you. Have some beverages, and check out the displays. If Lester wants to speak to you, he'll find you."

Hadder nodded thanks to Gondo and stepped over the whining bag of bones on the ground, making sure to come down on his outstretched hand on the way in. Standing in the entrance, Hadder straightened his clothes, something he always did when anxious, and moved forward, walking into the mind of a maniac.

———

LESTER MIDNIGHT'S *Biomass* was a true freak show, a living Ripley's Believe It Or Not museum. Only the creatures that adorned the walls and nooks of *Biomass* weren't the unlucky recipients of genetic mutations, bad genes, or horrific accidents. Instead, they were accomplices in their disfigurement, willing palettes upon which Lester Midnight wreaked his stomach-churning brand of art.

The entire building was mainly one large middle chamber surrounded by side rooms. As Hadder cleared the first hallway and entered the main showcase, he was greeted by a woman standing on a pedestal. Tall and lithe, she stood utterly unclothed, proudly displaying her artistic Elevation. The woman's skin was completely transparent, allowing anyone an unencumbered view of her inner workings. Hadder watched her lungs as they heaved, saw the direct effects of her pounding heart beneath her ribcage, and observed muscle flex as she moved. To enrich the show, the woman steadily ate from a basket of fruit next to her, giving the audience a peek into the entire digestive process.

A strange little man with an Elevated pixie nose saddled up to him and spoke conspiratorially. "There's a man in one of the outer rooms with the same Elevation. If you stay long enough, they'll perform a sex show. You haven't really seen the intricacies of sexual performance until you've witnessed the Transparent go at it."

"Good to know," said Hadder as he moved on, glad to be away from the repugnant little man.

Continuing through the main chamber, Hadder was hammered by all manner of visual assaults. One woman had been "reptized," her skin now scaly, her eyes like a viper, and her face pulled forward like that of a lizard. A far cry from the sensual Elevations of Helen and Nestra, Hadder felt no attraction to this changeling, only revulsion.

Many "exhibits" were residents that had been sewed together at various locations, with pretentious titles like "The Sharing Ideal," and "True Commitment." Other exhibits were residents who had their bodies rearranged, legs and arms reversed, heads turned around, and mouths that been placed on chests. Visitors walked around and gawked, some laughing, others cringing, and several discussing the artistic merits of each piece. "What do you think LM was trying to say with this one?"

Hadder rolled his eyes and continued on. At the back of the main exhibit hall, near an open door that read "Biomass" above it, Hadder had to stop and swallow down the urge to puke. Next to the door, hanging from wall supports, was a man whose skin had been flayed and pinned back like a frog in biology class. Beside the man, a woman whose mouth had been sewed shut, wearing a white nurse's uniform, regularly sprayed water onto the man's muscles, keeping them moist and protected from the dry chamber air.

Hadder looked into the man's eyes, convinced that he would see agony there, a silent call to set him free. But as he stared, Hadder only saw confused ecstasy staring back at him, with an oddball sense of pride lurking beneath.

Shaking his head, Hadder walked through the open doors that led to the "Biomass," shaking his head. Whether from pity, discomfort, or anger, Hadder wasn't sure.

———

IF THE MAIN exhibit hall was disturbing, then the "Biomass" room was genuinely confusing. The entire back of *Biomass* was comprised of one long, thin room. As Hadder entered, he saw that soft benches ran down both directions, facing the most beautiful garden Hadder had ever seen. While the gardens scattered around Station and tended to by the manikins were wondrous, this was beyond description. Flowers the size of umbrellas and supported by stalks as large as thin women were peppered throughout the display. Massive chunks of colorful pollen were spit out by one flower to be gobbled up by another. Below these behemoths, equally exotic plants played out similar scenes in shades of purple, blue, orange, and red.

Hadder thought it impossible that such a diversity of plant life could exist in one location. It indeed was a "Biomass," as all the shapes of nature were in full display - bells and funnels, trumpets and bowls, saucers and tubulars, and sphericals. For several minutes, Hadder lost himself in that wondrous garden, for every square yard held a vastness of natural beauty that would take years to note and accurately describe in words. How could the man responsible for the wickedness in the room behind him also have created such beauty? This thought plagued Hadder as he relished in his recognition of the garden's perfection.

As Hadder stood appreciating, he noticed that several other residents had entered the "Biomass" exhibit. Unlike himself, however, they paid little mind to the lush garden before them, giving it minimal attention before descending stairs that appeared at the long room's opposite ends. Curious, Hadder bid adieu to the nursery and walked down the stairs to his right.

Upon reaching the bottom, Hadder's eyes widened, and his stomach churned with increased bile as he discovered the real "Biomass" exhibit. Against the back wall, directly below the garden above, was a glass enclosure of soil, some of it classic black and brown, but the majority of which was a clear substance that had obviously been added to give the audience an improved view of the actual "Biomass."

Within the soil swam nearly a dozen Elevated residents. Their limbs had been removed, their bodies thinned and elongated, and their mouths enlarged, making them essentially large worms who wove their way through the dirt. Hadder watched in shock as they devoured soil as they made forward progress, simultaneously expelling dark material from their open anuses and leaving black trails in their wake. Without thinking, Hadder stepped forward, closely approaching the glass, a perverse curiosity over-taking his disgust as he studied the human worm farm.

A voice coming from beside Hadder wasn't enough to tear his attention from the bizarre scene. "True art doesn't exist without sacrifice. Would you sacrifice that which is most precious to you, namely your humanity, to create a beauty not found elsewhere in this universe? These brave souls have just done that. Their vermicast, or humicast if you will, can only be produced one way, and is absolutely essential in creating the enchanting garden found above. To have that kind of dedication, that kind of spirit, that kind of courage - that is what true art is all about."

Hadder didn't need to turn his head towards the effeminate, dramatic voice to know who he was talking to. "I notice you didn't rush to butcher your own body to join them, Lester."

"I concede your point, darling, but allow me to retort. Because of their sacrifice, they are now helpless creatures, only living in the now, only surviving in the name of art. Their shit is responsible for endless, unparalleled beauty. What's your shit responsible for?"

"Bad smells."

"The question was rhetorical, darling. Anyways, someone must remain to care for them, to make sure that their sacrifices continue with purpose.

Without the beauty of the garden above, this is just an experiment in biology, is it not?"

Hadder finally looked over at Lester Midnight, taking the man in for the first time. The man was tall and more muscled than Hadder anticipated. He had dark black skin, short white hair, white painted lips and nails. Lester wore a suit of molten gold, reminding Hadder of his friend Goldie, with ankle-length pants that showed off crystal loafers. He wore five earrings in each ear, five severed fingers that had been dipped in gold and swung freely like a morbid mobile. Rings adorned each finger, and his eyes were white on white, with flecks of gold that drifted through his irises. In his right hand, Lester held a solid gold cane, atop of which, cast in crystal, sat a human eye, complete with dangling nerve endings. "And what do you call that freak show in the main exhibit hall?"

Lester laughed gently and smiled. "Experiments in biology, of course. Come, enough of my art, darling, I want to hear of your own. Or maybe you have something else to discuss, new resident Marlin Hadder? Yes, I know who you are. There is very little that happens in Station that escapes my attention. Somewhere more private, perhaps?"

Hadder nodded and followed Lester Midnight back up to the garden, through the main exhibit hall, and up some stairs to an expansive office. During their walk, Lester regularly stopped to bask in the adoration of visiting residents, some stating their desires to be the subjects of future projects. Hadder looked around as they entered the large room. Sketches were scattered throughout the room, many which looked like early renderings of H.R. Giger, foretelling the horror of later artistic endeavors. Lester walked to his enormous desk, made seemingly of gold resin and white human bones, spun around dramatically and sat on its edge. "So tell me, Marlin Hadder, why are you here, fellow artiste?"

There was an obvious sarcasm, an outright challenge in those last two words. "I seek information, a name to be exact. But that could change quickly if I can't find the answers I need. In that case, I may seek something else. Your blood on my hands, perhaps."

Lester Midnight stared darkly at Marlin Hadder, the golden flecks in his white eyes spinning faster. Hadder watched as Lester's knuckles tightened on his cane and prepared for an attack. He maintained a safe distance and had already identified a thick sketchpad he could turn into an impromptu shield, if needed. Fortunately, it wasn't required, as the storm that roared in Lester Midnight passed as quickly as it came on. He dropped his cane and slapped his hands together in glee.

"Ahh, that tricky Royal! Always knowing when to play that fucking Key card to force me into something interesting. Of course, I immediately knew you weren't of the art world, but nonetheless, I have to tell you, I am a bit relieved. The last thing I wanted to do was hear about some hack's derivative art. I'm much more interested in what I see before me. Yes, I didn't quite notice it out there, but I see it now. Oh, how I see it. You know what makes me special, Hadder? I see what others cannot or refuse to see. And you know what I see in you?"

"Tell me."

Lester smiled and jumped off the desk, stood within arm's reach of Hadder. "I see the newest resident, one who isn't yet resigned to this existence. One who holds onto a Rage that all the joy in the world cannot repress. Rage, one of the purest emotions, one of the few sources of real art. How long has it had you?"

"It's been there forever, but it just recently took hold."

"Ahh, and these answers you seek, the questions attached to them are the cause of the takeover?"

"Yes."

"How delightful." Lester began to pace around the room. "But before you ask me *the* question, Hadder, ask me another. Indulge me. What is it you want to know about me? I am nothing if not an egoist."

Hadder didn't need to ponder a question; it was on the tip of his tongue. "Do you know that you're insane?"

Lester cackled, slapped his hands together again. "Yes! That's what I like! The Rage has no place for niceties or half-truths. Who told you I was insane? Royal Winters, that boring echo of the Before? Or some other equally terrible Key. I never had much in common with them, you know.

They thought me unbalanced, I thought them confused. Do you know why I thought them confused, dear Hadder?"

"No, tell me."

"Because. I'm the only person who seems to understand what this place is, darling. Do you know what Station is, Hadder?"

"Tell me."

"It is an experiment, a grand experiment, conducted by the divine. It is a way station, a temporary thing. We're meant to push the envelope in our short time here, discover that which we could not in the Before. You can't do that dancing the night away or coupling up and pretending that this is an earthly place. This city had a specific beginning. It will have a specific end. I have maximized my time here, created things never before seen. Where the other Keys have failed, I alone have succeeded. The other Keys are frightened; they want this limbo to continue forever, to live as small gods in their small worlds."

"And you, Lester? What do you want?"

Lester stared at Hadder crazily. "I want to create, to feel as the true gods feel until my time is up. Then I will relish in the Fall, and know that in the collapse, I will finally be an integral piece of this overarching project. The telling of the art that is Station will not be able to be told without Lester Midnight. My sacrifice will finally be made real."

Lester sank into one of the couches, finally drained of that which he had wanted to say for a long time. He waved a hand at Hadder. "Now, give me your real question, darling. Why have you come to me today, Marlin Hadder of the Rage?"

"There was a girl who was murdered a few Haelas ago at *The Soiree Noire*."

"Reena Song."

"Yes. I think the killer was a Riser that crossed the Skirt. I need to know the Riser's name."

"And why do you need a name, dear Hadder?"

"To find him. To kill him."

"Did you love this girl, dear Hadder?"

"I loved her. I wasn't in love with her."

"There's a vast space between those two things. Is it enough? The Rising is usually no place for a plain man like you, even with the Rage walking beside you."

"It is enough. I cannot resume life until she is avenged."

Lester rose, put his face close to Hadder's. "And this revenge? What if it jeopardizes the life that you currently enjoy? Actions have consequences, dear Hadder. I am sure that the other Keys fear you; maybe you've seen it in their eyes yourself. You mark a potential imbalance in the city, and imbalance could lead to destruction."

Hadder sighed deeply, tried to explain that which he did not fully understand. "I cannot be who I was, who the girl I am in love with needs me to be, until this killer is dead. Whatever happens because of my actions, the choices I am determined to make, so be it. I'm cursed, either way, Lester. I'd rather run headlong into the darkness than curl up into a ball and let it slowly eat me from the inside. And I feel the same about Station. If it's as you say, if it has an end, let us rush to it with our heads high, not let it crumble around us as we fight for scraps and become less and less human."

Lester smiled and put his palm to Hadder's face. "Said like a true harbinger of the Fall. In that case, Marlin Hadder, the man who killed Reena Song is an Elevated wretch named Skeelis. He's a thug for hire and has been bouncing from Bar to Bar for some time now, so I can't tell you exactly where he is located in the Rising. But know this, the Riser Wars have consolidated all the Bars into two main factions now sparring for control. In South Rising, Ego Rounds holds domain. He is a tough man, but principled, even if those principles are foreign to you and most others. You can work with him. In North Rising, a man who calls himself The Krown runs the show. His Elevations have made an unbalanced man near-insane, more beast than man, so you'll need some luck in getting through to him."

Hadder turned to leave. With his answer in hand, he didn't want to spend any more time with Lester Midnight than necessary. Lester called to his back. "Oh and Hadder, darling, I hope you don't plan on marching in there and then simply marching out."

Hadder stopped. "That's exactly what I planned. Why?"

"Dear boy, once you cross the Skirt, you're barred from returning. You're considered a Riser from then on."

"What are my options?"

Lester shrugged, a wry smile caked on his dark face. "Get your revenge and live your life out as a Riser, or make a stop before heading out."

"Stop where?"

"Why to see Albany Rott, darling. For certain situations, he may be coerced into providing you with a reentry pass back into the Setting. Or he'll kill you on the spot. Either way, it won't be boring."

"Thanks, Lester. Don't carve up too many more residents."

"By the way, love the outfit. Blood red suits you."

Hadder continued his exit. "I thought if I had to massacre you, best to wear something that would help me pass through your minions unscathed."

"Don't threaten me with a good time, darling." As he descended the stairs, Hadder heard Lester calling after him. "You're most welcome, Marlin Hadder! Good luck with your Rage and vengeance! I'll see you at the Fall! Oh yes!!! I'll most definitely see you at the Fall!! I'll be the one laughing!"

17

"He's right. If you willingly cross the Skirt, the Caesars won't let you back into the Setting. Unless you're willing to live out your probably short life as a Riser, you're going to need to talk to Mister Rott."

Much to Hadder's disappointment, Royal had concurred with Lester Midnight's take on the situation. He was hoping to avoid a visit to Mister Rott, was impatient to begin the hunt. And truth be told, Hadder had had enough of needing favors from the barely human, and he didn't know if Albany Rott even qualified as that.

Lilly retired to their living quarters as soon as Hadder returned. It was deep Haela now, and she had stayed up just long enough to see him still alive. Anything beyond ensuring his continued breathing, she wasn't interested. Hadder understood her anger. If anyone understood anger, it was him, but he had been set on this path and was unable to shift directions until he reached his destination.

"To the North, right?"

"Yeah. Just follow the Lethe River up. It emanates from Rott Manor."

"What's he like?"

Royal thought for a moment. "Been years since I saw him last, and that was from a distance, just his speech initiating the Skirt. He was much more hands-on in the beginning."

"What about back then? How was he?"

Another pause, this one longer. "Rott tries very hard to seem human. He tries very hard to look like he doesn't have all the answers. But he does. He tries very hard to seem interested, but I think he's bored."

"Any tips on dealing with him?"

"Yes. Be careful. This isn't some madman like Lester Midnight, whose ego you can feed into and whose desires you can tempt. I know you're a tough guy, Hadder. You've shared your training, and I can see the fighter in you. You walk with a confidence that says you can handle yourself. But if you try to talk tough with Albany Rott, he'll turn you into a pink mist in the blink of an eye, leaving nothing but a fading memory. Don't be scared, but don't be disrespectful either."

"I know when I'm dealing with serious men."

"But would you know when you're facing a serious god?"

———

BEFORE LEAVING *THE ROYAL JELLY*, Hadder had a manikin make him a new set of his usual clothes - gray pants, black shirt, black jacket, and black/white high tops. After bathing and changing in one of the empty communal showers, Hadder sat alone at the ground floor bar and drank beer alone. It was nearing the end of Haela, and Hadder didn't want to return to his living quarters. One, he wasn't tired, his single-minded purpose leaving no room for rest. And two, he couldn't face Lilly, especially with no good counterpoints to her numerous objections.

After finishing his third beer, Hadder walked outside to find that the Idol Moon was snowballing and set out to see Albany Rott. Taking various thoroughfares and garden paths due north, Hadder eventually came upon the Lethe River and followed it upstream, keeping the river on his right. North he went, farther than he ever had before, and before long, his eyes grew large, and his mouth fell open as he looked upon the grandest construct in Station - Rott Manor.

Although it was called a mansion, Albany Rott's home looked much more like a gothic cathedral. Built of the whitest marble Hadder had ever seen, the building was absolutely shining in the rays of the Solay. Taller than it was wide, two monstrous towers dominated the left and right side of the building, while the center was marked with a rose window above several pointed tympanums that topped large red doors. Situated as it was on a large hill, marble stairs fell to the left and right and ran headlong into footpaths, one upon which Hadder now walked. A torrent of water poured forth from the center of the landing, between sets of stairs, becoming what those lesser folk downstream would call the Lethe River.

As Hadder traversed the footpath towards the mansion, he passed through an impressive sculpture garden. All of the figures had been hewn from crimson marble and depicted humans, angels, and devils in various poses of battle. As Hadder passed under them, he felt eyes move along to follow his path and wondered what these frozen sentinels could do if they detected a threat to their master.

As he approached and ascended the stairs, Hadder was greeted by cool mist from the source of the Lethe, the refreshing spray removing the few lingering effects of his earlier beverages. Walking up to the red doors, Hadder brushed his hands over his clothes and calmed his nerves before raising his hand to knock.

Just as his knuckles were to make contact with the doors, they swung open silently, revealing a man waiting in the entryway. He was small and thin, wearing a white doctor's coat over brown pants and a yellowed dress shirt. His hair, neatly parted to the side, was blonde to the point of near transparency, and his blotchy skin looked like it would burn even under the Idol Moon's soft rays. Behind his John Lennon glasses, pale blue eyes stared out in the world, calculating every variable and determining optimal courses of action.

But there was something more in those computer eyes, something only someone with a similar affliction could see. Something Marlin Hadder could see all too clearly.

In the uncomfortable silence, Hadder looked down to see that the man held two books to his side. Hadder cocked his head to read the titles. One was Frank Herbert's *God Emperor of Dune*, and the other was Jeff Vander-Meer's *Veniss Underground*. Hadder, once an avid reader, was familiar with both books and didn't like what it said about this man that he chose these two dark texts to carry with him like a rosary.

After a while, the uncomfortable silence grew unbearable. "I'm Marlin Hadder, requesting a meeting with Mister Rott."

The small man cracked a victorious smile as if he had just won some secret game. "We know who you are. We know why you're here. Follow me."

The man spun on his heels, and Hadder followed, stepping onto a plush red carpet that ran from the entrance, down the length of the mansion's main room, and up multi-leveled stairs the width of the interior to disappear in the darkened distance of the floor above. Soft classical music greeted Hadder as he entered, coming from hidden niches high in the building's domed ceilings. Looking around as he walked, Hadder marveled at the tapestries that decorated the walls, antiques that sat on small pedestals throughout the room, and handcrafted furniture that looked too expensive and uncomfortable to sit on. As Hadder started up the stairs, he noticed ancient paintings hanging from the walls between levels, several of which were reminiscent of the works of some of history's most influential artists.

At the top of the stairs, the man in the doctor's coat spun back to face Hadder, barely able to hide or disguise his disdain. So much for first impressions, thought Hadder as he fantasized about punching a hole in the diminutive man's chest. "Wait here. Don't move." With that, the man moved against the righthand wall, books held in his crossed hands at his belt.

Hadder did as he was told and remained standing on the red carpet just a few steps from a dangerous fall, staring into the darkness of a long hallway that seemed to have no end. The small man stood against the wall unspeaking, his beady blue eyes fixated on Hadder.

Hadder chose to ignore the little man, his plate currently full of bizarre characters he had to maintain dealings with. As he looked into the abyss, Hadder worked hard to slow his breathing, a constant battle to control the Rage. Slowly, two towering figures began to emerge from the dimness, walking on either side of the red carpet. As they came into focus, Hadder saw that it was two Caesars who had joined them, just as large and imposing as those he had seen before. The monster on the right had black skin, a silver mohawk, and a clear vest while his companion on the left had beige skin, twin black braids that fell over his shoulders, and a black muscle shirt that swirled with color.

Approximately fifteen feet from Hadder, both Caesars stopped, crossed their massive arms over too-large chests, and waited, their looks threatening to wither Hadder's confidence. In the quartet's muteness, Hadder noticed that the Caesars observed the small man as closely as they watched him, something to put in his back pocket for later. With no words being exchanged between parties, Hadder simply looked down the endless hall, unsure of what was going to peer out from the darkness.

As he waited, the lights around the mansion began to dim almost imperceptibly. Hadder looked to the others, but none seemed to take notice. A warm breeze caressed Hadder's face and body, increasing in heat until it was uncomfortable, like standing in front of the oven door. Beads of sweat began to form on Hadder's brow and upper lip, forcing him to wipe them with the back of this hand. As the hot air was radiating from the darkened hall, Hadder stared harder into the black maw, searching for any sign of life.

And then he saw it, so faint at first that he had to rub his eyes to ensure that they were not playing tricks on him. Two embers could be seen bouncing through the darkness, growing closer by the second, first mere specks, then floating marbles of glowing red. As those lit coals approached, the darkness congealed and split down the middle.

A man of indescribable power emerged from the murk.

He stopped his approach ten feet from Hadder and waited, accustomed to people needing time to adjust to his presence. Tall and slim, the man's skin was as white as the marble which surrounded him. His hair, dark red like dried blood, was slicked back, just grazing his shoulders. He wore a fitted suit of the blackest material Hadder had ever seen; it seemed to selfishly pull light from the room, refusing to reflect it back.

A red button-up shirt was open at the collar, revealing a sparkling tattoo of light at the top of his sternum. It was a familiar form that tickled something in the recesses of Hadder's memory.

For some reason, Hadder's attention was captured by the symbol. It whispered secrets to him as he looked upon it, the light it gave off piercing his skin and fingering his heart. After several seconds that felt like minutes, Hadder was able to tear his eyes from the compelling design.

Three other characteristics, however, were equally striking about the man before him. First, his eyes were like a blacksmith's forge, simmering heat that crossed from deep red to black and back again. They didn't look at you, but rather through you, to your innermost thoughts, fears, and desires, rendering lies exercises in futility. Next was a fiery red scar ran across the man's pale face from left to right, starting at his temple and ending at his jawline. As it pulsed gently, Hadder began to believe that it was a constant source of agony for the man. Finally, the man's age was completely indeterminate; Hadder couldn't decide if he was early middle-aged or thousands of years old.

The man smiled at a joke that only he heard. "Salutations, Marlin

Hadder. I am Albany Rott, creator of this fine city that you now call home." His deep voice matched his appearance. There was limitless power between words that were spoken with an unidentifiable accent, a mashup of all the world's various intonations.

Since Rott already knew his name, Hadder skipped the introduction and remained quiet. "This small creature standing next to you, who was probably too rude to introduce himself, is Doctor Milo Flowers." The little man continued to stare daggers from behind his glasses. "Doctor Flowers was instrumental in helping me design and build the Caesars, an unfortunate necessity of the modern Station experience." The two Caesars behind Rott remained as they were. "I know he's a bit antisocial, but he truly is a brilliant synthetic biologist, second only to yours truly, in fact." Hadder thought he saw those blue eyes narrow at this remark, even hidden beneath the thick lenses. "Thank you, Doctor Flowers, you may leave us. I'll meet you in the testing room later." Milo Flowers nodded and then walked down the main staircase, cutting Hadder with another look before descending.

Rott watched Flowers go, waiting until he exited the mansion before continuing. "What do you think of my doctor, Marlin Hadder? I know he's awkward, but we cannot deny his craft and his work."

"He's not awkward."

Rott's red eyes widened a bit, unused to residents disagreeing with him. "Really? Pray, tell me what he is."

"What I meant was, he's not awkward for the reasons you think he is. He's not awkward because he is antisocial, although he probably is antisocial." Rott seemed to be leaning in; Hadder felt it more than he could see it. "He has the Rage. I'd be careful with that one."

Rott digested what Hadder said, smiled to himself. "And what about my fair city? Care to share your penetrative insights."

Hadder felt safe in assuming that honesty was the best policy when facing Albany Rott. "Other than the self-mutilation, monotonous debauchery, and murder, I quite like it."

"I didn't sense any sarcasm there."

"There wasn't any. I've made a home here. Or at least, I had made a home. It was stolen from me. I want it back."

Rott began to pace. "And who took this home from you, Marlin Hadder? Surely you still have living quarters? Surely your precious Bar remains standing? Surely you still have a warm body to wake up to each Solay?" As Rott walked, Hadder noticed that two hatchets, black wood handles with crystalline blades, were tucked neatly into his belt on each side, kept hidden under his suit jacket. "Station still stands, does it not? How, then, has your home been taken?"

"There was a murder several Haelas ago. A Riser named Skeelis snuck across the Skirt and killed Reena Song in *The Soiree Noire*."

Rott paused his pacing. "An unfortunate crime to be sure. Reena Song was a good girl, and her presence will be missed deeply. Was she your woman?"

"No, but she was my friend, and I've never had many of those."

"Because of the Rage?"

Hadder stepped back instinctively, surprised that Rott had seen through him so easily. "Yes."

"And now, with her death, the Rage is making demands, is it not?"

"It is."

"And these demands currently dominate you, allow for nothing else in your life right now? Certainly not allowing for any semblance of home?"

Hadder bowed. "You see it all, Mister Rott. I am unworthy of your presence."

Rott grimaced, then moved in a flash, was upon Hadder in an instant, his pale face hot against Hadder's own. "Don't falsely fawn, Marlin Hadder. I have enough doing that already. What is it that you want from me?"

"Doctor Flowers said that you already knew."

"I want to hear it from your mouth."

The embers in Rott's eyes had been fed, were now small flames. "I want to cross the Skirt, find this Skeelis, and kill him."

"You seek retribution?"

"I need retribution."

"Then go. No one will stop you from crossing the Skirt. Your Rage will mix well with the Risers." Although Rott's voice had not changed, there was a dangerous undercurrent to his words, made more frightening by his proximity. "What do you need from me?"

Hadder worked hard to maintain a brave face but was languishing under Rott's red stare. "I need permission to cross back into the Setting once my work is complete."

"To reclaim your home?"

"Yes."

Rott retreated a few steps and then spoke again. "The Risers are an unforeseen byproduct of Station. Who could have known that such anger could persist in the face of an idealized existence?"

"Thousands of years of history could have told you that." Hadder immediately regretted the words, was relieved when Rott waved them aside.

"Anger, sure. But such violence, to foster and then embrace a dependence on violence, even my wildest projections did not see this. Tell me, Marlin Hadder, what makes you think you'll survive the Rising? You're a violent man, but these people live violent lives, steel sharpened daily on steel."

"I'm not sure I will survive, haven't given it much thought, truth be told. But if I do survive, I want to know that I'll be allowed back into the Setting."

"It's an almost certainty that you will die, Marlin Hadder."

"I've died once already."

"But I won't be there to cradle your fall next time."

"I understand."

"And this does not dissuade you."

"This isn't a choice. Trust me, I'd rather not wade into a pack of weaponized animals. This isn't my idea of fun. But then things we are forced to do rarely are."

Albany Rott stood for a moment, studying Hadder, before letting loose a laugh from deep within, showing his perfect too-white teeth. "Oh, but there's something I like about you, Marlin Hadder! I speak your language, understand your words, but am, as of yet, not fluent. I would like to know more of you, discover that which remains hidden to even me. Very well, your reentry is granted."

Rott walked again, began speaking as if to himself. "But I know this Skeelis, and the little mutation will be hard to kill. That is if you ever find him. The Risers don't just let tourists pass through. If you're not recognized as belonging to a particular Bar, you'll be butchered on the spot. And then if you do happen to locate Skeelis and do happen to kill him, how do you intend to get back? They'll not sit idly by and allow you to take one of their own."

Rott stopped, a sign that a decision had been made. He looked to the Caesar on the right. "Otho, who was it that found this human incapacitated on the Skirt all those Haelas ago."

The behemoth answered in the voice of a boulder. "I believe that was Cal, Father."

"Of course, you're right. Otho, take Cal, and the two of you meet Marlin Hadder on the Caesar Bridge at Solay's break tomorrow. You're to accompany Marlin Hadder on this little sojourn of his and inform any Risers that he is under the protection of Albany Rott. After his business, on the slim chance that he survives, accompany him back across the Skirt and report to me."

For a walking statue, Otho momentarily appeared confused. "And if we are attacked?"

Rott waved his worry away. "By all means, those that break my edict can be disposed of."

Otho bowed deeply, and Rott folded his hands together. "Then, it is settled. Our business is concluded, is it not?"

Hadder, unsure of how to close the conversation, followed Otho's lead and bowed deeply. "Thank you, Mister Rott."

"Good luck, Marlin Hadder. I really mean it. Should this be the last I see of you, I want you to know that I have enjoyed this conversation. Rarely do humans interest me."

Hadder forced a smile and began to turn before Rott stopped him. "One more thing, Marlin Hadder. This home that you hope to reclaim, what will you do if, when you get there, it's not as you remember? What if the smells are different? What if broken glass cuts your bare feet as you walk? What if the creaks, once ignorable, now keep you up at night?"

"Why would it be different?"

"Maybe it's not different. Maybe it is you that is different. After you swim in blood, the bathwater will also change, will it not?"

Hadder nodded sadly, understanding Rott's point while conceding that he had no choice. As he walked back down the red carpet, Hadder could feel Albany Rott's fiery eyes on his back, making calculations he could never comprehend in a language he would never understand.

18

The Caesar Bridge differed significantly from the others that crossed the Lethe River. While those such as the Bridge Gab'Riel were works of arts, the Caesar Bridge was purely utilitarian. An add-on to the original blueprint of the city, the Caesar Bridge was where the Skirt crossed the Lethe River. Made of simple, sturdy timber, it was rarely visited by anyone other than the Caesars as they made their patrols along the Skirt.

Marlin Hadder walked towards the Caesar Bridge, happy to be away from the stuffy atmosphere of *The Royal Jelly*. For the better part of a Solay and all Haela, Hadder had anxiously bided his time, getting new clothes made while waiting for his opportunity to cross the Skirt. Royal had little to say, knowing that any words of discouragement would prove futile, and Lilly Sistine had even less. A coldness had fallen over Lilly, sheets of ice that barricaded the warm heart that he fell in love with. He understood, however, that this was her way of proactively dealing with loss, extra padding for the inevitable hit that was to come.

Unable to take the worried looks, disappointed glances, and angry words, Hadder had spent the majority of the Haela alone in the courtyard, practicing stretching and breathing exercises he hadn't done in years. When

Haela began swelling with Solay, Hadder was already sitting on the front steps of *The Royal*. All he had to do was grab his jacket and be gone.

As Hadder closed the distance to the Caesar Bridge, he could see that both giant Caesars were already waiting there for him. Otho, black skin and a silver mohawk, stood professionally, looking up and down the Skirt, perhaps more out of habit than anything else. He had a massive battle-ax strapped to his back, a figure cut straight from the pages of a D&D novel.

The other Caesar must have been Cal, the one that saved him so many Haelas ago. Slightly larger than even Otho, he had dark orange skin, a mullet of blonde hair, and matching yellow muttonchops, making him look like an oversized 80's wrestler from Venice Beach. Cal had a much more playful demeanor than his solemn colleague, casually throwing stones into the river as he waited. While Otho wielded an ax, Hadder could see that Cal had two regular-sized swords crossed and strapped to his back, the pommels sticking out above each shoulder for ease of reach. While Otho donned his transparent vest, Cal went shirtless, showing off a variety of pale scars against his tanned skin.

Hadder stepped onto the bridge and approached the monstrous duo. Unsure of how to interact with these intimidating constructs, Hadder simply nodded in greeting. "Otho. And you're Cal, I believe. I think I owe you thanks for saving my ass many Haelas back."

Otho simply continued his intense searching up and down the Skirt. Cal, however, halted his rock-throwing and walked towards Hadder. He stared down at Hadder with purple eyes, an elephant surveying a mouse. "You want to kill a man." If Otho had the voice of a boulder, then Cal's was the sound of thunder.

Hadder met the giant's stare and did his best to maintain his confident facade. "That's right."

"He murdered your woman?"

Hadder saw no point in arguing semantics. "That's right."

Cal continued his stare. "You were ready to die, that Haela I found you. Are you again ready? Are you ready to die for this woman?"

"I am."

"Then let's go."

Cal walked past Hadder and resumed throwing rocks held in his meaty palm into the raging waters of the Lethe. Otho stepped forward, a soldier ready for orders. "Direction?"

Hadder's face screwed up in confusion. "I'm sorry?"

"Direction?"

"We're going into the Rising."

"Direction?"

Hadder looked helplessly towards Cal, who simply chuckled as he threw the last of his rocks. "He wants to know which way into the Rising." He began to move his arms. "To the left, or north, are Bars that belong to The Krown. To the right, or south of the Lethe, are Bars loyal to Ego Rounds. Which one you need to see?"

"I don't know who this Skeelis works for. Which way would you recommend?"

Cal shook his head. "Not how this works. Otho and I weren't built with a lot of what you call 'free will.' So when my brother says, 'direction,' he needs you to pick a direction."

Hadder took Otho's silence for his agreement of Cal's assessment. "Well, I heard that this Ego Rounds is much more reasonable than his counterpart up north, so let's start with him and hope that Skeelis is there. And that he was acting alone."

Cal moved to the side of the bridge, waving Hadder on towards the southwest. "You go. We follow. Someone other than Skeelis tries to kill you, we stop them. You get your revenge, or we bring your body back."

"Simple as that, huh. Well, let's get going, fellas. I hear the Risers are like the Celebration Cluster, sleeping all Solay. Perhaps we can get there and back with limited issues."

With that, Marlin Hadder exited the bridge and began to cross the Skirt to the south of the Lethe River. Cal and Otho followed, but not before sharing a look that spoke volumes. A look that said, this resident has no fucking idea what he's walking into.

———

WHILE THE STATION that Marlin Hadder knew, the Setting, was a place of indescribable beauty comprised of manicured gardens, enchanting plant and animal life, and tended pathways, the Rising was that same place, if it had been hit by a nuclear warhead.

Where the gardens hadn't been eradicated, they grew haphazardly, breaking free of their designated areas to jut out from broken walkways and creep up the skeletons of long-abandoned Bars.

The remnants of great battles could be seen everywhere Hadder looked. Bloodstained walls held up roofs that looked ready for collapse. Sharp cuts marred the faces of the few buildings left standing. Char marks along the ground told the tale of countless fires being lit, perhaps to light a battle, maybe to celebrate a victory.

Bones littered the ground, some picked clean and others holding on to the last remaining strips of skin or hair. Manikin parts were strewn about, refusing to deteriorate at the same rate as the dead residents. At one particular crossroads, someone had compiled various manikin components into a makeshift scarecrow. While indeed off-putting, Hadder was unsure of the actual message it was intended to send.

Near the Lethe, Hadder only found disaster, beauty devolved into a post-apocalypse existence. As the trio walked, Hadder could sense they were being watched from the shadows of broken buildings. "Cal, you see anyone out there?"

The Caesar didn't hesitate or break his stride. "Spies. Ego Rounds' spies."

"So, he knows we're coming?"

"Of course, he does."

"Does that worry you?"

"Nothing worries me. But it should worry you."

They walked south in silence for a while after Cal's heartening words. Soon, Hadder saw dramatic changes in the landscape. Where there had been chaotic destruction, there now seemed a bit of order to the ravaged city. Buildings that were damaged had been patched up, obviously more for utility than ascetics. Watchful eyes could be seen from upper windows, and some Bars even had small groups milling outside.

Faces dirty with soot and grime, the Risers all wore matching black leather and fingered a variety of weapons, from iron rods to homemade machetes to darkened wooden staffs. They put on their best intimidating faces as Hadder passed. Without the accompaniment of Cal and Otho, Hadder was sure he would have already been met with violence.

As they progressed, glimmers of tactical moves began to appear. Trenches were dug at various locations, forcing Hadder and his guardians to take a zigzag approach south. Barricades were set at several thoroughfares, made from the rubble of fallen Bars, and topped with sharped metal rods. Groups of Riser soldiers were stationed at strategic locations, some with crafted crossbows that made Hadder feel especially vulnerable.

On several occasions, a particularly feisty Riser would move to intercept the trio, only to be pulled back by a seemingly higher-ranking soldier. As Hadder moved through the increasingly organized grounds, it became painfully clear that Albany Rott was correct; he would not have made it very far alone.

Past rudimentary watchtowers and within the sights of various projectile weapons, Hadder, Cal, and Otho continued their journey, growing increasingly surprised by the organization through which they marched. More military base on acid than uncontrolled chaos, Hadder watched as Risers moved with purpose, reinforcing roadblocks, mending building weak spots, and repurposing debris into weapons.

Eyes followed them everywhere, and soon they were shadowed to the left, right, and behind by several groups bearing arms. Although they maintained a safe distance, the threat of violence hung heavy and real in the air. If this was Riser downtime, Hadder wanted to do his best to avoid the Rising at Haela.

The further south they trekked, the more ornery the Risers became. Taunts began to fly at them from all directions, then the occasional stone. Hadder made sure to pay close attention, dodging several, while Cal and Otho just allowed them to bounce harmlessly off their thick skins. One lone

Riser, cutting a ridiculous shirtless figure in leather shorts held up by suspenders, sprung out from behind a slab of marble and clumsily swung a makeshift mace at Hadder's head. Hadder quickly ducked the strike and, seeing how unbalanced the swing put the man, dropped a vicious elbow across the attacker's nose, shattering cartilage and sending a fountain of blood into the air.

As the Riser screamed and cupped his hands over his broken face, Hadder simply kicked the man over and continued walking. Although he refused to turn around, he could feel Cal, and perhaps even Otho, cracking small smiles behind him. All three knew that that would be the last of the lone Riser assailants. If another attack came, it would be a coordinated effort.

The skeletons and dilapidated buildings that defined the early goings of their travels were soon left behind as an increasing number of fully functioning Bars appeared. Loud music could be heard coming from the open front doors of several, sharing an aggressive quality, whether metal or hip hop. Sentries were stationed on the roofs of almost all buildings, a blatant show of organization and force that contrasted with the secretive nature of the spies and scouts further north.

A large Bar sat heavy in the near distance, clearly the most important building in South Rising. A sturdy wall had been constructed around the Bar, making it more compound than place of leisure. With Risers blocking their left and right, the trio had no option but to walk towards the compound, stopping when they reached a metal gate that guarded the entrance.

As soon as they stopped, Risers moved in and tightened around them, forming rudimentary battle positions and wielding an array of wicked-looking weaponry. The metal gate slid open slightly, allowing just enough space for a tall, slim woman to pass through. It quickly slid shut as soon as she was through and facing Hadder and the Caesars. Black leather pants, boots, and tube top matched her black skin and black hair, which was pulled into a tight ponytail that cascaded down from the top of her head. Confident, fierce, and beautiful, she cut an impressive figure.

"I am Kamaria. State your business," she said to Hadder, ignoring Cal and Otho. "If I don't like what I hear, I'll have you cut down where you stand.

Nobody comes this far south without announcing themselves, Caesar guard or not."

"I'm looking for Ego Rounds."

"And what do you want with Ego Rounds."

"To talk. Just to talk. I have a question to ask."

She looked up to Cal and addressed him. "Who is this fool, Cal? Why do you accompany him? Who is he to Mister Rott?"

Cal shrugged. "He's the new resident. He want's revenge. Father said help him get it."

"Revenge?" Back to Hadder. "Revenge for what, Setter?"

"A friend of mine was killed by a Riser who snuck over the Skirt. I want to find this Riser."

"No one from our clique would cross the Skirt," stated Kamaria. "We have enough to deal with on this side of the border. To go poking around in the Setting? Tempt the wrath of Rott? Not us."

"Fair enough," replied Hadder, "But maybe Ego would know of who I seek. Could point me in the right direction."

Hadder could see the wheels turning in Kamaria's mind. Head down, she began to think out loud. "New resident. Seeking revenge in the Rising. Rott sending a Caesar guard. Is this the start of the Fall?" Kamaria's head snapped up to stare darkly at Hadder. "Who are you?"

"Marlin Hadder."

"But what are you?"

"Just a man who has a name that needs a location."

"No. I think you're much more than that. And I think that the fact that you don't know what you are is the only reason that you're alive right now. I'll permit you to speak with Ego."

Kamaria then moved like lightning. One moment she was standing several feet from Hadder, the next she was jammed up against him, her long, sharpened metal nails pressed against his throat hard enough to draw blood. Cal and Otho reached for their weapons but left their hands on the pommels without drawing them. Everyone stood frozen.

"Just know," Kamaria whispered in Hadder's ear, "if this is some trick to harm Ego, I will kill you. All the Caesars in force wouldn't be enough to keep my nails from your heart. Know this."

"I understand," said Hadder, his voice straining against the pain in his neck.

Kamaria slowly lowered her nails and yelled over her shoulder. "Open the gates! Tell Ego he has visitors!" The metal gate slid open on her command, wide enough to accommodate the large trio walking shoulder to shoulder. "A word of advice. Ego is smarter than you. Speak only truths. He doesn't tolerate liars or fools. You've proven yourself a fool already by coming here. Don't make it two for two. That math usually leads to your head on a pike."

Hadder simply nodded and moved forward, torn between fearing Kamaria and wanting to kiss her.

———

HADDER and his entourage walked through the courtyard surrounding Ego Rounds' command center, a Bar whose name read *Thug's Passion* above its large golden doors. The yard was much different than the landscape just outside its walls. Perfectly manicured grounds greeted the trio. Manikins could be seen carving shapes into hedges and planting those wondrous flowers that were common in the Setting. A small stream ran around the building, populated with iridescent golden coy that waited greedily near the surface for food.

Hadder crossed a small bridge that traversed the stream and looked back in concern as the two behemoths followed, their weight making the poor bridge groan under strain. The golden doors swung open at their approach, pulled from the inside by two men wearing black jeans and matching black vests. Both men shared an Elevation that caused Hadder to look twice - the back skulls of the men had been replaced by metal casings, making them look like robots with human faces. After opening the doors, they moved to the side and waited at attention.

Hadder passed through and into a long common room. Tables were placed to the left and right, where Risers looked up from their meals to look at the new visitors. Despite the plethora of furnishings and buzz of activity, the center of the room was left clear, lending Hadder and the Caesars an open path towards the back, where Ego Rounds could be found sitting on a golden throne placed upon a raised platform.

Guards were stationed in front of the platform, long spears at the ready, and Hadder spotted additional protection to the left and right, where women draped in leather fingered hand crossbows. Hadder halted his approach a safe distance from the platform, not ready to invite violence from this imposing new character.

And imposing was the word that immediately came to mind when Marlin Hadder looked upon Ego Rounds, a giant of a man who, although not near the height of the Caesars, probably exceeded their weight. Ego's girth reminded Hadder of the hippopotamus, that most dangerous of nature's creations whose enormous size hid layers of muscle and belied tremendous speed.

Ego lounged on his golden throne covered in plush pillows and animal skins. He wore loose black harem pants, black high tops, and went without a shirt, showcasing his unbelievable girth and a myriad of tattoos that were hard to make out against his black skin. Several gold dookie chains accented his golden-brown eyes that shone of light of their own, two bits of color that stood out against Ego's black face and thick, dark beard. Ego's hair was short and nicely shaped, with designs carved into it that had also been dyed gold.

As Hadder stared at the hulking man, his eyes fell to Ego's giant hands, where he noticed metal knuckles peering out from black skin. Hadder imagined that a blow from those Elevated hands could fell a Caesar and would put a hole in Hadder's comparably frail chest.

Two scantily clad women sat on either side of Ego, one petting his bare chest while the other peeled fruit with a knife. The knife seemed too at home in her hands, and Hadder understood that these two were not mere window dressing.

Hadder and Ego stared at each other for a long while, Hadder determined to allow the intimating man to speak first, which he eventually did. "I see you met Kamaria," Ego said in a soft but powerful voice.

Seeing the confused look on Hadder's face, Ego pointed a ringed finger at Hadder's throat. Hadder reached up and felt the blood that he had forgotten to wipe off before entering. "Impressive woman. I commend your tastes in sergeants."

Ego laughed. "If I had a hundred of her, this war would be over tomorrow. But, alas, she is a rarified creature and one that I am lucky to have as a partner." Ego motioned to Cal and Otho. "I see you have made powerful allies yourself. Rott doesn't take a shine to many. What is it that makes you so special, Marlin Hadder?"

"There is nothing special about me. Rott simply sympathizes with my plight."

Ego spat out some of the wine he had been drinking. "Albany Rott? Sympathy? Oh yes, I'm sure that's all it is." The words were dripped in sarcasm and sprinkled with condescendence. "And what is this plight of yours, Marlin Hadder? Does it bring you to me today?"

"It does. A Riser snuck over the Skirt a few Haelas ago and murdered a friend of mine. I need to find him."

"And what will you do when you find him, Setter? Bring him to justice? Serve him a strongly worded letter? Gather a jury of his peers and hold a trial?"

"No."

"What then?"

"I'm going to cut his fucking head off."

Ego's eyes went wide. "Oh, now I see it. Yes, yes, you hide it well, but it leaks out in moments of passion, does it not? It eats at you, I know this. How have you managed to remain a Setter? How have you tolerated the pain of holding it back?"

"It's an acquired skill."

"I can see that. Well, you have to know, my men and women are under strict orders not to cross the Skirt or harm any Setters. But, I concede that even the tightest ships have leaks. Give me a name. If it's one of my own, you'll have your vengeance."

"The Riser's name is Skeelis." Ego shifted uncomfortably on his throne. The woman peeling the fruit stopped mid-cut. Hadder grew impatient in the extended silence. "Do you know this man?"

"I do."

"And is he one of yours?"

"He is not."

"What can you tell me about him?"

"You sure know how to pick your enemies, Marlin Hadder. Skeelis is a Riser in every negative sense of the word, perverted in mind and body. He floated around as a mercenary during the Riser Wars, working for whoever promised the most kills, whoever proved the most violent. He belongs to The Krown now, is one of his most treasured killers. You're going to have a hard time with that one."

"How can I find him?"

"You'll have to go north. The bastard should be hanging around The Krown's compound, a Bar called *King's Head*."

"Thank you. Any advice?"

"Yes. It's a long walk through a den of vipers. You and your Caesars should dine with me. I'd like to learn what you know before you march off to your death."

"But I don't know anything of value."

"I agree. You don't know shit. But you are something. Otherwise, Kamaria would have slit your throat in the street. We don't do favors on this side of Station. Everything has a price, comes with a cost. Your cost is a meal with me, time I need to discover what you are and what that means to me."

"What could it possibly mean?"

"Oh, not much. Just the fate of Station. And perhaps the world outside these walls."

———

EGO TORE off the leg of an unrecognizable, turkey-sized bird that had been wholly smoked and placed on the table between him and Hadder. Cal and Otho sat at a nearby table, eating quietly under the watchful eyes of Ego's followers. Ego spoke through mouthfuls of meat. "You have no idea why people take such an interest in you, do you Hadder?"

"None at all. I feel very insignificant. I always have."

Ego swung the half-eaten leg in the air as he spoke. "I'm sure that the Moon, when it looks down upon the grandeur of the Earth, also feels insignificant. When it looks down at its small, pockmarked gray body, I'm sure it feels trivial standing next to the blue oceans, lush green forests, and snowcapped mountains of Dunia, or Earth. How could it know the giant effects it has on the world, from creating tides to stabilizing axial tilt to lighting the night skies? It does nothing, and yet it exerts tremendous power. It feels small, but wields dangerous control."

"Dangerous control without purpose sounds like chaos."

"Yes, Hadder. Chaos. Perhaps that's what you are, a chaotic variable dropped into Station like a new virus, spreading throughout both Rising and Setting."

"But why? Why would Mister Rott want such a thing introduced?"

Ego sat back on his broad haunches, laughed softly. "Ahh, but now we're guessing as to the whims of a god, aren't we? The short answer, Hadder, is that I do not know. The long answer, however, is just that."

"I have questions. But I also have time."

"Very well." Ego signaled, and a petite Asian woman appeared with a tray of beverages, most of which Hadder recognized as typical Station concoctions. The young woman cut darkened eyes at Hadder, and he returned a smile that disappeared quickly as his eyes found the large whip strapped to her black belt, a small blade attached to its tip. Ego took an orange drink and slid another over to Hadder.

"As I'm sure you're aware, Station was founded as a utopia for those who rejected or felt rejected by the natural world. What we call the Before. But Rott didn't account for something."

"The Risers."

"Yes. Not everyone is happy in a world of leisure. For many of us, that is a fate worse than the Before. Sitting around all day, manikins to feed us, clothe us, wipe our asses. There is a need for action, a call to violence in us that needs an outlet, and that just doesn't gel with many of Station's residents."

"To what end?"

"To give purpose to our daily lives. A reason to get up early, an excuse to train our bodies, a camaraderie built on more than casual sex and shared drugs. You've heard of the Soldier's Plight?"

Hadder shook his head in the negative.

"In times of war, bonds form that can never be broken or copied. Men count on each other in a way that isn't required away from the battlefield. It's terrifying, but in that fear you find real family, are truly alive. When the war ends, you grow to miss it, what it brought you. If the man next to you doesn't hold your life in the palm of his hand, what manner of friend is he really? When the bullets stop whizzing by your head, is a rollercoaster or scary movie gonna duplicate that thrill? Men fight for many reasons. But common to all is what war brings, something that no one talks about - a sense of being and community."

"And you had that in the Before?"

Ego downed his drink in one extended sip. "Yes, twice. First, as a military soldier. After I put in my ten, I got out and applied those skills to the streets. Within a few years, I had my city on lock, and my name echoed from coast to coast. And it was known, if you stepped in my city, you paid tribute, or you got got. Simple as that."

"Sounds like you had everything you wanted. What happened?"

A heavy sigh spilled from the heavy man. "My children. I never wanted them to follow in my footsteps. My baggage of dark needs was my own, and I didn't want them to carry it as well. When Charles Jr. got shot in a night-club over some bullshit, it hurt, but I thought I could move on. But when my baby girl got caught up, was gunned down with this piece of shit drug dealer she was with, the fight I had for that world flamed out."

"But you found it again in Station."

"I did."

"And now you want to destroy the city."

"No!" Ego slammed a meaty hand down on the table, his metal knuckles catching light from above and sending refracted rays around the table. The Caesars at the table over stopped their eating, waiting for a call to violence. "That's where the fucking Setters have me all wrong, have lumped me in with that psychopath The Krown, all because they cannot understand what it means to live a life of consequences."

Hadder was honestly confused, and it showed clearly on his face. "Then what is it you want, Ego? I crossed the bones and ruins up north. I've seen the effects of the Riser Wars. Looks like destruction to me."

"Nas said you have to destroy and rebuild." Another confused look from Hadder. "I am pleased with the way things are, Hadder. I don't want Station destroyed. In fact, right now, I'm the only thing preventing its annihilation. I want my half of the city, the Rising, to control it as I wish. I have no desire to take more or harm any Setters. I like playing games of strategy and violence, where losing means the forfeiture of lives. I was the best in the streets and I'll be the best here. But as I did in the streets, I only want to play with those also in the game. Shoot an enemy on disputed ground and you're a gunner. Shoot a woman on the way to the store and you're a murderer. I love my gunners, but I won't tolerate murderers."

"I still don't understand."

"Rott wanted to create a utopia, but he thought one size would fit all. It wouldn't. But two sizes will. I want the Rising to be that other size, for those who are willing to pay the ultimate price for living the ultimate life."

"And The Krown?"

Ego's face darkened, something Hadder thought impossible. "Ronald Cronowski. Juice head. Woman abuser. Dog kicker, for all I know. Rumors are he had it rough growing up, with a dad who kicked the shit out of him on the regular and a mother who turned tricks while daddy was at work. Sometimes, the young boy at home was thrown into the deals. As he got old, he got angry. As he got angry, he got nasty. As he got nasty, he got violent. Gym, juice, and violence was all he engaged in. He was in and out of jail before he found his way here. And once he discovered that he could inflict pain with Elevations, there was no stopping him. There were many reasons for the raising of the Skirt, yours truly included, but none played a bigger factor than Ronnie, who now called himself The Krown."

"You obviously see a difference between the two of you. Maybe I don't. Help me see."

"I want to control the Setting. I want it to play out like the streets. I welcome little factions or crews to spring up, try to usurp my control. I want smaller Bars to jostle for power, I want to move them around like chess pieces. My dream is to make the Rising an alternative to Station's floundering existence, where stakes are high and decisions always come with drastic repercussions. But most importantly, I want it to be a *choice*. You want to experience this life? Cross the Skirt and it's yours. Sounds horrible? Fine, stay in the Setting and enjoy the luxuries that soften your muscles and dull your minds."

"And The Krown? What does he want?"

"He only knows carnage, only wishes to invoke pain. The Rising is just a stepping stone for him."

"Stepping stone to where?"

"First to the Setting. Then, my guess is he wants out."

"Out? Out of the city?"

Ego leaned in and his eyes flashed in seriousness. "Yes, Hadder. Think about it. Think about the damage he could do in the Before. He has a head full of rage and an army of disciples, all with combat Elevations. Right now, the walls of Station, the Caesars, and yours truly keeps him confined, but out there they've never seen a monster like him. His fire will rage unchecked; he will destroy all in his path."

Hadder finally understood. And it terrified him. "He wants revenge against the world. For what it did to the boy he was."

"Not just him, Hadder. Many in Station want the same. We've taken bad chickens out of the coop, tied blades to their claws, and could now place them back among the group. I see tremendous blood ahead if that happens."

"One thing I don't quite get; how do I fit in all this?"

Ego took another drink, handed another to Hadder. "We've reached an uncomfortable stalemate. The Krown and I are equally matched. While he has many more followers, my men and women are much more organized and disciplined. Likewise, he doesn't have the numbers necessary to simply power through the Skirt. Remember, Risers are homicidal, not suicidal. The Caesars are beyond formidable, and Albany Rott hasn't begun to show his real power, much less where his loyalties lie. However, if The Krown were to defeat me, absorb my army and resources, he may have what he needs to overtake the Skirt, run ramshackle over the Setting. From there, he may have what he needs to bring the Wall down."

"Usher in the Fall."

"Yes, you know?"

"I heard it spoken of. But this still doesn't account for my role in all this."

Ego mulled this over for several seconds before speaking. "Honestly, I think Albany Rott tires of this balanced imbalance. Maybe he grows bored. But he wants to see chess pieces moved, and I think you are his pawn to e4, a chaotic element introduced to a stagnant layout. A drop of blood in a pool of piranhas. Something to stir the pot, mix the elements, force hands."

Now it was Hadder's turn to think for a moment. "Do you think The Krown sent Skeelis over the Skirt to kill my friend?"

Ego gave the question real consideration. "Maybe. Maybe not. Perhaps he sent Skeelis to test the Caesars' defenses. Perhaps he sent Skeelis to create fear and foster anger. Remember, if the Setting gets to the point where they want to attack the Rising, The Krown still gets his way, achieves his objectives. But most likely, Skeelis got high on some brain-melting gas and wandered over with bad intentions, found doors ajar, discovered a young girl in the shadows."

Hadder remembered the smile on Skeelis's face when the fiend saw Hadder in *The Soiree Noire*, like he knew the pain he was about to inflict was going to cut deep. But Skeelis failed to see that he had cut too deep, that he had unearthed something Hadder had worked hard to bury. He decided not to share this with Ego Rounds.

"Penny for your thoughts, Hadder. You look like you're stewing over something there." Hadder's eyes rose and Ego's head snapped back a bit from what he saw in them, something he was sure Rott had seen long ago.

"I was wondering if I should just kill both Skeelis and The Krown while I'm in the North. Put an end to all this bullshit."

Silence. And then deep laughter that sent waves across Ego Round's shirtless body. Other Risers who had been holding guard and listening in also began to laugh. Even Cal and Otho shared a small chuckle between sips of drink. Ego grabbed another leg from the cooked carcass. "You would be doing me a great service, Hadder. But you should know, The Krown would quickly impale you on those spikes of his and walk around with you for a week, allowing your body to decompose in front of everyone. Stick with Skeelis for now; you'll have your hands full with him. In fact, I give you a one in three chance of making it back alive." Ego could see Hadder's eyes flare, so he added, "Oh, I don't question your heart, Hadder. And Lord knows I don't doubt your Rage. But you're going against a man every bit as crazy as yourself, but with years of combat Elevations. I'm sorry, my friend, but it doesn't look good."

"I'm counting on that. And I hope Skeelis's face is frozen in a disdainful laugh when I bring his head back across the Skirt."

Ego's meaty hand hit the table again, almost splintering the weathered wood. "Oh, but Hadder, you would make an excellent Riser! When your business is done in the North, and when you realize that the Rage is not quieted, join me here and we'll conquer the Rising together."

"Something tells me it wouldn't end there."

"Well, of course not. Then we would have a falling out, split the Bars amongst ourselves, watch as loyalties are divided, and wage a proper, respectable war against each other. What do you think?"

"I think your utopia is my nightmare."

"No, Hadder, you'll be walking into your nightmare shortly."

19

V iktor Krill Lives!

There it was again, spray-painted on the lone wall where a Bar once stood. This was the third time Hadder had seen the message since the trio crossed over into North Rising, also known as the dominion of The Krown.

After his conversation with Ego Rounds, Hadder was once again invited to join the party of violence that defined Station's eastern third, but not before Ego provided Hadder with the general location of The Krown's encampment. Like Ego's, it was far from the Lethe, which separated their two controlled territories, and could be found in the northeast corner of the city.

Not wanting to run the entire Rising gauntlet, Hadder, Cal, and Otho simply went west from *Thug's Passion*, hitting the Skirt and following it north, back across the Caesar Bridge, where Hadder left his now-stifling jacket, and high into the city. When the northern Station Wall was in view, they cut east, entering the post-apocalyptic Mad Max world of The Krown.

This far from the Lethe, Hadder expected the landscape to mirror that of The Krown's nemesis to the south - defensive fortifications, military preci-sion, and controlled chaos. Other than chaos, the uncontrolled kind, Hadder saw none of these things. North Rising was a complete wasteland, complete with razed buildings, half-eaten carcasses, and scorched earth where wild-fires were employed as weapons.

Ten minutes into The Krown's territory, Hadder had seen very few Risers, and those he did seemed little more than scavengers, carrying trash they found back into sad, flapping tents that served as home. With very little else to note, the repeated graffiti messages were even more glaring. Hadder was unable to wrangle his curiosity.

"Who the hell is Viktor Krill?"

Cal and Otho shared a strange look, one Hadder had grown accustomed to in his short time with the behemoths. The look said that they knew something, didn't like what they knew, and weren't about to share what they knew with Marlin Hadder. Hadder kicked a loose stone in frustration, hurting the top of his foot, and made a mental note to ask others about this man who seemed so popular in the Rising.

On they walked, seeing more of the same, namely destruction of the highest order. With almost no organized protection to be seen, Hadder wondered why Ego couldn't easily take this turf with his sophisticated military tactics. Just ahead, a previous Cluster of Bars must have been the scene of a vicious fight. The bones of the Bars remained intact, decorated with burn marks, deep divots, and more of the same message.

Viktor Krill Lives!

The spaces between the ghosts of Bars had been filled in with large debris, probably taken from demolished buildings farther south and closer to the Skirt. The large piles of wreckage effectively cut off many of the options the trio had, forcing them to pass between two large buildings that faced and mirrored each other, most likely co-themed Bars from another, less violent time in Station's history.

As it was fast becoming late in the Solay, with the Idol Moon quickly retreating into itself, thicker darkness was descending on the city. This darkness only deepened as Hadder and his escorts passed between the towering buildings, sad things that seem to cry out for a return to the days when beautiful women and smart-looking men waited anxiously to gain entrance through their grand doors.

As they marched headlong into shadow, Cal and Otho began to look around, their large noses twitching. Cal looked down into Hadder's questioning eyes and said, "Risers. Lot's of em." Hadder kept a constant pace, not wanting to appear startled, but began searching the constrictive space around him. He saw the briefest of motion in a darkened window on the third floor. The soft sound of feet on dirt could be heard everywhere but seen nowhere.

The three continued on, wanting nothing more than to be free of the two monoliths at their sides, having had enough of feeling like cattle being herded to slaughter. As they approached the end of the twin buildings, a figure stepped out to block their path. Hadder, Cal, and Otho halted, taking a measure of the man. Although dark, the man stood beyond the deep shadows of the large alley, allowing the last rays of Solay to illuminate his frightful form.

Wearing only dirty jeans and worn black boots, the man didn't need clothes to look dramatic. That effect was created by the metal tusks that adorned his face, jutting out from each side of the man's jaw to kiss the air before him with a pointed touch. Although he had thick, should-length hair, few would notice, their eyes instead being drawn to the metal horns that leaped from the man's forehead, curling slightly backward. Not large, the man was imposing nonetheless, with tensed muscles looking prepared to uncoil on anyone foolish enough to get close.

As usual, Hadder was the first to break the uncomfortable silence. "I'm seeking a meeting with The Krown. I have a question for him, nothing more."

The man chuckled, making his blue eyes flash brightly in the dim surroundings. "You think this is a conversation? Or maybe even a negotiation? I can assure you it is neither. Take them."

Cal and Otho immediately dropped into fighting stances, their weapons appearing in their hands as if by magic. Hadder followed their lead, cursing himself for not bringing an instrument of his own. For the first time, Hadder felt that he may have put too much into Rott's promise of safe travel. Had Rott already lost more power than he imagined?

To either side and behind the trio, men began to emerge directly from the walls of the twin buildings. As they stalked forward, Hadder saw that their skin moved strangely, shifting from that of concrete to a grayish complexion that helped them blend into the shadowy background. Scores of the mimics appeared at once, surrounding the trio on all sides. From above, each window became occupied by a Riser, projectile in hand.

Caught in a trap, Hadder and the Caesars touched backs, guarding against sneak attacks. As the throng of mimics tightened around them, Otho grew tired of the posturing, slamming his broad ax through the meager defenses of a closing mimic and the metal pole it wielded as a weapon, splitting the man in half like a piece of firewood. Gore shot up like a paint bomb, covering mimic, Caesar, and man alike, forcing everyone to literally see red as battle rage engulfed all.

Hadder welcomed it, giving in to the Rage.

An explosion of action followed, the instantaneous violence reminding Hadder of the kung fu movies of his youth. Cal chopped down with his right sword, which was deflected by a mimic's oversized machete, but immediately backhanded with the same weapon, neatly slicing off the top half of the defending mimic's head.

Hadder wanted nothing more than to enjoy the scene but quickly found himself fending off attacks from two other mimics. The first came at his chest with a curved knife while the second swung a hammer overhand at his head. Hadder caught the wrist of the knife-wielder, pushing the blade out to pass in front of his body. In the same motion, Hadder executed a front kick on the second assailant, a perfect defensive Muay Thai technique for creating space. Catching the mimic squarely in the chest, air flew from the creature's lungs as the hammer flew from his hand. Hadder plucked the hammer from the sky and came down in a single move, caving in the skull of the first attacker, whose body went limp, sending the curved knife to the ground. Not wanting to leave himself open, Hadder simply kicked at the curved blade, sending it flying towards mimic two, who easily dodged the sloppy attack. But in doing so, he left his side unguarded, which Hadder happily took advantage of, blasting his shoulder with the hammer. The mimic fell to one knee as his clavicle shattered, turning to face Hadder, a curse forming on his lips. The curse fell flat, however, as his jaw was separated from his face by Hadder's next blow.

Pandemonium followed, rendering Hadder unable to even account for his own actions. Otho swung his giant ax in an arc, keeping fiends at bay, occasionally sending entrails high into the air. Cal took a more calculated approach, selecting targets and executing deft attacks and defensive maneuvers. A mimic's throat was slashed here, an eye was removed there.

Meanwhile, Hadder had to work extra hard to remain alive, fortunate that most mimic attention was on the imposing Caesars. Facing a variety of opponents, Hadder traded his hammer for a pickaxe, which he gladly left in the chest of a mimic in exchange for a slim rapier-like blade that almost made him a eunuch. After piercing a charging mimic's heart with the rapier, Hadder was surprised to see that his area had cleared, with overwhelming attention being placed on the Caesars.

Looking forward, there was nothing between Hadder and the tusk-faced man, who was obviously calling the shots in the battle. He remained standing at the end of the twin buildings, body cocked for violence as he surveyed the battle. He looked to Hadder and smiled, a natural act rendered unnatural-looking by the metal implants. Something snapped in Hadder, and he charged ahead, desperate to cut the accessories from the man's face and end this fight.

As he ran, Hadder planned his strike, considering potential attacks and counterattacks, readying himself for a bloody affair. Closing in, however, Hadder was surprised to see that the man had barely moved, had only brought his fingers to his mouth. A shrill whistle rang out across the alley, and Hadder doubled his efforts, afraid of what he knew was coming next. The tusked man was just outside of striking distance when the first quarrel struck him in the neck, his legs immediately turning to jelly. Hadder pressed on, readying his blade as two more bolts hit home, one latching onto his forearm and the other catching him just under the jaw.

Hadder took two more steps and fell face first at the feet of the tusked man, who remained unmoved during the whole ordeal. As unconsciousness fell over Hadder, he heard another whistle, sounding as if from a far-off land, and the ringing of metal on metal fell quiet.

———

ICY COLD WETNESS ripped Hadder from his deep slumber, transplanting him from a nightmare of blood-stained concrete, crumpled metal, and torn flesh into another only slightly less uncomfortable. As his eyes fought their way open, Hadder became aware of the pain in his hands, a thousand needles piercing his soft flesh. He raised his head and looked over, blinking away the water that had been unceremoniously thrown in his face, to find that his wrists had been tightly bound to a wooden board that ran across his shoulders. After feeling another board that ran vertically from the floor, Hadder quickly realized that he had been strapped to a crudely made cross. Out of mere reaction, Hadder tested the bindings, only to discover that they had been tied by a skilled hand.

Deep laughter, heavy and evil, tore Hadder from his physical predicament and demanded attention. Hadder raised his eyes and fought back a wave of terror that momentarily threatened to overtake him. Panic avoided, Hadder took note of the monster that sat before him. The beast that could only be The Krown.

While not as girthy as Ego Rounds, The Krown was a giant nonetheless, one that didn't hide his muscle under layers of fat. Looking as if he was chiseled from white marble, the hulking man sat on a throne of bones that was bound together with a clear epoxy, allowing one to view the remains that made up the macabre chair in all their glory.

The Krown wore black leather pants, black combat boots, and, like Ego Rounds, went without a shirt. Red, pink, and white scars crisscrossed the man's enormous white chest, a timeline of battles and wars. Putting aside Ego's unimaginable mass, The Krown was the largest man Hadder had ever seen, only marginally smaller than a Caesar. His jade eyes flared from a wave of deep anger, highlighting snakelike pupils, apt given that Hadder felt like a mouse cornered by a viper.

As Hadder continued his silent assessment, he soon understood how the behemoth came by his unusual name. Six long metal spikes stuck out from the man's skull, one positioned directly in the middle of his forehead, surrounding his shaved head like a small army of pikemen. Between each long spike, which Hadder had no doubt was used during fights, was a smaller one, probably more for decoration than its utility. Despite the frightful appearance, a small part of Hadder admired the man.

How do you ensure that your crown cannot be worn by another? Weld it to your fucking head.

Removing his stare from The Krown, who was still looking at him as if he were a steak, Hadder swept his gaze from side to side, making a note of what he could. They were in an enormous tent, heavy carpets were strewn about for comfort and lounging. To his left, Hadder saw Cal and Otho, standing at attention. Although they were not bound in any way, at least a dozen risers surrounded them, aiming cocked crossbows at their faces. Behind him, Hadder could hear wild laughter, the occasional argument, and a few choice insults thrown his way. This, coupled with the thick smoke that permeated the tent and stank of meat, told Hadder that he was in a kind of meeting or dining hall, not dissimilar to the one he visited in the south.

Four women, naked except for the leather hot pants and knee-high boots they wore, knelt to either side of The Krown's throne, pawing at him occasionally. Farther to the right of The Krown, the tusked man waited patiently, his eyes fixed solely on Hadder, offering a challenge.

The Krown shifted on his throne, leaned forward threateningly, and removed the hands of one of his concubines from his veiny shoulder. "The Caesars have informed me of why you have come, Marlin Hadder." His voice was deep and melodic, almost operatic in quality. Tremendous power resonated in that voice. "Tell me why I should do as you ask, and not burn you alive to feed my army." A cheer went up from behind Hadder, something soft and wet struck him from the side.

Hadder did his best to sound confident, a boy throwing stones into a tornado. "One of your men broke the cardinal rule of Station. Not only did he illegally cross the Skirt, but he murdered an innocent woman while there, someone who was beloved by the community."

"I don't see what any of this has to do with me, Setter."

"Some say that you ordered the attack, that you are testing the Skirt. If this is true, Albany Rott may have something to say about your rule here." A murmuring trickled through the hidden crowd. "But allow me my vengeance, and everyone will chalk it up to a lone wolf, acting only in selfish bloodlust."

"And you think I fear Albany Rott?"

There was a danger in the question. Hadder knew he needed to tread lightly before the unstable man-beast. "No, I don't. But I think you're not ready yet for an all-out war with him. You're still consolidating power in the Rising. Until that's done, you can't win a war against the combined forces of Rott's Caesars and Rounds' forces. You'd be stuck in a vice, squashed from both sides."

The Krown wanted to throttle the small man before him, wanted to tear him limb from limb, tossing the pieces to his dogs of war. But he couldn't deny the truth of what Marlin Hadder was saying. The war with Rott would come soon enough, but not now. All the pieces were yet to be put in place. "And who is it that you think wronged you, plain man? I would make sure that he is even one of mine before I entertain your proposal."

"The fiend's name is Skeelis." An eruption occurred behind Hadder, too many different sounds to pick out one general reaction.

The Krown smiled wickedly. "Ahh, yes, Skeelis. My treasured mercenary, my skilled killer. A valuable resource to me, Setter. Not one I will simply give away."

The tusked man walked over and whispered into The Krown's ear. The Krown's green eyes went wide, and his evil smile grew, showing teeth filed to sharp points, something Hadder had missed upon first glance. "I believe you remember Wagner here. He was the one who captured you and your Caesars."

"Easily captured, my king," added Wagner, his tusks bouncing with the words.

Hadder ignored the tusked man and addressed The Krown. "I don't see how he would know how easy it was. Pig-face here stayed so far from the battle, I thought him another Setter tourist."

Wagner stepped forward, a murderous scowl on his face, but was restrained by The Krown.

"Enough! Wagner here has come up with the most grand compromise - a chance at vengeance for you, some entertainment for me and my men. It's been too long since our last fight, and we miss the sight of blood." To no one in particular, "Someone, bring me Skeelis! And quickly!"

Hadder simply hung uncomfortably for the next few minutes, the pain in his wrists not being helped by the looks still being shot at him by Wagner, who had returned to his place on The Krown's right. Cal and Otho spoke quietly amongst themselves. If they were concerned about Hadder's safety, they positively refused to show it. Before long, Hadder heard the tent's large front flap open, and Skeelis lumbered past on warped legs to stand between him and The Krown, facing both. Thick leather encased his forearms, scabbards for his bladed arms.

"Skeelis, my pet, do you know this Setter who has come to us?"

The fiend known as Skeelis looked over to Hadder, recognition flashing in its dark eyes and on its scarred gray face. That wicked smile again, the same he'd seen when immobilized on the Skirt and in *The Soiree Noire* moments before Reena Song's brutal murder. A forked tongue poked out between pointed teeth as if tasting the air around Hadder, testing for fear. "I know not this Setter, my king," hissed the fiend in a high-pitched gravelly voice. "Most of those I meet join my collection of lovely masks, but I have not this face."

Hadder's eyes fell to Skeelis's belt, where there hung several masks of human flesh, reminding Hadder of their first meeting.

"Well now, Skeelis," The Krown continued, as if speaking to a child, "This man says you crossed the Skirt and hurt one of his lady friends."

"Skeelis doesn't hurt. Skeelis butchers." The fiend giggled.

"Butchered one of his lady friends, then. Why would you do such a thing, sweet Skeelis?"

Skeelis looked to The Krown, a questioning look on his abused face, as if he didn't know where The Krown wanted him to take this. "Poor Skeelis would *never* do such a thing, my king. But if poor Skeelis *were* to do such a thing, maybe he would do it because she poisoned the air with her sweetness. Maybe she made poor Skeelis's eyes water. Maybe poor Skeelis had to taste the source of this poisoned air. Maybe poor Skeelis wanted to see what she looked like holding her own head. But I would *never* do such a thing, my king. So I cannot say for sure."

The Krown chuckled to himself, obviously tickled by Skeelis's ridiculous half-confession. "All of us here are convinced of your innocence, dear Skeelis. Are we not!?" The crowd behind Hadder broke into a cheer. "But this man, this Setter, and these Caesars, they think you guilty. They want retribution from sweet Skeelis." Skeelis hissed at Hadder as the crowd began to boo. Another piece of half-eaten food struck Hadder from behind. "But I think I've come to a solution, one that will satisfy all aggrieved parties, myself included." The Krown stood up, began feeding into the crowd's growing excitement. "Sweet Skeelis, would you meet this man, this Setter, this accuser, in one-on-one combat!? To clear your good name and that of your cherished king?!"

Skeelis's wicked grin was back. He began to anxiously scratch at the leather hiding the razor-sharp blades that ran down his forearms. "I accept the challenge, my king."

The Krown spread his arms, speaking more to the throng than to the combatants. "Then, in one hour, let it be known that sweet Skeelis will face the Setter Marlin Hadder. The two will settle their differences once and for all - in the Meat Show!"

Cheers exploded across the meeting tent, a palpable buzz falling over the entire encampment. Hadder could hear Risers quickly exiting the tent, most likely to fill their heads with chemicals before securing good seats to the show.

The Krown spoke to Skeelis, showmanship all gone. "Skeelis, go prepare yourself. I want to see you wearing this man's face at dinner tomorrow. You'll be my guest of honor." Skeelis bowed and marched away, sliding the tube of leather down and showing the inside of his forearm to Hadder before passing out of sight. The Krown motioned to Hadder. "Cut the Setter down. Let him prepare for his fate."

Two Risers approached and cut the leather bonds from Hadder's wrists. He dropped to his knees from the assault of weight and rubbed his raw flesh, working to get feeling back in his hands. After a needed moment of recovery, Hadder worked his way back to feet to face The Krown, who had returned to his throne, a topless woman now on his lap.

"I have another condition to discuss regarding Skeelis."

The Krown, who was playfully choking the woman atop him, refused to look in Hadder's direction as he responded. "I'm a busy man, Marlin Hadder. A king has much to do, many moving pieces to control. I don't have time to waste. And negotiating with dead men is something I consider a major waste of time. You have your one-on-one fight, as promised. And you'll have your martyr's death, this I promise. Now get out of my sight. I'll see you soon. In the Meat Show."

20

Hadder and the trailing Caesars were marched due east towards the Station Wall, a small battalion of Risers encircling them with weapons at the ready. Cal and Otho were without their impressive blades, those having been confiscated when they were first captured. As Hadder walked, he tensed and released various muscles of his body, ensuring that each was primed for an explosion of movement. There would be no warmup period, Hadder knew, no feeling out rounds. He needed to be ready out of the gate. While he readied his muscles for a fight, he worked hard to control his breathing, using several relaxation methods he had picked up in his years of training across disciplines and teachers.

Within a few minutes, the group came upon a sizeable makeshift coliseum, crafted from discarded timber, and filled in with loose concrete. Although wide, with a large circumference, the arena wasn't very high, rising maybe thirty feet above the ground. There was only one entrance to the coliseum, a simple gap in the construction that had an ugly gate made of bones that was now pulled to the side. Risers poured through the hole, hooting and hollering, seemingly having made good use of the hour of preparation.

Every Riser that Hadder saw had some kind of extreme combat Elevation

- spiked knuckles here, a blade replacing a forearm there. Each wore scars from numerous battles, and all walked with the swagger of those who were confident in their ability to come out on top in physical confrontations. What they lacked in discipline and military precision, The Krown's army made up for in numbers, hatred, and a passion for bloodletting. If it came to open battle, Hadder questioned if Ego Rounds could hold up to The Krown's disciples. And if Ego Rounds fell, the remainder of Station was in grave danger.

Hadder finally reached the entrance gap and was welcomed by the decomposing bodies of two fallen Risers, one hanging on each side. Both had been up there for a while, with rib bones peeking through strips of falling skin and chunks of flesh missing, perhaps meals for some lucky scavenger. The corpses had been posed on their perches, arms swinging towards the gate to invite participant and spectator alike, zombie ringmasters welcoming everyone to a circus of death. To the right of the entrance, a large wooden sign had been nailed to the outer wall. In a shaky hand, three words had been written in blood, which had dried to a dark stain - The Meat Show.

"Last week's Meat, Setter," said one of the Riser guards to Hadder, drawing his attention back to the bodies. "I wonder how you'll look up there?"

"I'll make sure you look good, handsome boy," a female guard chimed in. "I'll pop that dick of yours out, carrion for the birds." All the Risers had a good laugh at that one.

As they passed through the gate and into the coliseum, Cal and Otho were pulled to the left, and all of the guards followed them save four who kept behind Hadder, guarding the gate, as he entered the arena. As he was about to step onto the sandy floor, a Riser poked his back with a metal staff. "Hey, Meat, can I have your shirt when you're dead?" The other three laughed at the question but stopped abruptly when Hadder turned back, a cold look in his eyes that chilled even their fiery hearts.

"No, you can't."

And with that, Hadder stepped onto the arena floor. It was supremely simple, with no obstacles or caches of weapons strewn about, just a sandy dirt floor that allowed for little in terms of sophisticated strategy. Large lights sat at the edges of the arena floor that, when coupled with the four spotlights that sat atop the coliseum wall, illuminated the show for all to see. The crowd of Risers roared as Hadder became clear to all, their collective noise rattling Hadder's eardrums and almost bringing tears to his eyes. Looking around, Hadder was surprised by the sheer number of Risers that The Krown had under his command. When all of his forces were assembled as they were here, Hadder could not deny that they were an impressive bunch.

To his left, Hadder could see The Krown sitting in what would be equal to box seats situated at the lowest level on the fifty-yard line. Concubines draped over him, The Krown sat comfortably, drinking from a horned goblet, waiting as if to see a movie to which he already knew the ending. On the other end of the arena, Skeelis paced back and forth, occasionally clasping hands with excited Risers in the crowd. Hadder supposed himself to be the away team.

A tiny man in a dirty orange tuxedo took the center of the arena to much fanfare. No more than four feet in height, the small man looked out of place in the Rising, where the meek certainly did not inherit the earth. A metal box gleamed at his throat, and three small horn speakers jutted out from his oversized head, one above each ear and another in the back. The Risers called out in unison, "Vizzano," and the man bowed in appreciation. He lifted his short arms into the air, sending the crowd into a frenzy, before dropping them and ushering in complete silence.

"My lovely Risers, how delicious it is to be joined here today." A giant's voice boomed from the diminutive man, multiplied many times over by the mechanism at his throat, and thundered into the air by his permanent head speakers. "How lucky are we, to serve The Krown, a just and noble king who knows what his people want. Nay! What his people need!" The crowd flared up, only to go quiet again. "On this beautiful Haela, under the Idol Moon, our benevolent king has put together, for our viewing pleasure, the resolution of a dispute between two men. One a fellow Riser, who shares in our dream of a fallen city. And the other, a cowardly Setter, whose name will be forgotten before it's even whispered on the lips of those who will mourn him.

"This will be a one-on-one affair, a fight of the purest sort, with no tricks or tomfoolery afoot. Hand-to-hand, that's what we like here, with nothing more than the man and his combat Elevations to prove his worth." Vizzano turned to face Hadder before continuing his speech. "And for those of us without combat Elevations, please kiss the reaper on your way out." Risers cried out in laughter, pointing at the fool who failed to even bring a knife to a gunfight. Vizzano faced the crowd once more, sucked in air for final delivery. "A fight! To the death! Two engaged in combat! One will leave as a man! The other will exit as Meat! My lovely Risers, I give you...The Meat Show!"

Super Bowls aren't this loud, thought Hadder as he watched Vizzano take another bow before stepping out of the arena, reappearing in The Krown's box seating, where he was promptly given a drink and a woman. The crowd had reached a new level of frenzy, would not be quieted until blood was shed, and a lot of it.

Skeelis began to stalk his way towards Hadder, that bowlegged walk more akin to primate than man. As Skeelis moved forward, he held both arms out wide to his sides, showing the razor-sharp blades that ran the lengths of both forearms. Although he was wearing one of his skin masks, that unmistakably cruel smile could still be seen through the mouth hole.

Hadder also began to move forward, bending low to scoop up a handful of sand on his way. Both men accelerated their paces as they approached the middle of the arena, Skeelis clearly out of control with bloodlust. When they were still several feet apart, Hadder noticed Skeelis's right arm cocking back for a sweeping blow aimed to neatly slice across Hadder's throat. Hadder immediately slowed his run and stepped into a front kick, catching Skeelis cleanly in the chest, his arm still out wide. The force of the kicked, increased by the fiend's forward momentum, blew air from Skeelis's lungs and forced him back. As he stumbled backward, Hadder threw his handful of sand into Skeelis's face. While the skin mask deflected some of the grains, many more found their way into the Riser's eyes.

Skeelis hissed a curse and threw his mask to the side before clawing at his eyes. Hadder moved in, delivering a straight right to the jaw followed by a leg kick that felt more like kicking a banana tree than a human appendage. As Skeelis stumbled, Hadder continued to throw blows, connecting with a left hook and right uppercut before finishing the combination with an overhand right that smashed into Skeelis's temple.

To Hadder's disappointment and surprise, the clean shots failed to drop Skeelis. Instead, they sent the twisted creature forward in a fury, arms hunting for flesh. With no time to move backward, Hadder pushed ahead instead, getting inside of Skeelis's blows and grabbing the Riser behind the head with both hands, securing a Muay Thai plum clinch. Pulling down with all his strength, Hadder forced Skeelis's head down while simultaneously bringing his left knee up, crushing the man's already destroyed nose.

As Hadder positioned himself for another strike, this time with the right knee, Skeelis brought his bladed forearms up to slash at Hadder in unison, opening deep cuts into the tops of his arms and forcing him to relinquish his grip.

Now it was Hadder's turn to stumble back, blood pouring from the long fissures that now adorned both arms. Skeelis continued forward, a hissing, manic laughter flowing from his crooked mouth. Hadder grew increasingly worried as his options became limited. The fiend's gnarly legs made leg kicks ineffective while its destroyed brain left head attacks impotent. Even worse, those devilish implants made clinch work a dangerous tactic that would leave Hadder a scarred mess even if he managed to win.

As these thoughts spun through Hadder's mind, his body also whirled, ducking a bladed arm from the right and jumping out of reach of an attack from the left. While Skeelis seemed invulnerable to tiring, Hadder certainly was not. His breaths grew labored, and his legs started to ache from the fast-twitch action he was demanding from his muscles. Hadder needed to make a move and fast.

After narrowly dodging another vicious combo that left a few more cuts on Hadder's arms and hands, the two combatants separated, circling each other warily. "Your woman cried when I held my blade to her throat,"

Skeelis shouted, his forked tongue dancing in the air. "A pity I couldn't enjoy her more. After I place your head next to hers, I'll find another to have more fun with. Any suggestions?"

Hadder had heard enough and reacted in seeming madness. He stepped into a sloppy, looping overhand left that rendered his entire side vulnerable, and Skeelis shrieked in delight. Quickly dropping under the telegraphed punch, Skeelis slid to the side and ran his bladed forearm against Hadder's open midsection.

Skeelis howled in glee as his blade ran the length of Hadder's abdomen, but stopped suddenly when he felt Hadder's left hand tighten on his right wrist instead of the warm entrails that he had anticipated. As Hadder spun around, his right hand joined his left in holding the Riser's arm out wide. In one smooth motion, Hadder leaped into the air, forcing Skeelis's controlled arm between his legs, and pulled back with all his strength.

Hadder's unanticipated weight pulled Skeelis to the ground, where he found himself on his back, Hadder's legs draped across his chest, and his cherished combat arm stuck between the Setter's thighs. Hadder arched his back, bending the fiend's arm across his body and exerting tremendous force on the elbow. Panic began to descend on the Riser as he realized the predicament he was in, stuck in a tight armbar with no referee to break the hold.

Desperate to extricate himself from the position, Skeelis began running his left arm along Hadder's legs in a sawing motion, hoping to remove the man's legs. Inexplicably, however, his razor-sharp blades would not penetrate the gray pant material. Hadder laughed from Skeelis's right. "What's wrong, my friend," Hadder said through gritted teeth. "Cannot cut through my Elevated clothing? I had it specially made for you - cut resistant. Amazing what the manikins can whip up for you if you're clear with your requests."

Understanding sinking in, Skeelis began to thrash, forcing Hadder to hold on for dear life. Showing unbelievable strength, Skeelis managed to roll to his left, sending Hadder up into the air to crash down onto the other side of the creature. Now both on their stomachs, Hadder continued to apply pressure, slightly readjusted his grip and pulled back with a lifetime of anger.

Skeelis screamed as his elbow bent in the wrong direction, a loud pop echoing across the coliseum and partially quieting the gathered masses. Skeelis arm now jelly in his hands, Hadder continued to twist and pull, taking grim satisfaction in the tearing of tendons and ligaments. Keeping a viselike grip on the Riser's wrist, Hadder positioned his feet against Skeelis's side and extended to his full length, taking a bladed arm along with him.

A fountain of blood erupted from Skeelis's right stump, covering Hadder in a crimson burqa. He stood up, towering over the whimpering creature writhing around on the red-stained sand. "Please! Please! Please!" cried the desperate Riser, "I've learned my lesson, really I have!"

Hadder stared at the now-silent crowd through blood-filled eyes, wanted them all to see him, wanted them to know what they would face if they crossed the Skirt. Skeelis rose pitifully as Hadder glared at the crowd, bowing to the man who had taken his arm. "Thank you, kind sir, they will sing songs of your.." Hadder would never find out the kind of songs they would sing as Skeelis launched into an attack with his remaining left arm. Anticipating the ruse, Hadder effortlessly sent the blow wide, blocking it with the appendage he held. He then swept the bladed arm in a horizontal arc, neatly cutting a line across Skeelis's exposed throat.

Skeelis dropped to his knees, a waterfall of blood appearing at his neck. He tried to say something through the bubbling river, but failed and fell forward, quite dead. The fight was finished, and Hadder was finished. But the Rage, it was far from finished.

Hadder bent over the body, his body shaking with angry energy, and used the bladed arm to remove the fiend's remaining arm, followed by both twisted legs. Finally, Hadder took Skeelis's head in his arms and sawed at the leathery neck until it came free in his hands.

Hadder left the head on the sand and collected the other appendages. With an armful of parts, Hadder marched over to the stands and began tossing the bloody appendages into the silent crowd. "You want meat! Here's your fucking meat, you fucking sub-humans!" Crowds parted where the meat landed; it seemed even these Risers had a limit to their insanity.

In the sandy sea of disbelief, blood-soaked Hadder walked calmly back towards the coliseum gate, picking up Skeelis's head on his way and cradling it under his left arm. As he approached the gate, the four guards remained unmoving. Hadder moved in close. "Get the fuck out of my way, Riser scum." The guards looked over to The Krown, who simply nodded, the hint of a smile on his pale face.

As the guards moved aside, Hadder stepped through and began exiting the coliseum. Behind him, he heard the familiar voice of Vizzano, addressing the audience. "Ladies and gentlemen, my lovely Risers, I give you...the Meat Show!" The place exploded in applause.

———

MARLIN HADDER SAT across from The Krown, caked in the fiend Skeelis's dried blood. Red flakes fell periodically, drifting down like ghoulish snowflakes to rest on the table between the two men. While Hadder had hoped to leave the Rising directly from the Meat Show, a regiment of Risers had met him outside the coliseum, stating that The Krown was requesting a private meeting. The word "requesting" fell out of the warrior's mouth coated in disbelief and annoyance. Apparently, the Risers were unaccustomed to their king making requests; he only dealt in demands.

To his credit, The Krown had offered a hose with which Hadder could wash off what was left of Skeelis, but Hadder declined, thinking it better to wear the badge of victory for a while longer. The two men now sat in a private tent, with only a table, two chairs, and three half-naked serving women holding trays full of drinks. Both The Krown and Hadder had drinks in front of them, Hadder's already almost empty. No guards were present, showing Hadder how little The Krown thought of his chances if he were to launch a spontaneous attack against the Riser leader.

Hadder leaned forward, elbows on the table, fingering his almost empty glass, adrenaline and Rage still present, but slowly fading into the background. The Krown leaned back comfortably, studying Hadder for an uncomfortable length of time. Finally, he spoke.

"I look upon you as if for the first time, Marlin Hadder."

Hadder looked up and met the giant king's green eyes. What may have passed for a smile hung heavy on the oversized man's face. "What do you want, Krown? Our business concluded with the death of that murderer Skeelis."

The Krown laughed lightly. "But business never concludes, does it? The execution of one deal simply leads to the next. And so on and so on. Our last deal was executed, successfully so I would say, and now I would like to propose another venture together."

"Let me guess, you want me to help you bring upon the Fall of Station."

The Krown's smile became a wicked grin. "Yes, you can certainly help me in toppling this infernal stalemate. But you're only looking at one side of the deal. What about what I can give to you?"

"There's nothing you can possibly offer me."

"How about a chance to play for the winning team? How about a chance to avoid a second, this time permanent, death? You see the numbers I have at my disposal. You see the animals that I lead. You think Skeelis special? He was an excellent killer, no doubt, but I have ten more just like him." The Krown's head cocked to the side as if he had just thought of something. "No one's told you, have they?"

"Told me what?"

"The tide has already turned, Hadder. The Riser crusade cannot be stopped. Every day more Setters cross the Skirt to join my ranks. Look around you; how do you think we run so deep? You think I have kidnapped these people? No, Hadder. The Station experiment has failed, as it was always meant to. These limited lives are no longer enough. The people demand possibility!"

"Possibility?"

"Yes. Possibility. Do you know why children, by nature, are happier than adults? It's because their lives are in front of them, with no limits. Dreams of being president, or a professional athlete, or a fucking astronaut abound; there are no restrictions. Our rebirth in Station made us children once more, another chance at life and the world at our fingertips. We even got tools that we didn't have before, tools that would ensure success in this new life." The Krown sighed heavily, took down the remainder of this drink in one large gulp. He motioned for one of the serving girls to bring more. As she delivered the beverages, The Krown stroked her bare breast absently, slapped her naked ass as she returned to the edge of the tent.

"But as the shine of this new life wore off, we became aware of the walls, became aware of the rules that control us. Our lives grew small, a Groundhog Day of experiences. And I saw us for what we really were - calves. Our movement was restricted, our activities were contained. Our muscles became weak and tender as we transformed into veal. And that's what we became - soft meat.

"It was this realization that led to the Riser movement. It is this realization that continues to drive Setters over the Skirt in record numbers. I am offering you a chance to join this inevitability, Hadder. And I only make offers once."

Hadder mulled over The Krown's words, had to admit that some good points were made. But in Hadder's mind, one key point trumped them all. "We had our chance in the world, Krown. We had it, and we blew it. All of us. We don't deserve another crack at it, and lord knows the world certainly doesn't deserve us showing back up, still full of anger and resentment, but now with Elevated bodies to act out our mania."

The Krown's jade eyes took on a hint of danger. "You talk of anger, but you have the Rage, Hadder. You have it like few I've ever seen."

Hadder took another drink, and his head fell. "I know this. But it's not something I welcome, it's not something I bathe in and cradle in my arms. And it's certainly not something I would want to be unleashed upon the world." The Krown had no reaction but to continue his serpent stare, so Hadder continued. "You say you tired of life in the Setting, and I get that. I also questioned what kind of life I could lead there, but I made a home and the best of the situation. You would rather wage war and play deadly games, and that's fine, too. But do it here in the Rising, ask Rott to extend the Skirt, but people don't deserve to die because of your boredom and ambitions."

The Krown leaned forward. "You dare speak Ego Rounds' words to me. What's next, will you spit in my face?" There was a challenge there, but Hadder would not take the bait. "Do you know what Ego Rounds is? He is someone who wants anarchy without chaos. He wants to organize lawlessness. He wants to control those who shun authority. He is a walking contradiction, a fat slob of a warrior. Why is it do you think that my numbers swell as his stagnate?"

"I think you promise the chance to hurt the innocent. And that appeals to most of these sick twists."

The Krown's hand came down on the table, almost splitting the thick wood. He deeply inhaled, an apparent attempt to calm himself. "I give my people something..." The Krown's large arms spread wide, "Grander."

Although Hadder grew tired of this conversation, there was something he remained curious about. "And why do you think you need me, Krown? I'm no one, have been in the city less than anyone."

"Oh, I don't *need* you, plain man. But you've been placed here by Rott for a purpose, at a time of great turbulence. The Rage you possess, the way you wield that Rage, makes you the perfect Riser. The respect you demand; yes, I see it already in my men, begrudging, but there, makes you a perfect wartime general. I'm going to win this war. I'm going to usher in the Fall. I'm going to conquer these walls. With you beside me, we could minimize casualties, charge the world with an armada of Risers. Take the world by the balls!"

"What makes you think Rott would ever allow you to escape these walls?"

The Krown shot Hadder a conspiratorial look. "It's been done before."

Hadder's eyes went wide. "Viktor Krill."

"Yes."

"Tell me about him."

"He was the first of us, the best of us. He denied Station and denied Rott. He almost singlehandedly ignited the Rising. Many of us thought as he did, but few would face the wrath of the Caesars. After setting off the Riser Wars, he retreated to the shadows, began to study the human form. He disappeared for months. When he returned, he was changed. He was more. Although he looked the same, he was faster, stronger, and smarter than anyone in history. This, coupled with unmatched nastiness, made him the most formidable man in the world. The Risers would have overtaken Station long ago were he still here."

"What happened to him?"

The Krown smiled. "One day, he was gone, and there was a dead Caesar next to the Station Wall. It was the first and only time anyone had gotten the best of a Caesar, and Viktor Krill did it by himself. He showed us that the Caesars could be killed, that the Wall could be overcome, that Rott could not keep us under his thumb forever. They try to say that Krill died in the desert, but we know better. Viktor Krill lives, and he's closing his fist on the world as we speak. It's our duty to join him."

"Well, I think that about covers it." Hadder rose to his feet, watched as The Krown's face darkened. "I thank you for your offer, but I'm afraid I must decline. You use intelligent words and some sound logic, but all of that is just to cover a fact."

"And what *fact* is that, plain man."

"That you're a killer. A killer with a reason is still a killer. You want to be a killer, be my guest. But you do it in the Rising. Not in the Setting. And not in the wider world. My Rage needs only a target. Proceed on this course, and you'll be next in its crosshairs."

After completing his speech, Hadder tensed, waiting for The Krown to attack. Instead, the giant king merely remained sitting, his face betraying two emotions - dumfounded respect and a desire to slay Hadder where he stood. When no actions unfolded, Hadder turned to leave but stopped to face The Krown again. "You never let me tell you my condition."

"What is your condition, Setter?"

Hadder held up the head he had been carrying with him since the Meat Show, Skeelis's dumb dead face staring out into the distance. "I'm taking this fucking head with me."

Hadder didn't wait for permission, simply turned and exited the private tent. Cal and Otho waited outside, their weapons returned to them. "Let's go. Quickly," stated Hadder as he passed between the Caesars and through the throngs of Risers still buzzing from the Meat Show. Hadder walked briskly and continued even when he heard the flap of the private tent rip open.

The Krown's voice chased him as he exited the Riser compound. "You had your chance, Marlin Hadder! After Ego Rounds kisses my crown, you'll be next! The Rising is mine! Station is mine! The world will be mine! Do you hear me, you Setter fuck! The world is mine!"

Hadder looked up to Cal as they walked. "I bet he wishes he had had me burned alive."

"There's still time," was all the Caesar said in reply.

21

Although Haela was quickly drawing to a close, with the first signs of Solay becoming visible, the Celebration Cluster was still buzzing with activity, residents stumbling from Bars giggling, not a care in the world. Hadder looked upon them as he would a child, knowing the atrocities that life had in store for them. Their custom outfits no longer looked chic and creative; they looked unnecessary, irresponsible. The residents skipping around, they looked like meat.

The Risers would feast upon these people.

Hadder limped forward towards the center of the Cluster alone, the Caesars having parted as soon as they crossed back over the Skirt, Cal stating that they had to report back to Albany Rott. Hadder's right leg throbbed where Skeelis's sawing had eventually made its way through the sturdy, specially-made fabric. His adrenaline had blocked the pain until they left The Krown's compound; now, it hurt like a bitch.

Eyes widened and followed Hadder as he slowly made his way through the groups of revelers, a crimson apparition come to rob them of their frivolity and innocence. Residents quickly cleared a path for Hadder, but remained a safe distance away; they were never much for missing a show. The broken metal pipe that Hadder had picked up in the Rising on his return made an uncomfortable noise as it dragged across the stone-laid plaza ground.

After what felt like a march for the ages, Hadder finally reached *The Soiree Noire*. Once a place of sanctuary, a place that helped heal a broken soul, the Bar now looked offensive, a museum for things that didn't matter. Hadder walked between residents gathered outside the Bar, slammed the jagged end of the metal pipe into the soft grass that surrounded the building, and completed his mission.

As he moved away, the screaming started. Men and women alike dove from the horrific sight, afraid that proximity to the installation may haunt their dreams. Fearful that the ghastly sculpture may reanimate, roll after them in their high heels and light-up shoes.

Hadder glanced back, admired his work. Under the bright lights of the Cluster, Skeelis had never looked better. The fiend's eyes had rolled back into his head, just showing the whites, and his long, forked tongue fell from his mouth to hang below his severed neck. Yes, Hadder thought, Skeelis had never looked better than with his head on a fucking stick.

A large crowd gathered, nearly everyone in the Celebration Cluster, to look upon the gruesome scene and its blood-caked creator. Hadder recognized countless faces in the group, but he was worlds away, unable to pull names from the space between them. A shrill voice cut through the collective murmuring.

"What is this? What *is* this?!" Monty the Mod swept down on his disk of light wearing a white Victorian suit, stepping off of the magical conveyance next to Skeelis's head. "Marlin Hadder, is that you? What in Station has happened to you, boy? And what is the meaning of this repulsiveness outside of my Bar? This is a place of celebration, not a horror show! I'm giving you five seconds to get rid of this repugnance, or I'm going to..."

Hadder's right hand shattered the little man's jaw before he could finish his idle threat. Monty crumpled to the ground and remained unmoving, his face looking extra stupid with a misaligned mouth. Hadder hadn't planned on a speech, but with every eye in the Celebration Cluster now squarely on him, he felt the moment called for one.

Hadder motioned to the spiked head. "This is the killer of Reena Song. Look at him! Scary, isn't he? There's a thousand more like him in the Rising, and they all thirst for your blood. It's only a matter of time before they cross the Skirt. That means, my well-dressed friends, that you all have a choice to make. Do nothing. Keep partying and fatten yourselves up for the slaughter. Or prepare. Get ready for the war that is coming. You like your lives here? Then you're going to have to fight for them." As Hadder began to limp away, he heard a voice from the gathered masses.

"But I'm a pacifist," said a man in the crowd.

"Then, your head will look good next to Skeelis's there."

———————

HADDER BARELY MADE it up the stairs of *The Royal Jelly*, his legs heavy from exertion, and his body drained of energy. As he entered the Bar, Royal turned quickly from his seat at the counter, his eyes red from exhaustion and worry. He ran towards Hadder, crushed him in a hug.

"I didn't think I was going to see you again, my boy. I thought you dead for sure." Royal separated, took a good look at Hadder. "But maybe I was right. Are you dead, Hadder?"

"Not yet. But soon, if I don't get some sleep."

"Of course, of course. You can tell me all about it when you wake. Let me help you."

Royal threw Hadder's arm over his shoulder and helped the weakened man to his living quarters. When the door opened, Hadder looked at Royal questioningly. "She took a room at *Cranesman*. Don't let it worry you. Once she sees you're back safe, you two will be peas in a pod once again before you know it. You want a shower?"

"No, just sleep."

Royal helped Hadder peel the crusty clothes from his body. "I'm gonna have these burned." Hadder simply nodded his assent. Royal walked to the doorway, stopped just before exiting. "What was it like over there? The Rising, I mean."

"Mad Max without the cool cars."

"Should we be worried?"

"Yes."

"Can we win?"

"I don't know. But we have no choice but to try."

———————

A TINGLING SENSATION in the pit of his stomach stirred Hadder from a deep slumber. Although he was still tired, Hadder was grateful for the intrusion that saved him from nightmares of Riser armies. As Hadder opened his eyes in the pitch-black space, he noticed something foreign on the other side of the room - red embers as if someone was smoking two cigarettes at once. Below those crimson lights, a symbol could be seen hovering in the air, humming with power.

"Light!" Hadder shouted in a panicked tone. Illumination filled the room, and twin cigarettes were revealed to be the eyes of Mister Albany Rott, who was resting in an armchair in the corner of the room, that jester's smile still plastered on his too-white face.

Mister Rott began to slowly clap; no traces of sarcasm were detected.

"Marlin. Hadder. Congratulations on your successful journey East. I must say, I'm a hard man to impress, but you've done just that. In a short time, you've run through the Celebration Cluster, made a home here in *The Royal Jelly*, met both Ego Rounds and The Krown, won a contest in the Meat Show, and made it out of the Rising alive. You've been in Station less than all others but have accomplished more than most everyone else. I was right to bring you aboard."

By now, Hadder had shaken the few remaining cobwebs of sleep, had moved to sit on the edge of the bed to face Albany Rott. "And why did you bring me aboard, Mister Rott? Ego Rounds and The Krown seem to think I am here to unbalance things, expedite some inevitability."

"And what do you think, Marlin Hadder?"

"I think I don't like being the pawn in some larger game."

"Tsk-tsk, Marlin Hadder. Larger game? Yes. But pawn? Oh, no, my dear boy. You are much, much more than a mere pawn. You are an essential piece. Not the king, obviously, that would be moi. But you are what dictates the game. The decisions you make will determine the future of Station."

"But why? This is your city. The future is your responsibility."

Rott stood, began to pace the room. "I'm a creator, Marlin Hadder, the greatest creator. But that's what I do, I create. I create, and I observe. I'm as excited as anyone as to how this will all turn out."

"Everyone's terrified, not excited."

Rott shrugged. "Same chemistry involved."

A thought struck Hadder. He narrowed his eyes at Rott. "If you really don't care about any of this, then why not open the doors? Allow those who want to leave to do so?"

"Impossible."

"Why?"

"There are larger rules at work, those beyond your limited comprehension. No one can leave the city."

"What about Viktor Krill?"

Albany Rott stopped his pacing. "My biggest mistake. My only real mistake. If I were a fisherman, he'd be the one that got away. I underestimated that evil little man. I never thought someone could decipher the code."

Hadder was at a loss. "What code."

"Why the code of the human body, of course. To its credit, humanity figured out some time ago that it fully utilizes a small percentage of its brainpower. What it never figured out, however, is that this inefficiency also applies to the human body."

"What do you mean?"

"I mean, dear boy, that that old body that you walk around in is a superpowered machine with restrictors installed throughout it. Somehow, Viktor Krill learned how to remove those restrictors. He discovered the code."

"Isn't that what Elevations are?"

Rott snorted derisively. "Elevations. Simple ways to spruce up your jalopy. Lipstick on a pig. No, I'm talking about abilities at the foundational level, real superhero shit." Rott's red eyes brightened as he spoke. "The stuff of gods."

"Like the Caesars."

Rott waved his finger in the air. "No, no. The Caesars are a completely separate construct. They are what you see, killing machines given simple, direct tasks. Viktor Krill is something much more sinister."

"And where is Viktor Krill? They say he lives. That he's out wreaking havoc on the world as we speak."

"He lives. But he'll be dealt with." Rott sat back down, thought a moment before continuing. "This is more than I've told anyone in forever, you know. For some reason, I feel comfortable speaking with you, Marlin Hadder. And that is an odd feeling for me."

"Why is that, do you think?"

"That. That, right there. You're inquisitive. You're riddled with anxiety but still do what needs to be done, ask what needs to be asked. You have compassion and kindness, but all of this resides under a blanket of barely controlled Rage, a Rage that is willing to do unspeakable acts. Tell me, how did Skeelis's head look on that pole?"

"Better. Much better."

Rott laughed, a strange sound from the powerful man. "Oh, but how I like you, Marlin Hadder!"

"If you like me, Mister Rott, then tell me the truth. Why do you tell me all this? Is it because you know I won't live long enough to do anything with this knowledge? Everyone speaks of the Fall. Is it inevitable?"

Rott's blood eyes tore into Hadder, reading his soul. "You want the truth, Marlin Hadder? I'll give it to you. I don't know why I divulge my secrets to you. I feel a strange compulsion to share with you. And for someone like myself, who controls so much, compulsion is a novel feeling that I wish to feed. Is the Fall real? Is the Fall inevitable? Much of that depends on the players involved. Much of that depends on you, Marlin Hadder."

And with that, Albany Rott rose, bringing an end to the conversation.

"Get some more sleep, Marlin Hadder. Unlike Viktor Krill, you haven't unlocked anything in that weak body."

"Tell me one more thing, Mister Rott. How do you know of this hidden code in the human body? What makes you such an expert on us?"

"An expert? Oh, you think so little of me, Marlin Hadder. I am *much* more than an expert. I am the warm hand that touched the soft, cold clay, making something from nothing."

As he finished his sentence, the room went dim, then dark, complete blackness enveloping Hadder. As quickly as it came on, it lifted, and Albany Rott was gone, leaving Marlin Hadder with disturbing thoughts and complicated truths.

———

AFTER TOSSING and turning for the better part of the Solay, Hadder finally gave up on getting any sort of restful sleep. He showered, obtained new clothes from a lemma manikin, ate a small meal, and headed out to find Lilly Sistine.

He first stopped at *Cranesman*, where Glen sat at his usual seat at the bar. Glen offered Hadder a slap on the shoulder and a smile as he sat down, tantamount to a raucous scream for the reserved Key. "Good to have you back, Hadder. All went well, I assume."

Hadder motioned for a beer from the manikin behind the bar. "As well as any trip to the Rising can go, I guess. Head still on my shoulders and all that."

"Which is more than we can say for the Riser that killed Reena Song."

The manikin delivered the beer, and Hadder drank deeply. "Word travels fast, I see."

Glen smoothed his beard. "Well, when someone mounts a head on a pike in front the Celebration Cluster's most popular Bar before knocking out said Bar's proprietor who is also an original Key, word tends to move like quicksilver. How was it on the other side?"

"Worse than I imagined." Hadder turned to Glen, looked him in the eye. "There's a war coming, Glen. The Risers won't be held back by the Skirt for much longer. If The Krown consolidates power, they're gonna try to bring the city down."

"The Fall."

"That's right. You know of it?"

Glen mulled over the question, took the opportunity to light a cigarette. He offered one to Hadder, who accepted and put it between his lips. Glen lit Hadder's cigarette before continuing. "Well, all of the Keys knew of the Fall, the inevitable end of the city. I'm sure you've heard the same from other sources, especially given the cast of characters you've met with recently, but Station was never meant to be permanent, was always just another pit stop on the way to the great beyond."

"Then what's the point? Why even create it?"

"You'd have to ask Mister Rott that one."

"So, what then? Are we just to let it die? Give up on our second chance the way we did the first time?"

"That's the question, isn't it, Hadder. What do you do in the face of the inevitable - fight or accept? Which is more painful?"

Hadder absently rubbed the gash on his leg. "Well, I can tell you first-hand that fighting isn't painless."

"Yeah, I see that you got a hitch in your giddy-up. You should get a manikin to look at that."

"I will." Hadder decided against avoiding the topic any longer. "Seen Lilly around?"

"Yeah, she stayed here last night. She heard you were back and went out a few hours ago. Check the usual places."

"I will, thanks." Hadder finished his beer and got up to leave. Glen stopped him with an upraised hand.

"You asked *why*. I think the city is either a test for us who have been given this second life, or it's just some grand experiment, and we're the guinea pigs. Or, hell, maybe it's both." Glen stopped to consider something, then resumed. "I'm not a happy man, Hadder, but I'm not miserable any longer, either. This place isn't much, but I made it, and I run it. And I ain't gonna run from it. Fight or accept? I choose to fight, but don't expect a similar answer from most residents. We've grown soft as the Risers sharpen themselves on each other. If you're gonna prepare for war, you're gonna have your work cut out for you."

Hadder nodded, made for the exit.

"And go gentle with Lilly. She thinks you chose a dead girl over her."

———————

LILLY SISTINE SAT ON A BENCH, staring into the magical waters of the Lethe River. Whether she was attempting to forget or remember Marlin Hadder was debatable. Hadder limped over and sat down next to her. She continued looking forward, sadness in her beautiful eyes.

"Something happened to your leg?"

"Yeah, someone tried to cut it off."

She laughed lightly, looked over to Hadder. "So, I guess you avenged your girl."

"Not *my* girl. *Our* friend. And, yes, she's been avenged. Our home is safe, for now."

"So that's it? I'm supposed to just forget that you left me, made a conscious choice to leave me, to run off into certain death, chasing the memory of a dead girl? You're right, Reena was our friend. But she's dead, and I'm alive. And you chose her over me."

Hadder had prepared himself for this moment, but the padding he erected failed to soften the blows. "I knew I'd come back, Lilly."

Sadness flashed into anger. "Bullshit, Marlin! You probably gave yourself a fifty-fifty shot at surviving, and that's because you're stupid. If Mister Rott didn't take pity on you and provide you with Caesar guards, you would have been dead thirty minutes into the Rising."

Hadder bit back a comment doubting that Albany Rott felt any emotion similar to pity. "But he did give me the Caesars. And I did make it back."

"But if he didn't give you the Caesars, you were still going to go."

Dishonesty seemed a poor tactic at this time. "I was." The slap came out of nowhere, sent Hadder's face to the side. Thrown with a shaking hand and powered by hurt, one of Lilly's large rings caught Hadder above the eye, opening a cut and sending blood streaming down.

Lilly's eyes went wide at the blood, and her hands went to her mouth. "Oh my god, Marlin, I'm sorry."

Hadder managed to smile through the pain, tried to blink away the blood. "I probably deserved that. Feel better?"

Lilly stood and began to wipe the blood from Hadder's face with her white t-shirt. The hint of a smile formed. "A little, actually."

"Want to try the other side?"

Lilly playfully hit Hadder on the shoulder. "Don't tempt me, Marlin Hadder. I can be more dangerous than any stupid Riser."

"I believe it. I was more frightened of seeing you than meeting The Krown."

"The who?"

"Doesn't matter. I'm here now. And I'm not leaving." Hadder pulled Lilly towards him, engulfed her in a passionate kiss, a tenderness to counteract the recent Rage. They separated, and Lilly had Hadder's blood on her face. "You've got blood on your face, Lilly."

"Leave it. Maybe I'll cosplay as Marlin Hadder tonight, the demon of the Celebration Cluster."

"You heard about that, too?"

"Everyone's heard about it, Marlin. You didn't exactly make a subtle return."

"It needed to be done."

"Did it? Or maybe you just got off on scaring the shit out of the Celebration residents."

"Can't two things be true?"

"I suppose they can. Come on, let's get that leg and those arms looked at. Who knows what kind of bacteria you picked up in the Rising."

Hadder rose on unsteady legs, found his throat seized in Lilly's small hands. "Promise me you won't go off again. Promise me the death wish and killing ends here."

"I promise," replied Hadder, grabbing Lilly Sistine in a tight embrace. As he held her, drinking in her sweet smell and soft body, Hadder smiled to himself, thinking that one out two promises kept ain't half bad.

———

THE NEXT FEW weeks passed uncomfortably, like Hadder was wearing a costume of wool. Lilly Sistine moved back into *The Royal Jelly*, but the honeymoon was over. Small missteps brought upon strong reactions and poorly selected words ushered in perfectly selected insults. Despite these tribulations, their relationship healed slowly.

Solays were spent much as they were in those better days - small concerts on the lawn, long walks to the Samsara, and trips to other Clusters.

When he could, however, Hadder would sneak off with Royal or Glen, visiting other Bar proprietors or Cluster leaders to warn them of the impending Riser attack. Some would listen; most would not. For many, total faith was placed in Albany Rott and his Caesars to protect the Setting and its vulnerable residents.

Whether they were receptive to advisement or not, Hadder always left them with some - begin preparations. This entailed fortifying areas, collecting or making weapons, and organizing watches. Despite Hadder's prominent status because of his victory in the Rising, time was all most residents would offer him, going back to their chemical drinks and smoky lounges once he departed.

"They just don't get it," Hadder said to Royal as they walked back from another set of fruitless meetings with impotent residents.

"They didn't fight hard for their lives in the Before. Chances are they ain't gonna fight hard for Station, either."

Royal's words rang true, and he couldn't help but recognize that he, too, surrendered his previous life. But he was another person now, walking hand-in-hand with a Rage that would not allow him to roll over. In Hadder's opinion, the Fall was only considered inevitable given that the people of the Setting were inevitably going to be fearful and docile, too consumed by paralysis to act. Hadder aimed to change that.

As Hadder and Lilly's injured partnership healed, rumors trickled out of the Rising. The Riser Wars, now merely a battle between two titans, was back on in full. Hadder felt a twinge of guilt as he climbed the Perch to see pillars of smoke emanating from South Rising. Perhaps his appearance had upset the balance, expedited the war. Or maybe he was just the excuse The Krown needed to drive his Risers into a frenzy of violence necessary to overtake Ego Rounds' organized defenses. Either way, things were progressing quickly now, the wheels of destiny turning.

Hadder took in the landscape, taking mental notes, using SWOT analysis to help guide his thoughts. There was much to do, but Hadder felt that there was time.

He was wrong.

———

THE MAIN DOORS to *The Royal Jelly* blew open, sending the last rays of Solay into the Bar. DD Bryce, a kind resident of no consequence, soon followed, his legs barely staying under him as he sprinted towards Royal, who was restocking the bar for the night's concert. Hadder and Lilly, setting up instruments on the stage, turned towards the ruckus.

"The Risers! The Risers!" repeated DD as he fell against the counter, trying in vain to catch his breath. Hadder and Lilly ran up as Royal poured the exhausted man some water.

"What are you saying," demanded Hadder as he reached DD. "What about the Risers? Talk, man!"

"Let him catch his breath first," said the always kind Lilly.

DD took huge gulps of air, chased them down with equally large swallows of water. He finally nodded his head, able to continue. "The Risers, they're gathering at the Skirt."

Panic seized Hadder. It was too soon, far too soon. "Where are the Risers from, the North or South?"

DD shook his head. "Hell if I know. But there are two large groups of them gathered just south of the Caesar Bridge. Looks like every fucking Riser in the city."

Hadder's face wore a mask of worried confusion. "Which way are the groups facing? Are they facing the Skirt?"

DD shook his head frantically. "No, no. They're facing each other. Looks like they're putting on a goddam show."

"So they are," whispered Hadder to himself.

"What was that, Hadder?" said Royal.

"I said DD is right. They are putting on a show. They want all of Station to see their forces, see who's going to come out on top. Ego Rounds versus The Krown. For all the marbles."

"Then what the hell do we do, Hadder?" Royal sounded legitimately concerned, the first time Hadder had sensed concern in his unflappable friend.

"We go watch."

————

RESIDENTS from across Station had gathered on the western side of the Skirt. Hadder, Lilly, and Royal fought their way through the masses to reach the front of the crowd. Several residents voiced their displeasure with being pushed out of the way, but quickly moved aside when they saw that it was Marlin Hadder parting the throngs.

As the trio reached the Skirt, they found Glen already there, staring across the barrier into the dark unknown. Simple nods were all that were exchanged in terms of greeting. The eleven Caesars stood on the Skirt dozens of yards apart like sentinels, weapons in hands ready to draw blood, daring the Risers to cross.

Across the Skirt, two Riser armies had gathered. The Krown's obviously larger, somewhat disorganized soldiers stood in stark contrast to Ego Rounds' smaller force that held tight formations, blades at the ready and projectiles aimed with steady hands. Looking at the collected warriors, it looked to Hadder that The Krown's numbers dwarfed those of Ego Rounds, even more so than previously thought. It seemed that the past few weeks of fighting had favored the North, tipping the scales even further in the direction of The Krown.

During their hurried trek to the Skirt, Solay had fallen into Haela, dimming the city and the battlefield Hadder now faced. The bright lights of the Skirt, however, clearly illuminated those Risers closest to the Setter audience while torches and bonfires lit the remainder of the armies. From the gathered Risers on the right stepped Ego Rounds, his massive form unmistakable against the backdrop of his men and their fires, light gleaming off the metal knuckles that adorned his hammer-like hands.

Ego Rounds continued forward, stopping about twenty feet in front of his followers. "The Krown! Let it be known that I, Ego Rounds, challenge you to one-on-one combat, to the death. May the victor control the Rising and the fate of Station. Do you accept? Or would you rather forfeit your power and retain your life? The choice is yours!"

Complete silence fell over the scene, stealing sound from both Riser and Setter alike before deep laughter cut through the muted air. The Krown stepped out from between his supporters, his jade eyes wild with excitement and bloodlust. He moved forward on light feet, more animal than man, also halting twenty feet ahead of his forces.

As Hadder looked on at the increasingly barbaric scene, puzzle pieces clicked into place, allowing Hadder to see the entirety of the picture. Over the last few weeks, Ego Rounds had clearly seen that his men, despite their superior discipline and tactical know-how, were no match for the North's vast numbers, insane combat Elevations, and unmatched ferocity. As the men and women under his command fell, Ego made a brave choice, a challenge that he knew The Krown could not shy away from, lest he loses the faith of his minions.

Ego Rounds was going to win or lose the Riser War here and now. Hadder's stomach churned. Whether from anxiety or a desire to join the fracas, Hadder was unwilling to ask himself.

The Krown, although half as girthy as Ego Rounds, towered over his enemy. While Ego was tall himself, he was dwarfed by The Krown, who came second to only the Caesars in terms of body intimidation. The Krown let the size discrepancy sink in for a moment before he spoke. "Ego Rounds! You know you are beaten; these last weeks have shown you the futility of your resistance. Anyone can see that this is a desperate attempt to steal victory from my jaws of defeat."

Ego Rounds shot back. "You sound frightened, my melatonin-deficient friend. Does The Krown fear a fair fight with a strong black man?"

The Krown laughed again. "Not at all, Ego. Just pointing out that I see the cause of your newfound bravery. This is the final card you have to play. Unfortunately for you, it's not the one you need."

"I tire of your words, you pale muthafucka. Accept or fuck off. Let all your men see who you are when you aren't hiding behind them."

The Krown's green eyes flared. "I accept. Happily."

"No weapons. No assistance. Just you and I."

The Krown grabbed ahold of one of the spikes jutting out from his head, pulled at it for effect. "These don't come off, Ego."

Ego held up his battering ram hands, showing his metal knuckles to The Krown. "These don't either. We'll call it even. You ready?"

"I've been ready. Tell me, when I open up that fat chest of yours, will blood or gravy come pouring out?"

"I'm going to rip those ridiculous rods out of your head, white boy. Maybe melt them down and fashion my own crown from your memories."

The Krown began to pace. Hadder could see the anger welling up in him. "You won't take my crown! But you will kiss it! Come now! Come kiss it!"

The Krown's army roared to the heavens, and Ego Rounds' minions, although fewer in number, matched their foes with a savage scream of their own, followed by chants of "Ego." Hadder's heart threatened to punch a hole in his chest as he watched the two titans face off.

Ego Rounds, finally tiring of the posturing, took off in a sprint towards his pale nemesis. Although massive, Ego moved impossibly fast, his light feet a blur against the Rising's broken ground. The Krown smiled wickedly, took five giant steps forward, and dug in. Ego came on like lighting, slamming into the taller man, and releasing a thunderclap that stole the air from everyone on the battlefield.

Although he was forced back, The Krown refused to fall, eventually holding his ground against the boulder that was Ego Rounds. The first attempt foiled, Ego separated and squared up, his metal knuckles waving threateningly. The Krown followed suit and initiated fisticuffs with a looping left hook that caught nothing but air. Two jabs also failed to find their target, and a straight right was blocked by Ego's left arm protecting his head.

Now it was Ego's turn. He immediately followed The Krown's blocked right with a right hook of his own, catching the man in the ribs and drawing a pained grunt. The Krown's arms fell slightly from the blow, and it was all Ego needed to launch a full-scale attack. A high left hook passed above The Krown's defensives to catch him on the temple while a straight right shattered his nose, sending a river of blood to cascade over the man's mouth and chin. Aided by his metal knuckle Elevation, Ego was tenderizing The Krown and wouldn't need many more clean shots to end the fight.

The Krown staggered back, wiping his messy face, and reset. Concern dotted the monster's visage as he began to truly understand the might of his foe. As Ego danced towards him again, preparing another vicious combination, The Krown clearly realized that he was no match for his dark-skinned competition on the feet, and took a new approach.

The Krown darted forward, getting inside of Ego's dangerous hands, and slammed his head down, looking to send his central spike into the South Rising leader's face. Ego anticipated the move, however, and caught the metal skewer with his meaty left hand. For a long moment, progress was halted in either direction, the massive men's muscles tense as they waged a war of attrition. Slowly but surely, The Krown's head began to lower, lance inching closer to Ego's exposed face.

With a primal yell, Ego twisted violently to his left, turning The Krown's weaponized head away from Ego's face and into the perfect position for what came next. Not only did the frantic maneuver, place Ego's face out of harm's way, it also freed up his right arm that had been previously contained by The Krown's left. Still controlling The Krown's head via his iron grip on the central head spike, Ego Rounds threw the hardest right hand of his life at the immobilized target, connecting squarely with the North Riser's jaw and sending him reeling backward. As The Krown stumbled, Ego moved in for the kill, fainting right and throwing a textbook left hook that caught the wobbly man on the tip of the chin with the metal knuckles, sending him to the ground, unconscious.

Both armies were shocked into stunned silence as the seemingly invincible Riser leader fell. Ego Rounds, shaking with adrenaline, lifted his hands to the sky in a sign of victory, sending his men and women into a frenzy. His people urging him on, Ego stalked towards his unconscious foe, his crazed eyes glazed over in bloodlust. "I told you," he yelled to the body at his feet, "That I was gonna rip those goddam spikes off your goddam head!"

Ego kneeled at The Krown's head, ready to finish the battle in gruesome fashion. Reaching for one of his foe's cherished Elevations, Ego stopped suddenly, seeing a wicked grin on The Krown's face. Recognizing the ruse for what it was, Ego lurched forward to grasp those deadly points.

But he was too late.

The Krown opened his evil jade eyes and thrust his head forward in a blink, his too-thick neck sending the central spike through the air like a spear to pierce Ego Rounds' enormous left knee. Ego roared in pain and fell back to land hard on his backside.

The Krown was up in an instant, readying a blow of his own. Ego attempted to stand but immediately collapsed, his enormous weight too much for the ruined knee. Just as Ego hit the ground again, The Krown connected with a looping uppercut that blasted Ego's head backward and sent the girthy man to his back.

The Krown fell upon him like a swarm, raining down heavy lefts and rights, many of which snuck through Ego's compromised defenses. With a useless left leg, Ego was unable to get to his feet. The remainder of the fight would take place on the ground, in The Krown's world. A downward left opened a cut over Ego's right eye, and a sharp elbow, although partially blocked, caused a significant contusion to form on his dark forehead.

With Ego clearly dazed, The Krown got back to his feet and launched into the second phase of his attack, firing heavy, booted kicks at his downed opponent's face and head. Hadder grew nauseous as he watched Ego Rounds, a man he hardly knew but had quickly gained respect for, eat kick after kick, punch after punch, from the beastly Krown.

After what felt like an eternity, The Krown stepped away to admire his work, also providing Hadder with a clear view of the downed man. Ego's face looked like a catcher's mitt, swollen beyond recognition, and he bled from a dozen wounds, leaving crimson liquid to pool on the rough ground. Ego, showing pure heart, tried to rise but fell back to his elbows, his body refusing even simple commands.

The Krown laughed deeply, a hateful sound that served as the perfect backing track for the dark scene. He yelled to the South Risers. "Is this your king? This tub of a man? No more!"

With that, The Krown stood above the prone Ego Rounds. "I told you, Ego. Everyone, especially you, must kiss the crown." A scream of pure heartbreak broke through the Haela, and Hadder looked over to see Kamaria burst from the crowd of South Risers, three men putting forth full effort to hold her back. The Krown glared at Kamaria and shot a cruel, sharpened-tooth smile at her, watching gleefully as her tears discolored the dusty ground.

"And so, the Riser Wars end," Royal simply stated at Hadder's side. Lilly gripped his hand in hers.

The Krown bent low, took Ego's head in his large hands, and ran his central head spike through the man's skull, pressing down until the two Riser legends touched foreheads. The Krown then kissed Ego Rounds gently on the lips as the life drained from his eyes. He held the pose for a moment, allowing all in observance to fully take in the scene, before rising and backing away, pulling the lance from the fallen Ego Rounds.

The Krown rose to his full height, and Ego's blood ran down the spike and fell across his pale face, giving the monstrous man a makeup job that made him even more terrifying. Hadder looked over and saw that Kamaria had stopped fighting, was now simply weeping into her leather-gloved hands.

The Krown took center stage, addressing everyone in earshot. "I am The Krown. And I claim victory over Ego Rounds, bested him in fair combat. The Rising, both North and South, now belongs to me. South Risers! You have until the end of the next Solay to report to my encampment, where you will finally join the winning team and aid our preparations. My army will sweep South at the turn of Haela to collect resources and establish bases. Any Riser found below the Lethe will be eliminated. Brutally. Do not die for nothing! Pledge allegiance to your new king, and together we will escape these walls and make the world pay for their crimes against us!"

The Krown's followers exploded into a cacophony of hoots, hollers, and applause. Much to Hadder's surprise, some of the South Risers followed suit, shouting and raising weapons into the air. The Krown continued. "Go now. Go, my Risers. Celebrate. Rest. Celebrate more. Rest more. For soon, soon, my precious Risers, we shake free of the shackles of our oppressors. Soon, we will slay the Caesars, conquer the weak Setters, and exact our vengeance on the world!"

The Riser jubilation reached a fever pitch, and Hadder feared an all-out riot and spontaneous advance across the Skirt. Risers from both sides moved closer to the Skirt, shouting curses at the row of Caesars. In return, the Caesars adopted fighting stances, battle-axes, cudgels, swords, hammers, sickles, and flails readied in the air.

The Krown laughed again but turned to face his followers with upraised hands. "I love the passion, but not yet, my pets. Let us cock the bow back farther before releasing our arrows. Then, we shall penetrate any resistance put up against us."

The Risers, whether from The Krown's words or the frightening, unified Ceasar front, backed away, slowly bleeding into the dim Haela before turning and disappearing into the darkness.

The Krown turned once more to face the Setter audience, looking through the line of Caesars. His fiery green eyes sought out and found Hadder among the residents. His wicked smile was gone, replaced with a look of what could almost be labeled disappointment. "Marlin Hadder. I see you looking on. I can feel your unrest. While you lie next to your woman like an old man, the Rage inside you begs for blood, thirsts for pain - two things you know I could give you. But don't worry, Hadder, this isn't an invitation. No, you had your chance. The only man to spit in my face and live. Well, rest assured, Hadder, I will rectify that issue, right that wrong. I called you a dead man before, and still, you are. Do not get comfortable in your small reprieve. Ready your weak Setter friends. I'm coming for you. Even Albany Rott cannot protect you forever." Having concluded his business and having said his piece, The Krown marched away, head held high and metal Elevations reflecting the small Idol Moon's rays.

A small contingent of South Risers remained behind, led by Kamaria. They approached the still body of Ego Rounds, each placing their hands on the large man's chest in a show of respect. They attempted to move the giant's corpse, failing three times before two Caesars joined them in their efforts. Eventually, the fallen Riser was successfully raised into the air and carried back towards his home in South Rising, where he would be given a funeral fitting a king.

Lilly quietly wept on Hadder's shoulder as Royal and Glen stood in respectful silence. Hadder and the other residents moved to return to their Clusters and Bars and living quarters, leaving the Caesars alone to guard the Skirt. As Hadder walked, he looked up towards the distant blackness of Rott Manor. There, on the roof of the building, two embers burned bright and clear, taking in everything beneath them, missing nothing.

But whether they cared or not, Hadder couldn't know.

PART III

AN INEVITABILITY CALLED THE FALL

22

"**M**ister Rott won't let that happen. The Caesars won't let that happen. They've always protected us, and I don't see why that would change."

Hadder threw his arms up in exasperation and readied some harsh words for Blindman Stu, the resident leader of a Cluster just west of *The Royal Jelly*. Hadder was stopped, however, by Royal Winter's gentle arm on his shoulder, selecting instead to stare daggers into Blindman's white eyes. Blind when he came to Station, Stuart Jenkins was gifted both his nickname and his sight by the city. Obviously, he felt a tremendous obligation to Station, but not enough to bleed and shed blood for it.

Royal put Hadder's thoughts into kinder words. "You were at the Great Duel, Blindman. You saw, with those fantastic new eyes of yours, the numbers the Risers now have. You saw the strength and brutality of The Krown. Did you know that since the Great Duel, Riser numbers have continued to grow? Our way life is at dire risk. If we don't do anything, we'll all be welcoming a second death shortly."

Blindman's white eyes moved between the two men making appeals. Although his sight had been restored, Blindman has chosen to keep the dead look of his eyes. Perhaps he was still dead inside, as well. He retorted, "No ten men, twenty men, can best a Caesar; they're demigods. And Mister Rott will never let his city fall; I refuse to think otherwise."

Even Royal now was becoming annoyed. "Blindman, the Caesars were created to manage a few bad apples, not truckloads of them. Soon, the Risers will have the numbers and the unity they need to overpower even our colossal defenders. And as for Mister Rott, I don't know that he cares for the city in the way that he once did. Perhaps he is simply waiting for its destruction, using its fall as an excuse to move on to other things."

Blindman's face remained impassive; he wasn't hearing anything Royal had to say. "Well, I thank you, gentlemen, for stopping by. I understand your concerns; I really do. But sometimes in this world, you have to have a little faith. I choose to put my faith in Mister Rott and the Caesars. They've yet to let me down."

Hadder and Royal walked away dejected. It had been five Solays since the Great Duel, and they had failed to reach even one significant resident leader. All wanted to go blindly about their lives, oblivious to the storm clouds forming in the East. Royal tried to offer some hope. "Well, the word is there's still fighting in South Rising. Looks like a lot of Ego's people aren't just gonna turn the keys over to The Krown."

"I'm sure Kamaria is putting up a hell of a resistance. But that just buys us time, not absolution. And right now, we're doing exactly jack shit with the time she's giving us."

"So, what do we do, Hadder?"

Hadder sighed deeply, bemoaning what he was about to say. "We're gonna have to wait for someone to die. Someone big."

———

MARLIN HADDER and Lilly Sistine laid together in the comfort of a freestanding hammock erected in the lawn of *The Royal Jelly*. As they swung slowly late in the Haela, they watched the iridescent insects and glowing flowers play their colorful games in one of the gardens that bordered the Bar. Lilly was exhausted, having delivered an especially powerful musical performance on stage hours prior. Water-filled eyes peppered the audience as she concluded the concert with Otis Redding's "Pain in My Heart." Now she rested, floating in and out of consciousness.

"Marlin?"

"Yes?"

"You think I'm good enough to make it in the Before?"

"I think the world wouldn't even know what to do with a talent such as yours, Lilly. I think you would set the music scene on fire."

"Yeah, but I guess we'll never know for sure, right?" Her voice sounded far away, as if coming from a dream.

"I think you're just going to have to take my word for it."

"Yeah, I guess so."

"But the world's loss is Station's gain. Your voice brings so much joy to so many residents. You really enrich our second lives."

Lilly nuzzled her face into Hadder's neck. "Thanks." Then she drifted back to sleep.

HADDER AND GLENN continued their trek through the city, making a note of possible defensive positions, resources to be utilized, and locations for potential ambushes, all while spreading the word - war is coming.

The Solay was quickly drawing to a close, with the two men having already swept south to take account of the Weep, the New Age Cluster, and another unnamed Cluster before hitting the Skirt and turning back north. The men kept a nervous eye to the East as they walked, waiting for berserkers to tear across the Skirt with mean-looking blades and angry hearts. And while none appeared, the spiraling smoke columns and occasional screams showed that the Rising was still far from a peaceful, unified territory.

From the south, Hadder and Glen eventually marched into the Celebration Cluster, which was just beginning to fill with life. Celebration residents moved quickly from Hadder's approach, fearful of the man who had entered the Rising with nothing and returned with a head - a head that he mounted in front of the poshest Bar in the area. Hadder ignored them and went about his work, making comments to Glen and taking in the older man's insightful opinions.

"What about *Inferno*," asked Glen as they passed the red monstrosity. "High vantage point, only a couple of entrances, strong foundation."

Although Hadder barely looked at the rose-covered building, he could still make out the human marionette hanging above the entrance doors, lording over her small, insignificant dominion. "Let the Risers have it if it comes to that. And if they don't burn it down, I'll do it my goddam self."

Glen began to formulate a retort, complete with logic and practicality but stopped when he noticed the smoldering in Hadder's eyes, a nugget of heat that threatened to become a wildfire. "Fair enough. Let it burn. Jackie Crone won't even have to change the sign."

As they rounded the corner and left *Inferno* behind them, Glen pointed out a man stumbling about, yelling at both residents and inanimate objects alike. "Jesus, look at this poor sonavabitch. Just turned Haela and he's already a mess, like the Weep shit him out directly into the Celebration Cluster."

Hadder squinted against the early Haela backdrop and sighed. Up ahead, making himself a fool while making others uncomfortable, was his old friend Jonny VV, someone who helped him when he much needed it. It was time to pay off a substantial debt. "I know him, Glen."

Glen wore a confused look. "Friend of yours?"

"Yes. Yes, he is."

Hadder approached the drunken Jonny VV, whose usually immaculate suit was stained with dirt and caked with grime. The man looked as if he had aged ten years since Reena's passing. "Jonny, Jonny," called Hadder as he came up behind Jonny VV, who turned and fell onto his backside at the sound of his own name.

Hadder rushed over to his friend. "Jonny, it's Hadder. Marlin Hadder."

Jonny VV looked up through unfocused eyes. "Hadder? Is it truly you, old chap?"

"Yeah, it's me, my friend. You don't look so good. Where are you going?"

"Oh, you know me, old boy. Just on my way to join the festivities." Hadder could barely make out the words Jonny's fat, swollen tongue was making. "I told Reena to wear something extra stunning, so I'm on my way to meet the old girl."

The bruise on Hadder's heart ached once more, and Glen moved a safe distance away in discomfort. "Jonny. Reena's dead, Jonny. She's gone, remember?"

Jonny nodded dumbly. "Oh yeah, that's right. Quite right, old chap." Jonny began to cry, tears leaving clean lines on his otherwise grimy face. "I loved her so. You know that, Hadder?"

"I know, my friend. We all did."

"She's the only one who got me. Really got me. She was mom, sister, and friend all in one. She was all I had."

"That's not true, Jonny. You have lots of friends here, but you need time to heal, away from the fucking Celebration Cluster and these soulless runners. What do you think, old friend?"

Jonny's eyes finally focused on Hadder, who leaned back on his heels from the pain he saw in those red, irritated eyes. "I think I'm tired, Hadder."

"Would you like to rest, my friend?"

"Yes, please. I would very much like that."

Hadder reached down and helped his friend up, throwing Jonny's arm over his shoulders and pushing down the feeling of nausea that erupted from the smell of his troubled companion. "Glen, I want to complete our loop, finish the analysis. Would you mind taking Jonny here back to *Cranesman* with you, find him a room, and some hot food? I owe this guy a lot."

Glen softened under the scene of Hadder holding up his bereaved friend. "Sure, Hadder. Happy to help." He looked to Jonny. "Jonny, my name is Glen. I'm gonna get you somewhere safe. We're gonna get you straightened out, ok?"

Jonny began to nod off in Hadder's grasp. His head came up at Glen's voice. "Any friend of Hadder's is a friend of mine. I accept your kind offer, dear sir."

Glen walked over and accepted Jonny from Hadder. "Jesus, he's heavy. And he's not gonna be much help. Don't know if I can get him there alone."

Hadder nodded and walked into the growing throngs of residents. He grabbed the arm of a large man with a bright orange duster and flat-top of bleached hair whom he remembered from his Celebration days. The man's name escaped him. "Hey, what's the fucking deal," began the man before recognizing Marlin Hadder and quickly altering his words. "Sorry, Hadder, you startled me, that's all."

"I need your favor."

The man bumbled, finding the words, and stammered when he unearthed them. "Sure, sure, Hadder. How can I help?"

"I need you to help my friend Glen here get our mutual friend Jonny VV back to *Cranesman* west of here."

The flat-topped man made a face. "But I was just heading to *Morning's Echo*. People are waiting for me."

"And I'm sure they'll be there when you return. You do remember Jonny VV, don't you? I'd hate to think of you as a guy who turns his back on his friends." The Rage was there, just beneath the surface, a lifetime of fair-weather friends and self-involved acquaintances fueling the fire.

The man could see the threat hiding behind the request, would be a fool to ignore it, especially from the now notorious Marlin Hadder. "Of course, Hadder. They'll be there when I get back. Happy to help."

The danger in Hadder's eyes vanished as quickly as it appeared, and he slapped the large man on the shoulder. "There's the good friend I knew to be there. Glen! This gentleman has offered to help you."

"I, I'm Nesto. Nice to meet you."

Glen had no time for Celebration folks. "Great. Get his other arm. We've got a bit of a hike."

"I'll come by and check on him after I'm done," said Hadder. Glen replied with a simple thumbs-up.

The pair began to walk Jonny west when the nearly unconscious man came to and turned his head back to Hadder. "Hadder, I heard you got the bastard. The one who killed my lovely Reena. Is it true?"

"I did, Jonny."

"Did he suffer as she did?"

"I cut his fucking head off, Jonny."

Jonny weakly nodded. "Good shit, old chap. Thank you."

Hadder simply smiled, and the three were off again, slowly making their way to *Cranesman*, where Hadder hoped his friend's heart would heal.

Before a Riser had the chance to rip it from his chest.

———

HADDER COMPLETED his work in the Celebration Cluster and continued north, planning to hit the Lethe River and follow it upstream until he reached *Cranesman* and could check in on Jonny VV.

As Hadder came upon the Lethe, he couldn't help but look back to the Skirt, imagining the army that waited for them across that empty strip of land. Hadder and Glen had spotted several Caesars making the rounds earlier in the Solay, giving them both a warm feeling that they weren't quite yet on death's door. With the Caesars still active and on their side, there was hope for victory.

With this thought running through his mind, Hadder looked to the Caesar Bridge, hoping that seeing another colossal ally stationed there would provide even more comfort. Looking closely, Hadder could see a hulking form on the bridge, but it was sitting down, as if at rest. Never having known a Caesar to rest when on patrol, Hadder reversed his course and decided to investigate.

A prickling air of danger enveloped Hadder as he closed in on the Caesar Bridge. Hadder looked around carefully, staring intently at the many shadows that fell across both sides of the Skirt, searching for signs of movement, glints of metal, or flashes of glowing eyes. With none found, he quietly made his way to the Caesar Bridge, anxiously checking under the bridge and around both sides for evidence of a trap. Again discovering nothing, Hadder stepped lightly onto the bridge, his eyes glued to the immense creature before him.

The Caesar sat in the middle of the bridge, his legs straight out ahead of him as he leaned against the railing. His head was down, chin against his chest, giving the appearance that he was fast asleep. His massive arms fell listlessly to his sides.

Hadder inched closer, trying to minimize noise on the rickety wood. Although the Caesar's white top-knotted ponytail hung low and blocked his face, the hair, coupled with the pale blue skin of his hands, told Hadder that this was Galba, his old Station welcoming committee member.

The last thing Hadder wanted to do was startle one of the city's titan enforcers, so he called out softly instead. "Galba. Galba. Are you ok?"

Nothing.

Hadder grew bolder, moved closer to the resting giant. Hunched over as he was, Hadder couldn't make out much, especially with the giant coat Galba was wearing. Finally, Hadder worked up the courage and knelt beside the guardian, lifting the massive head up and back.

Dead, open eyes stared back at Hadder, set in a face frozen in a moment of surprise and horror.

"Fuck me," blurted Hadder as he dropped the head and fell back, his pulse racing and his breath coming in short, inadequate bursts. Hadder rotated on his backside, putting his back to the grisly scene, keeping the rushing waters of the Lethe before him as he calmed himself and collected his thoughts.

Several deeps breaths later, utilizing techniques he had learned so long ago, Hadder managed to regain control. He turned to once again regard the dead Caesar. With no blood to be seen, Hadder was curious as to the cause of death. He crawled over to the body and, this time, pushed Galba's entire upper body back against the railing, unveiling the death-wound.

"Fuck me," he repeated, staring open-mouthed at the Caesar's bare chest, which had been caved in by a blow of unbelievable power. The size and location of the crater in Galba ensured that the Caesar's oversized heart would have detonated upon impact.

"He's dead."

The voice from the other side of the bridge sent Hadder reeling once more to the ground, a razor simply touching a violin string under extreme tension. Cal stepped into the light of the Caesar Bridge.

"Jesus Christ, Cal, my heart almost exploded. You want two bodies on this goddam bridge?"

"He's dead."

"I see that. You know anything about it?"

"No. I found him a little while ago. Been patrolling since. High alert."

Hadder got to his feet, walked closer to Cal to ease both conversation and his mind as it seemed the safest place at the moment. "What the fuck happened here, Cal?"

"Dead Caesar."

"I see that. But who did it? Who could do it?"

"Don't know."

Hadder returned to the body, pushed the shoulders up with his foot, revealing the wound. "What could have done this, Cal?"

"A hammer. A big hammer."

Hadder looked at the wound again, mentally measuring the width and depth of the crater. Unless someone in Station had figured out a way to launch tree trunks end first at terminal velocity, Hadder had to agree with Cal's assessment. "I think you're right. But who the hell could wield such a heavy weapon? The Krown? Sure. Ego Rounds before he died? Maybe. I know I haven't seen but a fraction of Risers, but I certainly don't think there are any that could best a Caesar. What do you think, Cal?"

Cal shifted from one foot to the other at the end of the bridge, looking anxious. The colossus' worry threw gasoline on Hadder's own bonfire of fear.

"Cal?"

Nothing.

"Cal, is there some other Riser that could have done this? Or do you think The Krown did the dirty work himself? He thinks himself too valuable. There's no way he would jeopardize himself like..."

"Maybe not The Krown."

"Ok, then there must be some other Riser that we haven't seen yet. Some Elevated freak who..."

"Maybe not a Riser."

Hadder could feel his face scrunch up in confusion. "You can't think a Setter did this? Their Elevations don't have any real value in..."

"Maybe not a Setter."

"Then who's left? Who else could do such a thing?"

"A Caesar could."

Hadder had forgotten what he had eaten that day, but he almost found out as his stomach lurched from Cal's terrifying words. He moved towards the frightening sentinel on wobbly legs. "Cal, do you really think another Caesar could have done this?"

"Looks like it."

Hadder was dumbstruck, words falling out as if from a dump truck. "But, but, I mean, how? Aren't you, you know, like programmed? To follow orders, I mean? Like, how does this even happen? What, what could make a Caesar want to hurt another Caesar? Aren't you all friends? Why? How could this happen?" Cal simply stared at the body of Galba as Hadder continued his blathering. "Cal! Goddamit, answer me! Please."

Cal turned away from the corpse of his colleague to stare at Hadder. Although no tears formed in his purple eyes, there was a sadness that had taken residence on his orange face. Still, he said nothing.

Hadder took a calming breath, tried another approach. "Cal, you told me the Caesars didn't have free will. If that's true, then how could this happen?"

Cal shot a look at Hadder that could almost be interpreted as pity. "The city is changing. Some of the Caesars are changing as well."

"How so?"

"We are starting to have dreams."

"Dreams of what?"

"Of lives beyond service."

"You mean lives outside of Station? You mean lives in the world?"

"Yes."

Hadder tensed, looking around with only his eyes for possible escape routes. Going over the railing to take his chances in the roiling waters of the Lethe seemed the only option. "Do all the Caesars feel this way, Cal?"

The monster shrugged. "Yes, but few will act on this, I think. Most are still loyal to Father."

"You mean Mister Rott."

"Yes."

"And those that aren't?"

Cal motioned towards Galba. "They are going to make trouble."

"Would they fight with the fucking Risers?"

"Maybe."

"Jesus Christ, Cal, do you know who they are?"

"No. They hide among us."

An overwhelming sense of despair attacked Hadder. If the Caesars, the only constant that Hadder had accounted for in the upcoming war, could not be trusted, then the Fall indeed could be an inevitability.

"What are we going to do about the body?"

"We? Nothing. My brothers will be here soon to help me take it away."

"Can you trust them?"

"No. But they are my brothers."

———

ANY ILLUSIONS that Marlin Hadder had about the Caesars moving the body of one of their own without attracting attention were dispelled early the following Solay when Lilly Sistine, returning from breakfast, burst into their shared living quarters, waking him from a restless sleep.

"Oh my god, Marlin. Did you hear? Did you hear?"

Hoping for a miracle, Hadder decided to feign ignorance. "Hear what?"

"They killed a Caesar. I mean, really. They actually managed to kill a Caesar. If they can do that, then what hope is there for us?"

Hadder needed to understand how much the general populace actually knew. "Wait, wait. Calm down. Tell me. Who killed a Caesar?"

Lilly looked ready to explode from Hadder's perceived stupidity. "Who killed a Caesar? Who do you think? The fucking Risers killed a Caesar, that's who!"

Despite Lilly's hysteria, Hadder was encouraged by the fact that the residents, much like himself, had not entertained the idea that another Caesar could have committed the murder. The Risers were a known entity, a defined enemy. Although terrifying, illicit killings were expected of them. A group of Caesars, however, turning oversized weapons on residents of the Setting, would be too much for the populace to bear.

Hadder wiped the sleep from his eyes. "Ok, well, they're obviously starting to test the Skirt. But this will cause the Caesars to tighten up. They won't be caught off guard again." The lies flowed like cheap gas station wine.

Tears welled in Lilly's cognac eyes. "Marlin, I'm scared."

Hadder motioned her over, buried her in a hug, whispered what she needed to hear. As the sweet words came out of his mouth, however, his mind went to other places, combing through potential strategies. If the residents were previously willing to rely on the Caesars for protection, perhaps Hadder could leverage the death of Galba to spur the Setters into action.

As he silently laid out the words he would use to persuade resident leaders, Hadder's bare shoulder grew wet from Lilly's Sistine's warm tears.

23

H adder listened as Royal did the talking. Tired of traveling across the city to meet one-on-one with resident leaders, often in vain, Royal had called a meeting of a select group of Setters at *The Royal Jelly*. Royal wisely held the meeting late in the Solay so attendees could simply stay put and catch the Bar's upcoming concert, where the increasingly popular Lilly Sistine would blow the audience's collective minds. Hadder stood to the side, arms crossed over his chest, his opinion of the average resident diminishing by the comment.

"It should be clear by now," said Royal to the leaders in attendance, "Although the Caesars are still our most formidable resource, they're not invincible gods as many of you had hoped. There have now been two Caesars who have met untimely fates at the hands of Risers. Will we let them fight our battle alone? Will we allow them to get picked off one by one until there are no guardians of the Skirt? Will we let the Risers take their time, crossing over the Skirt unencumbered when the time is right?

"The Caesars against the Risers is not a fair fight. The Setters against the Risers is not a fair fight. But our combined might, fighting together shoulder-to-shoulder, might be enough to turn the tables, allowing us to win this upcoming war and protect the lives that we have worked so hard to rebuild. In this city that is ours!"

There was some applause from the gathered audience, but not enough for Hadder's liking. Had anyone but Hadder known the actual cause of Galba's death, there would be no applause, only soft weeping from both men and women. What else did these people need to see?

Things were moving quickly now, at least on the Riser side of things. In addition to the death of a Caesar, there were reported attacks along the Skirt. Risers were sneaking through Caesar defenses to wreak momentary havoc before returning to the safety of the Rising. While most assumed it was merely the result of increasing attempts, Hadder wondered if something much more sinister was afoot. Hadder wondered if perhaps some Caesars were letting Risers through, aiding them in their terrorist efforts.

Equally worrying was the continued trend of Setters defecting to the Rising, eschewing their soft lives for those of hardened warriors. The over-arching thinking of these individuals must have been that it's better to be a heartless raider than a literal heartless corpse.

Hadder sighed deeply as Royal continued to work the crowd. Although they were slowly gaining support, it would be too little, too late at this rate.

"How's it looking," asked Lilly as she came up beside Hadder.

"Grim. It's not easy convincing anyone to fight, much less a group that has been atrophying for years - no work, no responsibility, no struggles. And now we want them to get out of their comfy beds and step into the fire. They're gonna need something extreme to wake them from this eternal dream."

"And the death of a Caesar wasn't enough?"

"Apparently, for some, but not for most."

"Then what do they need?"

"I wish I knew."

"Marlin." Hadder looked down into her sweet eyes, saw the fear and sadness there. "Are we going to die?"

Hadder tried to find the words to comfort her. He wanted nothing more than to do just that at that moment. But when his hands raked through the sands of reassuring sentences, they came out empty. "I don't know, my love. But I'm going to do everything I can to prevent that."

"I don't want to die again; the first time almost killed me."

Hadder looked back to the resident audience, unable to hold her desperate gaze. "Yeah, me neither. But I'm not going back to the Before as a goddam angel of vengeance, either. So, I'm going to fight."

Pressed close against him, Hadder could feel Lilly's body deflate a bit, as if the last bit of hope for a peaceful resolution slipped through her slim fingers. "I need to get ready for the show."

Hadder, his attention squarely fixed on a resident leader who was speaking to Royal, simply nodded absently. Lilly Sistine slipped away like a ghost, floating backstage to get ready for her performance.

———

"How's he doing?"

Glen shook his head. "Sad sack of shit won't leave his living quarters. I check on him occasionally and have a manikin bring him three squares. Poor bastard's broken, but he can be fixed. Just needs time. And to stay away from the fucking chemicals."

Hadder put his hand on Glen's shoulder. "Thanks, brother, means a lot to me. Jonny VV and Reena pulled me from a dark place that I had called home for a long time. I can no longer repay Reena, but I can sure as shit try to do right by Jonny."

"Some say you did right by Reena, too."

"Vengeance ain't repayment."

"No, I guess it isn't. Well, don't worry. I'll keep an eye on him."

"You coming to *The Royal Jelly* this Haela?"

Glen shook his head in the negative. "Nah, got too much to do around here. See these guys here?"

Hadder looked around *Cranesman* to the dozen or so men and women gathered around the simple wooden tables. "I see."

"They're all in with us. Gonna fight to the end, if it comes to that. We're all gonna get a nice buzz on and start to work. Gonna get the manikins started on some weapons and then continue work on fortifying this place."

"Good to hear, Glen."

"The Risers think they're bringing Hell with them, but if they attack this group head-on, they're gonna find out who the real demons are."

Hadder couldn't help but crack a smile at his friend's dark words. Mostly, he was happy to see that some were coming to the same conclusion as he had, that fighting was the only way to preserve life. But a small part of him was smiling for another reason - the thought of blood spray caressing his skin as he cut down Riser after Riser, filling the Rage's hungry mouth with the lives of others.

"I'll leave you to it, then." Hadder turned to leave.

"Oh, shit, I almost forgot." Hadder turned back to Glen, who handed him a small tan envelope made from strange material. "Someone dropped this off for you. No one was here at the time, so it was left with the manikin."

Hadder looked at the envelope, on which his name was written in masterful calligraphy. He fingered the odd veiny paper before releasing the soft seal and taking out the note within. He read over it several times before putting it back and placing the warm envelope in his jacket pocket.

"Good news, I hope."

"Too early to tell. Good? Bad? No idea. But whatever it is, it will be bizarre. With this one, it always is."

———

MARLIN, darling, I absolutely must see you. Whispers in the shadows suggest much. Meet me atop the Perch at the fall of Haela. Kisses. LM.

Hadder reread the note as he stood on the Perch, his mind returning to his first Solay in Station when Miles provided the worst orientation to the city possible. Hadder had no idea how long he had been in the city; time worked differently in Station, but it certainly felt like a lifetime since he had first looked down from this height.

"Thank you for joining me, darling."

Hadder glanced to his right and watched as Lester Midnight precipitated from the darkness, his white eyes and hair appearing first, his golden clothing next, and his black skin completing the arrival.

"I never thought you'd leave *Biomass*, Lester."

"Drastic times call for drastic measures, now don't they."

"Would you call these drastic times?"

"Well, if these aren't, then I don't know what is, darling."

Hadder held up the beige note. "Whispers in the shadows, Lester?"

Lester Midnight moved in, uncomfortably close. Hadder could feel the enigmatic man's breath on his face, could make out the flecks of gold dancing in his white eyes. "Whispers to most. Shouts to me and my network. I hear all, eventually, darling."

"And what do you hear, Lester?"

Lester's white lips twitched. "There is a viper in your house, darling."

"I don't follow."

"A traitor. A betrayer. This person walks among you, wearing the skin of a Setter."

Hadder straightened at the ominous news. "Who?"

A pained look flashed across Lester's face. "I'm sorry, darling. We don't know. A figure was seen passing into the Rising late one Haela. Now, this is not strange as it happens more and more these days. But none return. None but this one. It was dark, and my spies were far, so that's all I know. But if this person was allowed back over, it was with devilish orders, you can be certain."

"Do you know where this person went? What Cluster he returned to?"

Lester looked almost sad. "My spy lost him in the gardens, darling. He could be anywhere in the Setting. I worry for you, Marlin."

"Risers want me dead. And now at least one Setter may want me dead. I better keep my head on a swivel. Thanks for the information, Lester. I truly appreciate it. But why? You seem so above all of this."

"There are so few true artistes left, Marlin. I would be sad to lose one of your stature, darling."

Hadder's face contorted in confusion. "But I'm not an artist, Lester. Remember? I don't paint, and I don't make meat sculptures like you."

Lester laughed. "Oh, Marlin, such a narrow definition of an artiste. Your Rage is your art. I see it acted out on your face and in your actions every day. I kick myself to this day that I wasn't able to see it, but my spies tell me that your work, *Skeelis on Stick*, was absolutely breathtaking. Not an artiste? I laugh at your humility."

"You know the Risers will come for you, too, Lester. Or will you also join them when the moment comes?"

Lester joined Hadder at the railing, looked down at the magical city beneath them, a black canvas decorated with immense bursts of color. "No, darling, there is nothing beyond Station for Lester Midnight. I am one of the few who always knew that this place was not forever, that it didn't matter in the grand scheme of things. Therefore, I can proudly say that I made the most of my extra time. I created art that the world will never see again, using the human body as both paintbrush and canvas."

"And when the Risers come?"

Lester straightened at the rail, his knuckles tightening around the metal. "Oh, I won't go easily, darling. Everyone is born with the understanding that death is coming, that each day it is fought off. I mean, that is what living is - the denial of an easy death. We all failed our first test on this subject. I refuse to fail another."

"Then, you will fight with me, Lester?"

Lester turned to face Hadder once more. "I told you before, darling. When the blood starts flying and screams fill the air, look to your right. Lester Midnight will be there, creating my piece de resistance. I have spent all my time carving up the bodies of my subjects. Now it is my turn, but they will have to work for it. Their blood will coat my blades long before mine covers theirs."

"And *Biomass*? What will happen to your installations?"

"Like Station, art installations are fleeting, doomed to be admired and then replaced. They served their purpose, just as I will serve mine. *Biomass* will become a pyre when the Risers attack."

Hadder nodded. "Fair enough. Thank you, my friend." Hadder put out his hand to shake Lester's, but the strange artist put his black hands to each side of Hadder's head, pulled him closer, and placed a gentle kiss on Hadder's forehead.

"I hope you make it to the final battle, darling. The Fall will be a thing of beauty."

"I'm trying to stop the Fall, Lester."

Lester shrugged. "Beautiful either way."

Hadder made his way towards the stairs but was stopped by more words from Lester. "And, Marlin, you may want to hang on to that note and envelope."

Hadder looked down at the leather-like message in his hand. "Why's that, Lester?"

Lester smiled coyly. "I'm not one to support the defacement of another's work, but we knew your installation wouldn't be left alone for long."

"Installation? Lester, what are you talking about?"

"My men took some skin from Skeelis's head before it was removed. I made stationary from the fiend."

Hadder looked down, half in horror and half in grim satisfaction. "This message is written on Skeelis?"

"Indeed, it is. You know I'm not one to waste perfectly good material. And now you have something tangible to remember your vengeance by. You're welcome."

Hadder laughed, placed the envelope back into his jacket pocket. "Thanks, Lester. You're never one to leave me disappointed in a meeting."

"The best is yet to come, darling. Trust me, the best is yet to come."

24

Meetings with the residents continued. Some were successful, others were not. As Royal spoke, Hadder and Glen would peruse the audience, looking for any sign of betrayal. While Royal knew most everyone in Station, many remained unknown to Hadder. Unfamiliar faces always looked suspect; Hadder imagined each of them fingering sharp blades hidden in their jackets and coats.

Progress also continued, with weaponry coming out of the manikin shops each day and residents fabricating any metal they could find into instruments of violence. Additionally, Solays were increasingly spent exercising, practicing martial arts, and drilling attack plans. Chemicals were still imbibed, but more to accentuate the training and help harden the body than to soften the mind. While they still had a long way to go, Hadder was encouraged to see some residents' willingness to die fighting for their lives.

Stories of brutal battles made their way across the Skirt as The Krown's forces put forth full effort in eradicating the remains of Ego Rounds' followers. Despite being insanely outnumbered and with no hope of victory in sight, those remaining of the South Rising loyalists fought valiantly, utilizing the traps, terrain, and fortifications that Ego Rounds had so brilliantly put into place. Hadder smiled when he thought of the beautiful and deadly

Kamaria defeating another of The Krown's battalions, stubbornly denying the death that she knew was right around the corner. Hadder believed that if she could hold The Krown off for a few more weeks, those in the Setting may have a chance.

———

HADDER AND CAL walked the Skirt in silence, the bright rays of Solay allowing them both to take in their surroundings completely, marking areas most susceptible to Riser attacks or crossing attempts. With the alarming news that some of the Caesars may be actively working with the Risers, Hadder took it upon himself to strategize with Station's guardians, only working directly with Cal, whom he trusted implicitly. Every now and then, Hadder would point something out to Cal, who would nod or offer some small counterpoint. Eventually, Hadder grew tired of the elephant in the room.

"Have you discovered which Caesars are supporting the Risers?"

Cal kept walking, kept scanning the landscape. "Not yet. We are good at hiding our emotions, hiding our thoughts. But I have my suspicions."

"If you have your suspicions, why not call them out? Let them know you're on to them. Force their hand now, not when your back is turned."

Cal shook his head. "I cannot. I'm not sure yet how many there are. An accusation would set off a fight. A false accusation would set off a more brutal one, and we could all kill each other in a single skirmish. Then where would you and your Setters be?"

Hadder closed his mouth, unable to argue Cal's point. They continued south along the Skirt, below the Celebration Cluster and the Perch, when a large field referred to as the Grasslands opened up on Hadder's right. Often used for large games of soccer or football, it now sat empty, the times for joyous frolicking a thing of the past. Hadder nudged the giant creature in the ribs. "You could wage a hell of a battle there."

"Silence," was all that Cal said, squinting as he walked. Hadder peered down the Skirt and saw what the Caesar was trying to decipher, a flurry of activity a few hundred yards further south on the Rising side, past the Grass-lands. "Let's go."

Cal tore down the Skirt at a trot, with Hadder running full speed at his heels to keep up with the sentinel's impossibly long stride. They slowed as they approached a smattering of Risers, perhaps two dozen in total, who were working on something on the ground, out of sight from their position on the Skirt. On the Setting side, thirty or so residents from the nearby Cluster had gathered, apprehensively watching the Riser activity.

Two Caesars were already standing guard on the Skirt before the Risers, a giant gray block of stone called Titus and a pink-skinned colossus named Jules. In his large hands, Titus held a hammer that probably weighed as much as the average resident. Hadder nudged Cal again, pointing his chin towards the hammer, before giving the guardian a suspicious look.

Cal bent down to whisper. "Many Caesars change up weapons, grabbing the first thing they see before patrols. Plus, there's no way the killer would have used his own equipment."

Hadder accepted Cal's explanation, but kept a wary eye on the Caesar Titus. As they joined the other two Caesars, Cal spoke with Jules. "What's this?"

Jules, not as broad as most Caesars but a head taller than all, looked down at Cal, his shoulder-length blue hair blowing across his face in the soft breeze. "Not sure. Just making sure they don't try to cross. Only been at it a few minutes."

Giving the Caesars their privacy, Hadder walked away, staring intently at the Risers not but thirty yards away. Work continued on the ground, men and women alike laughing over the traces of pained cries. A glint of light caught Hadder's attention, and he looked over to see Wagner standing to the side of the Risers, staring daggers at his old nemesis, his metal tusks and horns polished to a high shine.

Hadder couldn't help himself. "Wagner! How's it hanging, pig-man? Having trouble with a few South Risers? How are you going to conquer the world if you can't even clean up your own backyard?"

Wagner smiled wickedly, and Hadder immediately recognized that he had read the situation wrong. "Hadder," the tusked man called, "You cannot imagine how happy I am to see you here. I mean, what are the odds? The Gods of war are truly smiling down on me this Solay."

Worry seeped in through crevices, a knot formed in Hadder's stomach. "What are you about Wagner, you lap-dog?"

"You must not have heard, Marlin Hadder. The Riser Wars are over. I mean, they were over the moment my king split the skull of that obese turd, but today even the denouement draws to a close. I am here to place a period at the end of that small chapter. So, without further ado, I give you the last of the resistance and the dawn of a wholly unified Riser empire."

His speech concluded, Wagner gave an upward motion to the Risers working on the ground. As one, the Risers knelt and lifted something substantial into the air, driving its base into a hole they had dug, locking the tall construct upright.

Although Hadder knew it was fated to happen, his heart still broke at the gruesome scene before him. A naked Kamaria hovered in the air, crucified, bleeding from countless wounds, and tattooed with numerous burns. Although obviously in tremendous pain, Kamaria's eyes still burned with defiance as she spat at her abductors below. One of the female Risers who was struck with spittle angrily picked up a rock and hurled it at the defenseless woman's head, striking Kamaria in the temple and sending her head lolling to the side. The Risers giggled like stupid children who had been sniffing paint.

Hadder made a move towards the Risers but was effortlessly held back with one arm by Cal, who looked down as if to say, "not here, not now." Hadder redirected his energy into glaring at Wagner, creating mental images of the man's chest exploding into a pink mist.

"She is more of a fighter than anyone you have in your soft Setting," said Wagner, addressing both Hadder and the assembled residents. "And look at her now. The great Kamaria, no more than a lawn ornament. Although I would rather burn you all alive, my king is a benevolent king. He has tasked me with spreading the word. Come to him now, pledge your allegiance, pick up arms against the lazy Setters, and prepare for world domination. Do this now, and you will enjoy all the benefits that we will reap as we harvest the world and take what is owed to us. Failure to do this will result in what you see here today."

Wagner motioned again, and a Riser wielding a wicked bladed staff slashed quickly across Kamaria's belly, sending her entrails spilling out to hang low on her body. The proud woman cried out once in pain, then remained silent, summoning a strength Hadder had never known. "Tough to the end," stated Wagner before motioning once more. Risers from the back stepped forward, carrying burlap sacks that shifted with activity from within. Standing at the base of the cross, the Risers emptied their bags, sending malnourished rats scurrying about the ground. Kamaria's eyes went wide with terror, and tears trickled down her dark cheeks as the rats began to climb the wood in search of the sweet, warm meat they detected.

Hadder's stomach lurched, and he looked away, turning back only when a scream from Kamaria demanded his attention. The rats covered her exposed organs, greedily devouring the soft flesh. Some had even begun to enter the wound, finding additional warmth and food in her body cavity. Kamaria shook from the torment, her eyes screaming when her mouth would not. Some residents ran from the horrible sight, others vomited where they stood. Many others looked on frozen, their minds unable to comprehend what their eyes were telling them.

Hadder locked eyes with Kamaria, hoping he could give her something to focus on, something to take her away from the gruesome reality of what was happening to her once formidable body. Minutes felt like days as the vermin continued their dirty work, sending Karmaria into convulsions of agony. Through it all, however, she kept her eyes on Hadder, eyes that were thankfully beginning to dim. Finally, the shaking subsided, and a look of gentle acceptance fell over Kamaria's face like a veil. Looking at Hadder, the corners of her mouth curled in a Mona Lisa smile, and she mouthed the words "kill them all" before letting out one last scream of defiance, shouting the word "Ego" as her head fell and her eyes glazed over.

A stillness fell over both Riser and Setter, with more than a few Risers looking off-put by the macabre display. Wagner sauntered to the edge of the

Skirt; the Caesars tightened their grips on their weapons. "Tell your friends what you saw here today. Let them know what awaits those who oppose The Krown. Come to us now and welcome a new life at the top of the food chain."

Wagner moved further up the Skirt to stand directly across from Hadder. "And Marlin Hadder. I'll see you on the battlefield. My tusks ache to touch your flesh."

"Just make sure you actually stand and fight this time, not let your lackeys shoot me from the rooftops."

"Do not worry, Setter, The Krown has outlawed projectiles for the Invasion. He wants every Riser to taste the blood on their hands. I can't wait to taste yours."

"I am going to kill you, pig-man. You need to know that."

Wagner pointed to the husk of Kamaria. "Funny, she said the exact same thing. Two days later, she's meat. You're all meat. You're just too stupid to know it." Wagner turned and began to walk away, shouting orders at his men as he passed. "Ten of you stay here. No one is to take down this warning. Kill any who attempt it."

The Rage boiled over inside of Hadder, a need to feel Wagner's death rattle against his cheek. In a fit of anger, Hadder bent down to pick up a rat who had enjoyed his fill of Kamaria before stumbling across the Skirt. Hadder chucked the swollen rat into the air, and internally rioted in laughter when it struck the back of Wagner's head with a dull thud. To Wagner's credit, he did not dignify the insulting assault with a response, merely choosing to continue his trek into the Rising, back to The Krown, no doubt.

Cal came up to Hadder. "What now?"

Hadder looked up at his giant ally. "I must tell Royal and the others."

"Tell them what?"

"That we're out of time."

———

HADDER HURRIED BACK to *The Royal Jelly*, stopping at a few select Bars he knew Royal's supporters frequented. The message he left at each was short and to the point - ready yourselves for battle; the Risers are coming.

As he walked, Hadder tried in vain to erase the image of the beautiful and powerful Kamaria turned inside out, left as food for emaciated vermin. The Rage coursed through his veins, demanding retribution in the form of Riser blood, threatening to take over his actions. Hadder fought it back with difficulty, reminding himself that there would be a time for the Rage to take control, but this was not it.

Hadder slowed when he entered the lawn surrounding *The Royal Jelly*, hoping to catch his breath a bit before he recounted the despicable scene he had witnessed. As usual, the yard was empty this time of late Solay, with everyone off preparing for the upcoming Haela's concerts and festivities. Taking his time across the lawn, Hadder was beset by an unsettling feeling, as if unseen Risers were hiding all about him - under the hammock, atop the Golden Bees, laying flat against the carefully mowed grass. Looking around with uncertainty, Hadder finally waved away his fears, chalking it up to the remnants of a troublesome Solay.

Just then, a scream cut through the air like a spear and brought those fears back in a rush. A scream that came from *The Royal Jelly*. A scream that came from the mouth of Lilly Sistine.

Hadder took off in a sprint, running faster than ever before, dark images spinning through his head as if on a carousel slide projector. A tiny hand sticking out from twisted metal, Reena Song's beautiful head laid carefully on her lap, Kamaria's eyes screaming things her mouth could not. He took the stairs three at a time, was at the top in a blink. He crossed the porch and threw open the heavy double doors, sending them crashing against the outside wall. He ran blindly into the Bar, not giving his eyes a chance to adjust to the unlit space, not caring about what sort of fiend he may discover inside.

Two long strides into the Bar, Hadder's feet flew out beneath him, and he fell heavily to the hardwood floor, plunging into something wet and sticky. As Hadder's eyes quickly dilated, he looked at his hands and found them to be covered in blood, still warm. The floor was coated in gore, running the length of the upper level, with splatter marks on the walls where brutal slashing had obviously taken place. Hadder's mouth stood agape as he took in the gruesome scene, so much blood in so many places.

"Marlin?"

Lilly's sweet, soft voice ripped Hadder from his shock faster than a dousing in ice water. Searching around furiously, Hadder finally found his love huddling in the corner of the Bar, covered in red stickiness. Knees pulled up into her chest, she shook uncontrollably and rocked back and forth as if willing herself to another time and place.

Hadder ran to Lilly in a panic, took her head in his hands, pulled her face up to look him in the eyes. "Lilly, it's me. It's Marlin. Are you hurt?" As he spoke, Hadder uncoiled the woman, looking for any signs of cuts or stab wounds. He found none.

"Marlin? Oh my god, Marlin. It's so horrible." Lilly wept openly as she spoke, her words running together in a tear-soaked jumble.

"Are you ok? Lilly! Are you hurt?"

Lilly shook her head in the negative, took a deep breath to calm herself. "I'm ok, Marlin."

"Is someone here? How many? Where are they?" Hadder looked around desperately as he asked, not wanting his own blood to join that which already painted the Bar's floor and walls.

Lilly again shook her head. "Gone. They're gone." Her words came out in bursts as panic refused to allow her breathing to normalize. "But. Marlin. Royal. Oh my god, Marlin. Royal." She broke down once more, words dissolving into indecipherable sobbing.

Hadder wiped the snot and tears from her face. "What, Lilly? What about Royal? Please, tell me."

Still unable to speak, Lilly simply pointed to the upper-level bar with a trembling hand. Hadder was scared to ask the question, frightened as to what he may discover. "Lilly, is Royal behind the counter?"

Tears continued to pour as she nodded before pulling her knees back up and hiding her head in her lap. Hadder rose carefully and turned to face the upper-level bar. He could see a river of red liquid emanating from behind the counter, running across the floor and down the stairs to the lower levels. Hadder moved towards the bar, anxiety slowing his movements, making each step feel like a slog through water. Eventually, he reached his destination and peered over the counter. And discovered precisely how Galba must have felt in his final moment as his chest caved in.

Behind the counter, in a lake of his own blood, laid Royal Winters, bleeding from a hundred wounds across a dozen locations. Royal's eyes went wide when he saw his friend, and Hadder recoiled at the realization that his companion still lived. After recovering from the brief paralysis, Hadder dove to the floor next to Royal, put his face close to the other man's.

"Royal, it's Hadder. I'm here, buddy, I'm here. You're gonna be ok. You hear me?"

Royal shook his head, blood flooding from his mouth as he attempted to speak. After several attempts, clearing liquid from his punctured lungs, Royal tried again. "Lilly."

Hadder smoothed back his friend's hair, fighting back the tears. "She's ok, Royal. I just checked on her. She's fine. Now let's get you some help."

Royal closed his eyes tightly, as if frustrated, swung his head side to side. He opened them again, looked at Hadder pleadingly. "Lilly."

Hadder's face softened, thinking his wounded friend couldn't understand that Lilly was safe. "She's ok, Royal. I checked on her already. Now let's get ready to move you."

Hadder got to his knees, ready to lift his friend from his bed of plasma, when he noticed Royal's eyes go wide, staring past him. "What is it, buddy? Does it..."

Hadder's words were cut off as a sharp blade plunged between his shoulder blades, forcing him to drop Royal to the floor. A second blow pierced his side, shattering ribs and clipping his liver. A third stab caught him higher, entering his right lung, and sent Hadder spiraling towards the ground to land atop Royal. Hadder spun onto his back, determined to face his attacker head-on, determined to inflict some pain of his own before he expired.

Unfortunately, that determination washed away like chalk in a rainstorm when he looked up to see Lilly Sistine standing above him, knife in hand, metal dripping more of his blood on the Bar floor. Gone were the tears and the snot. Gone was the terrified girl who curled up in the corner, waiting for Hadder to save her. A woman of consequence stood before him, content with her decision, comfortable in her execution.

Too dismayed to find words, Hadder scooted back using his elbows and feet, sliding in the muck that would soon be all that remained of Marlin Hadder and Royal Winters. Lilly came forward, knife leading, a mask of stoicism covering her once-enchanting face.

In a burst of denial, Hadder threw himself up and over the counter, crashing down on the other side and causing ripples of agony from his three wounds. He rose quickly and attempted to make for the entrance, but slipped on the wet surface and collapsed to the ground once more. His breath became increasingly labored as his right lung filled with liquid. Walking now out of the question, Hadder began to crawl towards the double doors, making little progress on the red-stained wood.

"Marlin, please. Don't make this any harder than it has to be."

The hard voice came from just behind Hadder. The wounded man flipped onto his back, found the face of the woman with whom he expected to spend the remainder of his second life. He chuckled silently, thinking he obviously still might. "Why?"

Lilly Sistine began to pace around Hadder, stepping carefully. "It's simple, Marlin. You and Royal and Glen are alright with dying for Station. I'm not. I didn't like dying the first time and don't figure on doing it again any time soon. Anyway, you said it yourself, I'll be a great success in the Before. It won't be like last time. With this voice I now have, I'm going to live the life I deserve."

Hadder couldn't believe what he was hearing, refused to acknowledge the truth of what was happening to him. "The Risers will kill you. You don't belong with them."

Lilly waved her knife at Hadder. "You think so little of me, don't you, Marlin? I already cut a deal with The Krown. I get you and Royal out of the way and punch my ticket into the Before. I get to sit out your stupid war and will walk calmly out of Station once the walls fall down. The deal couldn't be simpler. And I couldn't be happier with it." Lilly moved closer to Hadder; he put up his hands, palms open towards her.

"Wait, wait. Lilly, please wait. Think about what you're doing." Words struggled to come out now, his eyes felt heavy as more and more blood escaped his body. "Please. I love you."

Lilly's hard face softened, again resembling the young woman he met, the young woman who showed him that another love was possible, another home was possible. Her cognac eyes shined in the dim Bar. She smiled sweetly at the fallen Hadder, echoing another time and place, a better time and place. "Oh, Marlin. I love you, too. It's nothing personal. The Fall is inevitable; I see that now. And isn't it better that's it's me and not some leather-clad Riser? Trust me, it's better this way." Lilly moved in again, hovered just above Hadder.

"Please. I'm not ready."

Lilly's face was inches from his own now. She kissed him deeply on the lips. "Oh, yes, you are. You were ready to die for fucking Reena Song in the Rising. Now you can fucking be ready to die for me." She kissed him again. "Now die for me, Marlin."

The knife tore into his stomach, retreated, then plummeted into his chest. The blade flashed before him, moving up and down in a blur. A face contorted in a release of anger. Darkness appeared at the edge of his vision, creeping inward, as the flash of metal ceased. He heard the knife fall to the hard floor and footsteps moving towards the entrance.

Light poured in as the large double doors opened, but Hadder was already reeling towards darkness. A voice chased him as he descended into the void with nothing to slow his fall.

"Now, you can go to your whore."

With those final words filling the empty space, Marlin Hadder died a second time.

25

H adder swam in the void, weightless in that cold, black vacuum. From the edges of nothing, voices could be heard, reminding Hadder that his story hadn't finished. Yet.

"This is far beneath my talent and skills."

"I understand, Dr. Flowers. But can you bring him back?"

"The bitch did a number on him, but, yes, I can fix him."

"Then, please do."

"I don't understand why you want to save this man. This *plain* man. The Great War is on the horizon. Surely, he'll be dead within a few changes of the Idol Moon. Why tend to the calf's hoof on its way to slaughter?"

"All good points, Dr. Flowers. But please continue your work. I don't know why, but I have an affection for this human. He's lived more in his short time here than almost any resident, even those self-aggrandizing Keys."

"You're not growing soft, are you, Mister Rott?"

"Watch your tongue, Milo. There're limits to my tolerance. Even for an artist such as you."

"My apologies, Mister Rott. I just don't see the point when we know what is coming."

"Maybe I don't know, either. It's something that pulls on me, a premonition, a gut feeling as you humans would call it. I get so few of those. I need to trust them when they appear. I promised the city a fair fight for its survival. Without this man, it stands no chance. I want to see if he can upset the balance. So, maybe I'm just curious."

"Well then, Mister Rott, curiosity is another thing completely. To satiate curiosity, almost any effort is substantiated. I'll get to work."

"Thank you, Milo."

———

LIGHT ATTACKED Hadder's eyes through their closed lids as he lay heavy on his back. He turned his head before opening them, his mind scrambling to recall his last moments, fighting to remember what had transpired. To his right, there was nothing, only an empty, cavernous room filled with color. His eyes continuing to adjust, Hadder faced up again to find a stained-glass dome ceiling sending rays of the Solay on a prismatic journey into the room beneath.

His brain continued to claw through bits and pieces, attempting to find purchase on something, anything that would propel him into remembrance. Focusing on the stained glass far above him, Hadder slowly began to make out images in the decorative ceiling. A winged angel, hand gripping a glowing knife, was being whipped in the face by an unseen force hiding in the cloudy sky above.

For some reason, the knife caught Hadder's attention, tickled something in his memory. He pulled at that strand, determined to find out where it would take him. He recalled a knife. Phantom pains began to dot Hadder's body, forcing him to clutch at invisible wounds. Questions began to form. How did he get here? Where was he? Would Lilly know how to find him? Lilly. Lilly. Knife. Royal.

Lilly stabbing him countless times in the chest, the dead eyes of a shark wearing her face. Was she here now, lurking, waiting to finish the grim job?

Hadder rolled off the cot on which he had been laid, crashing to the polished marble floor. He tried to stand quickly but immediately fell, his legs still weak, and his equilibrium off. Hadder spun on his backside, hands out defensively, eyes darting in every direction, waiting for his lover to tear out from the shadows, sharp blade leading the way, hungry for the last of his blood. He twisted on the floor like a madman for several seconds, seeing a danger at each turn, terrified of feeling cold steel inside his body again.

"You're quite safe, Marlin Hadder."

The familiar voice halted Hadder's frenetic movements like a pause button. Stuck in a crab-walk position, Hadder looked over to where the sound came from and was surprisingly comforted by what he saw there.

Albany Rott sat cross-legged in an antique throne chair, his glowing red eyes standing out even in the brightly lit, empty cathedral. Both the symbol at this throat and the jagged scar that journeyed down his face continued to pulse with power as he puffed on an ancient-looking silver dragon cigarette holder. The twin crystalline hatchets remained tucked neatly into his black belt.

Hadder twisted to face the city's creator, putting his back to the cot on which he woke. "Where am I?"

Rott exhaled a lungful of smoke, smiling as it took the shape of a skull momentarily before spreading out into nonexistence. "You're in a cathedral on the backside of Rott Manor. I thought it would be the most beautiful place for you to awaken in. But it seems like the nightmares chased you here."

"Not nightmares. Ex-girlfriend."

"Yes, I know what happened to you. Humans never cease to surprise me with the lengths they will go in the name of self-preservation. Or self-improvement."

Hadder rose to his feet, only to immediately sit down on the cot. A grimace crossed his features.

Rott smiled again, showcasing those too-white teeth. "You're completely healed, but the mind remembers your numerous wounds, your carved-up flesh. It will take time for those muscle memories to fade."

"How long have I been here?"

"This is your third Solay here."

"Damn it. So much time lost."

"You were dead, Marlin Hadder. I think we did pretty well, considering."

"We?"

"I had Dr. Flowers return you to the realm of the living."

"Why?"

"He asked me that very question. And I'll give you the same answer I provided him with - I don't know. Maybe I didn't like how your story ended. Maybe I think you can do better."

"I don't know whether to thank you or curse you. You fixed me up only to send me to battle against an unbeatable force."

"Dr. Flowers said that as well."

"And your response?"

"Maybe I have more faith in you than you do."

"Well, that warms my heart to hear." The words dripped with sarcasm. Hadder leaned forward, pressed his hands to his thighs for aid, and stood on shaky legs. Pain ripped through his body like his veins had caught fire, forcing Hadder to close his eyes tight. He silently argued with his brain, chiding it for reacting to the ghosts of trauma, urging it to forget about Lilly Sistine and her betrayal. Through sheer will, the agony subsided, retreated to become a pervasive ache. It would have to do.

Hadder opened his eyes once more. Albany Rott was now also standing, smiling as if only he knew the punchline to some secret joke. "See. Better already."

"Thanks for the second chance. Again. But I have to get back. We still have many preparations to make. And we're almost out of time."

Rott nodded, took another pull from his silver dragon. "Of course."

Hadder gingerly made his way towards the cathedral's entrance, each movement giving voice to another repaired wound. As he walked, something gnawed at Hadder. Step by step, Hadder grew increasingly annoyed, increasingly confused, and increasingly angry. By the time he reached the ornate entryway, he could keep quiet no longer.

Hadder turned to face Albany Rott once more. "I don't understand your game, Mister Rott." Rott only lifted a dark red eyebrow in response. "I appreciate you fixing me up, but we need much more if we're gonna put up a fight in this war. I know the Risers fear you. I know for a fact that The Krown fears you. You could stop this madness with a snap of your fingers, and yet you sit on the sidelines like some blood-thirsty spectator. We need you."

Rott's ember eyes studied Hadder, head cocked to the side as if he were a hunter considering whether to eat an animal it had cornered. "You know, Marlin Hadder, you're one of only a handful of people to ever have the nerve to ask something of me directly. I respect that. You'll never understand how much I respect that. But this I cannot give you. I am but the creator of this city. Have I made changes here and there? Have I dictated certain things? Sure. But ultimately, the fate of Station falls on the shoulders of its residents. My hands are tied."

Hadder's anger grew, pushing aside the few remaining strands of restraint, making way for the Rage to take over. "That's bullshit."

"Excuse me?"

"You heard me. I'm not that smart, but I can sense power. And I know that you could end this with a word. But you won't. And I don't understand why."

"It's not for you to understand, human." There was a hint of a threat in Rott's tone, perhaps a reaction to Hadder's Rage.

"Fuck you. You brought us here to build better lives for ourselves. Some of us fucked that up. But many of us succeeded, built real homes here, did our best to learn from the Before and apply it to our new lives, our second chances. And what's our reward for that? To get slaughtered by a bunch of combat Elevated psychos that just want to punish the world for their own unhappiness?"

"Perhaps you'll win."

"Bullshit. Even if we win, this city will become a mausoleum. You can't erect a new city on a foundation of bones. Station will die either way. Or maybe that's what you want."

"I don't want anything, Marlin Hadder. Only to observe."

"Not good enough. Not nearly good enough." The Rage hummed now, ignored any signs of danger from Albany Rott. "You created Station. You ripped all of us from death. You had us make homes and find new families here." Hadder's voice amplified, echoing off the cold, hard walls of the cathedral. "You have a responsibility to that which you concocted! You owe us better!"

Embers became wildfires that threatened to exit the confines of Rott's eyes. "I owe you nothing! You are all nothing! I gave you all the greatest gifts - second chances and time - and you have squandered it. You say I must protect my creation; mustn't you answer for the actions of your fellow humans. The Risers are you, and you are the Risers. I see no difference between you all. I only see the failure of humanity. You would have succeeded as a group. Now, most of you will die as a group."

"You must fight with us. If not to save us, then to save those outside Station's walls, who will feel Riser blades at their throats if the city falls."

"Strong words from one who cannot keep his own heart beating. You tire me, Marlin Hadder. Maybe Lilly Sistine also tired of your empty words, your broken promises of a safe home. Tell me, Marlin, what will you do if you meet her on the battlefield? Will you be able to plunge a dagger into that beautiful creature? You know, for the good of the city?"

Hadder's Rage had reached its threshold for talking. He held onto a tenuous leash, and had much to do if any were to survive the upcoming fighting. "I'm going to go now, Mister Rott. I'm going to prepare my friends the best I can for war. We're going to fight to the last. And if I somehow survive this unnecessary conflict and you weren't around to aid in that survival, I'm coming back here. Station doesn't need an absentee landlord."

"Good luck with that, Marlin Hadder."

Hadder spun angrily and exited the cathedral, kicking himself. If he did somehow survive the Great War, he was sure that he had just signed his death warrant with the enigmatic Albany Rott. Lost in frustrating regret, he failed to look back as he made his way through Rott Manor; the broad grin on Rott's face went unnoticed.

———

HADDER STAYED SOUTH of the Lethe as he exited Rott Manor. Following the banks of the river, he made his way back home, a word that meant much less than it did three Solays prior. As he walked, Hadder finally looked down at himself. Rott had replaced his black t-shirt with a white one but had somehow replaced his gray pants with an almost exact replica. His high-tops were the ones his corpse arrived in and still wore much of his blood from the ordeal. Still, Hadder had to admit that he didn't look half bad for a dead man.

As Hadder approached *Cranesman*, he noticed a flurry of activity around the Bar. Men and women were moving with purpose, fashioning weapons from metal and wood, digging trap trenches, and practicing fighting maneuvers. They stopped to stare at Hadder as he passed, convinced they were observing the ghost of their former friend.

Hadder dramatically kicked in the doors of the Bar, sending the Solay's light into the dim building and making the mass of residents inside jump as they clutched weapons. Glen, standing amongst the Setters discussing strategy, fell back upon seeing Hadder and grabbed at his chest. Recovering quickly, he moved towards his friend, a look of bewilderment painted on his bearded face.

"Hadder? By the gods, could it be you, son? We thought we had lost you." Glen placed his hands on Hadder's shoulders, gripped up and down his arms as if to ensure that the man before him was real. Tears began to well up in the stoic man's eyes.

"You did lose me, Glen. Mister Rott brought me back. Again. For what reason, I can only guess. But those are questions for another day. We have work to do and little time to do it."

Glen collected himself, nodded solemnly. "Yes, of course. Another day. And I fear we have less time than even you think. Much has transpired since your...untimely exit." Hadder raised a questioning eyebrow, prompting Glen to continue. "The Risers have officially crossed the Skirt. There's a large group of them who made it over in the northernmost part of the city. Right now, they're stationed east of Rott Manor and just north of the Samsara, residing in a Cluster that they conquered in short order. This was two Solays ago. They haven't made any other movements, so I'm sure they're just waiting for the main assault from the east to sweep down and pinch us in a death grip."

"How did this happen so fast?"

Glen looked frightened, a strange look on the strong man. "Word is a couple of Caesars let them through before accompanying them west. We have one who escaped the slaughter. She said she saw Caesars cutting down residents two at a time with their giant blades. From the descriptions she provided, sounds like Tiberius and Dom have officially joined the Riser ranks."

"So at least two, probably more Caesars will be fighting against us."

"Yeah, our aces in the hole have officially become jokers, complete wildcards."

Hadder nodded, trying to process this new information, this unfortunate turn of events. He looked sadly at Glen, already knowing the answer to the question he was preparing to ask. "Royal?"

Glen's face sank for his old friend. "Afraid he didn't have a guardian angel like you did. Poor bastard bled out on the floor."

"And Lilly Sistine?"

"The bitch escaped into the Rising. But not before she killed two others and severely hurt a third making her departure. We're lucky someone spotted her across the lawn running out covered in blood; otherwise, we may have just chalked the whole thing up to a Riser assassination. Before we could even get to you, a Caesar had come in and removed your body. How he got there so fast is beyond me. But those that saw you get carried out swore you were a goner. Said you had more holes in you than Swiss cheese." Glen took a moment. "But I said if anyone can find a way back, it'll be that sonavabitch."

"You were right, my friend. Now tell me where we're at with preparations."

"Hadder?"

"Yeah."

"I'm truly sorry about Lilly. I thought she was one of the good ones. We all did."

The phantom wounds began to throb. "Maybe she still is, Glen. Facing death is no easy task, especially for those of us who have faced it before, stared down the gullet of the abyss. Truth be told, if she had just asked me, I would have plunged that knife in my own heart for her safety and happiness."

"But she didn't ask you. And she sure as shit didn't ask poor Royal."

"No, she didn't. She just acted out of self-preservation."

"Well, if I see her across from us in the Great War, I'm going straight for her. And I'm going to kill her."

Now it was Hadder's turn to place his hand on Glen's shoulder. "That's good, Glen. Because I don't think I'll be able to."

———

"YOUR RETURN HAS EMBOLDENED THEM. Not just here, but all across the Setting. And just in time, too. I think more bad news may have crushed everyone's spirit."

Hadder didn't respond to Glen's words, instead choosing to keep his attention focused on the work being done on *The Royal Jelly*. Although he knew that Glen spoke the truth, Hadder was unnerved by his role of savior. One that had been thrust upon him by many residents. But given that it was a necessary burden to bear, Hadder simply decided to remain quiet on the matter. His mantle of messiah would be proven bullshit soon enough.

Ten feet from where the two men stood, twin guitars stuck up from the ground, marking where their friend Royal Winters lay buried. Hadder's chest rose and fell quickly as he continued to mourn his lost companion. Hadder looked over at the fresh grave and repeated a promise he had made several times in the past few Solays - we will fight to the end, Royal.

"We're making good progress," Hadder said to Glen as they both watched their deceased friend's Bar acquire needed defenses and offensive surprises. "If we dig in at various locations like this, it will be a real pain in the ass to uproot us. We should be able to hold out for months, if not more. Let's see how much these bastards are really willing to work for their precious freedom in the Before."

"Agreed. We'll be like the Afghanis, defending our labyrinthine positions and striking when and where least expected. We'll try the patience of these impatient freaks." Glen nudged Hadder hard in the ribs, pointed his chin across the lawn to the north. "Now, what the fuck is this?"

From one of the many garden pathways that spilled out into the vast lawn of *The Royal Jelly*, a female Riser stepped out, flanked on three sides by residents who each held a long blade to her throat or neck. The Riser wore a skin-tight black leotard with leather boots and leather bracelets that ran up and down both her arms. Although she bore no apparent weapons, Hadder looked carefully and spotted two small blades, sticking straight up from her knees, perfect for a deadly Muay Thai contest. To finish off her look, the woman bore a leather mask, pointed in the front like a human falcon mask, with eyeholes that revealed dark, calculating orbs.

Glen motioned the quartet over, placing his hand over the pommel of the sword he kept strapped to his side. When it came to Risers, no precaution was too much.

The Riser strode over, a confident march that would have been at home on both catwalk and battlefield. When she was fifteen feet from Hadder, Glen held up his hand. The Setter guards tightened their weapons against the woman's throat and neck, forcing her to a stop. An uncomfortable silence settled in as Riser and Setter stood face to face, sizing each other up. It was the woman who broke the muted stare-down. "Usually, the captor speaks first. And, as you can see, I am successfully captured. You must feel so powerful right now." Sarcasm dripped from her words like blood had surely trickled from her bladed knees.

Glen responded, "What is it you want, Riser? And know that if I don't like what I hear, I'll have you sent back to the Rising in pieces."

"Tsk tsk. That's no way to treat a war messenger."

"Is that what you are?"

"Well, I have a message, so you tell me."

"What's the message?"

The woman ignored Glen, turned her leather mask to face Hadder. "Marlin Hadder, officially back among the land of the living. The Krown wants you to know, the Great War wouldn't have been the same without you."

Hadder shot back. "Is that why he sent Lilly Sistine after me? It seems like he wanted to take a shortcut."

The Riser shrugged, the movement showcasing her toned body and fighting muscles. "Well, you can't blame him for trying. The more Risers that make it out of Station, the more havoc we can wreak on the world. Simple math, really. He had to give it a go. But he wants you to know that he's delighted that death didn't take. We all ache for a true test of our combat Elevations. Only Marlin Hadder can provide that."

Glen cut in. "Is that your message? That The Krown is happy Hadder is alive? You're wasting all of our time."

The Riser turned quickly to Glen, so fast that Hadder's hand went to the knife in this belt. "No, plain man. That is not the message; that is a senti-ment. The message is this. The Krown invites you, and however many resi-dents you want to a meeting at the Samsara. Early this Haela. He has one last proposition for you. One last chance to save your weak lives."

Glen looked to Hadder. "An obvious trap."

"That's why I don't think it's a trap."

"It's no trap, stupid Setters. My king, although all-powerful, has a weak-ness for the people of Station. He wants to grant all residents one last chance to join him, to free themselves of these suffocating walls, and show the world the next evolution in mankind. You owe your people one last option. After all, that is what your ethos is based on, is it not? Freedom of choice? Let them hear the offer straight from The Krown's mouth. After that, we can commence with war."

Hadder stepped forward, stopped just in front of the Riser. "Is that all?"

"That is all, Marlin Hadder."

Hadder seized the woman by the throat, squeezing until her dark eyes went wide. "If this is a trick or some other ghastly display, I'm going to put a knife between those fucking shark eyes of yours." He released, and the woman coughed through a bruised windpipe. "Tell The Krown I'll be there, with any others who choose to come. Now get this bitch away from me."

Hadder and Glen watched as the Riser was escorted from the lawn. "This is a mistake, Hadder."

"The Krown is confident he'll win this war. Assassinating Royal and me was one thing. But he won't want to look weak to his followers. And a cheap trick would do just that. No, he wants to gloat. He wants to instill fear in those of us who will face him, weaken our resolves before he drops the ax."

"Then why go?"

"Because I think he might fuck up. Plus, we're dead anyway, Glen. What could it hurt?"

26

Almost two hundred residents crossed the Bridge Gab'Riel with Hadder and Glen after the onset of Haela. While many wanted to trek with a full arsenal, Hadder talked the anxious group out of this approach. He was confident that The Krown was merely using this meeting as the last opportunity to strike fear into the hearts of those he was soon to conquer, enslave, and destroy. Coming to this gathering armed would merely incite a battle, one the Setters would surely lose.

Hadder heard the grumbling behind him as the group walked. Most were against accepting The Krown's invitation, but something nagged at the base of Hadder's skull, urging him to visit the Risers one last time before the Great War, allowing residents to truly see who it was they were up against.

"I sure hope you know what you're doing," said Glen as they made the final turn into the path that would empty into the Samsara clearing, passing the onyx statue of the man raising his fists to the heavens. In this moment, the figure had added meaning and impact.

"I don't know what I'm doing, Glen. But I know this is what needs to be done."

Hadder had spent the remainder of the Solay rolling the potentials of this meeting over in his mind. From what he could gather, the conference would have a two-pronged effect for The Krown. First, he would terrify the Setting one last time, making sword arms quake and knees wobble at the thought of the Riser invasion. Second, he may gain new converts through scare tactics. Hadder had to continually remind himself that The Krown was playing at a more ambitious game, one that entailed venturing out into the wider world and bringing chaos to that hurtful land. To accomplish that, The Krown would need to minimize losses and take significant numbers into the Before.

What Hadder was unable to calculate was how The Krown could possibly dishearten the residents who accompanied him to the assembly. What could be said that wasn't already said? What could be done that hadn't already been seen or spoken of?

As Hadder and Glen crossed into the Samsara clearing, he quickly had his answer. And it turned his stomach and shot pins into his heart.

Tied to the Samsara's glistening black bark with rough rope stood a wet Lilly Sistine, her arms pinned to her sides. She violently shook her head to break free, liquid shooting from her long hair. A hundred Risers stood behind the Samsara, many holding torches that lit the clearing with an eerie glow. The Krown stood on the white sand just to the right of Lilly, his massive arms crossed over his enormous chest. Although he remained quiet, his jade eyes laughed at Hadder and the pain that was evident on the man's fallen face. Next to The Krown stood the Riser female from earlier; Hadder could imagine the smug smile she wore under her leather mask.

Amidst her struggles, Lilly spotted Hadder as he came to a stop in the clearing. Her red eyes went wide. "Hadder! Please! Help me!"

Without thinking, Hadder moved forward, a knee-jerk reaction to a friend in need, but was stopped by Glen's firm hand on his chest and two other residents holding down each of his arms. Hadder looked to his friend, desperation welling up behind his eyes. Glen shook his head. "She made her choice, brother. Remember Royal. He didn't have that opportunity. Lilly stole it from him."

Hadder stopped fighting his restrainers, and instead shot an angry glare at The Krown. A disconcerting quiet fell over the clearing, only the sounds of hissing torches and a pleading Lilly Sistine preventing total silence. Hadder quickly grew tired of this standoff.

"You called this meeting, Riser," called Hadder. "Say your piece and let us be on our way. We have a war to prepare for."

The Krown smiled. "Always one to cut to the chase, aren't you, Marlin Hadder. Never one to understand the power of theatrics."

"Is that what this is? I thought you had a message. Or was I misinformed by your walking bird-bitch?"

"The theatrics *is* the message, Setter fool. But since you want to play obtuse, I'll spell it out for you. And when I say *you*, know that I am speaking to all of you Setters who stand here this Haela. But not you, Hadder. I'll repeat it; you had your chance, and you tossed it back in my face. You're already dead." The Krown took his eyes from Hadder, began to pace on the white sand before the Samsara and the wet girl strapped to its trunk. "My dear Setters, you are all very fortunate. You're fortunate for the fact that I am a magnanimous king and that I don't hate you. I hate these walls. I hate these rules. And I hate the world that chewed us up and spat us out into this sunless prison. Now, on the eve of our escape and the Great Return, I am feeling especially generous."

The Krown paused his pacing. The torchlight flickered off his metal spikes, creating a halo around his bulbous head. "Any Setter who comes to our encampment north of the Samsara before the close of Solay tomorrow will be welcomed with open arms and given opportunities to prove their worth in the coming Great War. We will walk over Station's ruined walls hand in hand, cross that damnable desert arm in arm, and wreak havoc on the Before as we stand shoulder to shoulder!"

The Risers in attendance let out a great howl of support for their leader, moved by his confident words. The Krown waited for their cheers to subside before continuing. "An inevitability is something certain to happen. Since the beginning, the Keys have known that Station was an ephemeral thing, a city that would appear then vanish in a blink of time's eye. They have known, and they have kept this from you. They knew the Fall was on the horizon, and yet they continued on as if nothing was amiss, lording over the other residents. Albany Rott has used all of us. We are but an experiment, pawns in a contest between the gods. Well, I tired of being a pawn, so I made myself a king. And now I welcome you all to huddle in the warmth of my leadership and protection."

"And the girl? What's Lilly Sistine doing there?" The unfamiliar voice cut in from the back of the grouped residents.

The Krown's evil smirk made a triumphant return. "Just as my charity knows no bounds, neither does my savagery for those who oppose or fail me. Those of you who stand against me in the Great War can expect the worst kind of death. We promise not to be quick, Setters. Let this image stay with you as you make your final decisions."

At those last words, several Risers holding torches moved towards the Samsara. Lilly Sistine began to hyperventilate as panic set in, her words coming out in short bursts. "I'm. So. Sorry. Marlin. Forgive me. Please. Forgive me."

As the torches touched the glistening black bark, fire sprinted across the flammable liquid that covered both tree and woman, filling the courtyard with a demon glow that reflected the devilish scene playing out in its center. Lilly screamed as the flames licked her face and engulfed her beautiful hair, which now danced high above her head on heated updrafts. Her perfectly tanned skin browned then blackened before peeling away to reveal raw flesh and bone beneath the fires. Lilly shook her head in vain to put out the ravenous blaze as her eyeballs exploded under the extreme heat. In seconds, her small form could barely be made out through the hues of red and yellow and blue; only her screams marked that she existed within the inferno.

The whole of the Samsara was now aflame, granting the great tree one last burst of color, a shitty reward for all that it had given Station's residents over uncounted time. Hadder looked over those who had followed him this Haela and found a mixture of fear, disgust, and sadness in their flickering faces. It appeared that The Krown's appalling show was having its desired effect. Could Glen have been correct? Could Hadder have made a grievous error?

Silence abounded as the flames raged and then began to subside, the

Samsara's black bark refusing to accept the fire after the combustible solution began to burn off. As the pyre began to die down, the hands that were holding Hadder back slipped away, and what was left of Lilly Sistine came into focus, now just a charred mound, looking like a natural knot that had forever been on the side of the magical black tree. For some strange reason, this image eased the pain in Hadder's heart.

The Krown stepped forward again, having retreated from the heat of the Samsara's fires. "Know that this act brought me no pleasure." His laughing green eyes showed him to be a liar in addition to his title of killer. "But I made dear Lilly Sistine a promise. Kill Marlin Hadder and join me in storming the Before. Fail me and get burned alive. As you can all plainly see, Marlin Hadder stands before me right now, quite alive. Setters! I am a king of my word. Take this last chance and join me. We will surf the waves of conquest together. Stand against me and being burned alive will be the kindest death I have to offer." The Krown looked again at Hadder. "And Marlin Hadder, don't forget my promise to you. You *will* kiss my crown, dead man."

No longer restrained, Hadder reached behind his back, fingering an object tucked into the back of his belt. "I'm not a king. Sadly, I'm just a man who's tired of people like you. But I, too, am a man of my word." In a flash, Hadder gripped the knife he had hidden away by the blade and flung it overhand in the direction of The Krown. The weapon sped past the giant Riser, missing his shoulder by inches, and buried itself to the hilt in the leather-masked forehead of the Riser woman. She stood dumbly for a moment, even reaching up questioningly to touch the foreign object protruding from her head, before falling straight back like a tipped over sculpture.

The Krown's face twisted in surprise and anger as he looked from the fallen woman to Hadder, who went on. "I promised that Riser that if I didn't like what I saw here, I would put a knife between her eyes. I didn't like what I saw. She now has a knife between her eyes."

The Krown's anger dissipated as quickly as it had arrived. His deep laughter filled the void left by the fire's extinguishment. "Well, look at us, Marlin Hadder. Don't we make an earnest pair? Enjoy that kill. You won't be so successful in the coming war." To the rest of the residents. "Life or death. Subjugation or suffering. The choice is yours, Setters. And it's the last time you'll be presented with options. My word is gospel, as you see here today. Whether that word brings you wine or fire, that is up to you."

With that, The Krown turned and exited the Samsara clearing, heading north back to his newly established stronghold. Slowly, residents also began to withdraw, not waiting for Hadder to lead the way. Hadder and Glen remained behind, staring sadly at the burnt remains of their dear friend who had made a tragic decision.

Glen spoke without looking over, tears streaming down his weathered face to find shelter in his thick beard. "What the hell just happened here, Hadder?"

Hadder blinked tears from his own eyes as he tried to make out the enchanting Lilly Sistine from the charred heap now stuck firmly to the Samsara. Despite his best efforts, he could not see her, did not want to see her. "Glen, I think I fucked up."

———

NEW NIGHTMARES JOINED Hadder's old bad dreams. A tiny hand jutting out from the wreckage and a wife's dead eyes were now accompanied by Kamaria's innards cascading down her body, a lover's face as a knife flashed before her, and a friend burning bright in the darkness of Haela.

Hadder sat up, covered in sweat. Despite the restlessness of his sleep, he looked over at the Moon Clock to discover that it was well into the Solay. Hadder dressed quickly into clean clothes laid out by a manikin and made his way through the underbelly of *The Royal Jelly*. Fleeting nausea came on as he passed the room he once shared with Lilly Sistine. Although Hadder wanted to flee this place that held tragedy alongside beautiful memories, he had few options. *Cranesman* was now too close to a Riser stronghold, and *The Royal Jelly*, with its thick walls and ample acreage, was currently the best choice for a Setter home base.

As Hadder made his way through the twisting hallways of the living quarters and up the stairs leading to the Bar's main level, he commented internally about the lack of residents to be seen meandering around. Coming out onto the ground floor, the Bar still rang empty, with only Glen sitting calmly at the counter closest to the entrance, the location where Hadder and Royal had been attacked by the treasonous Lilly Sistine. Carpets had been laid down where the two men's blood had stained the hardwood floor.

Hadder slid in next to his friend, who poured a beer from across the counter and passed it over. Both men stared forward towards the empty stage. "You're not here to kill me, are you, Glen? I don't think I can survive another betrayal." Hadder was only half-kidding.

Glen took a long drink. "Nah, partner, just waiting to talk with you."

"How many?"

Glen looked confused. "Come again?" How many what?"

"How many residents left for The Krown's encampment? I imagine a lot after word of last Haela's show got around."

Glen laughed softly into his beer.

Hadder misinterpreted the reaction, grew angry. "Look, Glen, I know I fucked up. I'm sure The Krown scared most residents into joining him, and those that are left will be shaking too badly to even hold a weapon properly. But at least let me know what we're working with here. How bad is it?"

Glen looked over, a twinkle decorated his eyes. "You don't get it, Hadder. You didn't fuck up. The Krown fucked up. Your original premonition was correct."

Hadder's face screwed up in confusion. "I don't understand."

"Last Haela's show didn't drive anyone to the Riser side. I mean, sure, maybe a few went in the Haela, but no one of consequence and surely no numbers of consequence. In fact, it did quite the opposite. Our people are more determined than ever to fight to the end. Look at what happened to Lilly Sistine. She killed a Setter leader in Royal, almost killed another in you."

"She did kill me."

"Even worse. So Lilly killed two Setter leaders, and what does she get for it? Burned alive like a fucking Salem witch. The Krown thought this display would give further weight to his threats while proving him a man of his word. All it really did was prove that he's a maniac who may kill you even if you do his wretched bidding. Not only does no one want to join him now, but most are also willing to die to see that he fails in reaching the Before. Most of us still have loved ones that we left behind in the world. If we can protect them from here, it's the least we can do for abandoning them."

A smile, full and honest, began to form on Hadder's face. His skin twisted strangely at the long-foreign action. "So, it's just what we needed to unify us?"

"Fucking A."

Hadder's mind whirled with possibility. "With a unified, motivated, pissed-off front, we can hold out for months, maybe even a year, slowly whittling down Riser numbers."

Glen looked down at his now-empty beer. "Yeah, well, that's the other thing I needed to talk to you about, Hadder." He peered over at Hadder, a look of Zen crossed over his leathery face. "The cluster leaders held a meeting first thing this Solay."

"And?"

"And the consensus was that no one wants to wait around to die. No one wants to hole up in a Bar, waiting for the Risers to get around to them. No one wants to fight like guerrillas, hitting and running, hoping to die rather than get taken alive. Everyone is tired of living in fear, and pretty pissed off. We gave up on our previous lives. Now our new ones are being taken from us. But whether Riser or Setter, we are all part of the same group. Meaning we did this to ourselves. We were given the keys to the kingdom and still managed to fuck it up. We collectively spilled the milk. Now we collectively have to clean it up. The Before doesn't deserve to deal with the monsters we created here in Station."

Hadder turned his stool to fully face his last true friend. "So, what are you saying, Glen? What did everyone decide while I laid in bed, struggling with nightmares?"

"They decided to fight. Head on. No running. No hiding. No digging in. No cowering behind fortifications. You said it yourself, we're all dead, anyway. It's just a matter of if we're willing to fight and how. Well, they're now ready to fight. And they want to play it straight. A Great Battle to decide the Great War and prevent the Great Escape."

"Glen, you have to know, we can't win in a head-to-head fight. The best we can hope for is that both sides lay in ruin at the end."

"That's enough for us." Glen thought for a moment, then continued. "The Krown was right about one thing, you know. Station was never meant to stand forever. It served some purpose for some higher entity, and now it's passed its expiration date. We were all given a great gift - more time. And some of us did great things with that time - loved again, danced again, sang again, lived again. Now it's time to pay it forward, make sure this chapter closes without its unseemlier pages drifting over into the real world."

Hadder sat in shock. That shock, however, quickly morphed into a healthy respect for the people of Station. Long he had felt they acted like children, willing to let others dictate how the rest of their second lives would play out. But it seemed like even the most tractable puppet eventually tired of its strings. "Ok, Glen, I'm in."

Glen stood up, grabbed Hadder by the elbow. "Don't tell me, partner. Tell *them*."

Glen led Hadder to the front doors of *The Royal Jelly*, flung them open. A deafening cheer rang out from the Bar's sweeping lawn, where thousands of residents had gathered, rallying for their chosen course of action and for the selected captain who would lead them all to their deaths. Chants of "Hadder" broke out from the din as bladed weapons were raised high to the large Idol Moon.

Hadder allowed the celebration to go on for several minutes before stepping forward and raising his hand. Silence fell over the resident mass. "So, you want to have a proper fight!" The lawn exploded once more in a cacophony of screams, cheers, and chants. Hadder held up his hand again. "I won't lie to you, my friends. We probably can't win. We probably can't live through this. But I'll tell you what we *can* do. We can make sure that most of those bastards don't make it to the Before. And those that do will make the trip with broken bones, bruised muscles, carved up flesh, and missing teeth. Yes, we'll probably all die out there, but we'll die on our terms, on our feet, not our backs. And we'll have a fucking great time doing it! Are you with me?!"

The crowd's reaction blew Hadder's hair back and caused tears to form in his eyes. Hadder looked over to Glen, who continued to stare at the gathered Setters through his mask of Zen. He looked to Hadder. "They're ready."

Hadder put his arm around Glen's shoulders, squeezed his friend. "We're all ready, Glen."

———

THE ROYAL JELLY became mission control for the entirety of Setter preparations. Each Solay, residents from across the Setting would come to drop off weapons they had crafted, train with others, and form bonds with those they would die next to in short order. As weapon creation and training went on, Hadder and other Cluster leaders walked through the organized commotion, offering words of encouragement while discussing strategy.

Given the group's desire for a one-and-done battle that would conclude the war in a single fell swoop, there was really only one location in all of Station that could accommodate both armies while allowing for complete freedom of movement. Therefore, the Grasslands were chosen as ground zero of the Great War, a place that would forever be littered with the bones of a city lost to time. Glen showed concern for the plan. "Why would The Krown even do this? Surely he would rather attack us here, surround us and pick us apart, minimize his losses."

Hadder responded. "You're right, Glen. The Krown would certainly rather do that. But he won't be able to."

"Why not?"

"Because we're going to openly challenge him in front of his army. He can't afford to appear weak or afraid, not to that crazed bunch. Any weakness he shows will surely welcome potential usurpers. Remember, this is the same man who was willing to fight Ego Rounds in single combat when he was dominating the Riser Wars. If we challenge him to what is essentially a fair fight, he'll be forced to accept. Losses be damned."

"And how do you plan on challenging him?"

"There's no easy way. Someone's gonna have to go up there and deliver the message."

————

"You're not going, Hadder. End of discussion."

"I can't ask anyone else to go. Wouldn't be right."

"Neither would abandoning your army on the eve of battle."

"He wouldn't dare harm me before the war."

"You forget. He already tried."

Hadder had no comeback for that particular point of Glen's. "What then?"

The group of Setter leaders continued their discussion on the porch of *The Royal Jelly*, throwing out various suggestions, from drawing names from a hat to opening up the dangerous job to volunteers. Dying in battle was one thing, getting butchered as a messenger was something completely different, much less honorable.

As the leaders bandied around solutions, someone escaped the mass of residents on the lawn, began to climb the porch steps. Hadder's mind spun to identify the woman closing in on the group. When who she was finally clicked into place, Hadder gripped the knife at his belt, readied it for blood.

Jackie Crone was almost unrecognizable in simple dark blue jeans, tennis shoes, and a sweater. Her white hair was pulled back into a tight ponytail that mirrored the too-tight old skin of her face. Her blue eyes were all that remained of the powerful Key who once lorded over the Celebration Cluster's most notorious Bar. They continued to blaze with hatred and judgment as she stopped a respectful distance from the group.

Hadder's palm hurt as he gripped the knife tightly, praying that the old woman did something, anything that would give him reason to plant the blade in her bird chest. "Jackie Crone. Tired of tormenting the unsuspecting? Or are you finally realizing that your wasted second life is coming to an end?"

Jackie fired back. "Still stinging from our time together, boy? But we had fun, no?"

The gathered leaders looked at Hadder with questions, some amused, but most disgusted. Hadder decided it best to keep the conversation moving. "What do you want, Crone? We're discussing important matters here."

"Like who to send to The Krown as a messenger?" Hadder's dumb look made Jackie smile a bit, showing her yellowed teeth. "Yes, yes, we all know what must be done. I'm here to make it easy on you. I'll take your message to The Krown. Give me details before I change my mind."

A snarky comment formed on Hadder's lips before he willed it away. "Before I give you the details, may I ask why, Jackie?"

The old bag of bones shrugged. "My time here has drawn to a close. As I feared, your appearance expedited that inevitability. I'm no warrior. And I'm no goddam Riser, either. The thought of returning to the wretched Before turns my guts. So I might as well put myself to some use. As you said, I tormented a lot of residents in my funhouse. And I loved every moment of it, drank each experience down like an aged bourbon. Now that the fun's over, maybe I owe some reparations for my actions. So, that's that. Now, what do you want me to tell that pointy-headed twat?"

Hadder grinned at the old woman. Although he stilled wanted to throw her from a building, he had to respect her dedication to her gimmick. "Tell The Krown that we will meet him in open battle five Solays from today, on the Grasslands, at the largest point of the Idol Moon. Winner takes all. No survivors. No prisoners."

Jackie Crone turned her head and spit on the porch; a dark green loogie hit the wood with a loud splat. "Well, you all are certainly letting your balls hang. No shame in that. I'll tell the freak."

With that, Jackie Crone began down the steps of the porch, her careful movements showing the effects of age. Hadder called after her. "Jackie, make sure you return swiftly after."

Jackie responded, but refused to turn back to the group. "Silly boy. You'll get the answer you seek, I'm sure. But I very much doubt that I'll be returning to deliver it to you."

———

SEVERAL OF THE resident Setters were former soldiers, had previous martial arts training, or simply had participated in numerous street fights in the Before. Hadder and Glen watched as these men and women trained small groups throughout *The Royal Jelly's* lawn. Looking to his right, Hadder watched as Jonny VV worked with a woman named Israel Izzy as she showed him various Krav Maga techniques. Near the edge of the lawn, his old friend Goldie was learning how to slip a punch from Tender Hollins, an accomplished boxer in his former life.

Glen commented from Hadder's left. "Well, we're all gonna die. But we ain't gonna go out like punks. Everything's going well, brother."

As Glen spoke, Hadder's attention was drawn to the south side of the lawn. "And it may get better yet, Glen."

From one of the southern pathways, Lester Midnight's muscled doorman Gondo entered the lawn, pulling a large cart behind him. He spotted Hadder from across the grass and approached, the wagon banging loudly. Gondo dropped the handles as he neared Hadder, wiped his brow as he panted. Although the doorman still wore his black suit pants and high-gloss dress shoes, he had stripped down to his wife-beater, showing off his impressive, no doubt Elevated, muscles. His bone mohawk shined white under the Solay's rays.

"Well met, Gondo. What brings you here today? Quite a load you have there."

"It's heavier than it looks," said Gondo as he shook Hadder's hand. "Good to see you, Hadder, I've been following your exploits from afar. No news or gossip fails to reach *Biomass*."

"So, I've learned."

"Anyway, I just wanted to say that I respect what you're doing here. We can't just let those monsters moonwalk into the Before. We all failed that place one time; no need to make it a habit."

"Well said, Gondo. Now, what have you brought?"

"A gift from Lester Midnight. Here's the note that goes along with it."

Gondo handed Hadder the folded message. Hadder was relieved to see that it was written on plain paper this time rather than someone's flayed skin. He opened the note and read the message aloud.

"Greetings, darling. While skin, muscle, and bone will always be my favorite medium, sharpened metal is a distant second. Please accept some of my past works as a donation to the cause. Please don't judge them too harshly. I know they appear a bit ostentatious, but trust that they'll sever bone like butter. See you at the party. Kisses. LM."

As Hadder recited Lester Midnight's words, Gondo peeled away the canvas covering from the cart to reveal a stockpile of ornate bladed weapons. Hadder shielded his eyes as the rays of Solay reflected off the highly polished surfaces of the handcrafted blades. Hadder and Glen moved towards the cart like children on Christmas morning who just received what they desperately wanted, but were too shy to request. An assortment of weapons littered the cart, including knives, hand axes, an array of swords, lances, halberds, and several unusual creations that were foreign to Hadder. Each weapon was decorated with scrollwork, gemstones, and other cosmetic embellishments.

Glen gingerly picked up a beautiful Bowie knife, tested its edge. "It's sharp. It's really fucking sharp."

"They all are," said Gondo. "And strong, too. They may look as if they were made for the movies, but Lester doesn't make things that don't function."

Images of Lester Midnight's "Biomass" display and his description of the exhibit assaulted Hadder. "I know what you mean. Lester has our sincere thanks. What about you, Gondo? Will you stay with us for a bit? We could use a man with your size and skills."

Gondo shook his head. "Nah, I must get back to Lester. But don't worry, we'll be by your side at the Fall. Which reminds me, Lester wanted to know when the Great Battle will take place."

"If all goes to plan, it will be four Solays from today, at the heaviest of the Idol Moon."

"Then, I'll let Lester know."

"Gondo, one more thing. The Haela before the Fall, we're going to gather one last time here on the lawn. Have one final Bash, say goodbyes properly this time. I would love you both to join us."

"I'll pass your invite along, Hadder. But no promises. Lester is in the process of closing down the museum, so he's been busy terminating his displays."

"Sounds somber."

"There's much cleanup. Now I will leave you. Don't worry if you don't see us at the Bash. Look to your right at the Great Battle. Lester and I will be there."

Glen turned to Hadder after Gondo left. "So, I guess we should start distributing these weapons."

Hadder sifted through the trove of weaponry, gleefully testing out various makes. "Absolutely. But not before we get our pick of the litter." Glen smiled and joined Hadder in pouring through the vehicles of butchery.

27

"It's been two Solays now and no answer, Hadder."

"The Krown's just trying to make us sweat it out. No need to make it easy on us."

"You sure about that? You don't think they're going to just attack in the middle of Haela, pinch us from two sides, end us that way?"

Hadder thought, but just for a moment. "No, The Krown wants a grand fight, something to unite his followers and bolster their energy for the trek into the Before. He's just making us twiddle our thumbs. Remember, he's a dick."

Hadder and Glen sat on the porch of *The Royal Jelly*, sharing a joint as they took in the beauty of the lawn and its surrounding gardens as Haela fell and the iridescent creatures of the night awoke. Glen seemed especially contemplative. "Are you scared, Hadder?"

Hadder didn't want to lie to his last remaining friend. "I've died twice now, Glen. And both times were terrifying. Now I'm staring down a third trip into the abyss. But this time, for the first time, I'm prepared, truly ready. So, no, I'm not scared. But that in and of itself is kinda scary."

"What makes you feel ready?"

"I know I was here for a short time compared to yourself, but I feel like I accomplished a lot in terms of living. I finally came to grips with losing my family. I made some close friends, lost a great friend, avenged a misdeed. I loved again, had my heart broken again. I have witnessed things never imagined, put my head in the jaws of a beast and took it out unscathed. I watched a Great Duel between two goliaths, met an artist of the flesh, and may have become acquainted with a god. If my life was empty those final days in the Before, it's overflowing in these final days of Station. The Rage that has plagued both my lives, I will release it all during the Great Battle and pass on with a clean slate. How about you, Glen?"

"I want to get one more piece of young ass, then I'll be good to go."

Hadder laughed and slapped his friend on the shoulder as the lawn filled with night bugs creating miniature fireworks shows. The yard hummed with natural light from hundreds of variations of life. As the two men sat smoking and drinking, looking out onto a world seen by so few, they would be foolish to feel anything but lucky.

———

THEIR ANSWER CAME LATE the next Solay, as residents finished up their training, many growing accustomed to their new weapons supplied by Lester Midnight, their swings becoming sharper, stronger, and more accurate. A Setter named Roco Roc, who had been stationed at *Cranesman* as a sentry tasked with watching if the Riser army crossed the Lethe, passed through the throngs of residents, carrying a black wooden box. He cut a straight path through the lawn, arriving at Hadder and Glen in short order.

"Hadder."

"Roco. What do we have here?"

"A single Riser dropped it off, left it in the middle of the Bridge Gab'Riel. One of our spotters retrieved it when the Riser left and brought it to me. I'm pretty sure it's for you."

Roco passed the box to Hadder, who stared nervously at its hinged top. "Did you look in it?"

Roco shifted uneasily from one foot to the other. "I did. I didn't want to bring anything dangerous here."

"Sound logic. What's in it?"

"I think it's best if you looked for yourself."

Hadder gently lifted the top of the box; the rusty hinges let out a scream as if in warning. On the underside of the lid, roughly carved into the dark wood, was a single word - *ACCEPT*. Inside the box, Hadder was greeted by a white bun of hair, which he grabbed and lifted. Hadder let the box fall to the ground as Jackie Crone's head came out in his hand. Her dangerous blue eyes had been plucked out, and a second message was scrawled into her head with a blade. An X had been carved into the middle of her forehead, with a simple sentence above.

GIVE US A KISS.

Hadder showed Glen, then dropped the old woman's head back into the box on the ground. He kicked the box closed with his foot. "Well, neither subtle nor classy, but at least we have our answer. Gather everyone. We need to let them know that we have one last Solay to train. And to plan for a Bash that will send us all off with smiles on our faces."

Glen smiled. "We may be shit at fighting, but when it comes to planning a Bash, no one does it like a resident of Station."

———

THE FINAL SOLAY of training went well, equal parts work and frolic. An infectious buzz and humming energy permeated the residents as they finalized basic blade techniques and prepared for the Haela's festivities.

Some of the furniture from inside *The Royal Jelly* was brought outside and laid out across the lawn. Hidden lawn speakers were checked and double-checked while additional speakers were brought out from behind *The Royal Jelly's* famous stage. Although the yard was reasonably lit during Haela thanks to the iridescent creatures and vegetation that surrounded the Bar, more lighting was brought out and set up. In short order, the lawn of

The Royal Jelly looked to be a breeding ground for one of history's grandest celebrations.

Hadder sat on the Bar's porch as the last of the residents trickled out to prepare for the Haela's Bash, deemed by most residents the Great Goodbye. Glen returned from making some alterations to the inside of the Bar and joined Hadder. Together, the two friends sat for a bit in silence, taking advantage of one final moment of quiet reflection as they admired the home that their lost friend Royal had created within this strange world that was Station.

Hadder was the one to break the silence. "I'm looking forward to hearing Miles sing one last time."

Glen shifted in his chair. "I guess no one told you. Miles went over to the other side. Was one of the few who joined them after that shit show at the Samsara. Probably thinks he's gonna be a huge star in the Before, the next Michael Jackson or some shit. That plan didn't work out so well for someone else we knew."

Hadder was unable to mask his disappointment. "I think he doesn't quite understand that the Risers aren't planning on being huge supporters of the arts. They're more likely to start burning books like a bunch of Elevated Nazis."

Glen shrugged. "Fear of death makes you rationalize crazy actions, I suppose. Not to worry, we still have plenty of talented singers and musicians on hand."

"Quite right," said Hadder, but in his heart, he knew the concert wouldn't be the same without Station's two most angelic voices. He changed subjects. "You feel ready, my friend?"

"Brother, I've been ready. I may look like a million bucks, but I feel like a shit-covered penny. I'm tired and heavy, with two lives being held together by one old body. But don't you worry, I'm spry enough to take a couple of Risers with me before it's all said and done." Glen thought for a moment. "You think there's any chance we win? And if so, what happens next?"

Having witnessed the ferocity and fighting prowess of the Risers first-hand, Hadder thought very little of their chances but saw no reason to piss on his friend's glimmer of hope. "There's always a chance, Glen. And if we do, showing our passion for these second lives, maybe Mister Rott keeps the city alive. Maybe he'll be curious to see if the process repeats itself, if another Riser faction crops up in time."

Glen simply nodded. Sometimes men just need the slightest of openings to keep pushing with all their might. Glen got up on obviously stiff legs. "I'm gonna go get ready. How bout you?"

Hadder continued to stare, past the lawn, to the Grasslands, where most, if not all, of his friends would meet their bloody fates. "Are the Elevation Centers still open, Glen?"

"I would assume so. It seems like the manikins are going about like everything's hunky-dory. Business as usual for them. Why?"

"Just asking. Look, I gotta take care of something, but I'll see you at the Great Goodbye."

"Everything ok, brother?"

"Just something I think I should do." Hadder's voice was distant, as if he was already on the Grasslands.

———

THE GREAT GOODBYE was everything it was hoped to be and more. The porch was transformed into an outdoor stage, where Station's remaining musical talents wowed the gathered residents with heartfelt renditions of everyone's favorite songs. More manikins than ever seen crisscrossed the lawn and made their ways in and out of the Bar, delivering a potpourri of drink and smoke to the celebrating Setters. People danced, hugged, and kissed throughout the Haela, giving thanks for second life friends and experiences.

Arriving a bit late, Hadder was given a king's welcome as he stepped out onto the lawn. McKintosh Reed greeted him with a handshake and a slap on the shoulder, his Elevated dreadlocks still moving of their own accord like octopus legs in the ocean. Yasmin Dash, her elegant wings tucked neatly behind her, kissed Hadder deeply as he passed through, returning to her sensual dancing as soon as he moved on.

"Old chap! Old chap!" Hadder looked past several residents to discover Jonny VV calling him from a leather couch that had been brought from inside. The two old friends embraced, held each other for a long while before separating.

"Good to see you, Jonny."

"Hadder, drink with me, old sport." He handed Hadder a glass of crimson liquid. Hadder didn't care to ask what Number it was. "To Reena Song. Always and forever."

"Cheers to that."

The two friends sat for some time, exchanging stories from Hadder's early months in Station. Jonny told a few tales of Reena Song from before Hadder's arrival, and the two men smiled dumbly together, feeling as if their lost friend was sitting there next to them. "You think she's in a good place, Hadder?"

Hadder didn't need time for his response. "I think if there's a heaven or some other utopian next life, Reena Song is there now, waiting for you."

Tears welled in the flamboyant man's eyes. "Thanks, Hadder." Jonny VV looked to his right, and his eyes went wide. Hadder followed his eyes to a beautiful young woman dancing provocatively in a miniskirt. "Now, if you'll excuse me. I plan on ending the Great Goodbye in the arms of another, and it won't be you, old chap. No offense."

Hadder laughed. "None taken. Go get her, Jonny."

Hadder spent the next few hours bouncing from group to group, sharing in stories, drink, and smoke. On one couch, he found Monty the Mod, offering his beloved Ophidian to any who showed interest. Hadder moved next to the small man. "Monty. Happy you made it. I mean that. How's the jaw?"

Monty looked up, his face giving nothing away. "Marlin Hadder. The man who stole any hope for extra time in my city. The jaw's fine, thanks for asking."

"Monty, I..."

"Stop. This Haela is not for that. Here, she misses you." Monty held up the Ophidian towards Hadder. The serpent raised its body and froze at face level with Hadder, who breathed in deeply as the snake opened its maw and released its powerful smoky breath. "Goodbye, Marlin Hadder."

"Goodbye, Montgomery Walls."

The party continued, rising to a feverish pitch as drugs took hold, old friends became reacquainted, and new friends were made. Hadder, a crazed smiled pasted on his face from the Ophidian, made his way towards the stage, feeling a fundamental need to be close to the music. Several residents were on the porch, playing instruments with practiced fingers, driving the crowd into a frenzy. Hadder danced frantically with everyone around him, feeling the same camaraderie that helped pull him from the darkest time of his two lives. In short order, Hadder was out of breath and thankful as the set concluded and the music died down.

Hadder began chatting with a man when a scream from the crowd brought his eyes to the stage once more. Inexplicably, Glen was crossing the porch to stand before the microphone, his thick beard glistening with sweat. A twinge of nervousness struck Hadder, desperately hoping his friend wouldn't make a drunken fool of himself. Glen called out to the band behind him, and the woman on guitar began the first notes of "Simple Man." Seconds later, a second lead guitar joined in, and the song was underway. Glen took the mic stand in his hands and leaned forward. "This is for my good friend and brother, Royal Winters." Glen went on to release the song's first lyrics, his voice vibrant and clear, and the equal of any recording Hadder had heard. The lawn erupted in applause, delighted to discover that one of the city's most beloved figures stowed away a hidden talent.

"I had no idea he could sing," said a woman next to Hadder as the crowd quieted to better hear Glen.

"Me neither," replied Hadder as he looked over to the owner of the voice. The young woman he found there was stunning, with porcelain skin and a full head of wavy red hair that fell down her back. Although her arms and legs were covered with tastefully done tattoos, one, in particular, drew Hadder's attention. The middle of her forehead was decorated with the image of an elaborate key. Beneath the art, Hadder was able to make out the faint lines of a scar. A memory tickled his brain before clicking into place. "What's your name?"

"I'm called Coral. You're Marlin Hadder."

"I am. Nice to meet you. By the way, Shirley says hello."

The young woman's face contorted in confusion before realization hit her like a Caesar's hammer. She instinctively reached up to touch the scar on her head. Hadder gently caught her wrist. "Long journey we took just to end up at the same Bar again."

Coral smiled coyly. "Must be fate."

"And who are we to fight fate?"

"We're nobody."

"Exactly."

Coral and Hadder went on to dance throughout the night, joined by Glen and another young woman once his set concluded. They danced, they hugged, they kissed, and they laughed. At the party's apex, Hadder was forced to take the stage, address those in attendance. With a headful of drugs and a swollen heart, he had no choice but to speak the truth.

"My fellow residents of Station. I want to thank each and every one of you. Not just for coming out this Haela, but for sharing your lives with me. Like many of you, I was a husk of a man when I came to this strange city. While it's never easy to find the broken pieces of yourself, much less to put them back together, this city and many of you helped me do just that. I would be lying if I said this place was without pain, for what life is worth living without pain. But we all forged on past the pain that we carried here with us, made new homes in our reset realities. I'm proud of what we did here. I'm proud of the improvements some of us made and the lives we created. Tomorrow, we'll prove our love for this city, prove that we are passionate about our second chances. Prove that everyone can change for the better. I love you all and will gladly end my second life among you. Now find someone you care about and show them how much you appreciate their place, however small, in your life. Long live the Setting and long live Station!"

Applause began slowly, with many residents wiping moisture from their eyes, but built to a crescendo of ovation. As Hadder stepped away from the microphone, music returned in full as the Great Goodbye continued. Walking down the porch stairs, Hadder looked past the back of the lawn, where deep in one of the dark pathways, two red embers took in the festivities. Hadder met those embers with his own eyes, watched as they faded away into the shadows.

As the Great Goodbye began to wind down, pairs, trios, quartets, and more slunk off to find more private quarters. Coral and Hadder followed suit, discovered their own intimate space deep inside *The Royal Jelly*. There, they shared each other without reservation, allowing fear to be replaced with lips and skin, fingers and tongues. Even if for only a single night, the two residents found real comfort in each other's naked embraces, felt truly at home.

28

M arlin Hadder basked in the rays of the Solay as he anxiously fingered the handle of the ornate samurai sword that hung from its equally decorated scabbard at his hip. A gentle breeze drifted through the Grasslands, caressing the thousands of faces that dotted the open field. The Rage slowly moved forward within Hadder, readying itself to take full control. Hadder took a deep breath and smiled.

It was a good day to die. Again.

To his right, Glen nervously shifted his museum-quality flanged mace from one hand to the other. To his left, Jonny VV's knuckles went white as he tightly gripped a bone-handled rapier, looking more at home in a fashion show than on a battlefield. Both men shook with fear, although Glen was doing a much better job of covering it. Hadder couldn't blame either man.

The Riser army was more impressive than even Hadder had anticipated, gathered all together for the first time on the eastern side of the Grasslands, their numbers now exceeding the Setters by two to one. The Risers shined like diamonds, the large Idol Moon reflecting loudly off countless sharp metal edges. The Setters also glittered, light bouncing off of the various self-made and Lester Midnight-provided blades. But while the Setters carried weapons, the Risers *were* weapons. Spiked knuckles, bladed elbows and knees, and encased heads screamed under the bright Solay, begging for the opportunity to darken under a coat of Setter blood.

Above the ocean of Risers, four figures towered over the others. In addition to Dom and Tiberius, the twin albinos Vespa and Vitellius had forsaken their duties as Caesars to join the Riser revolution. With six Caesars to the Risers' four, the Station loyalists still held the advantage in that regard, but it was much more slight than initially hoped.

Standing front and center, shouldering a broadsword the size of a child, was The Krown. The beast stared directly at Hadder, his jade eyes blazing with the promise of pain and sorrow. While most Setters trembled, The Krown quietly chuckled, basking in the moment, his greatest so far as a king.

Hadder tore his gaze from The Krown to look up and down his makeshift group of defenders. Their six Caesars stood emotionless, equally spaced down the frontlines. The only Caesar that Hadder could remotely consider a friend, Cal, stood closest, only six Setters to his left. Cal looked down at Hadder and nodded, slapping his two swords together. Hadder continued to look back and across the Grasslands, praying for any signs of Albany Rott. There were none.

A familiar and welcome voice came at the perfect time, preventing resignation from taking hold. "Sorry, we're late, darling." Cutting through the Setter lines, Lester Midnight appeared behind Hadder with Gondo in tow. "I'm afraid I'm guilty of longwinded farewells, and my *Biomass* was hard to leave behind."

Hadder smiled at both men, shook their hands. "Just happy you're here, Lester. Good to see you, Gondo." The bone-hawked man nodded in return as he took off his suit jacket and let it drop to the ground, showing almost a dozen daggers tucked into his belt. In his right hand, the large man expertly held a metal police baton. True to form, Lester Midnight carried the most fanciful scimitar Hadder had ever seen. Hadder forced himself to look away lest he got caught up admiring the inlays and scrollwork. "Thanks again for the weapons, Lester. Beautiful work."

Lester smiled broadly. "Oh, just wait until you see them in action, darling."

A voice from across the Grasslands demanded Hadder's attention. It seemed The Krown tired of the dramatic standoff. "Marlin Hadder! Brave of you to join us. I must admit, I thought we would waste months ripping coward Setters from their Bars. I appreciate you expediting the process. Your recognition of the inevitability of the Fall pleases me. Not as much as your head hanging from my neck will, but still." The Krown kept his eyes squarely on Hadder but spoke to his followers. "Risers! No prisoners. No survivors. No mercy. They are all that stand between us and these walls, which will crumble soon. Go take your freedom! It can be found in the chest of a Setter!"

The Risers released a loud, singular roar that ripped across the Grasslands; Hadder could almost feel their unified breath on his cheek. Riser captain Wagner stepped out from the screaming mass, walking forward to stop in the center of the two groups, a long saber dangling from his right hand, trailing the tusked man. "Which of you weak men will taste my blade first? Come to me. Don't worry about the women you leave behind. I will tongue their cheeks before I take their heads."

Wagner's words rang hollow to Hadder, but they deeply triggered something in his friend Jonny VV, who sprinted forward, a primal cry emanating from his soul. Hadder tried to grab his fragile friend's shoulder, but reacted too slowly, catching only air in his gloved hand. Instead, he watched wide-eyed as Jonny ran towards the Riser, rapier cocked back in his right hand, quickly covering the seventy-five feet.

As he neared Wagner, Jonny thrust forward with his slim rapier, putting all the anger, fear, and sorrow he had into that blinding lunge aimed for the Riser's chest. Unfortunately, the tip of Jonny's blade caught only air as Wagner pirouetted in the blink of an eye, pulling his long saber behind him. Jonny flew past his intended target and hit the brakes, intending to spin back to face his enemy. But it was too late.

As Jonny slid to a stop in the grass, Wagner executed a perfect backhand that sent the devilish saber directly through Jonny's waist, neatly cutting the fashionable man in half. As Jonny's bottom half froze immediately, the upper part of the Setter's body flew forward, rolling to a gory stop several feet from the man's legs. A geyser of blood flew upwards from what was left standing of Jonny VV, creating a macabre statue that stole noise from the battlefield.

From behind him, Hadder could hear Lester Midnight comment. "Beautiful."

Seconds later, Jonny VV's legs gave way to gravity and collapsed to the ground, offering the first of what would become many stains on the grassy turf. Hadder held his breath, worried about the effect that Jonny VV's death would have on his army.

His concern was misplaced.

As one, the Setters howled in rage, furious at the death of the well-liked Jonny VV. Hadder released the last few threads of control, allowing the Rage to guide him, drive him. He merged his Rage with that of the group, drew his samurai sword, and held it up to the Idol Moon. "For Station!" Hadder screamed, and the Setters moved forward as one. The Risers met the roar with one of their own and launched their assault.

The Battle for Station was on.

———

THERE WAS NO THINKING, only reacting to the chaos that surrounded Hadder. Red mist hung on each breeze through the Grasslands, forcing Hadder to continually wipe his eyes. During one such wipe, a knife flew from the mass of fighting, aimed for Hadder's throat. He lurched sideways at the last second, and the blade cut a deep chasm in Hadder's neck, narrowly missing his carotid artery.

"Fuck!" Hadder yelled, his hand reflexively going to his wounded neck. When his hand returned wearing a crimson glove, Hadder's Rage rose a level, forcing him to wade into a trio of Risers. The first Riser was trying to communicate with her companion, working to refine their fighting strategy. Hadder's samurai sword sliced downward angrily from the side to land just behind the forehead, and the woman's face slithered off her head, leaving the other Riser to stare into an open nasal cavity. The shocked male Riser tried to react, but Hadder had already begun a backswing that tore open the man's throat and created a waterfall of blood that cascaded down his bare chest.

The final Riser moved in quickly, swinging an arm that had been transformed into a wicked-looking blade below the elbow. With Hadder's sword out wide from the vicious backhand, he was utterly exposed, unable to get his weapon back in time to parry the strike. Hadder tensed, waiting for the cold steel to penetrate his body.

Instead of stabbing pain, however, Hadder felt only swift air as something flashed before him too quickly to register. The Riser howled, and a moment later, Hadder was hit with a stream of warm blood from the stump of his arm. Both Riser and Hadder looked down to see the arm-blade on the ground, then looked again at each other. Hadder shrugged, and the Riser's head flew from its shoulders as Lester Midnight completed his kill. "Stay sharp, darling. I may not be there next time." Having saved Hadder's life, Lester rejoined the battle, moving like quicksilver as he floated from one Riser to the next, giving out five wounds for each one he received.

With some space now around him, Hadder took a moment to evaluate the battlefield. Lester Midnight's cache of weapons was having a more substantial impact on the battle than Hadder had anticipated. Although more aggressive and experienced, the Risers were enduring an unforeseen disadvantage in that many of their homemade weapons were shattering when encountering Lester Midnight's superior craftsmanship.

Unfortunately, only about fifty residents were wielding Lester's creations. Where they didn't have that advantage, the Risers were decidedly winning. Hadder winced as a familiar Riser woman tore the right eye from Star, the first resident other than Miles to welcome him to the city. Speaking of Miles, Hadder watched as the traitor-singer hid behind the Caesar Tiberius, jabbing out at Setters with a long halberd from the safety of the creature's immense shadow.

Elsewhere, Setters fought bravely, swelling Hadder's heart with pride. McKintosh Reed fought off a quartet of Risers with a fury. He struck out against the two combatants facing him with two machetes while the Risers to his left and right dealt with McKintosh's whirling dreadlocks, each one tipped with a small knife. McKintosh took the hand from one Riser with a machete while simultaneously taking spiked knuckles to his shoulder from the other. He fell back, his dreadlocks keeping the other two at bay, the blade falling from his injured left arm. In a release of fury, McKintosh shot forward, driving his remaining machete deep into the shoulder of the spike-knuckled Riser. As the Riser fell, McKintosh was pulled down, his lone blade stuck in the man's clavicle. The Risers pounced on the grounded resident, one sending a thin sword through McKintosh's back while the other repeatedly kicked his sides with edged boots. McKintosh spat blood onto the lifeless face of the Riser beneath him before he, too, dropped dead. The attacking Risers both leaned down, screaming profanities at the deceased Setter, but quieted suddenly as two dreadlocks leaped up from their owner's corpse, taking both men through the throat.

Hadder fought through the crowd, his sword shattering Riser weapons, stealing arms from torsos, and fertilizing the soft ground with Riser innards. He passed the Caesar Titus, who, although teetering on one leg, battered Risers with his frightening battle-hammer. Further north, an area had opened up where the albino twins Vespa and Vitellius teamed up against their fellow Caesar Otho. The ground shook as the titans went at each other, Otho narrowly missing the traitors with his double-headed ax. But as impressively as Otho fought, he was no match for the twins, who moved with practiced synchronization, each wielding a matching glaive that allowed them to strike from a distance, rendering Otho's ax ineffective. Otho moved forward without fear, trying to get inside those demon spears, but was eventually caught in the side by Vespa. Otho clutched his wound, and it was all the opening that Vitellius needed to slip his own glaive between the loyal Caesar's ribs, pushing down the pole to drive the blade up and into Otho's gigantic heart. Otho fell face-first into the grass, and the twins moved on quickly, cutting a swath through the Setter lines.

As Hadder reengaged in the center of the melee, he was bleeding from a dozen wounds, although none of them incapacitating. He felt no pain as the Rage coursed through him, driving his body faster, strengthening each blow. Hadder batted away a trident aimed for his stomach, then carved a path through the Riser's face on the backswing, taking out both eyes in the process. Feeling danger to his left, he spun without thinking, narrowly avoiding becoming split in two by a vicious sickle. The Riser swinging the blade smiled, his face studded with metal and his eyes tattooed entirely black. He attacked again, and Hadder leaped back, again moving just out of the curved blade's path. Hadder moved in as the weapon passed. The Riser flipped the handle over and regripped for a backswing attempt. Hadder, inside now, blocked the backswing with a right front kick while bringing his sword down atop his foe's head, which split down the middle like a melon.

A scream from behind Hadder saved his life, forcing him to react by diving to his left. Despite the fast movement, a long blade caught Hadder in his right side, neatly slicing through his cut-resistant clothing and ripping open a deep wound that showed off the white of his ribs. Hadder quickly rolled onto his back on the ground, bringing his right sword arm up to defend while covering his injured side with his left. Hadder cursed under his breath as the Riser captain Wagner stared down at him, brown teeth showing between metal tusks. No insulting words or cute sayings were delivered as Wagner began stabbing down with his long saber. Hadder knocked the first blow out wide to his left, and the second was backhanded to the right, although it still nicked his shoulder, adding to Hadder's laundry list of wounds. Hadder knew that Wagner would adjust; that one of the next few strikes would find a vital organ. In desperation, his left hand felt around the soft grass, hoping to grab dirt, pebbles, or anything else which could be thrown in the bastard Riser's eyes. His hand found nothing. It was time to die.

Wagner came on again, both hands on the pommel of his sword to resist deflection, determined to drive the saber through the despised Marlin Hadder's heart. As Wagner started his downward thrust, two giant dark orange hands appeared from the red mist, reaching down from above to grasp a metal tusk in each hand. With a grunt and jerk, the tusks were ripped from Wagner as the man screamed. The metal inserts each took one half of the Riser's jaw with them as they were removed and thrown across the Grasslands. Wagner fell to his knees, a gurgling cry caught in his throat as his tongue hung in midair like red rope licorice. Ignoring the pain in his side, Hadder pushed off with his left arm, propelling himself forward, bringing his samurai sword around to cleave the captain cleanly through the neck. Wagner's head sat motionless for a moment before falling forward and rolling to a stop between Hadder's legs.

Cal offered an oversized hand to Hadder, helping him to his feet. "That's two times you've saved my life," Hadder said to the Caesar.

"Father Rott's orders," was all that Cal said before rejoining the battle, his twin swords leading the way.

Hadder looked across the fighting once more, the Rage working hard to overcome pain and exhaustion. Although the Setters were fighting admirably, felling at least one Riser for every Setter that was killed, the numbers were simply becoming too much. Yasmin Dash performed a dance of death, spinning through the Riser ranks, her now-bladed wings out wide, carving up enemies as she twisted and rolled. A knife soared from the crowd around her and managed to miss her twirling wings, burying itself to the hilt between the beautiful woman's shoulder blades. Yasmin arched her back in pain, and three Risers moved in like lightning, driving metal though her neck, chest, and stomach.

Elsewhere, every Setter seemed to be fighting at least two Risers, a disadvantage even seasoned warriors would have a hard time overcoming. Friends died wherever Hadder looked. Monty the Mod floated just over the battle on his light disc, striking down at Risers with the Ophidian, which was no longer dispensing psychoactive smoke but fast-acting poison through its curved fangs. Riser faces swelled up like balloons when they were bitten, cutting off air passages and leaving suffocated bodies dead on the ground. Monty celebrated one such successful strike before a spear thrown by the unfaithful Caesar Tiberius caught him in the chest and drove him from his disc. Monty disappeared into the crowd of Risers below, never to be seen again.

Hadder's body began to betray him as blood continued to leach from his multiple wounds. Stumbling his way towards Glen, whose mace was thick with Riser flesh as he faced off with three Risers, Hadder tripped on something and fell hard. Looking back as he rose, he found both Helen and Nestra butchered on the ground, holding each other in a death embrace. Hadder shook off the disturbing image and limped towards his friend, who still managed to swing his weapon like a madman, holding the Risers' attentions. Hadder slipped in behind Glen's combatants, driving his sword through the back of one and taking the arm of another before anyone even knew he was there. Glen took the final Riser in the face with his mace as the man stared at Hadder in surprise.

"How you holding up, brother," asked Glen.

"I don't know how much more I have in me."

"Me neither. But we've had a good showing, no?"

"Absolutely."

"Then let's finish strong, shall we?"

"Absolutely."

"See you on the other side." And with that, Marlin Hadder's friend Glen waded back into the fray. It was the last time Hadder would see him.

An especially loud fracas caught Hadder's attention towards the edge of the battle. Lester Midnight faced off with six Risers, his scimitar dancing in the air, blocking a sword here, taking a finger there, sending a knife wide here, removing the top half of a Riser head there. By the time Hadder got there, Lester had narrowed it down to four Risers. One peeled off to face Hadder while the others continued to wear down Station's most notorious artist.

The Riser woman with the bladed whip cracked her weapon towards Hadder, testing the distance. With very little energy remaining, Hadder disregarded any strategies that required sudden dives or quick dodges. He was just going to have to take one to give one and hope that he gave better. Remembering what the Riser woman did to Star, Hadder baited his foe, dropping his sword low to the right, with no chance to parry the blinding strike. The woman screamed in triumph, showing fangs, and cracked the whip in Hadder's direction. The whip flew true, as Hadder knew it would, heading straight for his left eye. Anticipating the move, Hadder's left hand was up, palm out, even before the Riser completed her arm movement. The blade drove into Hadder's palm and stuck. Using the pain to fuel the Rage, Hadder circled his wrist around the whip and pulled forward suddenly, catching the woman off-guard before she could release her weapon. She stumbled forward, no defense in place, and met Hadder's samurai sword with her head, which fell with a thud to the crimson ground.

Hadder turned back to where Lester was fighting and found the man lying on the ground, four Risers dead around him and another hovering above him, poised for a killing thrust. Hadder cut the Riser in half from right shoulder to left hip and chuckled darkly as the top half slid from the bottom. The laugh quickly stopped, however, when he saw Lester on the ground. He dropped to his knees next to the artist, whose guts were spilled out onto the grass next to him.

Lester smiled as he recognized Hadder. "So good of you to come, darling. You're the only one to attend my funeral."

Hadder began to choke up, pushed it down. "You're going to be fine, Lester."

"Lying doesn't become you, darling. Just tell me this. How does it look?"

Hadder looked down at his strangest friend's entrails, a sticky mound of red and pink, glistening curves catching the rays of the Solay, sending starlight back into the air. "It looks beautiful, Lester. A true work of art."

Lester's smile widened, his eyes now looking at something far past Hadder, at something more beautiful than Hadder could ever imagine. "Ahh, thank you, darling. That's all I ever wanted." And with that, Lester Midnight died.

Hadder spun away from his friend, sat on his backside as hell played out around him. Setter blood was spilled across the battlefield, and even the Caesars were beginning to fall. Hadder watched as Jules was piled on by ten Risers with long spears, looking like a pincushion when they fell away. Risers laughed as they chased after retreating residents and cut them down from behind. Despite battle continuing across the Grasslands, both sides knew. The Battle for Station was effectively over.

Risers now took their time, their victory all but ensured. They chanted the name of their king as they carved up pleading Setters. They sang crude songs about what they would do in the Before. They pounded fists as Setters were raised into the air, impaled on long spears. Hadder put his head in his hands, the sounds of mockery too much to handle, cutting him deeper than any wound he had received.

Then all went silent.

Hadder removed his face from his hands, was immediately confused. The battlefield had grown dark, and Hadder looked up to see black clouds moving in to cover the Idol Moon, something never before seen in Station. Lightning jumped between the charcoal clouds, and thunder shook the Grasslands. Risers and Setters alike had stopped their fighting, all now facing east, staring slack-jawed. Hadder limped through the remaining warriors, finally reaching the edge of bodies to glimpse a view.

Manikins lined up and down the Skirt, more than Hadder had ever seen in one place. In the center of the manikins stood Albany Rott, his red eyes ablaze with fire and his crystalline hatchets in each hand. Lightning continued its dance above their heads, and thunder threatened to crack open the ground beneath their feet. Hadder felt a drop on his arm, then another as the skies opened up, sending a deluge of liquid to assault the Grasslands. Looking at his arms, Hadder jumped to see them covered with blood, thinking he was wounded worse than thought, before realizing that it came not from him, but from the skies. It was raining blood.

"People of Station," Albany Rott cried out, his voice booming across the Grasslands, forcing Hadder's chest to tighten. "I gave you paradise, and you turned it into Abaddon. Let me be the first to congratulate you on proving me correct. Your prize? Obliteration." As Rott completed that final word, the eyes of all the manikins changed suddenly, trading in their milky nothingness for the fires of Rott's red orbs. Rott motioned forward with one of his crystal axes, and the manikins poured into the Grasslands, moving with impossible speed, eyes ablaze with unknown anger.

They tore into the Risers, fighting like mechanized zombies, ignoring cuts and stabbings to rip the eyes from heads, throats from necks. Albany Rott followed after them, his twin axes a blur as he dispatched three Risers in the blink of an eye.

For a moment, Hadder's heart swelled, thinking he had reached the enigmatic Mister Rott; thinking they had proven the love many residents held for the city; thinking Rott had come in their time of need to save them.

Hadder was wrong on all accounts.

Manikins attacked Setters as readily as they did Risers. Hadder watched in horror as Gondo's body was ripped into four pieces by a group of manikins, who took no time to admire their handiwork. Instead, they ran off to leap upon the Caesar Augustus. Unable to tear apart the Caesar, like a mere resident, the manikins instead held on tightly to the giant before exploding, sending fiery manikin parts flying while opening smoldering holes across Augustus's body. With white bone and pink muscle peering out from four craters, the Caesar let out a roar before falling to the wet ground, an unmoving pile of scorched flesh.

Explosions went off around Hadder as Setters and Risers both ran in fear and confusion. Thunder continued to shake the ground, which eventually opened small crevices across the Grasslands from which fire poured out, engulfing resident, Caesar, and manikin alike. Hadder stumbled around the shaking ground, the flames lighting up the battlefield as if it were a stadium. Red rain continued to fall in sheets as manikins, even those on fire, persevered, killing all in their path.

Hadder looked on as Titus batted away a dozen manikins with his warhammer before three took hold and detonated, sending the Caesar to his knees to be swarmed by more manikins. To the left of that, Hadder found Coral sprinting west, two manikins closing quickly. Hadder moved to follow but was sent flying to the side as something smashed into his ribs, breaking most of them. His sword flew off into the crowd.

Hadder sucked in deeply, trying to breathe in through broken bones, and flipped over onto his back. He cursed under his breath as The Krown stepped out from the sheets of crimson rain, looking like a demon of the apocalypse. He stalked towards the fallen Hadder, his face twisted in anger, his usual cruel smile firmly in place.

"It's over, Krown," Hadder said breathlessly. "Rott's had enough of us. There will be no Before for you."

The Krown continued to march forward. "I can see that, plain man. But I am nothing if not a man of my word. Have I not proven that? I promised I would kill you, promised that you would kiss my crown. Now come to me!"

Hadder pitifully attempted to scoot away from the Riser leader but ate the sole of The Krown's oversized boot for his troubles. His head lolled to the side as The Krown took Hadder's face in his large hands, pulled him up to his feet. The Krown's serpentine jade eyes burned brightly as he stared down at Hadder, the sad little man who thought he could best a king. "And now, Marlin Hadder, you may kiss my crown." The Krown slammed his head downward, his central spike aimed directly for Hadder's forehead. Hadder felt the spike pierce his skin a moment before their foreheads clashed together angrily, and stars erupted across Hadder's vision. The two men held that position for a moment, darkness threatening to overtake Hadder, before The Krown dropped the smaller man and staggered backward, a dumb, baffled look pasted on his face.

Gone was the central spike, and Hadder laughed from the blood-soaked ground, a tiny trickle of his own blood running down his face, mixing with that which fell from the sky. The Rage was back, and despite his wounds, Hadder got to his feet, moved towards the wobbling king, who reached up to feel for his central spike. The one that had been driven back into his own brain.

Hadder limped over to The Krown. "Not a plain man anymore, Krown," said Hadder as he pointed to the small hole in his forehead. "Diamond-plated forehead Elevation; just got it done last Solay. Just for you, you predictable fuck. Now die for me."

With that, Hadder pushed The Krown in the chest and watched in delight as the former king fell backward into a pool of blood on the Grasslands turf.

The moment of elation passed, taking with it the last of Hadder's Rage, leaving a void that was quickly filled by the effects of a severe concussion. Hadder's head spun like a top, forcing him to bend forward, hands grasping knees, and puke all over The Krown's lifeless body. As the world circled around him, Hadder fell to his backside, watching the city explode and burn through bleary eyes. Darkness again crept in from the edges of his vision, telling him that the last sands of consciousness were running down the hourglass.

Hadder sat helplessly as four manikins ran at him, said goodbye to the two worlds that he failed, and waited to be ripped apart, unable to even bring his arms up in defense. Just as they were upon him, though, the manikins broke off to either side to attack a Setter woman to Hadder's left and a Riser male to his right. Hadder was disregarded completely.

What the fuck, was the last thought that passed through Hadder's mind before it shut off completely, sending him careening to the Grasslands floor, ready to accept his third death.

————

BACK IN THE VOID AGAIN, Hadder feared that this was becoming a habit. Although he was unable to open his eyes, move his extremities, or even mouth words, Hadder could still hear the city crumbling around him. The screams of men and women mixed with explosions, blood rain downpours, and raging fires to create a cacophony of sound. Soon, however, even those noises faded, and Hadder felt relief in the fact that he was finally going to meet his maker. Again.

He vowed that this time, he wouldn't turn down the handshake.

Hadder thought of how this new meeting would go, even as he felt his body being lifted off the wet ground and slung over a thin shoulder. Hadder bounced up and down as his bearer ran, all the while imagining himself begging the glowing figure for another chance, apologizing profusely for the random act of violence that sullied their first encounter, promising that the Rage was a thing of the past.

While the sounds of battle faded in the distance, the heat of wildfires, the rumble of the ground shaking, and the compressed air of eruptions continued to assault Hadder's motionless body. Just as Hadder had grown accustomed to the bouncing stride, he was weightless, thrown powerfully into to the smoke-filled air to crash into freezing water.

The cold attacked Hadder's skin as he sank, soaked through muscle to chill bone, and still, he was unable to move. So, this was the end, he thought as he came to rest on the muddy bottom. Darkness then overtook him, his conscious mind finally clicking off.

But not before a splash was heard far above him.

29

Hadder's sense of touch returned to him first. He felt the hard, sandy ground beneath him, could detect itchy grains sneaking into his most sensitive crevices. Sound returned next, with Hadder hearing the continued destruction of Station from afar. Smell followed, the scents of blood, smoke, ash, and death thick in the air. Finally, Hadder worked up the energy to open his eyes, frightened of what he might find.

The red eyes of Albany Rott stared down at Hadder. Gone were the fiery blazes that filled Rott's eyes on the battlefield; his usual red embers were back in place. Hadder threw a weak punch at the man's face from his back, which Rott smoothly dodged. Hadder stumbled to his feet, stood there on wobbly legs, furious to be alive.

"Not again! Not again! Why won't you let me die?"

"I'm sorry, Marlin. I couldn't allow it."

"Where the hell are we?"

"Well outside of the Walls of Station. Look."

Hadder turned around and saw the city of Station in the distance, clear under the large Idol Moon. The entire city was ablaze, including its impass-able walls, and shook as if the desert ground was threatening to swallow it whole. "Why have you done this, Rott? Why let the city fall? Why kill every resident?" Hadder refused to look away from the imploding city as he spoke.

"You still live."

"Everyone but me then!"

"I had to, Marlin."

"I don't believe it."

"In some things, even I am without choice."

"Tell me why."

"You might not understand."

"Tell me!"

"Before you can understand, you have to know who I am."

Hadder finally turned back to face Albany Rott. "And who are you, Albany Rott? Beyond a mass murderer."

"You cannot murder that which has already died."

"Semantics. I ask you again. Who are you?"

Rott reached up and fingered the glimmering symbol beneath his throat. "Do you know what this is, Marlin?" Hadder shook his head in the negative. "This was my original blueprint."

Confusion twisted Hadder's face. "Blueprint for what?"

"For what would become the human race."

Hadder felt his jaw fall open, realization hitting harder than the cold water had struck. "Are you trying to say that you..." Hadder's voice trailed off as he found himself unable to lend words to the idea that was forming.

Rott saw his difficulty and answered for him. "I am your creator, Marlin. I am the creator of all mankind and more. The birds you hear, the dogs you pet, the cows you eat; I am responsible for all of it. The Earth, as you humans call it, was my project. And mankind was my crowning achievement, an entity that could love so deeply one moment, and act so cruelly the next. My project was the envy of all, and humankind, especially, drew the attention of the heavens. You all were complex and vexing, surprising and disappointing. As you evolved under my care, even more attention fell upon you. Until you drew the greatest attention of all."

Hadder could barely believe the words he was about to speak. "You mean God?"

"That's what you humans would call him. We have more accurate terms for him, but let's stick with God to make things easier and prevent your brain from melting. God took a liking to my little project, wanted more and more say over what was to be done here. Things got messy, too many cooks and all that. Then one day, he decided that he wanted total control over the Earth. In the language of the cosmos, I told him to fuck off. He didn't like that one bit."

"You told God to fuck off?"

"No worse than punching him in the throat, I suppose." Hadder's mouth snapped shut. Rott continued. "Anyway, God has a low tolerance for disobedience, can be a real prick, truth be told. He told me that if I loved the humans enough to quarrel with the Almighty, I could live among them for eternity. And so, he sent me here to play in the dirt with the mortals. Never again to see the glories of the Heavens. As you can see, the ruler of this existence is a petty creature indeed."

"How long have you been here, Rott?

"A long, long time, Marlin."

"Do you miss your home?"

"More than anything. This brings us to Station. God reignited a dialogue with me many years ago, complaining about human behavior and what he perceived to be your lack of growth. He wondered why I didn't create a utopia for you all, one that would allow you to more effectively develop both emotionally and intellectually, one that would remove the need for violence or melancholy. I told him that this was impossible, that these things were intrinsic in humans, were essential to their makeup. He disagreed. And, thus, our bet was made."

"What exactly was the bet?"

"I told him to provide me with some throwaways, humans who had completely given up or disrespected life. I would create a world for them, where the negative triggers of the Earth wouldn't exist. Money and jobs wouldn't be necessary. Anything they disliked about themselves could be changed. All of the stressors of the world would be removed. Life would essentially be perfect."

"And the bet?"

"I said, given all this, the humans would still destroy the city from within. He didn't believe me. The bet was made."

"How were you so sure you would win, that we would still manage to fuck everything up?"

Rott shot Hadder a wry smile. "Because I molded you in my image, Marlin. As I have always fucked things up, I knew that you would follow in my footsteps."

"And what do you receive now that you've won?"

"A ticket home, of course."

As the truth slowly settled in, the Rage in Hadder began to bubble up once more, unable to accept the fact that they were all merely pawns in a game played by the gods. Unable to accept the fact that in their own ways, both Ego Rounds and The Krown were correct. Hadder turned back to the sinking city. "Then why are you still here, Rott? Why haven't you flown skyward, or whatever it is you do to get back to Heaven?"

"Loose ends."

"Come again."

"There are some loose ends. Well, one loose end, really. There were stipulations of our bet, and one of them forced me to kill all the residents of Station. Once our experiment was complete, God didn't want any of these test subjects returning to his Earth to corrupt his stock."

Hadder spun back. "Viktor Krill."

"That's right. Viktor Krill. The one variable I didn't see. I couldn't chase after him, with the experiment still ongoing. But nothing holds me back now. I will catch him. He will feel my wrath. And I will earn my trip home."

Hadder's legs grew tired, his body still weakened from the concussion and loss of blood. He sat on the sandy ground, looked up at Albany Rott. "Rott, what am I doing here?"

"The Lethe River passes under the city walls and comes out in a cave just over that hill. It's too far for a human to make the trip without drowning, but these problems are not mine. I took you out via that path, using some tricks to keep you alive."

Hadder's head dropped into his lap. "No. I mean, what am I doing *here?* Alive. This is the third, no fourth or fifth time I should have died. Why are you keeping me alive? I'm so tired. So very tired."

Rott walked over to Hadder, hovered above him. "I empathize with you, Marlin. I really do. I, who have lived here on Earth for a millennium, understand more than anyone the exhaustion that accompanies extreme living. For countless years, I have dedicated my existence to returning home, ignoring relationships, and caring nothing for enjoyment. And now that my time on this Earth is drawing to a close, I want to make up for lost time, have one last adventure that's driven by excitement and fun as much as end goals. And I don't want to do it alone, Marlin. I've been alone for too long now. I'm tired of talking to myself."

Hadder looked up into Albany Rott's crimson eyes. "You're telling me that the Devil wants a buddy?"

"I never cared for that term, or any others that have been bestowed upon me. I have had many names over the years. But right now, yes, Albany Rott needs a friend."

"Why me?"

"I don't know, but I have felt it since discovering you by accident. You have the Rage, but it is tempered by kindness. You can bend like a reed in the wind, or you can dig in and hold your ground against tremendous forces. You value life now but are unafraid of death. I think we can have some good times together, really shake the pillars of Earth. Give those boring cunts up there something to really talk about. What do you say?"

Rott held his hand out to Hadder, reminiscent of another time, in another life. Hadder took his hand, was quickly lifted to his feet. Together, the two men stood and watched as the city called Station continued its descent into the desert. As the last of the city disappeared into the sand, a cry of "Father" cut through the barren land. The Caesar Cal was still alive as Station vanished forever.

Hadder looked over to Rott and was surprised to see a single black tear fall from his eye. Rott wiped it with the back of his too-white hand and clapped Hadder on the shoulder. Hadder noticed that the man still had his crystalline axes tucked into this belt. "We should get a move on. This desert can be tricky to escape, even for me."

"Where are we going," asked Hadder as the pair began to walk.

"To find Viktor Krill. He'll be hard to locate and harder to kill."

"How will we find him?"

"Simple, really. We'll just follow the shadow of blood."

Hadder accepted the vague explanation and walked on. As the sadness of his friends' deaths began lessening with each step, his excitement for the dawning of a new adventure began to rise. But if man and fallen angel were going to spend significant time together, the two would need to increase their capacity for small talk. Not everything could be life and death, Heaven and Hell, philosophy and theology. He decided to move forward with a first attempt. "Rott?"

"Call me Albany or Al."

"Ok. Tell me, Al. Since it appears we've got a lot of time on our hands, how'd you get that nasty scar on your face?"

Rott remained impassive as he marched on. "Well, Marlin, when you get struck down from Heaven, it tends to leave a mark."

Hadder sighed, understanding that on this next, most thrilling adventure, one that would find him rubbing shoulders with a god, *small* talk would be hard to come by. So be it, he thought as they crossed the seemingly endless desert. Marlin Hadder had died twice and welcomed a third. With Death sitting on his shoulder and the Devil walking in his shadow, Hadder was sure that the future could be anything.

Anything but boring.

ABOUT THE AUTHOR

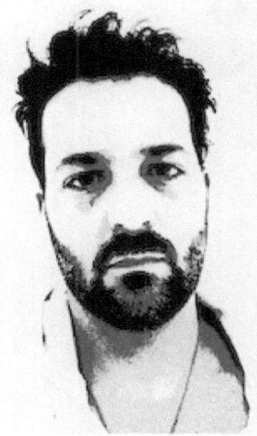

Jarrett Brandon Early splits time between Virginia Beach, VA and Thailand. He lives with his wife Natthicha and daughter Alexandra Beam. He is hard at work on two sequels to Station – The Rott Inertia and Ill Messiah. Learn more at jarrettbrandonearly.com.